DUDLEY PUBLIC LIBRARIES

The loan of this book may be renewed if not required by other readers, by contacting the library from which it was borrowed.

X

D0716864

000003115709

Romantic Escapes

Romantic Escapes:
Greece

REBECCA WINTERS

MICHELLE DOUGLAS

JENNIFER FAYE

MILLS & BOON

First Published in Great Britain 2021
by Mills & Boon, an imprint of HarperCollins*Publishers* Ltd,
1 London Bridge Street, London, SE1 9GF

www.harpercollins.co.uk

HarperCollins*Publishers*
1st Floor, Watermarque Building,
Ringsend Road, Dublin 4, Ireland

ROMANTIC ESCAPES: GREECE © 2021 Harlequin Books S.A.

A Wedding for the Greek Tycoon © 2015 Rebecca Winters
Miss Prim's Greek Island Fling © 2019 Michelle Douglas
The Greek's Nine-Month Surprise © 2016 Jennifer F. Stroka

ISBN: 978-0-263-30299-8

MIX
Paper from
responsible sources
FSC™ C007454

A WEDDING FOR THE GREEK TYCOON

REBECCA WINTERS

To my wonderful grandsons, Billy and Jack.

These two brothers show a love and devotion to each other that touches my heart.

CHAPTER ONE

August 9, New York City

THE BEARDED OLDER DOCTOR looked at Zoe. "Young woman. You've been cancer-free for eight months. Today I can say without reservation that it's definitely in remission. We've already talked about the life span for recovering patients like you. But no one can predict the end of life for any of us."

"I know," she said as he continued to explain the survival expectancy statistics for patients like her. But she'd read about it all before and didn't really listen. The adage to take it one day at a time and rejoice for another day of life was the motto around the hospital.

Zoe's physical exam had gone without incident. Her labs looked great. But she would never outgrow her nervousness. Fear lurked in her that the next time she had to have a checkup, the cancer would have come back. She couldn't throw it off.

The therapist at the center had given her a book to read about dealing with the disease once it had gone into remission. Depression bothered many patients who feared a recurrence and that was a problem they needed to deal with. Since Zoe was a prime example, she could have written that section of the book herself.

But for today she was filled with relief over the lab results. In fact she was so overjoyed with the news she had difficulty believing it. A year ago she'd been told she had a terminal case, but now... She looked at the doctor. "So what you're saying is—it's really gone."

His brows furrowed. "Believe it, girl."

She believed it for today, but it would come back.

"I'm pleased that the terrible fatigue you felt for so long is now gone. You seem much stronger physically and emotionally. Your therapist and I believe you're ready to leave the center today if you wish."

That was the news she'd been waiting for. She had plans and there was no time to lose.

"Here's hoping that from now on you can live a normal life."

Normal... It would never be normal when she knew the cancer would return. But she smiled at him. "How can I thank you for everything you've done for me?"

"You already have by working so hard to get well. You have a beautiful spirit and are an inspiration to the other patients here in the hospital. All the friends you've made here will miss you."

Tears stung her eyes. "I'll miss them more." With this checkup behind her, she could put her plan into action.

"I doubt that."

Zoe folded her arms to her waist. "My bill has to be astronomical. If it takes me the rest of my life, I'm going to pay back every cent of it."

"It's been taken care of by the generosity of the Giannopoulos Foundation Charity."

"I'm aware of that." So aware, in fact, she needed to thank the members of the Giannopoulos family personally and one day she would. "But everyone who works here is an angel, especially you. I don't know what I ever did to deserve such care."

When she'd been admitted to the hospital, she'd read the material given to every patient. The first time she'd gone to the chapel inside the hospital she'd read the plaque. It had been named for the Church of Agii Apostoli in Greece.

In honor of Patroklos Giannopoulos and his wife Irana Manos who survived the malaria outbreak on Paxos in the early 1960s.

In honor of her brother Kristos Manos who survived the malaria outbreak and emigrated to New York to build a new life.

In honor of Patroklos Giannopoulos who died from lymphoma.

"I'm here by the grace of the foundation here in New York too," the doctor reminded her. "It was established for Greek Americans with lymphoma who have no living family or means for the kind of help you've needed. There are some wonderful, generous people in this world. Do you have a place to go?"

"Yes. Father Debakis at the Sacred Trinity Greek

Orthodox Church has taken care of everything. I've known him since I was young. Throughout my ordeal he's been in constant contact with me. I owe him so much, and Iris Themis too. She's from the humanitarian council at Sacred Trinity and has arranged to take me to their homeless shelter where I can stay until I find a job and a place to live. All I have to do is phone her at her office."

"Splendid. As you know, you'll need another checkup in six weeks, either here or at another hospital depending on what's convenient. It will include a blood test and physical exam for lumps. But you can contact me at any time if you have concerns."

Zoe dreaded her next checkup, but she couldn't think about that right now. Instead she stood up to give him a hug. "Thank you for helping me get my life back. You'll never know what it means."

After she left his office, she hurried through the hospital and walked along the corridor that led to the convalescent center. She had a room on the second floor. Having lost her family, this had been her home for twelve months.

In the beginning, Zoe didn't dream that she'd ever leave this place alive. At first the man she'd been dating had called her often, but the technology company Chad worked for transferred him to Boston and the calls grew fewer and fewer. She understood, but it hurt her to the core. Even if he'd told her he was crazy about her, if he could leave at the darkest moment of her life, then she couldn't expect any man to accept her situation.

Though there were family friends from her old

neighborhood who phoned her every so often, the inmates had become her choice friends. With all of them
being Greek American, they shared stories of their family histories and had developed a camaraderie so strong
she didn't want to leave them. It was here that her whole
life had passed before her.

Once inside her room, she sat down on the side of
the bed and phoned Iris. They planned to meet in front
of the convalescent center in a half hour. One day Iris
and the priest would receive their crowns in heaven.

Zoe had emerged from her illness wanting to help
people the way they'd helped her. College could wait. If
she could go to work for the Giannopoulos Foundation,
that was what she wanted to do. Of necessity Zoe would
have to approach Alexandra Kallistos, the woman who
managed this center, but any experiences with her were
unsettling. The other woman was standoffish. Whether
that was her nature, or if she just didn't care for Zoe,
she didn't know.

Earlier today when they'd passed each other in the
hall, Ms. Kallistos hadn't even acknowledged her.
Maybe it was because Zoe was taking up a bed someone else needed, but the therapist had insisted she
still needed to be here. Because she'd lost her parents
and required more time to heal mentally, the arrangements had been made for which Zoe would be eter-
nally grateful.

Ms. Kallistos had an office at the hospital and was
officially in charge. All the staff, doctors, nurses, thera-
pists, lab workers, X-ray technicians, orderlies, kitchen
help, volunteers and housekeeping people reported to

her. She was a model of efficiency, but Zoe felt she lacked the bedside manner needed to make the inmates comfortable enough to confide in her.

Alexandra was a striking, brown-eyed, single Greek American woman probably in her early thirties. Her dark brown hair flounced around her shoulders. She wore fashionable clothes that made the most of her figure. But she seemed cold. Maybe that wasn't a fair judgment, but the thought of approaching her for a position made Zoe feel uneasy.

If there was a problem, maybe Father Debakis would have better luck in bringing up the subject of Zoe working here.

August 10, Athens, Greece

Vasso Giannopoulos was nearing the end of the audits on the Giannopoulos Complex in Athens, Greece he co-owned with Akis, his younger married brother, when he heard his private secretary buzz him. He'd been looking over the latest inventories from their convenience stores in Alexandroupolis.

"Yes, Kyria Spiros?"

"Ms. Kallistos is on the line from New York. She's calling from the hospital in New York, asking to speak to you or your brother. Do you want to take it, or shall I tell her you'll call her back later? I know you didn't want to be disturbed."

"No, no. You did the right thing." The Giannopoulos Hospital and Convalescent Center were located in Astoria. But why she would be calling when he was scheduled to meet with her tomorrow seemed odd. His head lifted. "I'll speak to her."

"Line two."

He picked up the phone. "Alexandra? This is Vasso."

"I'm sorry to bother you, Vasso. I thought I could catch you before you fly here. You're very kind to take my call."

"Not at all."

"Everyone knows that you and your brother established the Giannopoulos Greek American Lymphoma Center here in New York several years ago. This is the fourth time that I've been contacted by a major television network to devote a piece to your lives.

"The managing director of the network wants to send a crew here to film the facility and interview some of the staff. More importantly they want to interview you and your brother for the featured documentary. I told him I would pass this along to you. I know you've turned them down before, but since you'll be here tomorrow, would you be interested in setting up an appointment?"

Vasso didn't have to think. "Tell the man we're not interested."

"All right. When can I expect you to arrive?"

"By two at the latest. I appreciate the call. *Yassou.*" As he rang off, Akis walked in the office. "Hey, bro. I'm glad you're back. Alexandra just phoned. One of the networks in New York wants to do a documentary on us."

"Again?" Akis shook his head. "They never give up."

"Nope. I told her to tell them no."

"Good. How soon are you leaving for New York?"

"I'm ready to head out now. I plan to meet with some of our East Coast distributors early in the morning. Then I'll go over to the hospital and take a look at the books."

"While you do that, I'll finish up the rest of the inventories for the northern region. Raina will help. She's a genius with accounts. You won't have anything to worry about."

"How's her morning sickness?"

"It hardly ever bothers her now."

"Glad to hear it."

"Before you leave, I have a question." Akis eyed him with curiosity. "How did your evening go with Maris the other night?"

"So-so."

"That doesn't sound good. We were hoping she might be the one who brings an end to your bachelor existence."

"Afraid not. She's nice and interesting, but she's not the one." He patted Akis's shoulder. "See you in a couple of days."

Vasso hadn't been dating Maris that long, but already he knew he needed to end it with her. He didn't want to lead her on. But Akis's comment had hit a nerve. Both of them had been bachelors for a long time. Now that Akis was married, Vasso felt an emptiness in his life he'd never felt before. His brother was so happy these days with his new wife and a baby on the way, Vasso hardly recognized him.

August 12, New York City

"Vasso!"

"How are you, Alexandra?"

The manager got to her feet. "It's good to see you."

"I walked through the hospital and convalescent center first. Everything seems to be in perfect order. My congratulations for running an efficient center we can be proud of."

"Thank you. I know you're busy. If you want to go over the books in here, I can order lunch to be brought in."

"I've already eaten. Why don't I look at the figures while you're out to lunch? If I see anything wrong, we'll discuss it when you get back."

"All right. Before I leave, I wanted to tell you about a young woman who applied here for a job yesterday. I told her she didn't have the education or background necessary for the kind of work we do at the center.

"Later in the day I received a phone call from Father Debakis at the Sacred Trinity Church here in Astoria. He knows this woman and finds her a very capable person. He wanted to know if he could go to someone higher to arrange for an interview. I wrote the priest's number on my sticky note in case you want to deal with him."

"I'll take care of it now. Thanks for telling me."

"Then I'll leave and be back in an hour."

"Take your time." Vasso's curiosity had been aroused by the mention of the priest. As she reached the door he said, "I want you to know my brother and I are very pleased and grateful for the work you do to keep this center running so smoothly."

He heard a whispered thank-you before she left the office. Vasso phoned the number she'd left and asked to speak to Father Debakis. Then he sat back in the chair.

"It's an honor to speak with you, Kyrie Giannopoulos. I'm glad Ms. Kallistos passed my message along. Since I don't wish to waste your time, I'll come straight to the point." Vasso smiled. He liked brevity. "A very special twenty-four-year-old Greek American woman named Zoe Zachos here in Queens would like to work for your charity. I've taken it upon myself to approach you about it."

"I understand Ms. Kallistos had reservations about hiring her."

"When I spoke to her on Zoe's behalf, she said this young woman doesn't have the credentials and flatly refused to consider interviewing her for a position. I disagree strongly with her assessment and hoped to prevail on you to intercede in this matter."

Vasso and Akis had flown to New York ten months ago to find a new manager after the old one had to give it up due to ill health. Alexandra had come to them with outstanding references and was the most qualified of all the applicants because she'd had experience working in hospital administration.

Akis, who'd been in business with Vasso from childhood, had flown to New York five months later to check on her. So far neither he nor Vasso had a problem with the way she'd been doing her work. She must have had good reason not to take the other person's application.

"Obviously this is important to you."

"Very." Vasso blinked in surprise at the priest's sobriety. "Perhaps she could be interviewed by you?"

He sat forward. "That isn't our normal procedure."

"Ah…" The disappointment in the priest's voice wasn't lost on Vasso, who'd been taught by his deceased father to revere a priest.

His black brows furrowed. "May I ask why you have such strong reasons for making this call?"

"It's a matter of some urgency."

The hairs lifted on the back of Vasso's neck. After the priest put it that way, Vasso didn't feel he could refuse him. "Tell me about her background."

"I think it would be better for you to discover that information yourself."

At this point Vasso was more than a little intrigued. In all honesty he found himself curious about the unusual request. "How soon could she be at Ms. Kallistos's office?"

"Within two hours."

"Then I'll be expecting her."

"Bless you, my son." The priest clicked off while a perplexed Vasso still held the phone in his hand. For the next hour and a half he pored over the books. When Alexandra returned, he told her everything looked in order and listened to some of her suggestions to do with the running of the hospital.

During their conversation, a polite knock sounded on

the closed door. He turned to Alexandra. "That would be Zoe Zachos. If you'll give us a half hour please."

After a discernible hesitation she said, "Of course." She showed remarkable poise by not questioning him about it. He watched her get up and open the door. "Come in, Zoe," she said to the blonde woman before she left them alone.

Zoe? That meant Alexandra knew her.

Vasso didn't know exactly what to expect other than he'd been told she was twenty-four years old. He got to his feet as the young woman came into the office.

"Kyrie Giannopoulos?" she said, sounding the slightest bit breathless. "I'm Zoe Zachos. I can't believe it, but somehow Father Debakis made this meeting possible." In an instant a smile broke out on her lovely face. "You have no idea how grateful I am to meet you at last."

Tears had caused her translucent green eyes to shimmer.

When she extended her hand to shake his across the desk, he saw a look of such genuine gratitude reflected in those depths, it reached places inside him he didn't know were there.

"Please, Thespinis Zachos. Sit down."

Her lissome figure subsided in one of the chairs opposite the desk. She was wearing a print blouse and khaki skirt, drawing his attention to her shapely body and legs below the hem. She had to be five-six or five-seven.

"I'm sure he told you that I'd like to work for your foundation."

He felt an earnestness—a sweetness—coming from her that caught him off guard. "He made that clear."

She clasped her hands. "When he spoke on my behalf with Ms. Kallistos, she said I didn't have the kind of background she was looking for."

"But Father Debakis feels that you do. Tell me about yourself. Why would you want to work for the foundation as opposed to somewhere else, or do another type of work entirely?"

"He didn't tell you?" She looked surprised.

"No. He's a man of few words."

"But he makes them count," she said with a smile that told him she'd had a running relationship with the priest.

Vasso agreed with her assessment. The priest had an amazing way of making his point. It had gotten Vasso to conduct this interview, which was out of the ordinary. "Why not start at the beginning, *thespinis*?"

She nodded. "I've been a patient here with non-Hodgkins lymphoma for the last year and was just released on the ninth of this month."

A patient...

Knowing what that meant, he swallowed hard. Vasso had thought of several reasons for the possible conflict between the two women. He thought back to a year ago when another manager had to resign because of health issues. When they'd hired Alexandra, Zoe Zachos had already been a patient here. The two had seen each other coming and going for months. But it didn't explain the problem that caused Alexandra to turn down Zoe's request.

"I was thrilled to be told I was cured."

The joy in her countenance was something Vasso would never be able to describe adequately. "That's wonderful news," he said in a thick-toned voice.

"Isn't it?" She leaned forward with a light in those marvelous green eyes. "It's all because of your family. The foundation you established literally gave me back my life!" The tremor in her voice resonated inside him.

He had to clear his throat. "To hear your testimonial is very gratifying, Thespinis Zachos."

"There's no way to pay you back monetarily. But I would love to work for you in some capacity for the rest of my life. I'm a good cook and could work in the hospital kitchen, or in the laundry, or give assistance to those convalescing. Give me a job and I'll do it to the best of my ability. The trouble is Ms. Kallistos told Father Debakis that without a college degree and no experience in the health field, there was no point in interviewing me.

"She wondered if I might not be better suited to becoming a nun if I wanted to be of service to others." A *nun*? "I'm sure she was just teasing. Father Debakis and I laughed over that. I'm hardly nun material. But I do want to make a difference."

Vasso's anger flared. Not so much at Alexandra as at himself and Akis. At the time they hired her, both he and Akis had decided she had the best credentials for the important position even if she was younger. But Vasso could see there was a great deal more to finding the right person for this particular job than what was put on paper. Since Zoe had been a patient here for such a long time, surely Alexandra could have shown a little more understanding.

"Whatever was said, you have a great advocate in Father Debakis. How did you come to know him?"

"My parents owned a Greek *taverna* and we lived in the apartment above it here in Astoria near the Sacred Trinity Church. Father Debakis was serving there when I was just a young girl and always took an interest in our family. If it hadn't been for him, I'm not sure I'd be alive today."

"Why do you say that?"

An expression of unspeakable sorrow brought shadows to her classic features, changing her demeanor. "A year ago I'd gone to a movie with some friends from the neighborhood. We walked home after it was over. It was late. My parents would have been in bed."

She paused before saying, "When we got there, it looked like a war zone. Someone said there'd been an explosion. I ran towards the fire chief who told me an arsonist had planted a bomb in the back of the laundry next door to my parents' *taverna* where I sometimes helped out part-time. Fire spread to the *taverna*'s kitchen. Everything went up in smoke. My parents died. So did the owners next door who'd run the laundry for many years."

"Dear Lord." Vasso couldn't fathom it.

"Everything burned. Family photos, precious possessions, clothes—all was gone. I've always lived with my parents and worked in the restaurant kitchen to save money while I went to college. The scene was so horrific, I collapsed. When I came to, I was in the ER at the local hospital. Father Debakis was the first person I saw when I woke up.

"He told me the doctor had examined me and had discovered a lump in my neck." Vasso saw her shudder. It brought out a protective instinct in him he hadn't felt since he and Akis were on their own after their father died. Though Akis was only eleven months younger, their dying father had charged Vasso to look after his younger brother.

"Honestly, I'm still surprised I didn't die that night. I wanted to. I was convinced my life was over. He, along with Iris Themis, one of the women on the church humanitarian council, wouldn't let me give up.

"They are wonderful people who did everything to help me physically and spiritually in order to deal with my grief. The diagnosis of cancer added another level of despair. My parents and I had never taken a handout from anyone. For them to shower me with clothes and toiletries lost in the fire besides being there for comfort, meant I felt overwhelmed with their generosity."

Vasso got up from the chair, unable to remain seated. Father Debakis had told him she was a very special young woman.

"Before the fire and my illness, I'd planned to finish my last semester of college to get my English degree. I'd even thought of going on to get a secondary school teaching certificate. Because I had to work at night and go to school during the day, my education had to be strung out."

A sad laugh escaped her lips. "At twenty-four I would have been one of the oldest college graduates around, but the enormity of losing my parents this last year along with the lymphoma has changed my focus."

"It would change anyone's." When Vasso's father had died of the disease, the world he and Akis had grown up in was changed for all time. They'd adored their father who was too poor to get the medical treatment needed. As he slipped away from them, they'd vowed never to feel that helpless again.

He watched as she re-crossed her elegant legs. "While I was still at the hospital, I met with a cancer specialist who discussed my illness with me. My student insurance would only cover a portion of the costs. There was only a little money from my parents' savings to add to the amount owing.

"With their insurance I was able to pay off my student loan. What I had left was the small savings in my bank account that wouldn't keep me alive more than a couple of months. I was trapped in a black abyss when Father Debakis and Iris came to get me and bring me here.

"I was told the center existed to help Greek Americans with lymphoma who had few sources of income to cover the bulk of the expense. They took me into the chapel where I read what was written on the plaque."

As she looked up at Vasso, tears trickled down her flushed cheeks. "At that moment I knew the Giannopoulos family truly were Samaritans. You just don't know how grateful I am." The words continued to pour out of her. "As long as I'm granted life, I want to give back a little of what your foundation has done for me. It would be a privilege to work for you and your family in any capacity."

As long as I'm granted life.

What had Father Debakis said? It was a matter of some urgency.

Zoe Zachos's revelations had left Vasso stunned and touched to the soul. He sucked in his breath. "Are you in a relationship with anyone?"

"I had a boyfriend named Chad. But he got a job offer in Boston around the time of the fire. I urged him to take it and he did. We've both moved on. So to answer your question, no, there is no special person in my life."

Good grief. What kind of a man would desert her in her darkest hour?

"Where do you live right now?"

"I'm at the church's shelter. I'm planning to find an apartment, but I hoped that if I could work at the center here, then I would look for a place close by."

"Do you have transportation?"

"Yes."

"And a phone?"

"Yes." She drew it from her purse. "Iris will pick me up here as soon as I call her."

He pulled out his cell. "Let's exchange phone numbers." After that was done he said, "Before the day is out you'll be hearing from me."

She got to her feet. "Thank you for giving me this opportunity to talk to you. No matter what you decide, I'm thankful I was able to meet one of the Giannopoulos family and thank you personally. God bless all of you."

All two of us, he mused mournfully. *Four* when he included Raina and the baby that was on the way.

After she left the office, Vasso went back to the desk

and sat down to phone Akis. He checked the time. Ten o'clock in Athens. His brother wouldn't have gone to bed yet. He picked up on the third ring.

"Vasso? Raina and I were hoping we'd hear from you before it got too late. How do things look at the center?"

He closed his eyes tightly. "Alexandra has everything under control. But something else has come up. You're not going to believe what I have to tell you." For the next few minutes he unloaded on his brother, telling him everything.

"When we created the foundation, it felt good. It was a way to honor *Papa.*" In a shaken voice he said, "But one look in her eyes taught me what gratitude really looks like—you know, deep down to the soul. I've never been so humbled in my life."

"That's a very moving story," Akis responded in a serious tone. "What do you think we should do? Since Alexandra has made her opinion obvious for whatever reason, I don't think it would work to create a position for Thespinis Zachos under the same roof."

"I'm way ahead of you. What do you think if we hired her to work at the center on Paxos?"

He could hear his brother's mind ticking away. "Do you think she'd be willing to relocate to Greece?"

"I don't know. She has no family in New York, but she's very close to Father Debakis and one of the women working for the Church's humanitarian program."

"What about a boyfriend?"

"Not at the moment. But I'm sure she has friends she met at college. There was the mention of friends she'd been out with the night of the fire."

"She's definitely one of the survivors of this world. What does she look like?"

How to describe Zoe Zachos...? "I can't explain because I wouldn't do her justice."

"That beautiful, huh?" Akis knew him too well. After a pause, "Are you thinking of asking her if she'd like to move to Paxos?"

It was all he'd been thinking about since she'd left the office.

"Just be careful, Vasso. I know you inside and out. If she does take you up on your offer of a job, you're going to feel responsible for her. Be sure that's what you want."

He lowered his head. Funny how circumstances had changed. Vasso used to be the one watching out for Akis. Now his little brother had taken over that role. It gave him a lot to think about, but there wasn't time if he expected to phone her before nightfall. "I'll consider what you've said. *Yassou.*"

On his way out of the office, Alexandra was just coming in. "You're finished?"

"That's right."

She looked surprised. "Are you staying in New York tonight?"

"No. I'm flying back to Athens." The beauty of owning a private jet meant he could sleep at night and arrive where he needed to be the next morning.

"I see. What have you decided about Ms. Zachos?"

"You were right. Her skills can best be used elsewhere." Her bilingual abilities in English and Greek played only a tiny part of what she could bring to the job. "That's what I'll tell Father Debakis. Keep up the good work, Alexandra. My brother and I are relying on you."

Relief broke out on her face. "Thank you. I hope the next time you come you'll arrange to stay longer."

Vasso nodded before leaving the center. After he got in the limo, he phoned the priest.

"Father? This is Vasso Giannopoulos. I've just come from the center and am pressed for time. Could I meet with you and Thespinis Zachos in your office ASAP?"

"That can be arranged. I'll ask Kyria Themis to bring her immediately."

"Excellent. In lieu of her parents who died in the fire, I look to you as someone who has her deepest interest at heart. I understand she has revered you from childhood. What I'd like to do is present an employment offer to her. I believe it's vital that you are there so she can discuss it with you." He paused, then said, "She regards you as her mentor."

"She's so grateful to everyone who helped her; her dearest wish is to work for your foundation. She lost everything. Now that she has survived, she wants to give back what she can."

"After talking to her, I believe that's true. I'll see you soon."

He hung up and asked the limo driver to take him to the Greek Orthodox Church a few blocks away.

CHAPTER TWO

ZOE DIDN'T KNOW what the meeting with the priest was all about. The incredible-looking man she'd met at the hospital earlier had told her he'd phone her before the day was out. Since leaving that office, she'd wondered if he'd really meant what he'd said.

But any concern in that department vanished the second she caught a glimpse of his black hair through the opening of the study door. Her pulse quickened for no good reason the second a pair of jet-black eyes beneath black brows zeroed in on her.

Both men stood when she walked in wearing the same skirt and blouse she'd worn earlier. She only had three or four outfits because no more was necessary living at the hospital. But now she needed to do some shopping for a wardrobe with the money she still had left in her bank account.

Over the years Zoe had been in the priest's study many times with other people, but she'd never laid eyes on any man as gorgeous as Vasso Giannopoulos. The thirtyish-looking male possessed facial features and a hard-muscled body that were as perfectly formed as her favorite statue of Apollo she'd only seen in pictures. No other man could possibly compare.

Her first meeting with him had been so important, she hadn't had the luxury of studying him the way she could now. He was probably six foot two and topped the priest by several inches, having an authority about him not even Father Debakis possessed. The dark gray suit toned with a lighter gray shirt gave him a rare aura of sophistication.

"Come in and sit down, Zoe. Kyrie Giannopoulos requested that I be in on this visit with you."

"Thank you." She found an upholstered chair next to the couch where he sat.

Father Debakis took his place behind the desk. He nodded to the younger man. "Go ahead and tell her why you've asked for this meeting."

Vasso sat forward to look at her with his hands resting on his thighs. Her gaze darted to his hands. He wore no rings. "After you left the hospital, I phoned my brother to tell him about you and your situation. We would be very happy to have you come to work for the foundation, but the position we're offering would be on the island of Paxos in Greece."

Zoe decided she had to be dreaming.

"Have you ever been there?"

She shook her head. "No, though I did go on a two-week university tour to England right before the fire broke out. As for our family, we took trips up and down the East Coast and into French Canada."

After a quick breath she said, "My great-grandparents left Florina in Macedonia to escape communism after the Greek Civil War and came to the US in 1946. It was in New York my father met my mother whose family were also refugees. They'd planned to take us on a trip back there for my graduation present, but it didn't happen."

"Maybe now it can," he said. "The center here in New York is fully staffed, and it might be a long time before there's a vacancy. But our center on Paxos has needed an assistant to the manager since the last one left to take care of a sick parent."

Zoe could feel her pulse racing. "You've established another hospital?" That meant she wouldn't have to work under Ms. Kallistos?

"Our first one actually. My brother and I have interviewed a number of applicants, but the manager hasn't felt he could work with any of them."

He? "What makes you think he would feel differently about me?"

"I have a feeling he'll welcome you because you have one credential no one else has possessed to date. It's more important than any college degree."

Her heart was pounding too hard. "What's that?"

"Compassion. You've lived through the agony of having been diagnosed with lymphoma, being treated for it and beating it. The year you've spent in the center here has given you the most valuable knowledge of what it's like to know you have the disease, and to have survived."

"Still, Ms. Kallistos said—"

"Let me finish," he cut her off, not unkindly. "For

that kind of learning experience, you've paid a terrible price. Yet it's that very knowledge that's needed to work with patients because you conquered the disease. Everyone in the hospital will relate to you and your presence alone will give them hope."

"She does that at the hospital every day," the priest inserted.

Her throat swelled with emotion. "What's the manager like?"

"Yiannis Megalos served as a rear admiral in the Greek Navy before his retirement."

A man who'd been an admiral. How interesting. "Then he must run a very tight ship."

The smile he flashed turned her heart over. "He's an old family friend and came to us about a position with the foundation after losing his wife to cancer, in order to work through his grief. In that respect you and he already share something vital in common by having a burning desire to help. I don't need to tell you his organizational skills and his work with the wounded during his military career made him an excellent choice."

"He sounds remarkable."

"Yiannis is a character too," he added on a lighter note. She felt his eyes travel over her. "If I have any concerns, it's for you. Leaving New York to live in a new country is a huge decision to make. If you've got anyone special you don't want to leave, that could prove difficult."

She shook her head. "There's no one."

"Even so, you may not feel that you can uproot yourself from friends. It might be hard to leave those here at the church who've helped you. That's why I wanted Father Debakis to be here in case you want to discuss this with him in private."

"Of course I'll miss everyone, but to be given a chance to work for your foundation means more to me than anything."

"We can come to terms over a salary you'll feel good about. You'll need a place to live. But all of those matters can be discussed once you've determined that you want this position. Talk it over with Father Debakis. Take as long as you need."

Zoe was so thrilled to have been offered a job it took a minute for her to comprehend it. She fought back her tears. "I'll never be able to thank you enough for this offer, not to mention the generosity of your family's foundation."

He got to his feet. Again she felt his scrutiny. "Be sure it's what you want," he warned in a more serious tone of voice. If she didn't know anything else, she knew deep down this was what she wanted and needed. "In the meantime I have to fly back to Athens tonight. You can phone me when you've made your decision."

Seize the moment, Zoe. "Before you leave, could I ask you a few more questions?"

"Of course."

"What's the weather like right now?"

"It's been in the low eighties all summer and won't drop to the seventies until later in September. Usually the night temperature is in the sixties."

"It sounds too good to be true. Are there shops near the hospital to buy clothes?"

"The center is on the outskirts of the small seaside village of Loggos. There are a few tourist shops, but I'd suggest you do your shopping in Athens first."

"Then that solves any problems I'll have about luggage. I lost everything in the fire so I'll replenish my wardrobe there."

He paused in the doorway, looking surprised. "Does this mean you've already made up your mind?"

She eyed the priest then glanced back at the other man. "I can't wait!"

"I can see you're a woman who knows her own mind." She thought his eyes might be smiling. "Under the circumstances, let's go out for dinner where we can talk over details. I'll drive you back to your shelter then leave for the airport."

She turned to the priest. "Oh, Father Debakis...I'm so happy I could take flight."

He chuckled. "I believe you could."

Vasso knew he'd never forget this moment. It was a nice feeling to make someone happy. He smiled at the priest. "It's been a pleasure to meet you."

"And mine, Kyrie Giannopoulos. Bless you."

"Shall we go, *thespinis*?"

After they walked out to the limo, he asked her to recommend a good place to eat.

Zoe swung around. "There's a Greek diner called Zito's a few blocks over. They serve lamb kebabs and potatoes so soft you can taste the lemon."

That sounded good to him. He told the driver who headed there, then concentrated on the charming female seated across from him. "We need to talk about your travel arrangements. There are dozens of flights to Athens every day. Once we know the date, I'll book a flight for you."

"Thank you, but I'll take care of that. This is so exciting, I can't believe it's happening."

Her excitement was contagious. He hadn't felt this alive in a long time. Once inside the diner they were shown to a table for two. The minute they were seated and Zoe ordered for them, she flicked him a searching glance.

"While I've got you here alone, I need your advice. If I were to take Kyrie Megalos a small gift from New York, what would he like?"

His lips twitched. "He collects naval memorabilia from all over the world."

That gave her a great idea. "Thanks for the tip."

"You're welcome. Before any more time passes, I need to know about your financial situation."

"I don't have one. I'm broke." A laugh escaped her lips, delighting him. "That doesn't mean I have no money, but it wouldn't be enough to keep me alive for more than a few months. That's why I can't wait to start work.

"When I look back, I'm pretty sure I know the reason why Ms. Kallistos didn't want me to work there. I took up a bed in the center for eight months after my first cancer-free checkup. That's because I was allowed to live in the hospital's long-term facility for the last eight months and get therapy to help me with grief issues."

Vasso surmised that was only one of the reasons Ms. Kallistos had problems with Zoe. No woman could compete with this female's effervescent personality. Her reverence for life sucked you in.

"After the chemo and bone marrow transplant, I was given all the time there I needed to recover, for which I'm grateful. I don't even have to wear a wig now. No one would ever guess that I'd once lost all of it."

Without her blond hair that had a slightly windblown look, she would still possess stunning classic features. "You seem the picture of health. If a long stay at the center was what made the difference in your recovery, then I applaud the therapist's decision."

She nodded. "I finally got it out of my doctor that the therapist was worried about my recovery. Losing my parents was so horrendous I had gone into a deep depression, and he could see I needed counseling. That part was certainly true. I was an only child and way too connected to them at the hip. They were wonderful and worked so hard, I tried to do everything I could to help them. In one night my whole world evaporated."

"That's the way my brother and I felt when our father died of lymphoma. The world we knew had gone away. Luckily we had each other."

"My therapist explained that if I'd had a sibling, it might have made a big difference. He made me realize why I had such a hard time letting them go. Grief hits everyone differently. In my case I was a twenty-four-year-old woman crying like a child for her parents. You don't know how much fun they were. We were best friends."

"Akis and I had the same relationship with our father." Everything she told Vasso rang so true with him about his own life he had trouble finding words. "I'm glad the priest prevailed on me to interview you. He's very persuasive."

Another quick smile appeared. "He is that. The other day when the doctor saw me for my six-weeks checkup and told me I was still cancer-free, something changed inside of me. I didn't want to stay there any longer and realized I'd come out of the worst of my depression. Father Debakis knew about my wanting to work for your foundation. So for you to give me a chance is like another miracle." Her voice trembled. "Thank you for this opportunity. I promise I won't let you down."

"I'm sure you won't."

The waiter brought their food, but Vasso hardly noticed what he was eating because emotions got in the way of anything else. Their conversation had reminded him of the father he and Akis missed. Their dad had treated them like buddies. He had laughed and joked with them.

Vasso always marveled over how smart he was. Their father knew everyone and had taught them to treat other people with respect. That was how you got ahead. He and Akis remembered everything their father had told them.

She finished her meal before looking up at him. "Your money saved my life and it's saving the lives of everyone at the hospital. Not just the patients, but the staff too. My oncologist is thrilled to be working there.

You and your family have done more for others than you will ever know."

"I hear you, Zoe. Now no more talk about gratitude. Because you'll be living on Paxos, I know of several places you can rent. By the time you reach the island, I'll have lined up some apartments for you to look at."

"That's very thoughtful of you, but I can do that myself."

"I'm sure you could, but you'll need a place close to the center and they're not easy to come by."

"Then I take your word for it. Thank you."

"If you've finished, I'll run you by the shelter."

She got up from the table. "I'll phone you as soon as I've made my flight plans."

"I'll be expecting your call and we'll go from there."

As he walked her out to the limo, he felt as if he too had undergone a life-changing experience. Of course he realized the foundation was helping many people. But for the first time since he and his brother had established the two centers, he had a personal interest in one of the former patients who had recovered.

She'd been so open about her family it triggered memories for him about his father and the life the three of them had enjoyed together before he'd died. Despite their poverty they'd had fun, too. He'd forgotten that aspect until Zoe started talking about her life. Because of her comments about family, he was seeing his own past through fresh eyes. Her story tugged at his heart and Vasso found he was no longer the same emotionally closed-up man who'd flown to New York on business.

August 17, Athens, Greece

Prickles of delight broke out on the back of Zoe's neck as the plane made its descent through a cloudless sky toward the runway. From her coach-class window seat she looked out at the sea, the islands. Closer still she made out the clay-roofed houses lining Athens's winding roads. This was Vasso Giannopoulos's world.

A sense of wonderment accompanied these sensations because she still couldn't believe she was coming to a place where she'd never been before and would be working. No doubt her ancestors experienced the same feelings when they arrived in the US, ready to embark on a new life.

How easy her life was by comparison! Instead of reaching the US by ship, she was on an airliner. Instead of having to undergo a holding time for immigrants, she'd been given safe passage right through to the Athens airport where she'd be taken care of. A job was waiting for her. So was the man who'd made all this possible. He was so wonderful she couldn't believe how lucky she was to have met him.

Kyrie Giannopoulos and his family were responsible for everything that had happened to her since she'd been admitted to the Giannopoulos Center in Astoria a year ago. Somehow he'd made it possible for her to work for his foundation. He'd said he'd be waiting for her when her plane landed.

The thought of seeing him again gave her butterflies. Surely meeting him a second time wouldn't cause her legs to almost buckle as they'd done the first time.

The mere sight of such a magnificent-looking man had haunted her thoughts whether she was awake or asleep.

After the plane touched down and taxied to the hangar, the seat belt came off and Zoe reached for her secondhand overnight bag. She followed the other passengers out of the plane to the terminal lounge where they went through customs. Her bag was searched. After she'd presented her passport and answered a few questions, a female airline attendant came up to her.

"You're Zoe Zachos?"

"Yes?"

"Come with me, please."

She got on a cart and was driven some distance to an elevator that descended to the ground floor. After another little ride the airline employee stopped the cart in front of a door. She got out and opened it. "Your ride is waiting out there."

The second Zoe walked through the door onto the tarmac where the hot sun beat down she saw a limousine in the distance. Once again her legs seemed to go weak when she spotted her benefactor lounging against the passenger side wearing sunglasses. This morning he'd dressed in a light blue sport shirt and tan chinos. He looked so wonderful she moaned before she realized he could have heard her.

"Thespinis Zachos, welcome to Greece."

No man should be this handsome. Zoe felt out of breath. "Thank you for meeting me."

"Of course. I hope you had a good flight." He took her bag and opened the rear door for her to get in.

"It was fine."

He went around the other side and got in with her bag so they sat across from each other. The interior smelled of the soap he must have used in the shower. Her reaction to him was over the top. Maybe there was something wrong with her.

"My driver will take us to the complex where my brother and I work. We'll stay in the penthouse. It's where we entertain guests and business people who must stay overnight. Tomorrow we'll fly to Paxos."

The limousine moved into the center of Athens. Another time and she might enjoy the scenery more, but right now she couldn't concentrate. After what he'd just told her, Zoe felt like a tongue-tied high school girl with a giant-sized crush on a man so far out of her league it was outrageous.

Glomming onto the safer subject of business she said, "Does Kyrie Megalos know you've hired me?"

"Not yet. I want him to meet you first."

She eyed him directly, but couldn't see his eyes behind the glasses. "Something tells me you're pulling the same thing on him that Father Debakis pulled on you." Vasso laughed hard. "He may not want me to be his assistant."

"In that case he'll give you another position. Don't worry. He won't suggest that you join a nunnery."

Laughter escaped her lips. His sense of humor was very appealing. "I shouldn't have said anything about Ms. Kallistos's remark. It wasn't kind of me."

"She should have known better than to say anything, so put it out of your mind."

"I have. Do you mind if I ask you some questions? Would you please tell me what kind of business you're in? I don't have a lot of information about you apart from your philanthropic work."

They'd driven into the heart of the downtown traffic. "If you'll look out your right window, you'll see a store coming up that says Alpha/Omega 24."

Zoe searched each shop. "Oh—there it is! *Everything from A to Z.* It's like one of the 7-Elevens in the States!"

"It's store number four, the first store we opened on the mainland."

"So you're a convenience store owner! Where are stores one through three?"

"On Paxos. My brother and I started our own chain years ago. They've spread throughout Greece."

"Now you're forcing me to guess." She eyed him with an impish expression. "Do you have as many as a hundred perchance?"

"We reached the hundred mark in Thessalonika."

Zoe gulped. "You weren't kidding, were you? Does your chain spread as far as Florina?"

"Farther, but it might interest you to know we have a store in Kozani. It's not far from the home of your ancestors."

She'd just been teasing, but he'd come back with an answer that filled her with awe. "So how many stores do you have altogether? Wait—don't answer that question." Heat filled her cheeks. "I'm being rude to pry. Forgive me."

"I don't mind. 2001, including the one we recently opened in Crete."

Zoe had tried to imagine the kind of money it took to run both centers. Now that she knew what kind of wealth was behind the foundation, she was blown away by the generosity of these men. "You really are perfect," she whispered.

"You have a lot to learn," he quipped, making her smile.

By now the limousine had turned down an alley and stopped at the side of a big complex. He got out with her bag and came around to help her. He had a remote on his key chain that opened the door to an elevator. They rode it to the top. When the door opened, she entered a glassed-in penthouse where she welcomed the air conditioning.

"If you'll come with me, I'll show you to the guest bedroom." She followed him through a hallway to a room with a fabulous view of Athens.

"What an incredible vista! Am I the luckiest woman in the world to sleep here tonight or what? You're far too good to me."

"We do this for business people who come to be interviewed for store manager positions."

"But I'm not exactly the kind of business person that generates a profit for you. I promise I'll do my best to help the patients at the hospital."

"I have no doubt of it." He put her overnight bag on the floor. "The en-suite bathroom is through that door. This area of the penthouse is all yours until we leave for Paxos. Now I'm sure you want to freshen up and relax, but first let me show you the kitchen."

She walked down the hallway to the other part of

the penthouse with him. "There's food and drink waiting for you if you're hungry. Please help yourself to anything you want while I go down to the office and check in. If you need me, just phone me, but I won't be long. After lunch we can go shopping if you're up to it."

"Thank you, Kyrie Giannopoulos." He was beyond kind and so many other things she'd lost count.

"Call me Vasso."

She smiled. "I'm Zoe."

He'd removed his sunglasses. "Zoe Zachos. Has anyone ever called you ZZ?"

Another laugh broke from her. He had a bit of an imp in him. "No. You're the first."

She felt the warmth from his black eyes long after he'd left the penthouse. Before doing anything else she walked over to the windows in the living room. The site of the Acropolis seemed as surreal as the whole experience of meeting Vasso Giannopoulos for the first time.

He had to be a very busy man, yet he'd taken time out to interview her himself. His insight about the emotions she would experience by moving to Greece revealed he was a man of empathy and compassion. Because of his goodness, her life was already being transformed.

CHAPTER THREE

"KYRIE GIANNOPOULOS?" VASSO's secretary spoke to him as he was passing through to his office. "Your brother said he'd be in after lunch. You've had two calls this morning from Maris Paulos who said it was urgent you get back to her."

In order to maintain his privacy, he gave out his cell phone number only to a few people. It forced Maris to reach him through his secretary. Until she'd mentioned Maris's name, Vasso hadn't thought about her.

"I'll call her now. Just so you know I'll be out of the office tomorrow. Akis will handle anything that comes up. If there's an emergency, he'll call me."

"Yes, sir."

Vasso went into his private office and rang Maris. After apologizing for not phoning her before his quick trip to New York, he asked if they could meet later that night. He'd stop by her condo. She sounded happy. That worried him because he didn't plan on seeing her after tonight. But Maris deserved the truth. She wanted more out of their relationship, but he didn't have it inside to give.

With that taken care of, he sequestered himself in his office for a couple of hours to do paperwork. Then he phoned Zoe.

"I'm glad you called. I've eaten lunch and was just leaving to go shopping."

"Then I'll take you."

"Oh no. You've done enough for me."

She was so different from other women he'd known whose interest in money seemed to be at the forefront. Both he and Akis felt the women they met were always assessing the worth of the Giannopoulos brothers, a real turnoff. But the Zoe he'd met so far seemed the exact opposite of a woman with that kind of hidden agenda.

"But you don't know where to go to shop."

"I'll be fine. I've lived in a big city all my life."

Vasso chuckled at her show of independence. "I realize that. But it would please me to accompany you this once. I'm coming upstairs now."

He was aware how grateful she was for everything. Pleased that she wasn't too tired, he arranged for his driver to meet them in the alley and drive them to the Attica department store near Syntagma Square.

She must have showered because she smelled sweet like a fragrant rose, dressed in a different skirt and blouse, when he helped her out of the limo. "You'll find everything you want here at a good price," he explained. "Shall we start in the luggage department? You'll need a large suitcase."

Her sculpted mouth curved into a smile. "You're reading my mind."

He liked the three-piece set of luggage she picked with a gold fleur-de-lis design on a dark red background. Vasso asked the clerk to find an employee to take their purchases out to the limousine waiting in front of the store.

Women's clothing was on the next floor. Zoe stopped him before they approached the counter. "Tell me something honestly. I saw Ms. Kallistos coming and going for a whole year. She only wore dresses or skirts and blouses. Would you suggest the same thing for me?"

"For work, yes. But you'll want other kinds of clothes, too. The island has a lot to offer when you're off of work. Among other things like jeans and shorts, you're going to need some good walking shoes and a bathing suit. Maybe a sweater or jacket when the nights cool down. Paxos is a different world from New York."

"I realize that. After living in the asphalt jungle, I'm relishing the quiet of a sun-filled island with no skyscrapers."

"You're going to undergo a big change. Tell me something. Do you have a laptop?"

"I had one for college, but it got destroyed in the fire."

"I was afraid that might be the case."

"Stop, Vasso. I know what you're going to say. I have enough money to buy another one."

"I believe you, but the foundation supplies all the equipment, so I have an idea. While you shop for clothes, I'll go to the electronics department and get you a computer. You'll need it when you're not at the center. It shouldn't take me long then I'll come back here for you."

"That sounds good. When we're through shopping, I'd like to take you to an early dinner. It will be on me. I'm afraid I won't have much money left to spend, so I'll let you pick a place my pathetic bank account can afford."

Those shimmering green eyes had him mesmerized. "I know just a spot in the Plaka. You'll love it."

"The old part of Athens," she mused. "To think I have Greek blood running through my veins, yet I've never been here. I promise to hurry because I can't wait to explore." Zoe's eagerness to live life made him see it through new eyes. "My father didn't like to go shopping with my mother because she took so long. I'll try not to be like her."

Amused by the comment he said, "Take all the time you need." He and Akis had grown up in a one-parent household, so he didn't know what it would be like to hear two parents going at it back and forth.

He left her talking to a saleswoman and headed for another part of the store. Besides a laptop, Vasso wanted her to have a new iPhone. He was still amazed by the extent of her loss, and even more astounded that she wasn't bitter or angry. She didn't know how to feel sorry for herself. That trait alone increased his admiration for her.

Fire had snatched away everything from her, including her parents. She was forced to build a life all over again. The woman was a survivor in more ways than one. He couldn't imagine another woman of his acquaintance who would be eager to throw herself head-long into an undetermined future.

She was beautiful inside and out. By some miracle the lymphoma hadn't taken her life. Her gratitude was over the top, yet it was that very quality that drew him to her. You couldn't compare her to anyone else. She'd maintained a great sense of humor even after the ordeal she'd been through, which put her in a class by herself.

As Vasso had discussed with Akis, he was happy they'd honored their father by creating the foundation. But at the time, neither of them had any idea that their money would be responsible for Zoe getting the medical care she'd needed to whip the terrible disease. Today he was thankful they'd had both centers built so he could give her the job she wanted.

She's becoming important to you.

An hour later he found her and they walked out of the store with their arms loaded. They were greeted by a rash of photographers and journalists taking pictures and calling out questions. Someone had tipped the paparazzi off that he'd come to the store. Vasso was furious this had happened, but Zoe seemed to handle it well by ignoring them. He helped her into the smoked-glass limo.

"You must be a celebrity," she said in a quiet voice.

"Anyone's a celebrity if they have money."

"There's a lot more to their interest in you than that!"

"It's because Akis and I came from a life of poverty. The media has been following us around for several years."

"How ghastly." He heard a sigh come out of her. "But

I think it's because you've done something extraordinary with your lives. To impart your fortune for the good of humanity puts you in a class all by yourselves. Surely you must realize how much people admire you for that. It's a great compliment to you, even if you don't like the publicity."

"Trust me, I don't," he muttered. "Let's forget them. I'm just sorry I couldn't protect you from them."

"I can understand that you don't relish being mobbed."

She understood a lot of things that made him feel closer to her. He was beginning to desire her company more and more. "It's one of the reasons why I don't spend all my time in Athens."

Her gaze darted to him. "I don't blame you. Under the circumstances, can we go back to the penthouse to eat dinner? Now that they've seen you, they'll probably follow us to the Plaka. If I can't pay for our meal, I can at least cook for you."

"I didn't bring you here to cook."

"You don't know how much I miss it. I was at the center for a whole year. No place of my own to have fun in the kitchen. Yours is a cook's dream, believe me! But please don't misunderstand me," she cried softly. "I just meant that now I'm well, I look forward to doing the things that once brought me pleasure. That is if you'll let me."

How could he say no to that? "Of course."

"If I say so myself, my parents' *taverna* brought in a lot of customers because of my mother's recipes that go way back."

Vasso couldn't hear enough about her life. "What was her specialty?"

"She had several, but my favorite main dish is *burek*."

His brows lifted. "You can make Macedonian *burek*?"

"So you like it?" Her eyes smiled.

"I had it once in Kozani and loved it."

"I'd like to make it for you if you'll let me loose in your kitchen. We'll see how it compares. But you need to start with an appetizer and some Mastika liqueur over ice. You probably don't have any of that on hand."

"Our number-four store should carry it. We'll stop there on the way back."

She reached in her purse and wrote something on a piece of paper before handing it to him. "Do you have all these items?"

He checked the list: dough ingredients, minced lamb, white cheese, spinach, *kasseri* yellow cheese, olives and tomatoes. They'd need to pick up at least half the items on her list. Vasso alerted his driver, then focused on her. "I'm already salivating."

"So am I." She chuckled. "There's nothing I'd love more than to fix you one of my family's specialties."

"Are you homesick for New York already?" He'd been worrying about that. To live on Paxos was going to be a huge adjustment for her.

"I'll never stop missing my parents, but there's nothing in New York for me now so I won't be missing it. Yet being able to cook up a meal in your kitchen will be a little like old times with my folks."

Her tremulous answer tugged on his emotions. He

had a longing to comfort her. "I can relate. So many times I've wanted to discuss business with our father."

"Every time I went into the hospital chapel, I would read the words on the plaque and wonder about him. When did he die?"

"Sixteen years ago."

She shook her head. "You were so young to lose him. That must have been terribly hard on your mother."

Vasso cleared his throat. "She died soon after I was born."

A slight gasp escaped her. "I had no idea. That means your father raised you and your brother alone. Did you have grandparents?"

"They died too, but that's another story."

"Will you tell me about it?"

"Maybe. Over dinner." Just then the limo pulled in front of the store. "I'll be right back." He got out and hurried inside the crowded interior.

"Boss?"

"*Yassou,* Galen. I'm here to pick up a bottle of Mastika liqueur."

"I think we've got one left. It's been on the top shelf in back for a while."

"The older, the better."

"I'll get it."

"Let me." Vasso found it and the other items needed. After putting some bills on the counter he said, "Talk to you later."

When he got back in the limo with the groceries, he handed the bottle to Zoe. "Is this what you wanted?"

She looked delighted. "I can't believe you stock it

here. No wonder your stores have been such a huge success. This is my lucky day. Now I'm going to have to produce a meal that will win the Giannopoulos seal of approval."

He laughed, realizing that she had a knack for bringing that out in him. When she'd walked into Alexandra's office last week, he hadn't been prepared for the effect this utterly feminine woman would have on him. But the first impression she'd made on him, with her wavy blond hair, had brought a spring-like newness into his life.

When they arrived at the penthouse, they loaded everything into the elevator and rode to the top. Before long they'd taken everything to her bedroom. Then they gravitated to the kitchen where he helped her gather all the ingredients to make their dinner.

It was fun working side by side. "This is a brand-new experience for me."

"How come?"

"I've never brought a woman to the penthouse, let alone allowed her to take over the kitchen."

"You're kidding! Not one girlfriend?"

"I have a confession to make. After Akis and I started making real money, we worried whether the women we met only wanted us for what we could do for them. We refused to bring them here. It was safer to take them to dinner. That probably sounds very cynical to you."

"No. Not after what you've told me about your life. There's a lot of avarice in the world. I imagine anyone who has the kind of money you make would have trouble trusting someone who wanted to get close to him."

"Akis had the same trust issues, but he's married now. When he first met Raina, he fell hard. But his fear of not being loved for himself caused him all sorts of pain."

"How did they meet?"

"She flew over to attend the wedding reception of her Greek friend Chloe who'd lived with her in California. Akis had been the best man. After running away from the maid of honor who was after him, he picked on Raina to dance with him until he could get out of the room safely. That accidental meeting changed his life."

Zoe chuckled. "When did he know she was the real thing?"

"He always knew it in his heart, but he needed a nudge. I did some research on her and learned she was Raina Maywood."

"What? Isn't she the famous American heiress to the Maywood fortune?"

He nodded. "When Akis found out, everything changed. He knew that she wasn't after his money, but he had another problem."

"Why?"

"He didn't feel good enough for her. Our lack of formal education made him worry that she'd soon grow bored of him. On the night she was leaving to go back to California, I called her and begged her to go to him. She was broken up, not understanding why he couldn't accept that she loved him. Luckily she took my advice and convinced him he was her whole world. They got married fast and I've never seen him so happy."

"Was that a little hard on you?"

He looked in those compassionate green eyes. "You have a lot of insight, Zoe. Until they said their vows, I never realized how connected we'd been throughout our lives. When you told me how close you were to your parents, you were describing me and Akis.

"I felt lost at first, but slowly that feeling started to dissipate. Raina has been a joy and makes my little brother so happy I can't imagine life without her now. With a baby on the way, Akis isn't the same man."

"A baby? That's wonderful!"

"When Akis and I were young and struggling, we couldn't have imagined this day."

She flashed him a smile. "And now there's a lot more to come. Your lives are a miracle, too."

The things she said…

They kept working in harmony. Zoe definitely knew her way around a kitchen. By seven o'clock, they sat down at the dining room table to eat the best home-cooked food he'd ever tasted.

They started with the Mastika poured over ice and served with a grilled *krusevo* cheese pie for an appetizer. The *burek* was out of this world. Layers of dough with white cheese, minced lamb and spinach garnished with tomatoes and onions marinated in a special herb sauce. It was so good he ate more than he normally did at a meal.

"You could open your own *taverna*, Zoe."

"What a lovely compliment. Before I decided to go

to college, I actually thought about it, but my parents insisted I try college first. You know the rest. Then the day came when the world as I knew it went away."

Vasso didn't want her to think sad thoughts. "We can be thankful you didn't go away with it or I wouldn't have been treated to such a feast."

"You're just being nice."

"Not true. Now it's my turn to pay you back by doing the dishes while you get your bags packed. Tomorrow we'll have breakfast here and fly to Paxos."

That was the plan, but he discovered he was loving her company so much he wanted to keep her here in Athens for a while and show her around. It shocked him that he could feel this attracted when they'd known each other for such a short while. How had he existed all this time before she came into his life?

"Before I do that, I want to hear about your grandparents. It's sad to think you didn't have them in your life either." She started clearing the table. It thrilled him she didn't want to leave him quite yet.

"Both sets of grandparents came from Paxos."

"Ah. I'm beginning to understand why the island has been so important to you."

"The grandparents on my father's side and their children—with the exception of our father—were victims of the malaria epidemic on Paxos. In the early sixties it was eradicated, but they didn't escape it."

"Amazing that your father didn't get the disease."

"No. Pockets of people were spared. No one knows why. Maybe he was naturally immune. A poor fisherman who lived on Paxos took care of my father. To-gether they caught and sold fish at the market in Loggos.

"After the fisherman died, our father continued to fish in the man's rowboat. It was in town he met our mother. She and her brother Kristos survived the epi-demic that had killed her family. He emigrated to New York to find a new life, but was killed crossing a busy street."

"How awful. That explains his name on the plaque!"

"Yes. Apparently my mother grieved when he left Greece. In time she and my father fell in love and got married. She worked in the olive groves. Together they scraped to make ends meet any way they could.

"I was born first. Then Akis came along eleven months later. But the delivery was too hard on *Mama* who was in frail health and she died."

He could see Zoe was trying not to break down. "It pains me that neither of you knew your mother. That's so tragic. I at least didn't lose my parents until a year ago, so I have all the memories of growing up with them."

His eyes met hers. "In ways I think your pain has been much worse. We never knew her. She didn't know about her brother getting killed, which was a good thing. We were so young when she died we had no memories except the ones our father told us about. But you lived, laughed and cried with your parents for your whole life, doing everything together. That's a loss I can't comprehend."

"Thanks to the therapy provided by your generosity, I'm doing fine these days. Truly your father had to be a saint to manage on his own. No wonder you wanted to do something extraordinary to honor his name."

"To be sure, he was our hero. I was six when we helped him in the store where he sold the fish. Neither Akis nor I went to school regularly because we needed the money too badly. Poverty was all my father knew. I know it hurt his pride that we boys were known as the poor Giannopoulos kids.

"Most people looked down on us. But no one could know the depth of our pain when he was diagnosed with lymphoma and died. At that point we only had each other in order to survive. *Papa* asked me to look out for Akis."

Zoe gasped. "How old were you?"

"Thirteen and fourteen."

"Overnight you two had to become men."

"All we knew was that we only had ourselves in order to survive. The man who owned the store died and his wife needed help. We asked if we could stay on and work for her. By then the woman was used to us and she really needed the help. So she let us work in her store.

"Akis and I traded off jobs. He'd wait on the customers while I went fishing and picked olives. Then we'd turn the schedule around. We worked long hours."

"When did you fit in some time to play, let alone attend school?"

"Not very often."

"I'd love to meet Akis."

"That can be arranged. But enough about me. Now I want to change the subject. Have you ever ridden in a helicopter?"

She shook her head, still haunted by what he'd told her. "No. I've always wondered what it would be like."

"Does the thought of it make you nervous?"

"Kind of." A hint of smile broke the corner of her mouth. "Ask me tomorrow when I actually have to climb inside it."

"Once you get used to it, you won't want to travel any other way."

"I'll have to take your word for it." After a hesitation… "Vasso?"

He'd started loading the dishwasher. "What is it?"

"You've been so kind to me my debt to you keeps growing. I told Father Debakis what I'm going to tell you. If it takes me the rest of my life, and it probably will, I intend to pay back every cent your foundation spent on my behalf.

"Every inmate at the center would like to tell you of their gratitude in person. You've saved the lives of many people who had no hope. It's staggering the good you've already done." Her lower lip started to tremble. "You're wonderful."

Her words moved him. "If I started to tell you all the things I think about you, there wouldn't be enough hours."

Color rushed into her cheeks. "You're full of it, but it's nice to hear."

"How could the man you had been seeing before the fire have walked away?" he whispered. That question had been gnawing at him since she'd first told him she'd had a boyfriend.

"I don't know." She half laughed as she said it. "He broke my heart when he made the decision to move to Boston. I went through a lot of pain, but with hindsight I can see he didn't love me in that heart-whole way or he couldn't have left.

"After several months I decided I was lucky. If there'd been no fire, would he have eventually asked me to marry him? I don't have an answer. But the fact remains that he wanted to go to Boston more than he wanted to be with me. I certainly don't blame him. To be with a terminally ill patient would mean he had to forget his dreams. That's asking too much of a man unless he's met the love of his life."

"Was he the love of *your* life?" Vasso needed to hear her answer.

"Let me put it this way. I had boyfriends. Some meant more to me than others. But I met Chad while we were both on that study abroad program in England. That was his graduation-from-college present. It threw us together for two weeks. You can learn a lot about someone on a trip like that. We had fun and didn't want it to end after we returned to New York.

"The more I saw of him, the more I thought maybe he could be *the* one. But the circumstances that brought me to this hospital put an end to the relationship we'd enjoyed. Now you know the story of my life."

"But not the pain you suffered when he didn't stay with you."

She took a deep breath. "It was awful. I won't lie about that. If ever I needed someone who loved me that was the time. But his love wasn't the forever kind. That was a hard lesson to learn. It taught me not to put my faith in a man." She looked up at him. "That's as honest as I know how to be."

The man had been a fool. Vasso's black eyes burned into hers. "Just look what he missed. Thank you for telling me."

"I've probably said too much." After taking a few steps away from him, she turned around. "Thanks for listening. I've talked your ear off."

"It was my pleasure. Just so you know, I have to go out again for a little while. I'll try not to disturb you when I come back in."

"Please don't worry about me. Good night." In the next instant she'd disappeared into the other part of the penthouse.

While Vasso stood there overwhelmed by tender new feelings she brought out in him, his cell rang. He pulled it from his pocket. When he saw it was his brother, he clicked on. "Akis?"

"I thought I'd check in. How's everything going with Thespinis Zachos?"

He held his breath. "Fine."

Low laughter bubbled out of Akis. "Come on. It's *me* you're talking to."

"I'm aware of that. I took her shopping, then we had dinner and now she's gone to bed. Tomorrow morning we'll fly to Paxos."

"I can read between the lines, bro. Let's try this again. How are things really going?"

"The press intruded as we left the department store, so we came back to the penthouse and she cooked dinner. It was probably the best Macedonian food I've ever eaten."

"I guess that makes sense considering her parents ran a *taverna*."

"She only has one more semester before she receives her college degree in English, but Alexandra didn't know about that. It's just as well Zoe will be working on this side of the Atlantic. Tonight she told me she wants to meet you and thank you for saving her life. If you want my opinion, she'll charm Yiannis until she has him eating out of her hand."

"It wouldn't surprise me considering she's already accomplished that feat with you. A woman cooking in our kitchen? That has to be a first. I guess it's too late to tell you to go slow, the same advice you once gave me. *Kalinihta.*"

"*Kalinihta.*"

Zoe was still on his mind when he arrived at Maris's condo twenty minutes later. "Vasso—you're finally here!" she said after opening the door. "I've missed you."

But when she would have reached for him, he backed away.

A hurt look entered her eyes. "What's wrong?"

Vasso hated to do this, but for both their sakes he needed to break things off with her. Zoe filled his thoughts to the exclusion of all else, but that made him anxious when he remembered how he'd once felt about Sofia.

As for Maris, he didn't like hurting her when she'd done nothing wrong, but as he'd told his brother, she wasn't the one. Still, he couldn't help feeling a little guilty about doing this to her.

"Let's sit down."

"I don't want to." Her chin lifted. "Why do I get the feeling you're here to tell me it's over with us?"

Being a journalist, she had good instincts and was always out for the truth. "To be honest, while I was in New York I had a chance to think. I don't believe there's a future for us and I thought it would be better to tell you now. I like you very much, Maris. We've had some good times, but—"

"But you're ready to move on," she interrupted him.

"Surely you know I don't mean to hurt you."

"One of my friends told me this was how it would end with you, but I didn't want to believe her. So who's the new woman in the life of the famous Vasso Giannopoulos?"

He stared her down. "Would you have preferred that I told you this over the phone?"

She had the grace to shake her head. "No. It hurts no matter what."

Vasso admired her honesty. "I've enjoyed the times we've spent together and I wish you the very best in the future."

Maris walked over to the door and opened it. "I'm afraid I can't wish you the same, but one day I'll get over it. I thought we had a real connection. Being with you has meant everything to me. Too bad it was one-sided. *Adio,* Vasso."

He left for the penthouse. After reflecting on what had just happened at Maris's condo, he realized this had been the story of his life since Sofia Peri had rejected his marriage proposal. That was ten years ago after he'd finished his military service. It had taken a long time to get over the pain of her marrying someone else. From then on he'd buried himself in business with Akis.

Over the last few years he'd been with different women when time permitted, but he'd ended every relationship prematurely and had pretty well given up on finding his soul mate.

Then Zoe Zachos had walked in Alexandra's office, causing his heart to beat so hard he hadn't been the same since. In the last twenty-four hours her effect on him had been staggering.

After getting used to being in a helicopter, Zoe was entranced by everything she saw. They passed over so many historic places in the Ionian Sea she'd only read about in books or seen in the movies she was awestruck.

From the copilot's seat, Vasso looked back at her through his sunglasses. Today he'd dressed in a white crewneck and white cargo pants. It wasn't fair one man out of millions could be so attractive. Using the mic he said, "We're coming up on Paxos."

She looked down from the window. "But it's so tiny!"

"It's only seven miles by three. Too small for an airport which is just the way all of us who live on the island like it."

Zoe leaned forward. "What do you mean *we*?"

A dazzling white smile greeted her gaze. "As I told you last night, my brother and I were born here. We had the center built here. *My* home is here."

Her heart pounded so hard she was afraid he could hear it. "*This* is where you live when you're not in Athens or traveling for business?"

"That's right."

In shock that she'd be working so close to this fantastic man's home, she turned to the window once more.

"We're flying to the center now. I've phoned Yiannis to expect me. Once inside his office you two can meet and talk about the position."

As the helicopter dipped, she made out several fishing villages with colorful harbors. Lower and lower now, she took in the lush deep greenery of olive trees sprinkled with pastel-colored clusters of small villas. Quaint waterside cottages came into view. One stretch of fine white sand scalloped the green coves and gave way to another seaside village. On the outskirts now she realized they were headed for a sprawling white complex peeking out of the olive groves.

She held her breath as they were about to land. This time it set down on the hospital roof, but she wasn't as nervous as when the helicopter had lifted off the penthouse roof.

"Are you all right, Zoe?"

"Yes. I was just thinking how my parents and I would have loved transportation like this all the years we lived in New York City. I'm spoiled already."

But the minute the words were out of her mouth, it made her realize she did too much talking. He brought that out in her. Now that they'd landed, she didn't want to prolong the conversation and unbuckled her seat belt.

She thanked the pilot and climbed out of the helicopter wearing one of her new outfits. The navy cotton dress with the white print had a crew neck and sleeves to the elbow. It was summery light, yet had a certain classy look she felt would be appropriate for the job.

When Vasso walked her to the stairs that led to an elevator, she felt his gaze travel over her. Hopefully he approved of her choice of dress. But the second Zoe entertained the thought she was irritated with herself that he was on her mind way too much. The fact that his home was so close to the center meant she'd probably see him more often than she would have imagined. It shouldn't thrill her so much.

"This is a private elevator," he explained as they entered. "The hospital takes up three floors. On the second floor there's a walkway to the three-floor convalescent center. Yiannis's office is on the main floor off the foyer at the main entrance."

They exited the elevator and walked along the corridor of one wing, passing a set of doors with stained-glass inserts signifying the chapel. Zoe looked around. "I love the Hellenic architecture." Their eyes met for a moment. "It flows like the sculpture of a Greek temple."

Her comment seemed to please him. "When we had it built, we tried to preserve the flavor of the island. The kitchen and cafeteria are in the other wing. The eating area extends outside the doors to the patio overlooking the water."

"A hospital built in the middle of paradise," she mused aloud. "If I'd been privileged to recover here, I know I would have lived on the patio. To be near the sea would be heavenly."

When they came to the foyer filled with exotic plants and tubs of flowers, he smiled warmly at a woman probably fifty years old who appeared to run the reception area. "Hebe." He kissed her cheek.

The other woman beamed. "Yiannis said you were coming. It's always good to see you."

"The feeling is mutual. Kyria Lasko, I'd like you to meet Thespinis Zoe Zachos from New York City. She's here for an interview with Yiannis."

"Ah? I hope it means what I think it means." Her friendly brown eyes were so welcoming Zoe was able to relax a little.

"How do you do, Kyria Lasko?" She shook hands with her.

"Call me Hebe."

After being around a cold Alexandra for a whole year, Hebe Lasko was like a breath of fresh air. "Thank you."

"Hebe is the head of our business office located down the other hall," he explained, "but she's been doing double duty as Yiannis's assistant."

Zoe turned to him. "You mean this front desk is where I would work?" she asked quietly.

He nodded. "Yiannis's office is through that door behind the desk. Let's go."

She followed him around the counter where he knocked on the door and was told to enter. Vasso ushered her inside and her first thought was that she'd entered a room in a naval museum.

There were models of ships on the shelving and several framed photographs of the former military leader in dress uniform. Other small photographs showed him with his striking wife. What an attractive man he was with gray hair and dark brown eyes!

As the two men embraced, she noticed he was shorter than Vasso and was dressed in a short-sleeved white shirt and dark trousers. They exchanged comments and his hearty laugh filled the office. Then his eyes swerved to Zoe.

"So, Vasso… I see you've brought along a visitor. A very lovely one at that. Is this some kind of announcement you're making?"

CHAPTER FOUR

THE INFERENCE COULDN'T have been more obvious. Zoe tried to repress a groan.

"In a way, yes! I've found you the assistant you've been needing. Yiannis? Meet Thespinis Zoe Zachos. She was born and raised in New York City, and she's a bilingual Greek American. I was so impressed with her I plucked her away and brought her here. I'm going to leave the two of you to get acquainted and take a look around the facility, but I'll be back."

He disappeared so fast Zoe felt like the foundation had just been knocked out from under her.

The older man smiled at her. "Sit down, Zoe. How come you're still *thespinis*?"

He immediately reminded her of her father who was always outspoken. "I haven't met the right man yet."

He frowned before taking his seat. "What's wrong with the men in New York?"

"I'm afraid the problem lies with me."

"What are you? Twenty-two?" he asked with a teasing smile.

"I'll be twenty-five next weekend."

His brows lifted. "That old." Laughter broke from her. "All right. Let's start from the beginning. Vasso wouldn't do this to me if he weren't a hundred-percent sure you're the person I'm looking for to help me run this place. Tell me about your background."

Without going into too much unnecessary detail, she told him about her family and education. When she got to the part about the fire, she managed to stay composed. Then she told him about her lymphoma and the year she'd spent at the center.

"My family priest knew how much I wanted to work for the center to pay back all it had done for me. When the doctor gave me another clean bill of health, Father Debakis arranged for Kyrie Giannopoulos to interview me. He said your assistant had to leave and you were looking for a new one."

The older man suddenly sat forward. "You're cancer-free?"

"At the moment, yes. But there's no guaran—"

"Forget that," he broke in on her. "You're exactly what's been needed around here. How long before you have to go back to New York?"

"I—I don't plan to," she stammered. "I told Kyrie Giannopoulos I'd like to work for the foundation for the rest of my life. It will take that long to pay his family back for all they've done for me. If I'm given a job here, this is where I'll plant new roots."

"You're hired, Thespinis Zachos."

Zoe couldn't believe it. "But you hardly know anything about me."

"Of course I do. Vasso wouldn't have brought you

here if he had any questions. This center needs input. Who better than you to see what we're doing right or wrong? When I was in the navy, we had informers who quietly gathered information helpful to the brass. With you around, I'm already feeling like I'm back on duty with a crew I can count on."

To hide her joy that he'd accepted her on Vasso's say-so alone, she reached in her tote bag and pulled out a seven-by-seven-inch box wrapped in paper showing various American naval frigates. "This is for you." She handed it to him. "I would have given it to you whether I got the job or not."

Yiannis eyed her in surprise before opening it. "What's this?" He pulled out a creamware mug and read aloud the words printed in dark red ink. "*We have met the enemy and they are ours.*"

"That's the image of Edward Preble," she explained. "He was a naval hero at the time of the war in Tripoli. Kyrie Giannopoulos told me you're a naval hero and have collected naval memorabilia. I knew he meant Greek memorabilia, but I thought you could add this mug as a piece to show your appreciation for an American naval hero. A little diversity makes things more interesting, don't you think? If nothing else, you could drink coffee from it."

He burst into laughter at the same moment Vasso joined them. "It looks like you two are getting along famously."

Yiannis lifted the mug. "Did you see this?"

"No."

"Take a look. Our new employee just presented me

a gift to add to my collection." Vasso shot her a knowing glance before he took it to examine.

The retired admiral sat back in his chair, eyeing the two of them with satisfaction. "The only thing I need to ask now is: how soon can you come to work? I needed you yesterday. Poor Hebe has been run ragged doing the job of two people."

Zoe liked him a lot already. For years she'd worked with her parents at the *taverna*. It would be nice to feel useful again with someone dynamic like him. Despite his grief over the loss of his wife, he had a buoyant spirit.

"Tomorrow morning? Today I need to find a place to live."

"Tomorrow at eight-thirty it is. You've made my day."

She got to her feet. "You've made mine by being willing to give me a chance. I can't thank you enough and I'll try not to make you sorry." Zoe shook his hand and headed for the door. She needed to use the restroom she'd seen down the hall.

After she emerged, Vasso caught up to her. "We'll fly back to my house for the car and drive into Loggos. When we reach the village I thought we'd stop for lunch and check out several furnished apartments I told you about. Hopefully one will suit."

Things were moving so fast she could hardly think. "Do all the people working at the center live in Loggos?"

"They come from all over the island, but Loggos is a good place for you to start out. The only bus picks up passengers in front of the main *taverna* and will bring you to the center. It makes three stops a day there in front of the fountain, so you'll always have a ride home. I suggest you give it a month. If it isn't to your liking, you can live wherever you want on the island, but you'll need a car. I'll help you with that when you're ready."

"Thank you, but I don't have a driver's license, Vasso. If I decide to buy a car, then I'll have to take lessons first." He'd already spoiled her so completely she would never be out of his debt. Vasso was so caring and concerned—the differences between him and Chad were like day and night.

The flight back to his house passed in a blur. There was too much to absorb. She couldn't take it all in. Once again she felt the helicopter dip and fly toward a charming, solitary white beach villa with a red tiled roof. They landed on a pad in the middle of a copse of olive trees, causing her breath to escape. There was no doubt in her mind this was Vasso's sanctuary.

She spotted a dark gray Lexus parked nearby.

Once the rotors stopped spinning, Vasso unbuckled the seat belt. While he removed her luggage, she jumped down so he wouldn't have to help her and reached for the train case. Without waiting for him, she headed for his car.

"Zoe? The house is in the other direction. Where do you think you're going?"

"To get in your car. I'm assuming I'll be able to move into an apartment today and don't want to put you out any more than necessary."

"We're not in that big a hurry."

"*I* am. Once I have a place to live and am on the job, I'm going to feel free. I don't expect you to understand. But being the recipient of so much generosity for so long has become a burden, if that makes sense. I hope I haven't offended you."

"Not at all."

Zoe tried to sound matter of fact about it, but it was hard to hide the sudden alarm that had gripped her. Vasso was already bigger than life to her. She'd been in the penthouse that he and his brother used for business. She'd even cooked a meal there! Because she was a future employee, Vasso had opened every door for her.

But to enter his home would be crossing a line into his private world she refused to consider. She might like it too much. No way did she dare make a move like that. Already she was afraid that her feelings for him might interfere with their professional relationship.

Yiannis Megalos had made an assumption about her and Vasso the second he'd seen them walk in the office. She could imagine how it looked. Obviously Vasso had gone out of his way to do something unprecedented to accommodate her desire to work for the foundation. But this last favor to help her get settled had to be the end of it. Her self-preservation instinct had kicked in to guard her heart.

If she came to depend on Vasso, how did she know he wouldn't be like Chad in the sense that he wasn't invested in the relationship to the extent that she was? Zoe refused to put her trust in a man again where it came to her heart. There was no point anyway since her cancer could be coming back. Better to concentrate on her work and give it her all. In the end she'd be spared a lot of heartache.

She waited for Vasso to bring the rest of her luggage to the car. He used a remote to open the doors and put the luggage in the trunk. Zoe took advantage of the time to get in the front seat.

When he got behind the wheel, he turned to her. Suddenly they were too close. She was so aware of him she could hardly breathe. "Why do you think you would be putting me out?"

Until now she hadn't felt any tension between them, but after what he'd just said, she feared she'd irritated him after all. "Because you've done so much for me, it doesn't make sense that you'll have to come back here later for my luggage."

"I'm in no hurry. Have I led you to believe that?"

She moistened her lips nervously. "No. Of course not. You're such a gentleman you'd never make anyone uncomfortable. But you and your brother run a huge corporation. Everything was going smoothly until you were asked to interview me. I know Father Debakis laid a big guilt trip on you, so don't try to deny it."

"I wasn't going to."

She took a breath. "Thank you. Since then you've had to deal with me. As if I'm not already indebted to you several hundred thousand dollars."

"Zoe—have you considered the situation from our point of view? Our father died a terrible death while Akis and I stood by helplessly. To know that the foundation has helped someone like you means everything to us. It's a pleasure to see you get back on your feet."

Her head bowed. "You're the two best men I know."

"That's nice to hear. What do you say we drive to the village? After lunch you can take a look at the furnished apartments available. One is over a bakery, the other over a gift shop."

She flicked him a worried glance. "A bakery?"

The second Zoe's question was out, Vasso realized where he'd gone wrong and gripped the steering wheel so hard it was a miracle he didn't break it. "Forgive me for forgetting where you'd lived." She'd never forget the fire that had traveled to the kitchen of her parents' *taverna*.

"We'll cross that one off the list. You'll like Kyria Panos. She's a widow who's been renting the apartment over the gift shop since her son got married. You'll have your own entrance in the back. The only drawback is that it's a one-bedroom apartment."

"I don't need more than one."

"You're so easy to please it's scary."

"Not all the time."

"Give me an example."

"If I told you some of my hang-ups, you'd send me back to New York on the next flight."

"How about just one?"

"A couple of my girlfriends wanted me to room with them in college, but I'd always had my own space at home and didn't want to give it up. They teased me about it and tried to talk me into it. But the more they tried, the more I didn't like it. I guess I'm really a private person and get prickly when I sense my space is being invaded. That's why I lived with my parents."

"There's nothing wrong with that. But maybe the day will come when you won't want to be alone."

"If you're talking about marriage, I'm not planning on getting married."

"Why?"

"I like my life the way it is." She turned to him. "I really like the way it is right now. I don't want some man bossing me around. One of the older patients at the center used to tell me about the fights she had with her husband. For the most part my parents got along great, so I couldn't relate to this woman's life. He pecked at her all day long."

Vasso's black brows lifted. "Pecked?"

"Yes. You know. Like a hen pecks at her food. That's what he'd do to her about everything. What she bought, what she ate, what she did with her spare time. Peck, peck, peck."

Laughter pealed out of Vasso. "Most of the older women in the center made similar comments about married life. I decided I was well enough off being on my own."

"My brother loves married life."

"Maybe that's true, but what does his wife have to say when he's not listening?"

She heard a chuckle. "I have no idea."

"Maybe it's better you don't know." He laughed louder. She loved hearing it. "I could see in Yiannis's eyes that he wonders why you aren't married, Vasso.

Admit you don't want some wife leading you around by the nose."

"Now there's a thought."

She laughed. "I'm only teasing." No woman would ever do that with a man like him. The female who caught his eye would be the luckiest one on the planet. No way did she dare dream about a romantic relationship with Vasso.

If it didn't work out, she wouldn't be able to handle it. Just admitting that to herself proved that her feelings for Vasso already ran deeper than those she'd had for Chad. The two men weren't comparable. No one could ever measure up to Vasso.

"You may be teasing, but I can hear the underlying half truths."

Time to change the subject. "Tell me about my landlady, Kyria Panos. Did she henpeck her husband?"

"As I recall they did a lot of shouting, but for the most part it was good-natured."

"That's nice. I bet you know everyone around here."

"Not everyone," he murmured, "but Akis and I rented an apartment along this waterfront when we started up our business years ago, so we're friends with many of the owners around here."

Vasso started the engine and drove them through the olive groves to the village. An hour later, after they were filled with spinach pie and ouzo lemonade, he carried the last of Zoe's luggage up the stairs to the furnished apartment. The front room window overlooked the horseshoe-shaped harbor. The minute he saw Zoe's expression, he knew she liked the view and the typical blue-and-white décor.

She smiled at him. "This place is really cozy and so colorful. I love it, and it's all mine."

After what she'd recounted earlier about needing her space, he could believe she was serious. But it bothered him that she was so happy about it.

"I'm glad you like it. Our number-one store is just a few doors down. You can grab breakfast there while you're waiting for the bus."

"If I do too much of that I'm going to get fat, but I want you to know I'm ecstatic to be here," she exclaimed. Vasso couldn't imagine her with a weight problem, not with her beautiful face and body. Her green eyes lifted to his. "Cinderella may have had a fairy godmother, but I've had the perfect godfather who has granted my every wish. Now that your mission has been accomplished, I release you to get back to your life."

Zoe could tease all she wanted, but he sensed she wanted him to leave. The hell of it was he didn't want to go. Since she'd flown to Athens, he'd been a different person and couldn't spend enough hours with her. She was so entertaining he never knew what was going to come out of her mouth next. The thought of her ever being interested in another man disturbed him more than he wanted to admit.

He'd only scratched the surface of her life, but she'd drawn the line at entering his home. Why? Was it because she didn't trust him after what Chad had done to her? Did she see every man through the filter put there by the other man's defection? Was she afraid of marriage because of that experience?

She didn't bat an eye over renting an apartment with one bedroom. Did that mean she really did like to be alone? He could hear Akis commenting on the subject. *Are you still feeling responsible for her, or is there something more eating at you?*

Vasso had to admit there were a lot of things eating at him. He sucked in his breath. "If you need help of any kind, I'm only as far away as the phone."

"You think I don't know that?" She walked him to the door. "I'm sure we'll see each other again. Hopefully by then Yiannis will have a good word for me."

As Vasso had predicted to Akis, she already had Yiannis eating out of her hand.

"Stay safe, Zoe."

"You, too."

He heard the slight wobble in her voice. It stayed with him as he left the apartment, taking with him the haunting image of her blond hair and sparkling eyes, not to mention the white-on-navy print dress that clung to her figure.

Once he reached the car, he took off for his villa. But he was too upset by emotions churning inside him to stay on the island till morning. If he did that, he'd be tempted to drop by the apartment with some excuse to see her again. Instead he alerted the pilot that he was ready to fly back to Athens.

After the helicopter touched down at the penthouse, he checked any messages his private secretary might have left. Apparently Akis had dealt with everything important. Grabbing a cup of coffee, he went back to his office to dig into the inventories still left to get through. But first he texted his brother.

I'm back in the office working. Zoe Zachos is living in the apartment above Kyria Panos's shop. All is well with Yiannis.

Not two minutes later his brother phoned him back. "Have you contacted Maris?"

"Yes."

"That's good. She phoned several times yesterday wanting to know about you."

"Sorry."

"I get it. So how are things with her?"

"I broke it off with her last night."

"I guess that doesn't surprise me. Whatever happened to 'slow down'?"

Vasso let out a morose laugh. "Look where it got *you*."

CHAPTER FIVE

August 26

ALREADY IT WAS FRIDAY. Five days without seeing Vasso felt like five years. In the time they'd been together, they'd confided in each other about the very personal things in their lives. He knew information about her she hadn't shared with anyone else. Zoe loved being with him. She ached for his company. He brought excitement into her life.

But she'd better get used to separations because the foundation was only a small part of the huge company he ran with his brother. And the more she heard about their generosity, the greater her need grew to do all she could to help in such a humanitarian effort.

Over the last five days Zoe had been able to introduce herself to every inmate except the twenty-four-year-old guy from Athens named Nestor. The resident therapist was worried about him. He'd been undergoing chemo in the infusion clinic and was in a depressed state, refusing to talk to anyone.

The therapist told her Nestor had been a receptionist

at a hotel that went bankrupt. He couldn't find a job and after a few months became homeless. Two months later, he was diagnosed with lymphoma. He usually lived on the steps of a Greek Orthodox Church but spent a lot of time under the nearby bridge with his other homeless friends.

This was the case of another kind priest who got in contact with the center on Paxos and arrangements had been made to get him admitted. Zoe found out that the helicopters owned by the Giannopoulos brothers helped transport patients like Nestor from all over Greece when there was no other solution.

Through Yiannis she learned more about Vasso and Akis. Born to poverty, they'd built a billion-dollar business in such a short period of time it stunned the Greek financial world. That was why the media was always in their face. It explained why Vasso made his home here on Paxos. Evidently his younger brother lived on the nearby island of Anti Paxos.

Just thinking about Vasso caused her breath to catch.

Already she was finding out that the homeless patients were afraid there'd be nothing for them to look forward to once they had to leave the center. That was an area needing to be addressed. Zoe had known the kind of depression that was drawing the life out of Nestor. Now that lunch was over, it would be a good time to visit him.

She took some oranges and plastic forks with her. When she reached his room she found him half lying in a recliner wheelchair. Every room had a sign that said,

"Reality is never as dark as the places your brain visits in anticipation." How true.

"Nestor?"

He opened his eyes. They were a warm brown. Despite his bald head, he was good looking, or would be if he were animated.

"If you're too nauseated to talk, I've been there. Mind if I sit down?" She pulled a chair over to him and set the items on the table. "I'm new here. My name's Zoe. I just got out of the hospital in New York City after being there a year. I had lymphoma too."

That brought a spark. "You?"

"I thought I'd be dead by now, but it didn't happen. I also lost my family in a fire, which made things much worse. I understand you don't have family either."

"No. My grandfather raised me, but he died."

"Well we're both very lucky that the Giannopoulos Foundation exists. They've given me a job here. What kind of a job do you want when you leave?"

"I won't be leaving," he murmured.

"Of course you will. As my priest told me, God didn't come to my rescue for nothing. I know how the nausea can make you think you'll never be better. But it will pass. I brought you some things that helped me.

"If you open and smell an orange before you eat, the aroma will make the food tolerable. At least it worked for me. Also, the metal forks and spoons sometimes make you gag. Try eating your food with a plastic fork and see if it makes any difference."

He eyed her with curiosity. Good!

"See you soon. Maybe one of these days we'll go

outside on the patio and have a game of cards. I'll bring a scarf and some snacks. I have an idea you'd make a dashing pirate. You know, young-Zorba-the-Greek style."

She left the room and continued on her rounds until the end of the day. Yiannis wanted her to be his eyes and ears. Besides keeping up on the paperwork, he expected her to make suggestions to improve their services. What was missing? That's what he wanted to know.

Now that she'd been hired full time, they would take turns covering for each other Saturday and Sunday. This coming weekend was his turn to work. Suddenly Zoe had more freedom than she knew what to do with.

When she walked out to catch the bus, the fountain of Apollo was playing. Again she was reminded of Vasso who, like the sun god in his chariot, was so handsome it hurt. She needed to get her mind off him. In the morning she'd take a long hike around the island.

On Sunday, she and Olympia, one of the cooks from the hospital, were going to take the ferry to Corfu from Loggos. While Olympia met with her relatives, Zoe planned to do some sightseeing on her own and was looking forward to it.

A group of workers got on the bus with her. They were already friendly with her and chatted. One by one they got off at different stops. Zoe was the only one who rode all the way into the village. By now the driver named Gus knew her name. Though she might be in Greece rather than New York, there was the same atmosphere of community she'd loved growing up.

When Zoe got off the bus, she headed for one of the *taverna*s that served *mezes* along the harbor front. At twilight the lights from the boats and ferry twinkled in the distance. It was a magical time of night.

Most of the tables outside were taken by tourists, but she finally found an empty one. She'd been anxious to try the various fish appetizers to see how they compared with her mother's cooking. The waiter brought an assortment of octopus, shrimp, sardines, calamari and clams.

Maybe she was biased, but she thought her mom's were better. Then again maybe she was missing her family. How they would have loved to come here for a vacation.

Don't look back, Zoe. You're the luckiest girl in the world to have been given this opportunity. You've been handed a second chance at life. You've been able to realize your dream to work for the Giannopoulos Foundation. You're living in one of the most beautiful spots on earth.

"Such a beautiful young woman sitting alone at the table looking so sad is a sin. Even if it isn't all right, I'm going to join you."

She'd know that distinctive male voice anywhere and looked up in shock. "*Vasso*—"

"Sorrow on a night like this is a tragedy."

Zoe made an odd sound at the sight of him. Tonight he'd dressed in a black silk shirt and tan trousers. Afraid she was staring hungrily at him, she averted her eyes. "I was just doing a little reminiscing about my parents. You caught me at the wrong moment."

He took a seat opposite her at the round table. His nearness did strange things to her equilibrium. "What's on that mind of yours?"

The waiter came, but Vasso only ordered a cup of coffee. She knew he was waiting for an explanation. "I've been sitting here counting my blessings."

"That sounds like you. So you're not missing home then?"

She sat back in the chair. "I stay in touch with my friends through email. As for Chad, he took my advice and is out of my life."

Her heart skipped a beat. "It was the right decision for both of us. Otherwise I wouldn't be sitting here on the island Kyria Panos calls the jewel of the Ionian, eating dinner with my benefactor. If you saw me in a sad mood just now, I was thinking how much my parents would have loved this island and how they longed to visit Florina. But my mother would whisper that these sardines were overly seasoned."

Following his chuckle, he took a sip of the coffee the waiter had brought to the table. "What are your plans for this weekend? I talked to Yiannis and learned it's your turn to be off work until Monday."

She glanced around as if she were afraid to look at him. "We've decided to alternate weekends. The security guards will take turns to cover for us while we sleep there."

"According to him you're turning the place around already."

"Yianni is just being nice."

"So it's Yianni now?" he questioned with a smile.

"The first time I called him that by mistake, he said his wife always dropped the 's' and he ordered me to keep doing the same thing."

"It's clear he's happy with you." Vasso finished his coffee. "How do *you* like your job by now?"

CHAPTER SIX

"I LOVE IT!" Zoe's eyes sparkled like the aquamarine sea around Akis's villa on Anti Paxos. "There's this one patient named Nestor I want to tell you about. But only if you have the time."

"I'm off work for the weekend too. If there isn't something you need to do, why don't we drive to my house to talk? There's a lineup of tourists from the ferry who would appreciate this table."

When she reached in her purse to pay the bill, he checked her movement and pulled out his wallet to do the honors.

"I don't expect you to pay for me."

"Not even when it's your birthday?"

She gasped slightly, but then she shook her head. "Why am I not surprised? You know everything about me."

"Almost everything," he teased. "This one is the big twenty-five. I remember having one of those five years ago."

"Did you celebrate with someone special?"

"If she'd been special, she and I would still be together."

She eyed him frankly. "Your fault or hers?"

"Most definitely mine."

"Don't tell me there hasn't been one woman in your life who meant the world to you?"

He helped her up from the table and they walked along the waterfront to the parking area near the pier. "Her name was Sofia Peri. I asked her to marry me."

After a measured silence, "How long ago?"

"When I was twenty. But the business Akis and I put together hadn't gotten off the ground yet. She needed a man with substance."

Zoe stared up at him before getting in his car. "Just look what *she* missed…"

Touché.

He closed the door and went around to the driver's seat to get in. They drove the short way to his house in companionable silence. "Where does that road go?" she asked before they reached his villa.

"To the pier where I keep my boat."

She turned to him. "Can we drive down to look at it?"

"If that's what you want." He made a right turn that led to the water's edge where she saw his gleaming cruiser.

There was an enchantment about the night. A fragrant breeze lightly rippled the water. This was Vasso's front yard. "It must be fabulous to go everywhere you want by water. Of course you go by helicopter too, but I can't imagine anything more fun than finding new coasts to explore."

Vasso shut off the engine and turned to her. "I had

those same thoughts years ago. When the rich people pulled into our little harbor to eat and buy things from the store where Akis and I worked, I always wondered what that would be like. That was long before it became an Alpha/Omega 24 store."

Her heart ached for how difficult his life had been. "Is that how you met the woman you proposed to? Was she a tourist who came in?"

"No. She lived in the village. We went to the same church and the same school, even though Akis and I were absent most of the time. Her parents didn't approve of me, but she defied them to be with me."

Zoe felt pained for him. "Was she your childhood sweetheart?"

"You could say that. I assumed we'd get married one day. We were crazy about each other, or so I thought. It helped me get through some difficult times, especially after our father died. Akis and I continued to work there and had saved enough money to buy it from the owner. By then I was nineteen and had to do my military service.

"While I was gone, we wrote to each other and made plans. At least *I* did. But I didn't realize that while I was away, she'd started seeing a local fisherman's son who was making a good living. She never once mentioned him to me until my return. The news that she'd fallen for someone else pretty well cut my heart out."

Zoe didn't know what to say. "My relationship with Chad never got as far as yours." The normal platitudes wouldn't cover it to comfort him because in truth, the woman sounded shallow. If she chose ready money over the true value of Vasso Giannopoulos whom she'd loved for years, then he was well out of it.

"Are you saying you were never intimate with him?"

"No. I was taught to wait for marriage. Guilt kept me from making that mistake. Thank goodness it did since Chad and I weren't meant to be. But I'm truly sorry about Sofia."

"That's past history. Fortunately for me, it was Akis's time to go into the military. I had to do the job of two people to keep our business running. By the time he got back, we went all out to make a success of our lives. Both of us were sick of being looked upon as the impoverished Giannopoulos boys who rarely went to school and had no education. I believe it was harder on Akis, but he's very sensitive about it."

"The poor thing," she said quietly. "Neither of you knew your mother who could have comforted both of you. I can't comprehend it."

"Our father made up for it."

"That's obvious. The two centers you've built in honor of him say everything." Her throat had started to swell. "If I could meet him, I'd tell him he raised the best sons on earth."

"If I keep listening to you, I just might believe it. As long as we're here, would you like to go for a boat ride?"

"I thought you'd never ask," she admitted on a laugh.

"I'll take us on a short drive to the harbor. It's very picturesque at night."

Zoe got out of the car before he could come around to help her and started walking to the boat dock. She turned to him. "What can I do to help?"

His white smile in the semi-darkness sent a rush of warmth through her body. "If you want to undo the rope on this end, I'll take care of the other."

His cruiser looked state-of-the-art, but small enough for one person to manage. She did her part, then stepped in and moved over to the seat opposite the driver's seat. Never in her wildest dreams would she have imagined spending her twenty-fifth birthday driving around an island in the Ionian Sea with a man as incredible as Vasso. If she was dreaming, it didn't matter. She was loving every minute of it.

He stepped in with a male agility that was fascinating to watch and handed her a life jacket to put on. As he started to sit down she said, "You have to wear one too. I'm not the world's greatest swimmer. If I had to save you, it would be kind of scary."

His deep chuckle seemed part of the magic of the night. When they were both buckled up, he started the engine and they went at wakeless speed until they were able to skirt the cove. Zoe got up and stood at the side. Other boats were out, but all you could see were their lights and other lights on the island.

She turned around and braced her back so she could look at Vasso. "I've been thinking about your childhood. Did they offer a class in English when you did go to school?"

He slanted her a glance. "Yes, but we were rarely there. Our major knowledge came from talking to the English-speaking tourists. The owner of the store gave us a book to learn from. Our father told us we had to learn it in order to be successful."

"My parents spoke English and I was lucky to be taught at school from day one. If I'd had to learn it from a book the way you did and teach myself, it wouldn't have happened, believe me."

"You would if it meant your living."

Her life had been so easy compared to Vasso's, she didn't want to think about it. "I'm sure you're right."

"What kind of books did you read?"

"For pleasure?"

He nodded.

"English was my major, but I have to admit I loved all kinds of literature. In my mind you can't beat the French for turning out some of the great classics. My favorite was Victor Hugo's *Les Misérables* about Jean Valjean, who listened to the priest and did good. One of my classmates preferred Dumas's *Count of Monte Cristo* whose desire for revenge caused him not to listen to the priest."

Vasso slowed the boat because they'd come to the harbor where she could fill her eyes with its beauty. "I've seen the films on both stories. We'll fly to Athens and take in a film one day soon, or we could go dancing if you'd like."

Zoe smiled. "That sounds fun, but finding the time might be difficult." *Don't torture me with future plans, Vasso.* "I have my work cut out here."

In that quiet moment Vasso reached out and caressed her cheek with his free hand. His touch sent trickles of delight through her nervous system. "Yiannis has been thanking me for dropping you on his doorstep. I do believe everyone is happy." In the moonlight his heart-melting features and beautiful olive skin stood out in relief. "Shall we go back to the house?"

More than anything in the world Zoe wanted to see his home, but there were reasons why she had to turn him down. He was her employer, but there was much more to it than that. She'd found herself thinking about him all week, wishing he'd come by the hospital. For her to be looking for him all the hours of the day and evening meant he'd become too important to her already.

She could feel her attraction to him growing to the point she found him irresistible. This shouldn't be happening. If she fell in with his wishes, she could be making the worst mistake of her life. And it would be a big one, because there was no future in it.

"I'd better not, but thank you anyway. This has been a thrill to come out in your cruiser. I've loved every second of it, but I've got a big day planned tomorrow and need to get to bed."

The oncologist had told her that because of her type of lymphoma, the odds according to the Follicular Lymphoma International Prognostic Index indicated she'd live five years, maybe more. No one could guess when there'd be a recurrence.

With that in mind, she needed to keep her relationship with Vasso professional. She was already having trouble separating the line between friendship and something else. By touching her cheek just now he'd stoked her desire for him. He'd mattered too much to her from the beginning and her longing for him was getting stronger.

Whatever the statistics said, Zoe was a ticking time

bomb. The breakup with Chad had been hard enough to deal with. But knowing the disease would come back had made her fear another romantic involvement. The only thing to do was stay away from any sign of emotional attachment that could hurt her or anyone else. Zoe had her work at the center and would give it her all.

On their way back to the car she hoped she hadn't offended him. He'd been so kind to find her at the *taverna* and help her celebrate her birthday. Yet once again she felt tension emanating from him, stronger than before.

When he helped her in the car he said, "Tomorrow I'm planning to look at a new property. I'd like you to fly there with me. It'll be a chance for you to see another part of Greece. We'll only be gone part of the day. Once we're back, you can get on with your other plans."

The blood pounded in her ears. "That wouldn't be a good id—"

"Humor me in this, *thespinis,*" he cut her off. "Since I came empty-handed this evening, let it be my birthday present to you."

She averted her eyes. "Did Yianni put you up to this?"

"No. I actually thought it up all by myself." On that note she laughed and he joined in. "I like it when you laugh."

Zoe didn't dare tell him how his laugh affected her... the way his black eyes smiled, the way he threw his head back, the way his voice rumbled clear through to her insides making them quiver. Oh no. She couldn't tell this beautiful Greek god things like that.

Her resistance to him was pitiful. "How soon did you want to leave?"

"I'll come by your apartment at eight-thirty."

If he was going on business, then she needed to dress for the occasion. When he went out in public he was targeted by the paparazzi. She wanted to look her best for him.

"What's on your mind?" he asked when he pulled up in back of the apartment.

"Things that would bore a man."

"Try me," he challenged with fire in his eyes.

"What lipstick should I put on, what shoes to match my dress, what handbag will be better. Decisions, decisions. See what I mean?"

He scrutinized her for a moment. "I see a lovely woman. What she wears doesn't matter."

"I'm a fake. If you saw me without my hair you'd have a heart attack." She'd said it intentionally to remind him who she was, and got out of the car. "Someday I'll lose it all again when I have to undergo another session of chemo, so I'll enjoy this momentary reprieve while I can. Thank you for this unexpected evening. I'll be waiting for you in the morning. Good night, Vasso."

She let herself in the back door, but was so out of breath it took a minute before she could climb the stairs. Even if her fairy godfather hadn't needed the reminder, *she* did.

Tomorrow has to be your last time with him, Zoe. Absolutely your last.

After a shower and shave, Vasso put on tan trousers and a silky, claret-colored sport shirt. While he fixed himself his morning cup of coffee, his phone rang. It was his brother.

He picked up. "*Yassou,* Akis."

"Where are you?"

"At the house."

"Good. Raina and I were hoping you'd come over this morning and have breakfast with us. We haven't seen you in two weeks."

"Thanks, but I'll have to take a rain check on that."

After a pause, "What's going on?"

"I'm off on business in a few minutes."

"We already closed the deal on the store in Halkidiki."

He rubbed the back of his neck. "This is something different."

"Then it has to involve Zoe Zachos. Talk to me."

Vasso let out a frustrated sigh. "I've been helping her settle in."

"And that includes taking her on a business trip?" His incredulity rang out loud and clear.

Vasso checked his watch. "I'm going to be late picking her up. I'll explain everything later. Give Raina my love."

The question Akis was really asking went to the core of him. But he couldn't talk about it. Once they got into a conversation, his brother would dig and dig. Zoe had said the same thing about him. They weren't brothers for nothing, and Akis wouldn't stop until he'd gotten to the bare bones. Vasso wasn't ready to go through that. Not yet...

Pieces of last night's conversation with Zoe had shaken him.

I'm a fake. If you saw me without my hair you'd have a heart attack. Someday I'll lose it all again, so I'll enjoy this momentary reprieve while I can.

Chilled by the possibility of the lymphoma recurring, Vasso started the car and drove to her apartment, unaware of the passing scenery.

When Chad heard I'd been told my disease would probably be terminal, he couldn't handle it. I told him I didn't want him to have to handle it and begged him to take the job offer in Boston and not look back. He took my advice.

Chad's pain would have been excruciating to realize he might lose her. But Zoe had to have been in anguish over so many losses.

Vasso's thoughts flew to his father when he'd been on the verge of death. The sorrow in his eyes that he wouldn't be able to see his sons grow to maturity—the pain that they'd never known their mother—the hope that they would never forget what a wonderful woman and mother she'd been—

Tears smarted his eyes. Not so much for the pain in his past, but for Zoe who didn't know what the future would bring. Their light conversations only skimmed the surface of what went on underneath. Her declaration that she never planned to marry was part of the babble to cover up what was going on deep inside of her.

All of a sudden he heard a tap on the window and turned his head. It was Zoe! He hadn't realized he'd pulled to a stop outside the apartment door. She looked gorgeous in a simple black linen dress with cap sleeves and a crew neck. The sun brought out the gold highlights in her hair.

He leaned across the seat to let her in. She climbed in on those well-shaped legs and brought the smell of strawberries inside. Her lips wore the same color and cried out to be kissed. Her eyes met his. "*Kalimera,* Vasso."

"It's a beautiful morning now, *thespinis*. Forgive me for staring. You look fabulous."

Color rose into her cheeks. "Thank you. After getting caught off guard by the paparazzi in Athens, I thought I'd better be prepared to be seen in the company of one of Greece's major financial tycoons."

Vasso took a deep breath. "I hope that's not the case today. Have you eaten breakfast?"

"Oh yes. Have you?"

"Just coffee."

Her brows met in a delicate frown. "That's all you had last night."

Zoe managed to notice everything. He liked it. He liked her. *So much in fact he couldn't think about anything else.* "I'm saving up for lunch," he said and drove the car back along the tree-lined road to his house where the helicopter was waiting.

"Where are we going?"

"I've decided to let it be a surprise. You'll know when we land at the heliport."

Before long they'd climbed aboard the helicopter and lifted off. Vasso put on his sunglasses and turned on the mic. When he looked over his shoulder he saw that Zoe had put on sunglasses too. She was beautiful and could easily be a famous celebrity. But he was glad no one knew about her. He liked the idea of keeping his find to himself.

He gave her a geography lesson as they flew northward to Macedonia. She knew more Greek history than most people of his acquaintance. Once they neared the desired destination, the land became more mountainous. He could tell her eyes were riveted on the dark green landscape that opened up to half a dozen magnificent lakes. Further on a sprawling city appeared. The pilot took them down and landed in a special area of the airport. When the rotors stopped whirling Vasso said, "Welcome to Florina, Zoe."

She looked at him in wonder. "Are you serious?"

"When you told me your parents had wanted to bring you here for your graduation, it gave me the idea."

"So you don't really have business here?" she asked in a softer voice.

"I didn't say that."

Zoe shook her head and took off her sunglasses. "You do too much for me, Vasso."

"I'd hoped for a better reaction than a lecture."

"I didn't mean to sound like that. Forgive me."

"Come on. I have a limo waiting to take us sightseeing." He got out first then helped her down. The urge to crush her warm body in his arms was overwhelming, but he held back.

The limo was parked nearby. He helped her inside, but this time he sat next to her. "I've asked the driver to take us on a small tour. When I told him your great-grandparents lived here until the outbreak of the Greek

Civil War, he promised to show us some of the historical parts of Florina and narrate for us over the mic."

She looked out the window. "I can't believe this is happening."

"I'm excited about it, too. I've never spent time in this area and am looking forward to it."

"Thank you from the bottom of my heart," came her whisper. When he least expected it, Zoe put a hand over his and squeezed it for second. But as she tried to remove it, he threaded his fingers through hers and held on to it.

"I think I'm almost as excited as you are. The cycle of the Zachos family has come full circle today. Seventy years ago your ancestors left this town to get away from communism. Now their great-granddaughter is back to put down her roots in a free society. That's no small thing."

"Oh, Vasso."

In the next instant she pressed her head against his arm. While the driver began his narration—unaware of what was going on in the rear—Vasso felt her sobs though she didn't make a sound. Without conscious thought he put his arms around her and hugged her to him, absorbing the heaves of her body. He could only imagine the myriad of emotions welling up inside her.

After a few minutes she lifted her head and faced straight ahead. "I hope the driver can't see us. Here he's going out of his way to tell us about the city, and I'm convulsed."

"He knows this tour has more meaning for you than most tourists so he'll understand."

"You always know the right thing to say."

For the next half hour the driver took them past buildings and landmarks made famous by the prominent filmmaker Theo Angelopoulos.

"Since the last war I don't imagine the homes my great-grandparents left are even standing," she confided.

"Probably not." Vasso asked the driver to drop them off at a point along the Sakoulevas River. "Let's get out and walk to Ioannou Arti Street so you can get a better view of the twentieth-century buildings along here. There's an archaeological museum we can visit."

She climbed out and put her arm through his as they played tourist. It felt so natural with her holding on to him like this. He could wish this day would go on forever.

"This is fabulous, Vasso. I had no idea the city was so beautiful. To think maybe my great-grandparents walked along this very river."

"Maybe it was along here they fell in love."

Zoe looked up at him in surprise. "I had no idea you're such a romantic at heart."

"Maybe that's because you bring it out in me." Obeying an impulse, he lowered his mouth and kissed those lips he'd been dying to taste. It only lasted a moment, but the contact sent a bolt of desire through him. She broke the kiss and looked away before they walked on.

The limo met them at the next street and they got back in. "If you've had enough, I'll tell the driver to run us by a market the Realtor told me was for sale. He tells me there's a *taverna* nearby where we can try out *burek*. We'll see if it compares to your mother's recipe."

"I'd love that."

Vasso alerted the driver and soon they pulled up in front of a store selling produce. He got out and helped Zoe down. Together they walked inside the busy market. The city was certainly big enough to support one of their stores. But he was curious to know the figures and approached the owner.

"While I talk to him, take a look around and see if there's something you want to buy to take back to the apartment."

She smiled. "Take as long as you need."

Zoe strolled around, eyeing the fruits and vegetables brought in by local farmers. Vasso noticed the customers eyeing her, even the owner who could hardly concentrate when asked a simple question.

When Vasso had learned what he wanted to know, he went in search of Zoe and found her at the back of the market buying a bag of vegetables.

"Don't they sell peppers in Loggos?"

Her face lit up. "No. These are sweet Florina red peppers. My mother remembered her mother and grandmother cooking these. They aren't like any other peppers in the world. I have the recipe. When we get back to Loggos, I'll cook some for you with feta cheese and we'll see if they live up to their reputation. The eggplant looks good, too."

His pulse raced at the thought of going back to Zoe's apartment. "Then let's grab a slice of *burek* at the *taverna* two doors down now, and eat a big meal this evening."

"That sounds perfect."

She hadn't said no. Their day out wasn't going to end the second they flew back to Loggos. That was all he cared about.

After telling the owner he'd be in touch with the Realtor, Vasso carried her bag of precious peppers and eggplant as they walked along the pavement to the outdoor café. He ordered *burek* and Skopsko beer for both of them.

When she'd eaten a bite, he asked for her opinion.

"I'm more curious to know what you think, but you have to tell the truth. If you like it better than mine, it won't hurt my feelings very much."

He burst into laughter and ate a mouthful of the pie. Then he ate a few more bites to keep her in suspense. She was waiting for an answer. Those green eyes concentrated solely on him, melting him to the chair. "It's good. Very good. Yours is better, but I can't define why it's different."

She leaned forward. "You mean it?"

Good heavens, she was beautiful. "I don't lie, *thespinis.* Let's drink to it." They touched glasses, but she only drank a little bit of hers while Vasso drained the whole thing. Food had never tasted so good, but that was because he was with her and was filled with the taste of her. He wanted more and suspected she did too otherwise she wouldn't be talking about their spending the rest of the day together back on Loggos.

"Excuse me while I freshen up before we leave."

Two hours later they arrived back at Zoe's apartment. While she got busy preparing the peppers, Vasso followed her directions for *moussaka*. "I'm glad you're staying for dinner, Vasso. There's something important I want to talk to you about."

Vasso darted her a piercing glance. His heart failed him to think she had an agenda. Was that the reason he'd made it over her doorstep tonight, and not because she couldn't bear to say good-night to him?

"What is it?"

CHAPTER SEVEN

"I DIDN'T FINISH telling you about one of the patients named Nestor. The poor thing doesn't think he's going to get better. He's depressed, but it isn't just because he's undergoing chemo. He lives with the fear that because he was homeless when he was brought in, he has no work to go back to even if he does recover.

"I've discovered that several of the older patients are afraid they won't get their jobs back if their disease goes into remission. So I was thinking maybe in my off hours I could set up a service to help those patients find a job."

"A service?" One dark brow lifted. "Have you discussed this with Yiannis?"

"Oh no. This would be something I'd do on my own. But I wanted to see what you thought about it."

He put the *moussaka* in the oven. "It's a very worthy project. Maybe even a tough one, but you're free to do whatever you want in your spare time. Surely you know that."

"So you wouldn't disapprove?"

Vasso frowned. "Why would you even ask that question?"

She carefully peeled the skins off the roasted peppers. "Because the people I approach will ask what I do for a living and your foundation will come up. You're a modest man. I don't want to do anything you wouldn't like."

He lounged against the counter while she prepared the peppers to cook with olive oil, feta cheese and garlic. "You couldn't do anything I wouldn't like."

Her gaze shot to his. His compelling mouth was only inches away. She could hardly breathe with him this close to her in the tiny kitchen. "You shouldn't have said that. I'm full of flaws."

His lazy smile gave her heart a workout. "Shall we compare?"

"You don't have any!"

"Then I'll have to break down and reveal a big one."

"Which is?"

"This!" He brushed her mouth with his lips. "When a beautiful woman is standing this close to me, I can't resist getting closer." He kissed her again, more warmly this time.

"Vasso—" She blushed.

"I told you I had a flaw."

She turned from him to put the peppers in the oven. When she stood up, he was right there so she couldn't move unless he stepped away. "I'd like to spend the day with you tomorrow. We'll tour the island and go swimming on a beach with fascinating seashells. What do you say?"

He could probably hear her heart pounding. She'd promised herself that after today, she wouldn't see him again unless it was for professional reasons.

Thank heaven she had a legitimate excuse to turn him down.

"Thank you, Vasso. That's very sweet of you, but I can't. I'm going to Corfu in the morning with Olympia."

Those black eyes traveled over her features as if gauging her veracity. "I might have known you'd strike up a friendship with her. She worked in the food services industry before coming to us."

Zoe nodded. "We have that and more in common."

He took a deep breath and moved away. "I'm sad for me, but glad for you to be making friends so fast."

"I found out she bikes with her husband. So they're going to lend me one of their bikes and we'll take rides around the island after work and on our free weekends." She'd added that to let him know her calendar was full.

Another long silence followed, forcing her to keep talking. "Everyone here has been so friendly. I already feel at home here. After moving heaven and earth for me, your job is done. You don't have to worry about me anymore."

Still no response. Needing to do something physical, she set the little breakfast table. After making coffee, she invited him to sit down while she served him dinner. When he still didn't say anything, she rushed to fill the void.

"I'll never forget the gift you gave me today. Seeing the city of my ancestors meant more to me than you will ever know."

"It was a memorable day for me, too," he murmured. "I want to spend more days like this with you, Zoe. I'd love to go biking with you."

"Between our busy schedules, that could prove difficult." She put the *moussaka* on the table and stood at his side to serve him a plate of peppers. "Tell me what you think about Florina's most famous vegetable."

He took one bite then another and another and just kept nodding.

That was the moment Zoe knew she was in love with him. The kind you never recovered from. To her despair, the thing she hadn't wanted to happen *had* happened. She adored him, pure and simple. His kisses made her hunger for so much more. His touch turned her inside out with longings she wanted and needed to satisfy. *Oh, Vasso... What am I going to do about you?*

Before Zoe blurted that she loved him, she sat down and ate with him. "Um... These really are good."

"You're a fabulous cook, and I've never tasted better *moussaka*."

"You put it together, so you get the credit."

After Vasso drank his coffee, he flashed her a glance. "The next time we're together, I'll cook dinner for you at my house and I won't take no for an answer."

Zoe let the comment slide. The way he made her feel was toppling her resistance. As she got up to clear the table her cell rang. She reached for her phone lying on the counter.

"Go ahead and answer it," he urged her when she didn't click on.

She shook her head. "It's Kyria Themis. I'll call her back after you leave."

"Maybe it's important, so I'll go."

Much as she was dying for him to stay, she knew this

was for the best. Their friendship needed to remain a friendship, nothing more. The kiss he'd given her today had rocked her world. That's why the less they saw of each other, the better.

She walked him to the door. "Good night then, Vasso. This day was unforgettable."

So are you, Zoe.

Vasso got out of there before he broke every rule and started to make love to her. In his gut he knew she wanted him, too. Desire wasn't something you could hide. Whether in the limo or the car, the chemistry between them had electrified him.

Though he didn't doubt she'd already made plans for tomorrow, he sensed she was deliberately trying to keep their relationship platonic. But it wasn't working. Despite her determination not to go to his house, she'd invited him to the apartment tonight and had cooked dinner for him.

There were signs that she was having trouble being too close to him. He'd noticed the little nerve throbbing at the base of her throat before he'd moved out of her way in the kitchen.

While she'd stood next to him to serve dinner, he'd felt the warmth from her body. It had taken all his willpower not to reach around and pull her onto his lap. She was driving him crazy without trying.

On the drive to his house he made a decision to stay away for a few days and let her miss him. He had no doubts it would be harder on him, but work would help him put things in perspective.

Tomorrow he'd do a tour of the stores where he needed to meet with the new store managers to make certain they were following procedure. That would take him the good part of a week. In the meantime Akis would be free to meet with their food distributors in Athens for the critical monthly orders.

Once he was home he phoned his brother to tell him his plans. Before hanging up he said, "I met with the owner of a produce market in Florina today who wants to sell. The Realtor has named a figure that's too high. I think I can get the asking price down, but wanted to know your feelings about us putting up a store there."

"I always trust your judgment, but why Florina? What were you doing there?"

He gripped the phone tighter. "I flew Zoe there for her birthday. Her great-grandparents emigrated from there to America in the mid-forties. Before her parents could take her there for a college graduation present, they died in the fire."

His brother was quiet for a minute. "*Vasso—*"

"I know what you're going to say."

"Since you've already disregarded my warning to take it slow, I was only going to ask if there's a boyfriend in the picture."

"He bailed on her when he found out her disease would probably be terminal."

"That, on top of all her pain," his brother murmured in commiseration. "It would have taken a committed man."

He exhaled sharply. No one knew that better than Vasso. If Chad had loved her enough, he wouldn't have let her talk him into walking away. He could say the same for Sofia who hadn't had the patience to wait until things got financially better for him. Today he rejoiced that he and Zoe were still single.

"How is she working out with Yiannis?"

"They're trading off weekends and he lets her call him Yianni. That's how well they've hit it off. Let me tell you about her latest idea."

After he'd explained, Akis said, "I must admit a job referral service for the patients is a brilliant idea. When are Raina and I going to meet her?"

"I was hoping next Friday evening before she has to go on duty for the entire weekend."

"Do you want to bring her to our house?"

"I fear that's the only way it will work. She isn't comfortable coming to mine yet."

"Then you *have* heeded my warning to a certain extent."

Akis couldn't be more wrong. "Let's just say that for now I'm letting her set the pace. But I don't know how much longer I can hold out."

"Before you do what?"

"Don't ask that question yet because I can't answer it. All I know is I like being with her." *That was the understatement of all time*. "I'll talk to you later in the week. *Kalinihta.*" He clicked off and got ready for bed.

Once he slid under the covers, Akis's probing question wouldn't leave him alone. Until Vasso knew what Zoe really wanted, he couldn't plan on anything. She'd been hurt by Chad who hadn't seen her through her life-changing ordeal. To have a relationship with Zoe meant earning her trust. He'd begin his pursuit of her and keep at it until she had to know what she meant to him.

After a restless night, he flew to his first destination in Edessa and emailed her to let her know what he'd been doing. He did the same thing every night. By the time Friday came, he couldn't get back to Paxos soon enough. Before he drove to the center, he stopped by the number-one store to check in with the managers and buy some flowers.

"Vasso?" a female voice spoke behind him.

He turned around. "Sofia."

Her brown eyes searched his before looking at the flowers. "I was hoping to see you in here one of these days. Can we go somewhere private to talk?"

After she'd turned down his marriage proposal, there'd been times in the past when he would have given anything to hear her say that she'd changed her mind and wanted to marry him. How odd that he could look at her now and feel absolutely nothing. Meeting Zoe had finally laid Sofia's ghost to rest.

"Why not right here? I'm on my way to the center, but I can spare a few minutes. How are you?"

"Not good. I've left Drako."

Somehow that wasn't a surprise to him, yet it brought him no pleasure. Akis had told him he'd seen her in town a few months ago and she'd asked about Vasso. "I'm sorry for both of you."

Her eyes filled with tears. "Our marriage never took and you know the reason why. It was because of you. I've never stopped loving you, Vasso."

He shook his head. "I think if you look deep inside, you'll realize you were young and ambitious. Drako was already doing an impressive fishing business."

"I was a fool."

"I'm sorry for both of you."

"All this time and you've never married. I know it was because of me, and I was hop—"

"Sofia," he cut her off. "I moved on a long time ago."

"Are those flowers for someone you care about now?"

"They're for the woman I love," he answered honestly. Her face blanched. "You have children, and they need you more than ever. Now if you'll excuse me, I have to get to the center. I wish you the best."

He waved goodbye to the owners and hurried out to the car needing to see Zoe. By the time he reached the center he was close to breathless with anticipation. But first he went by Yiannis's office to let him know he was there. The older man told him she was out on the patio with several of the patients.

"When you have the time, I'll tell you about all the changes she's made around here for the better. We're lucky to have her, Vasso."

"I agree. Will it be all right with you if I steal her away for an early dinner?"

"Of course."

"Good."

Without wasting another second he hurried down the hall to find a container for the flowers, then he headed for the doors leading to the patio. She'd arranged four round umbrella tables to be close together with two patients at each one in their recliner wheelchairs. One man and one woman to a table. All wore some kind of head covering and all were playing cards. Zoe was obviously running the show using a regular chair.

She hadn't seen him yet. He stood watching in fascination for a few minutes.

All of them had to be in their late forties or were older, except for one man who looked to be in his twenties. He wore a red paisley scarf over his head like a pirate. As Vasso moved closer, he could tell the younger man was fixated on Zoe. Why wouldn't he be? She was by far the most beautiful and entertaining female Vasso had ever seen. Today she was wearing a soft yellow blouse and skirt.

They were all into the game and the camaraderie between them was apparent. This was Zoe's doing. He reached for a regular chair and took it over to put down next to her. "Can anyone join in?"

He heard her quiet intake of breath when she glanced up at him with those translucent green eyes. "Kyrie Giannopoulos—this *is* a surprise. Please. Sit down and I'll introduce you."

One by one he learned their names. They were profuse in their thanks for his generosity. "We're having a round-robin that's timed," Zoe explained. "Nestor here is on a winning streak." She smiled at the younger man.

"Then don't let me interrupt," he whispered, tamping down his jealousy. "I'll just sit here and watch. Maybe later you'll tell me why the emails you sent back to me were so brief."

For a moment their eyes met. He saw concern in hers. Before the night was out, they were going to talk.

It appeared Nestor couldn't take his eyes off her. When he could see that Vasso wasn't about to leave, the younger man glared at him beneath veiled eyes. The fact that he was recovering after chemo didn't stop the way he studied her face and figure. Was Zoe interested in him?

Vasso couldn't prevent another stab of jealousy, but when he thought about it that was absurd. If there was a bond between them, it had to do with the fact that both Nestor and Zoe had their illness in common. They had an understanding that drew them together. If she suspected the younger man's infatuation, she didn't let it show.

Soon a couple of the nurses came out to take the patients back to their rooms. But Nestor declined help and wheeled his chair out of the room.

"Don't forget movie night tonight!" she called to them. "I'm bringing a treat!"

"We won't forget!" said one of the older men.

Vasso watched her clear up the cards. She was nervous of him. Did he dare believe that she was equally thrilled to see him, and that's why she'd been caught off guard? He desperately wanted to believe she was in love with him, too.

"What's this about movie night?"

She nodded. "During my chemo, there were nights when I couldn't sleep and wished there were something to do. I asked Yianni about it and he told me to organize it. Anything that could increase everyone's comfort was worth it."

Zoe never ceased to amaze him. "You're already revolutionizing this place. What time is your movie night?"

"After nine-thirty. That's when the demons come."

He didn't want to think about the demons she'd lived through. "In that case I'd like you to have an early dinner with me first. Please don't turn me down. My brother and his wife want to meet the new assistant manager. They've invited us over. Maybe you can get Raina to unload about Akis's imperfections. Maybe he pecks at her, too."

She laughed, causing her nervousness to disappear for the moment. "As if I'd ask her a question like that!" There was green fire in her eyes. "I'll have to let Yianni know I'm leaving for a while."

"I've already asked if it's all right, but if you'd rather not leave the center, just tell me. We can arrange dinner with them for another time."

"No." She shook her head. "That sounds lovely. I've wanted the opportunity to thank Akis. How soon do you want to leave?"

"As soon as you're ready. We'll leave from the hospital roof."

"Let me just freshen up and then I'll meet you at the private elevator in ten minutes."

"Before you go, these are for you." He handed her the flowers.

"Umm. Pink roses. They smell divine."

"They smell like you. I noticed the scent the first time you climbed in the limo."

Color filled her cheeks. "Thank you, Vasso. They're beautiful."

"Almost as beautiful as you."

She averted her eyes. "You shouldn't say things like that to me."

"Not even if I want to?"

"I'll just run to my desk and put them on the counter, then I'll join you."

He could have no idea how much the flowers meant to her. She loved him... Too many more moments like this and all her efforts to keep distance between them would go up in smoke.

After receiving his newsy emails all week, to be given these flowers had her heart brimming over with love for him. It was clear he wasn't about to go away, and now he was whisking her off to his brother's villa.

She was filled with wonder as the helicopter flew over the tiny island next to Paxos. Vasso pointed out the vineyards on Anti Paxos. "If you notice the surrounding water, it's Caribbean green. Your eyes are that color, Zoe."

Every comment from him was so personal it made it harder for her to keep pushing him away. *That's because you don't want to, Zoe. You're in love and you know it.*

As they descended to a landing pad, she could see that the water *was* green, not blue, putting her in mind of emerald isles she'd never seen except in film. Vasso helped her down and kept a hand on the back of her waist as they made their way toward the small stone villa.

"Look at these flowers!" Zoe exclaimed. "It's breath-taking." They lined the mosaic stone pathway.

"Vasso?" she heard a female voice call out.

"Nobody else!" he called back.

In the next instant Zoe caught sight of the lovely American woman who'd married the other Giannopoulos son. She was a blonde, too. Zoe's first impression was that she glowed with health. Vasso had told her they were expecting a baby.

"Zoe? This is my favorite sister-in-law Raina."

"Your only one," she broke into English, rolling her violet eyes. "I'm so glad you could make it." Raina shook her hand before hugging Vasso. "Akis just got back from Athens and will join us after he gets dressed. Please come in. We've been excited to meet you."

Zoe followed her into the most amazing living room. A fireplace had been built in a wall carved out of rock. Between the vaulted ceiling and arches, the stone villa reminded her of pictures from the old family photos that had gone up in flames. The curtains and pillows added marvelous colors of blue and yellow to the décor. Zoe loved it.

"While Vasso goes to find Akis, come out on the terrace, Zoe, and have some lemonade with me."

They walked past the open French doors where the terrace overlooked a kidney-shaped swimming pool. Glorious shades of red, purple and yellow flowers grew in a cluster at one end. Beyond it the sea shimmered. "You live in paradise, Raina."

Her eyes sparkled with glints of blue and lavender.

"Every day I wake up and can't believe any place could be so beautiful."

"I know. When Vasso took me on a helicopter ride, I thought I had to be dreaming."

"May we never wake up." Raina Giannopoulos had a charming manner Zoe found refreshing. "Come and sit. I've wanted to meet you ever since we heard you were coming to Greece to work." She smiled. "Don't get me wrong. I love it here, but I miss talking to another American once in a while. Do you know what I mean?"

Zoe liked her very much already. "I know exactly. It's nice to speak English with you."

"I'm working on my Greek, but it's slow in coming."

"I may be Greek in my DNA," Zoe confided, "but I'm American in my heart."

"I thought I was, too, before I married Akis. Now the Greek part has climbed in and sits next to it."

Zoe laughed while Raina poured them both a glass of lemonade. "Before the guys come out, may I tell you how much I admire you for handling everything you've been through? My grandfather died of stomach cancer and my grandmother from heart failure. I watched them suffer and can only imagine your agony."

"It's over now."

Raina nodded. "You don't know it, but both brothers have been very touched by your story and are astounded by your desire to pay them back. Their father meant the world to them. Until you came along, I don't think either of them realized what good they've really done."

"I know," Zoe whispered, moved by her admission

about her grandparents. Raina had known a lot of pain too. "It's hard for Vasso to accept a compliment. I'm afraid all I do is thank him. I'm sure he's sick of hearing about my gratitude."

"If that were the case, you wouldn't be here now."

"That's the thing. He got me this job so fast he couldn't know how important that is to me. One day my lymphoma will come back, so I want to do all I can for as long as I can."

She saw a shadow pass over Raina's face, but before anything else was said, two black-haired men with striking features came out on the terrace, dressed in casual trousers and sport shirts.

Zoe stared at Vasso's brother, then turned to his wife. "I didn't realize how closely they resemble each other," she whispered. "I thought Vasso was the only Greek god flying around Greece in a helicopter."

"Do you want to know a secret?" Raina whispered back. "When I first saw Akis on the street in Athens, he seemed to be the incarnation of the god Poseidon come to life from the sea."

"I thought you met at a wedding reception."

"That's true, but we almost bumped into each other first on the street."

Zoe smiled. "And you never recovered."

"Never."

"Would you believe my first thought was that Vasso was the sun god Apollo? The statue in the fountain at the center looks just like him. With a husband like yours, it makes you wonder if you're going to give birth to a gorgeous god or a goddess, doesn't it?" After that comment they both laughed long and hard, cementing their friendship.

The men came closer. "What's so funny, darling?"

While Zoe sat there blushing, Raina smiled up at her husband. "We were discussing the baby's gender."

"What's funny about that?" Vasso wanted to know. His intense gaze had settled on Zoe. She knew he wouldn't let it go without an answer.

"Maybe Raina will give birth to a little Poseidon carrying a trident. That's why we laughed."

A knowing look entered Akis's eyes before he kissed his wife on the cheek. "My choice would be an adorable Aphrodite like her mother."

The two of them were madly in love. Zoe could feel it. She was terribly happy for them and about the baby on the way. Zoe would never know that kind of joy. To get married, let alone have a baby, when she knew her cancer could come back wasn't to be considered.

She could see the hunger in Vasso's eyes when he looked at his brother's family. It was killing Zoe, too, because marriage and babies weren't in the cards for her. They couldn't be.

"Akis, let me introduce you officially to Zoe Zachos. Yiannis tells me he doesn't know how they ever got along without her."

"So I've heard." Akis came around and shook her hand. "Apparently your round-robin card game was a huge hit today. We'll have to lay in some chips to make things more interesting for your future poker games."

"That would be fantastic! Thank you. Before another moment goes by, I have to thank you for allowing me to work at the center. I've been given a second chance at life and will always be indebted to you and Vasso." Zoe fought to hide the tears quivering on the ends of her lashes.

She put up her hands. "I'll only say one more thing. I know you're God-fearing men because of your father's example. Christ said that when you've done it unto the least of these, you've done it unto me. Well, I'm one of the least. It's my joy to give back what I can."

Vasso stared at her for the longest time before Raina told the men to sit while she put on an American dinner California-style in Zoe's honor. Fried chicken, potato salad and deviled eggs along with Raina's Parker House rolls recipe.

Zoe had never enjoyed an evening more. Vasso told them about their trip to Florina and discussed the wisdom of putting in a store there. The time passed so fast she protested inwardly when she looked at her watch and saw that she needed to get back to the center.

Raina walked her out to the helicopter. Zoe smelled a haunting fragrance coming from the flowers. "I've never seen Vasso this animated since I met him. He never used to laugh the way he does now. It must be your effect on him. We'll do this again soon," Raina promised.

No. There couldn't be another time. Zoe wouldn't be able to stand being around these wonderful people again when it hurt so much. "Thank you for making me feel welcome, Raina. I've loved it. Vasso told me how you two met. Apparently Akis was running from the maid of honor at the reception and asked you to dance."

"Did he tell you I'd just sprained my ankle and was on crutches?"

"No."

"I was glad I couldn't dance with him because I didn't want anyone to know I was there. The paparazzi were outside waiting. Chloe's wedding was the event of the summer for the media."

Zoe nodded. "They mobbed Vasso the day we went shopping at the department store in Athens. With them always being in the news, it doesn't surprise me that women are after those two brothers. It's really a funny story about you two. Akis is a lucky man. For your information, you could open up your own restaurant serving the food we ate tonight."

The other woman hugged her. "After I heard from Vasso what a great cook you are, that's a real compliment."

Vasso came from behind and opened the door so she could climb in.

"Thanks again, you two. It was wonderful meeting you."

He followed her in. Once they'd fastened their seat belts, the rotors whined and they climbed into the twilight sky.

Zoe could see Vasso's profile in the semidark. He was a beautiful man who'd taken over her heart without trying. She was prepared to do anything for him. That meant weaning herself away from him. He deserved to meet a woman who had a lifetime ahead to give him love and bear his children.

Because of the foundation, she'd been granted five

years, maybe a little more, to live life until her time ran out. But it would be a selfish thing to do if she reached out for love. It would be asking too much to deliberately marry a man and have his baby, knowing she would have to go through another period of illness before leaving them. Zoe refused to do that to any man.

"Zoe? We're back at the hospital." Vasso's low voice brought her back to the present.

She thanked the pilot and got out of the helicopter. When Vasso started toward the elevator with her, she turned to him. "I had a marvelous evening and loved meeting your brother and his wife."

"You and Raina really seemed to hit it off."

"She's terrific. Between you and me, your brother doesn't have anything to worry about. She's crazy about him. No talk of his pecking at her."

Vasso grinned.

"It's obvious they have a wonderful marriage. Now I need to go inside and set things up. You don't need to come all the way to make sure I'm safe."

His dark brows furrowed. "Why are you pushing me away, Zoe?"

After taking a deep breath, she folded her arms to her waist. "Let's be honest about something. Our relationship has been unique from the beginning. The normal rules don't apply. You've done everything humanly possible to help me relocate to a new life, but I'm acclimatized now. For you to do any more for me will make me more beholden to you than ever. I don't want that."

"What if I want to be with you, and it has nothing to do with anything else?"

Zoe lowered her head. "If that's true, then I'm flattered."

"Flattered," he mouthed the word woodenly. "That's all? So if you never saw me again, it wouldn't matter to you?"

"I didn't say that," she defended in a throbbing voice.

"Then what *did* you say?"

"You're trying to twist my words." She pressed the button that opened the elevator door. When she stepped in, he joined her.

"Why are you running away from me?

"I'm not! I'm supposed to be back at work."

"Work can wait five minutes. I want an answer."

"*Vasso—*"

"Yes? I'm right here. Why won't you look at me? I lived for your emails, but you didn't open up in them."

Her cheeks felt so hot she thought she must be running a temperature. "Because... I'm afraid."

"Of me?" he bit out, sounding angry.

"No—" She shook her head. "Of course not. It— It's the situation," she stammered.

"If you're afraid I'm going to desert you the way Chad did, then you don't know me at all."

"I never said that."

"But it's what you were thinking. Admit it."

"You've got all this wrong, Vasso."

"Then what are you worrying about?"

"*Us!*" she cried.

"At least you admit there *is* an us," he said in a silky

tone. In the next breath he reached for her and slid his hands to her shoulders, drawing her close to his rock-hard body. "You're trembling. If it's not from fear, then it means you know what's happening to us. I'm dying to kiss you again. But this time we're not standing in the middle of Florina for all to see."

She hid her face in his shoulder. "I'd rather you didn't. We'll both be sorry if you do."

"I'll be sorry if we don't. Would you deny me the one thing I've been wanting since we met?"

All this time?

"Help me, Zoe," he begged. "I need you."

His mouth searched for hers until she could no longer hold out. When it closed over hers she moaned. Thrill after thrill charged her body as they began kissing each other. One led to another, each one growing deeper and longer. She was so lost in her desire for him she had no awareness of her surroundings.

Vasso's hands roved over her back and hips, crushing her against him while they strained to get closer. She was so on fire for him it wouldn't surprise her if they went up in flames. This wasn't anything like her response to other men, to Chad. All Vasso had to do was touch her and she was swept away by feelings she'd never thought possible.

"Do you have any idea how much I want you?" His voice sounded ragged. "Tell me now how sorry you are." His mouth sought hers again, filling her with sensation after sensation of rapture. But his question made it through the euphoric haze she was in and brought her back to some semblance of reality.

"Vasso—we can't do this any longer," she half gasped, struggling for breath.

"Of course we can."

"No." She shook her head and backed away from him. "I don't want a complication like this in my life."

"You see me as a complication?" he ground out.

"Yes. A big one. You're my ultimate boss. I'm here because of you. We crossed a line this evening, but if we stop right now, then there's been no harm done. I look upon you as a blessed friend and benefactor. I don't want to think of you in any other light."

His face looked like thunder. "Don't make me out to be something I'm not."

"You know what I mean. I need to be here on my own and work out my life without any more help from you. I don't have to explain to you how much I already love it here. But when Father Debakis asked you to interview me, he had no idea what a kind and generous man you really are or how far you would go for the welfare of another human being."

"You're confusing my human interest in you with the attraction we feel for each other, which is something else altogether. Admit the chemistry has been there from the beginning."

"How can I deny it after the way we kissed each other? But it doesn't change the dynamic that I'm an employee of the Giannopoulos Foundation. It would be better if we remain friends and nothing more. You admit you've had other girlfriends. I'm positive there will be more. When another woman comes into your life who sets off sparks, you'll be able to do something about it without looking back."

His black eyes glittered dangerously. "What about you?"

She threw her head back. "I told you the other day. I'm not interested in romance. I want to make a difference in other people's lives. In ways, Ms. Kallistos had the right idea about me after all."

"What rubbish. You know damn well you don't believe what you're saying. I know you don't, but for some reason I have yet to figure out, you've decided to be cruel."

"Cruel?" Her face heated up. "I'm trying to save both of us a lot of pain."

She heard a sharp intake of breath. "You're so sure we'll end up in pain?"

"I *know* we will."

He shook his dark head. "What do you know that I don't?"

Zoe didn't want to say the words. "Think about it and you'll see that I'm right. There's another Raina out there waiting for you to come along. She won't be an employee and she'll be able to give you all the things you've been longing for in your life. Trust me in this. Your turn is coming, Vasso. You're a dear man and deserve everything life has to offer."

Frown lines darkened his handsome features. "Why do I feel like you're writing my epitaph?"

No, my darling. Not yours. Zoe swallowed hard. "I'm not the woman for you."

A haunted expression entered his eyes. "You're not making sense."

"In time, it will be clear to you. Good night, Kyrie Giannopoulos. From now on that's how I'll address you coming and going from the center."

He pushed the button that took them down to the main floor. "Since I'm your boss, I'll accompany you to the entertainment center to offer help if you need it."

Oh, Vasso…

When they reached the game room, there were twelve patients assembled with several nurses standing by. "We've been waiting for you, Zoe," one of the women called out.

Nestor shot her a glance. "Did you forget the treat?"

"Of course not. It's something we chemo patients enjoyed when I was convalescing at the other center. I'm curious to know if you'll like it. But you have to be patient while it cooks."

"What are you going to pull out of your magic bag now?" Vasso said *sotto voce*.

After their painful conversation, his teasing comment made her smile. She ached with love for him and moved over to the microwave. "See these?" Zoe picked up a packet of popcorn lying on the counter.

"They don't sell this in Greece," Vasso murmured.

"True. I brought a supply in my bag when I flew over."

She put a packet in the microwave and pressed the button. In a few seconds the kernels started to pop. Her eyes met Vasso's as that wonderful smell started to permeate the air. When it stopped, she opened the door and pulled out the filled bag. Taking care, she opened it.

Vasso had first dibs. After eating some, he started nodding and took a handful. He couldn't stop with just one and kept eating and nodding. Zoe knew it was a winner and smiled. "I'll let you keep this bag and I'll do another one."

She started cooking it. "Since you're the bird down in the mine and you're still breathing, they'll be willing to try it."

His burst of rich male laughter warmed her heart.

"You think it'll catch on?" she asked.

"Like wildfire. In fact we'll have to stock these in our stores."

"You'll have to tell your managers to cook a batch to entice the customers."

His black eyes smoldered. "You've enticed *me*, Thespinis Zachos."

The popping stopped, but her heartbeat pounded on. She hurriedly pulled out the bag. Vasso took over and opened it before passing it around to those who were willing to try it.

In a louder voice she said, "The popcorn helped some of us at the other center. But if you're too nauseated, then wait till next Friday night," she urged. "Now I'll turn on the film. It's the one that got the most votes to watch. *The Princess Bride* in Greek."

Everyone started clapping.

Vasso turned off the overhead light and came to stand by her with a lazy smile on his face. "Where did you find that?"

"When I went to Corfu with Olympia. This film is a winner with everyone. Have you seen it?"

"No. Any chance of my cooking another bag while we watch?"

If Vasso was trying to break her down, he was doing a stellar job. Those roses had been her undoing. "You don't have to ask me if you want more popcorn. You're the boss."

CHAPTER EIGHT

EVERYTHING HAD BEEN going fine until Zoe reminded Vasso that she worked for him. But that was okay because he wasn't going to let her get away with ignoring him. She would have to put up with him coming to the center on a regular basis. Little by little he would wear her down until she confessed what was going on inside her.

Throughout the entertaining film, he noticed Nestor watching her rather than the movie. One day the younger man would be better. Since Zoe had voiced her concern, Vasso had been thinking about him. Their company had two thousand and one store managers throughout Greece. On Vasso's say-so, any one of them would take Nestor on as an employee.

When the movie was over and the lights went on, the nurses started wheeling the patients back to their rooms. Vasso volunteered to take Nestor. He felt Zoe's questioning glance on him while she straightened up the room. He kept on going and soon they'd entered his hospital room where Vasso sat on the chair near the table.

"You didn't have to bring me," Nestor murmured. "Thank you."

"You're welcome. Before I leave, I wanted to discuss something with you. I know you're in the recovery phase of your illness. When you're ready to be released, I'm curious to know where you want to go."

"I was born and raised in Athens."

"But I understand you have no family now."

"No," he said, tight-lipped.

"If you could do anything, what would it be?"

"Anything?" Vasso nodded. "I'd like to go to college, but that would be impossible."

At Nestor's age, Vasso had wanted the same thing, but he and Akis were too busy building their business. There was never the right time. "Maybe not."

The younger man looked shocked.

"There are scholarships available for hardworking people. If I arranged for you to get a job in Athens, you could attend college at night."

Nestor's eyes opened wider. "That would be amazing, but I don't know if I'm going to get well."

"I understand you're better today than you were a week ago. Have faith and we'll talk again when the doctor okays your release."

He left Nestor thinking about it and headed for the private elevator. There was nothing he wanted more than to find Zoe and talk to her. But she needed her sleep so she could be in charge tomorrow and Sunday. The one thing that helped him walk away tonight was knowing she wasn't going anywhere. She loved her job and he would always know where to find her.

For the next week he kept busy coordinating work with Akis and continued to send emails to Zoe. He knew his brother wanted to ask him more questions, but Akis kept silent. That was good because Vasso didn't want to get into a discussion about Zoe. They debated the pros and cons of putting up a store in Florina, but didn't come to a decision. The city wasn't growing as fast as some other areas.

On Friday afternoon he flew back to Paxos. After a shower and shave, he put on casual clothes and headed over to the center. Seven days away had made him hungry for the sight of her. But first he checked in with Yiannis who sang Zoe's praises. "We can be thankful all is well with that young woman."

"Amen to that." He expelled a relieved sigh. "I'm going to go over the books with Kyria Lasko in accounting if you need to find me." Vasso knew he wasn't fooling the admiral, but he appreciated the older man for not prying into his personal life.

Two hours later he walked down the hall. When he couldn't see Zoe at the front desk, he headed for the entertainment center. Friday night was movie night. He had a hunch she was in there setting things up for later. But when he went inside, he only found a couple of patients with a nurse.

"Have you seen Thespinis Zachos?"

"She just left, but she'll be back at nine-thirty."

Vasso thanked her and left the hospital in his car. En route to the town center he phoned her. By the time she picked up, his pulse had jumped off the charts.

"Vasso?"

She sounded surprised. He'd missed her so much just the sound of her voice excited him. "I'm glad you answered. Where are you?"

After a pause, "At the apartment."

"No bike riding today?"

"No. Our plans fell through. Her husband hurt his leg biking, so she's home taking care of him this weekend."

"Sorry to hear that. I flew in earlier and worked with the accountant at the center. I didn't see you anywhere. Have you eaten dinner?"

"Not yet."

"I'd like to talk to you about Nestor. Would you like to meet me at Psara's? I don't know about you but I'm craving fish."

He could hear her thoughts working. "That's the *taverna* down near the parking area?"

"Yes. I'm headed there now if you'd like to join me. But if you have other plans, I'll understand."

"No—" she exclaimed, then said no in a quieter voice. "Nestor told me you talked to him last week."

"That's right."

"You…planted a seed."

Good. "If you want to discuss it, I'll be watching for you." Without waiting for a response, he clicked off and pulled into the parking. He got out and hurried toward the *taverna* to grab a table before the place filled up. Being that it was a Friday night, the paparazzi were out covering the waterfront. Celebrities from Athens often came to Loggos for dinner. Vasso couldn't escape.

In a few minutes, every male young or old stared at the beautiful blonde woman making her way toward him. She'd dressed in a leaf-green blouse with a white skirt tied at the waist. He experienced the same sense of wonder he'd felt when he'd seen her the first time. She was like a breath of fresh air and walked with a lilt on those fabulous legs.

When Vasso stood up to pull out her chair for her, several journalists caught her on camera. She couldn't have helped but see them. "Ignore them," he muttered. "Pretty soon they'll go away."

"Not as long as you're here." But she said it with a smile. "I knew I was taking a chance to be seen with you."

"You're a brave woman, but then we already know that about you." His comment brought the color flooding into her cheeks.

The waiter came to pour coffee and take their order. They both chose the catch of the day. Once they were alone again, he studied her classic features. "Thanks for answering my emails. You've kept me abreast of everything going on at the center. But you never share your personal feelings. How *has* your week gone?"

"Every day is different. I couldn't be happier," she said through veiled eyes. "What about yours?"

"I can't complain as you know from my messages to you, but thanks for asking."

Considering what it had been like to get in each other's arms last week, this conversation was a mockery. But he'd play her game for a while longer. "How much did Nestor tell you?"

Now that he'd changed the subject to something important to her, she grew animated. "He mentioned that you talked to him about a scholarship so he could go to night school. He's been in disbelief that you really meant it."

Vasso sucked in his breath. "I would never have brought it up if I weren't serious. Earlier this week I talked to the manager of our number-four store in Athens. He'd be willing to give Nestor a job. I have no idea if he would want to work in a convenience store after being employed at a hotel, but—"

"I'm sure he would!" she cried out excitedly. "Oh, Vasso—there's been a light in his eyes that hasn't been there until now. It's because of you."

No. That light had to do with Zoe. She ignited everyone she met. "How much more chemo does he have to go through?"

"He's had his last treatment. The doctor has high hopes for his recovery."

"In that case I'll come to movie night tonight and tell him."

His news made her so happy he realized she couldn't tell him not to come. "Hope will make him get well in a hurry."

The waiter chose that moment to bring their dinner. When he walked away Vasso said, "That's the idea, isn't it. We all need hope."

That little nerve at the base of her throat was pulsing again. She started to eat her fish. "Between you and Father Debakis, I don't know who will deserve the bigger reward in heaven."

"Your mind is too much on the hereafter," he teased. "I'm quite happy with life right here."

She flushed. "So am I. It's just that I'm so than—"

"Don't say that anymore, Zoe. I'm quite aware of how you feel. I want to talk about how we feel about each other. I can't stay away from you. I don't want to. So we need to talk about where we're going to go from here. I *know* you feel the same way about me."

Her head lifted and their gazes collided. "I admit it, but you'd have to be in my shoes to understand why it wouldn't be a good idea for us to get any more involved."

"I can't accept that."

Zoe's expression sobered. "You're sick of hearing the same thing from me, aren't you?"

If he dared tell her what he really thought, she'd run from him. He couldn't handle that. "I'm not saying another word while we're the focus of other people."

One journalist had stayed longer to get pictures of the two of them. Vasso shot Zoe a glance. "If you're through eating, let's head for my car and ruin that guy's evening."

Her sudden laugh always delighted him. He put money on the table and got up. She was still chuckling when they reached the Lexus and he helped her inside. Zoe looked over at him as he drove. "Even paradise has its serpents."

"They have to earn a living, too."

Her eyes rounded. "You feel sorry for them?"

"No, but I understand that the need to make money in order to survive makes some people desperate enough to take chances."

"You're right, of course. I've never been in that position." She glanced at him. "I've never gone to bed hungry in my life." There was a catch in her voice. "Because of your foundation, I've been taken care of in miraculous ways. Sometimes I'm overwhelmed by your generosity."

Vasso couldn't take it anymore. "Overwhelmed enough to do me a favor?"

"I'd do anything for you. Surely you know that by now."

"Then come to my house after movie night is over. There's something I have to discuss with you, but we'll need privacy."

He heard her quick intake of breath. "That sounds serious."

"It is. Don't tell me no. I couldn't take it."

Zoe trembled, wondering what had happened to put him in this cryptic mood. If he was unhappy with some of the innovations she'd made at the hospital, all he had to do was tell her up front. Maybe Yianni had confided that she wasn't working out, but he didn't have the heart to tell her to her face because he was such a sweetheart.

When they reached the center, he parked the car and they entered through the front door.

She saw the clock. "It's almost time. I need to hurry to the game room and set up."

"Go ahead. I'll be there in a minute."

Did he want to talk to Yianni again?

Zoe went to the restroom first so she could pull herself together. She had the idea he was going to discuss her future here at the foundation. Could he be going to let her go? Fear stabbed at her. Maybe coming to work for him hadn't been a good thing after all. The passion enveloping them last week had only muddied the water. Tonight things were crystal-clear.

If Father Debakis hadn't intervened, she wouldn't be in this precarious position now. It wasn't his fault, of course. If she hadn't been so desperate to repay her debt, she wouldn't have caused all this trouble.

That's what Vasso had been alluding to earlier. Desperation was responsible for all kinds of mistakes. Her biggest one had been to accept his offer to relocate to Greece and continue taking his charity for the rest of her life.

Of course she was earning a salary now, so she hoped that wasn't what it looked like to him. She buried her face in her hands, not knowing what to think.

She wished her mother were around to talk to her about this. The great irony about that was the fact that if her parents were still alive, Zoe wouldn't be thousands of miles away from home. She'd be finishing college and getting on with her life, never knowing of Vasso's existence. Instead she'd dumped all her problems on Vasso who hadn't asked for them in the first place.

Zoe was terribly conflicted. She'd acted besotted in his arms, but as he'd reminded her, the emails she sent back to him didn't say anything about her feelings. In her heart she'd been watching for signs of him all week. When he hadn't come to the center before tonight, she was desolate. But she couldn't have it both ways, not when she'd told him she wanted to keep their relationship professional.

What a laugh she must have given him. No doubt he saw her as the worst kind of needy female. If she kept this up much longer, he'd be forced to find her something else to do in order to get her out of his hair. But he was such a good man he would never fire her without a new plan.

When she'd washed the tears off her face, she headed for the entertainment center. Eight patients showed up. The other four had just been through another session of chemo and wouldn't rally for a few days.

Vasso had singled out Nestor. While he thrilled him with a job offer, she popped more popcorn and started a movie. This time it was the Greek version of an old film, *Zorba the Greek*. The audience would complain that Anthony Quinn was Mexican, not Greek then they'd pull the crazy plot apart. Hopefully it would entertain them enough for a little while to forget how sick they felt.

By the end of the film, no one wanted the evening to be over. It proved to her that movie night worked. While the nurses took the patients back to their rooms, she tidied the place. But when she followed Vasso out of the center to his car, her heart felt as if it weighed a stone. She dreaded what was coming and her legs felt like dead weights.

On the drive to his house she turned to him. "How did your conversation go with Nestor?"

Vasso let his wrists do the driving. "He sounded just like you when I told him I'd find him an apartment near the number-four store. That way he could walk to work and take the bus to the university after he was released. I don't think he could see the film through the tears."

No. Nestor's gratitude would know no bounds for their benefactor, but she refrained from saying anything because Vasso didn't want to hear it.

Zoe tried to gear up for what was coming. How awful that a conversation with him would take place in his house, the one personal area of his life she'd tried to stay away from. She loved it already just seeing it from the air.

He drove around the back of it. It had been built near the water's edge. They entered a door into the kitchen area with a table and chairs. Though small like a cottage, huge windows opened everything up to turn it into a beach home, making it seem larger. No walls.

Everywhere you looked, you could see the sea. All you had to do was open the sliding doors and you could step out on a deck with several tubs of flowers and loungers. Beyond it, the sand and water were at your feet.

A circular staircase on one side of the room rose to the upper floor. It had to be a loft. The other end of the room contained the rock fireplace with a big comfy couch and chairs.

"Would you like a drink?"

She shook her head. "Nothing, thank you."

"Let's take a walk along the beach. The sand feels like the finest granulated sugar. I do my best thinking out there. We'll slip off our shoes and leave them inside. You can wash your feet later at the side of the deck."

After she did his bidding, she followed him outside. Night had descended. A soft fragrant breeze with the scent of thyme blew at her hair and skirt. She knew it was thyme because there was the same smell at the center. Yianni had explained what it was. He was a walking encyclopedia of knowledge.

She could talk to him the way she did with Father Debakis. The wonderful man had great children who looked after him, but he'd loved his wife to distraction and talked to Zoe about their life together. How heavenly to have enjoyed a marriage like Yianni's.

When they'd walked a ways, Vasso stopped and turned to her. The time had come. Her body broke out in a cold sweat. To her shock, he cupped her face in his hands and lifted it so she had to look at him. Zoe couldn't decipher the expression in his eyes, but his striking male features stood out in the semidarkness.

"I want to start over."

She blinked. "What do you mean?"

"I mean, I'd like us to do what two people do who have met and would like to get to know each other better."

After everything she'd been thinking as to what might be the reason why he'd brought her here, Zoe was incredulous. "That's the favor?"

"I know it's a big one. Last week you made it clear you didn't want anything more than friendship from me, but we moved past that after your arrival in Greece. I want to spend this weekend with you and all the weekends you're available from here on out."

The ground shifted.

She was positive she'd misunderstood him.

"Did you hear me?" he asked in an urgent voice.

"You *can't* be serious." She grasped his wrists, but he still cradled her face in his hands.

"Why are you acting like this, Zoe?"

"Because you're carrying your sense of responsibility to me too far."

"Does this feel like responsibility?" He lowered his mouth to hers and kissed her long and hard until she melted against him. Zoe was delirious with desire after being away from him for a whole week. "Tell me the real reason you're fighting me," he said after lifting his head. They were both out of breath. "I know you're attracted to me. You told me there's no one else in your life." The warm breath on her mouth sent a fire licking through her body.

"There isn't, but Vasso—" she moaned his name, "I can't be with you. If I had known this was going to happen, I would have changed my mind and stayed in New York. I would have found another place to work."

His brows met. "You don't mean that. You're lying to cover up what's really wrong."

Making a great effort, she eased herself out of his arms. "You're a very intelligent man. If you think hard about it, you'll know why this won't work. My cancer is in remission, but no one knows when it will come back."

She heard him suck in his breath. "Guess what? Tomorrow I could go down in the helicopter and never be seen again. It could happen. But if I looked at life like that, nothing would get accomplished."

"A possible helicopter crash one day compared to a recurrence of cancer are two different things."

He raked his hands through his hair. "No. They're not. No matter what, life is a risk."

"But some risks are more risky than others, Vasso. To get close to you is like buying something you want on time. One day—much sooner than you had supposed—you'll have no choice but to pay the balance in full. It will be too heavy a price to have to come up with all at once. I won't let you get into that position."

This time his hands slid up her arms. "You honestly believe you're going to die soon? *That's* what this is all about?"

"Yes. But I don't know the timetable and neither do you. What I do know is that you watched your father die of the same disease. No one should have to live through the trauma of that experience a second time in life. You and your brother have fought too hard to come all this way, only for you to get involved with a time bomb, because that's what I am."

He drew her closer. "Zoe—"

"Let me finish, please? I saw the love Akis and his wife share. With a baby on the way they're totally happy. He doesn't have to worry that Raina is going to be stricken by the inevitable.

"Don't you understand? I want you to have the same life *they* have. No clouds on the horizon. To spend time with me makes no sense for you. I'm a liability and I made Chad see that. He was smart and did the right thing for both of us."

Vasso's features darkened. "How was it right for you?" his voice grated.

"Because I would have been more depressed to watch

his suffering over me when I could do nothing to alleviate it. Just think about what it felt like when your father was dying, and you'll understand exactly what I'm talking about. It would have been so much harder on me if Chad had been there day and night. I couldn't have handled it."

"I'm not Chad." His hands slid to her shoulders. "Did you love him?"

Vasso's question caught her off guard. "I…thought I did. There are all kinds of love."

"No, Zoe. I'm talking about that overpowering feeling of love for another person that goes so deep into the marrow, you can't breathe without it."

He'd just described her feelings for him and pulled away before he read the truth in her eyes. "I don't want to talk about this anymore. If it's all right with you, I'd like to go home."

She turned back and hurried toward the deck where she could wash the sand off her feet. By the time he'd caught up to her, she'd gone inside and had slipped on her shoes.

"Before we go anywhere, I need to tell you something important, Zoe. Will you listen?"

They stood in the middle of the room like adversaries. Spiraling emotions had caused her to shake like a leaf. "Of course."

"Something unprecedented happened to me when I flew to New York to interview you. I didn't ask for it, but it happened. I haven't been the same since. Like you with Chad, I thought I loved Sofia. She'd always been there. We'd been a couple for such a long time, it just seemed normal for us to get married.

"Luckily, she got impatient. While I was in the military, she couldn't wait for me. Though I didn't know it at the time, she did me the greatest service in the world because it was apparent she wasn't the one for me.

"After surviving that hurdle, Akis and I led a bachelor existence for years. When Raina came into his life, it was as much a shock to me as to him. He'd been with other women, but she knocked him sideways without even trying, and transformed his life. I can promise you that if she'd been a recovering cancer patient, it would have made no difference to him."

"That's what you say because it's what you want to believe." She shook her head. "I can see there's no way to get through to you on this."

"You're right. There's only one solution to end our impasse."

"Exactly. By ending it now."

"I have a better idea in mind."

Zoe couldn't take much more. "I need to get back to the apartment."

"I'll take you, but I want you to think very seriously about my next words."

She reached for her purse and started for the kitchen. "Will you tell me in the car?"

Without waiting for him, Zoe went outside and walked along the path to his Lexus. Afraid to have contact, she quickly got in and shut the door.

Vasso went around to his side of the car and started the engine. But before he drove them to the road, he slid his arm along the seat so that his fingers touched the ends of her hair. Immediately her body responded, but she refused to look at him.

"We need to get married."

Her gasp reverberated in the interior. "*Married*—"

"The sooner the better. According to your timetable, we might have five years together before everything comes to an end. I want to give you children. I'd rather take those five years and live them fully with you, than walk away from you now and leave us both in pain."

"I won't be in pain," she defended in a quiet voice while her heart ran away with her at the thought of having his baby.

"Well, I will." He tugged gently on her hair strands. "After the way you kissed me back tonight, I know for a fact you'll be in pain, too. I don't need an answer yet, but I'll look for one soon."

"No—" she whispered in agony. "You mustn't."

"If I'd let the *no*s and the *mustn't*s get in the way, I wouldn't be where I am today. You and I don't have the usual problems that beset couples. We know who we are and exactly what we're getting into. We've learned how precious life is. We've been made brutally aware that there are no guarantees for the future, only what we're prepared to build together."

She swallowed hard. "What it proves to me is how far you would go to honor the wishes of Father Debakis."

"He has nothing to do with this!"

"Then why would you be willing to make the ultimate sacrifice by marrying me and giving me a home when you know I have a very short life span."

"Because I love you."

"I love you, too, but I wonder if you remember the warning you gave me in New York. You said, 'Be sure it's what you want.' How sad someone didn't warn you to be sure it was what *you* wanted."

"You're putting up a defense because of your own insecurities." He drove the car to the road and they headed for the village.

"Vasso, you don't want to marry me. We're both temporarily attracted to each other. You're like any red-blooded bachelor might be, but you're not in love with me. I refuse to be your personal project.

"I came here to work and pay you back for your generosity. Wouldn't it be a great way to show my gratitude by becoming your wife? Then you'd be forced to take care of me for however long I have left.

"Forget children. No way would I want to leave a baby for you to raise on your own. Your father did that. I won't allow history to repeat itself. You and Akis have been through so much, you deserve all the happiness you can find.

"Sofia Peri didn't know what she was doing when she let the most marvelous man on earth slip through her fingers. If you'd married back then, you'd probably be a father to several darling children. I should never have come here."

Yianni had gotten along fine before Zoe had arrived. The center would run smoothly whether she was there or not. If she flew back to New York, she could get a job as a cook. When she'd saved enough money she could finish her last semester of college. Then she could get a job teaching school and send money to the foundation every month. It was the best plan she could think of under the circumstances.

When she got back to the apartment, she'd phone Father Debakis and have a heart-to-heart with him. He was probably at dinner and could talk to her when he was through. The priest would understand her dilemma and give her the guidance she needed because heaven help her, she couldn't make this decision without his blessing.

Vasso drove around to the back of the shop. She opened the door before he came to a stop. "Thank you for bringing me home. You made Nestor a happy man tonight."

"And what about you?"

"You already know what I think."

"We're not finished, Zoe."

"How can I convince you that this just won't work?"

"I didn't realize you were so stubborn."

"Then be thankful I'm not the marrying type. You've dodged a bullet. Good night."

CHAPTER NINE

FOR THE NEXT week Vasso worked like a demon, traveling from city to city to check on stores while Akis worked out of the Athens office. After the last conversation with Zoe, he knew she needed time to think about their situation without being pressured.

Now that it was Friday evening, he couldn't stay away any longer and flew to Paxos. She would be on duty this weekend and couldn't run away from him. After they watched a movie with some of the patients, he'd get her alone to talk until he convinced her they belonged together.

At five to six he tapped on Yiannis's half-open door and walked in. Zoe wasn't out in front, but he didn't expect her to be.

He found the admiral pouring himself coffee from a carafe brought in on a cart from the kitchen. The older man was using the cup Zoe had given him. He turned to Vasso. "Ah. You're here at last."

By his sober demeanor Vasso sensed something was wrong. "Did I miss a call from you?"

"No, no." He walked back to his chair. "Sit down so we can talk."

Not liking the sound of that, he preferred to remain standing. Yiannis looked up from his desk. "I have a letter here for you. It's from Zoe. She asked me to give it to you when you came by and not before."

His heart plummeted. He took the envelope from him, almost afraid to ask the next question. "Where is she?"

"She flew back to New York on Tuesday."

The breath froze in his lungs.

"On Sunday she came over, white as a sheet, and submitted her resignation. Zoe's the best assistant I could have asked for, but the tragic expression on her face let me know she's been suffering. She told me she was so homesick she couldn't stay in Greece any longer. The sweet thing thought she could handle being transplanted, but apparently it was too big a leap. Kyria Lasko is helping me out again."

His agony made it hard to talk let alone think. "I'll find a temporary accountant from headquarters until we can find the right person to assist you," he murmured.

"You'd better sit down, Vasso. You've gone quite pale."

He shook his head. "I'll be all right. Forgive me. I've got things to do, but I'll be in touch."

Vasso rushed out of the hospital and drove to the village at record speed. He parked the car and ran along the waterfront to the gift shop. The second Kyria Panos saw him she waved him over with an anxious expression. "If you're looking for Thespinis Zachos, she's left Greece."

He felt like he was bleeding out. "I heard the news when I was at the center earlier. Let me pay her bill."

"No, no. She paid me. Such a lovely person. Never any trouble."

Not until now, Vasso's heart cried out.

He thanked the older woman and drove back to his house. After making a diving leap for the couch he ripped open the envelope to read her letter. She'd only written one short paragraph.

Forgive me for accepting your offer of employment. It has caused you so much unnecessary trouble. I'm desolate over my mistake. One day I'll be able to start paying you back in my own way.

My dear, dear Vasso, be happy.

Blind with pain, he staggered to the storage closet and reached for his bike. He'd known pain two other times in his life. A young teen's loss of a father. Later a young man's loss of his childhood sweetheart. This pain was different.

Zoe thought she could spare him pain by disappearing from his life. But with her gone, he felt as if his soul had died on the spot. Vasso didn't know how he was going to last the night, but he couldn't stay in the house.

He took his bike out the back door and started cycling with no destination in mind. All he wanted to do was keep going until he got rid of the pain. It was near morning when he returned to his house and took himself up to bed.

The next time he had cognizance of his surroundings, he could hear Akis's voice somewhere in the background urging him to wake up. He couldn't figure out where he was. How had he made it upstairs to his bed?

His eyelids opened. "Akis?"

"Stay with me, Vasso. Come on. Wake up."

He groaned with pain. "Zoe left me."

"I know."

"Did you see her letter?"

"That, and your bike lying on the ground at the back door."

He rubbed his face with his hand and felt his beard. "How did you find out?"

"Yiannis called me yesterday worried about you."

"What's today?"

"Sunday."

He opened his eyes again. "You mean I've been out of it since Friday?"

"Afraid so." His brother looked grim. They'd been through every experience together. "You've given me a scare, bro. I was worried you might have driven yourself too hard and wouldn't wake up. Don't ever do that to me again."

Vasso raised himself up on one elbow. "A week ago I asked her to marry me. Friday night she left her answer with Yiannis. I wanted her so badly I pushed too hard."

"It's early days."

"No. She left Greece to spare me. Zoe's convinced the disease will recur."

Akis sighed. "Raina picked up on that the night you came for dinner."

"For her to give up the job she wanted was huge for her. There's no hoping she'll come back."

"Why don't you get up and shower, then we'll fly to my house. Raina has food ready. Once you get a meal in you, we'll talk. Don't tell me no. This is one time you need help, even if you are my big brother."

September 23, Astoria, New York

"Zoe? Come in my office."

She knew what the doctor was going to say and was prepared for the bad news. This was her first checkup since she'd left the hospital six weeks ago. The month she'd spent in Greece was like a blip on a screen, as if that life had been lived by a different person.

She'd decided not to call Father Debakis. No one at the church knew she was back in the US. Zoe prayed Ms. Kallistos hadn't seen her slip in the hospital and would never know about this appointment.

Zoe had made up her mind she wouldn't depend on the charity of others ever again. While she was staying at the YWCA, she'd been going out on temporary jobs to survive. There was always work if you were willing to do it. This was the life that had put Nestor in a depression. She could see why.

If any good had come out of her experience on Paxos, it had been to introduce him to Vasso who had not only saved his life through his charity, but had made it possible for him to go to college.

Vasso... Zoe's heart ached with a love so profound

for him she could hardly bear to get up every day and face the world without him.

"Zoe? Did you hear me?"

She lifted her head. "I'm sorry. I guess I was deep in thought."

He frowned. "You've lost five pounds since you were released from the hospital. Why is that?"

"With the recurrence of cancer, that doesn't surprise me."

"What recurrence?"

Zoe shook her head. "You don't need to be gentle with me, doctor. Just tell me the truth. I can take it.'

He cocked his head. She had to wait a long time before he spoke again. "I'm beginning to think that if I told you the truth, you wouldn't recognize it, let alone believe me. I *am* a doctor, and I've sworn an oath to look after the sick."

"I know," she whispered.

"But you think I'm capable of lying?"

She bit her lip. "Maybe not lying, but since you work with cancer patients, I realize you're trying to be careful how you tell a patient there is a death sentence in the future."

He leaned forward. "We all have a death sentence awaiting us in life. That's part of the plan. In the meantime, part of the plan is to live life to the fullest. Something tells me that's not what you've been doing."

Those were Vasso's words. It sent prickles down her spine.

"There's no recurrence of cancer, Zoe. I'm giving you another clean bill of health."

"Until another six weeks from now, then it will show up."

He made a sound of exasperation. "Maybe you weren't listening to me the first time I told you this. In people like you with none of the other complicating factors, the statistics prove that about ninety-one out of every one hundred people live for more than five years after they are diagnosed. And seventy-one out of every one hundred people live for more than ten years. Some even live to the natural end of their lives."

She'd heard him the first time, but she hadn't been able to believe it. *Was it really possible?*

"Since you're cancer-free and in perfect physical shape, I want to know the reason for your weight loss. It has to be a man."

She struggled for breath. "You're right."

"Tell me about him."

Zoe had refused to give in to her feelings since returning from Greece. But with the doctor who'd been her friend for a whole year pressing her for an explanation, she couldn't hold back any longer and blurted everything in one go. The tears gushed until she was totally embarrassed.

"Before I see my next patient who's waiting, do you want to know what *I* think, girl?"

Girl? He hadn't called her that in a long time. Surprised, she looked at him, still needing to wipe the moisture off her face. "What?"

"You're a damn fool if you don't fly back there and tell him yes. I don't want to see you in my office again unless you have a wedding ring on your finger!"

September 25, Athens, Greece

When the ferry headed toward the familiar docking point at Loggos, Zoe was jumping out of her skin with nervous excitement. She'd taken the cheapest one-way night flight from JFK to Corfu and caught the morning ferry to Paxos Island. While on board she changed into walking shorts and sneakers. Everything else she owned was in her new suitcases. Luckily the largest case had wheels, making it easier for her to walk along the waterfront to the gift shop.

Kyria Panos looked shocked and anxious when Zoe entered her store. "I didn't know you were back. If you want the apartment, I've already rented it. I'm sorry."

"Don't be. That's good business for you! I just wondered if I could leave my luggage here. I'll pay you and be back for it by the end of the day."

"You don't have to pay me. Just bring it behind the counter."

"You're so kind. Thank you."

"Did you know Kyrie Giannopoulos tried to pay me for your rental?"

"No, but that doesn't surprise me." There was no one in this world like Vasso. "I'll buy one of these T-shirts." She found the right size and gave her some euros. "Mind if I change in your bathroom?"

"Go ahead. Whatever you want."

Having deposited her luggage and purse, she left and was free to buy her favorite snack of a gyro and fruit at Vasso's number-one store. Once she'd eaten, she rented a bike from the tourist outfit at the other end of the pier and took off for Vasso's beach house.

Though she hadn't lived on Paxos for very long, it felt like home to her now. The softness of the sea air, the fragrance, it all fed her soul that had been hungering for Vasso. Raina had said it best. "I thought I was American too before I married Akis. Now the Greek part has climbed in and sits next to my heart." Zoe could relate very well.

She had no idea if Vasso would be home or not. If she couldn't find him, she'd bike to the center and drop in on Yianni. He was a sweetheart and would be able to help her track him down without giving her presence away. She wanted, needed to surprise Vasso. It was important she see that first look in his eyes. Just imagining the moment made it difficult to breathe.

The ride through the olive groves rejuvenated her. Every so often she'd stop to absorb another view of the azure sea and the white sailboats taking advantage of the light breeze. She removed her helmet to enjoy it. While she was thinking about Vasso, she saw the local bus coming toward her. It slowed down and a smiling Gus leaned out the window.

"*Yassou*, Zoe! Where have you been?"

"In New York, but I'm back to stay!"

"That's good!"

"I agree!"

After he drove on, she put her helmet back on and started pedaling again. She went through alternating cycles of fear and excitement as she contemplated their reunion. Zoe wouldn't allow herself to be bombarded with negative thoughts again. She'd weathered too many of them already. Because of a lack of faith, she'd wasted precious time, time she and Vasso could have had together.

Zoe stopped every so often to catch her breath and take in the glorious scenery. She had no way of knowing if he'd be at the house, but it didn't matter. This was his home. He would return to it at some point, and she'd be waiting for him.

Akis looked at Vasso. "What do you think about him?" The last person they'd interviewed for the assistant's job at the hospital went out to the lounge to wait. Over the last week there'd been a dozen applicants for the job before him.

"I think he's as good as we're going to get."

"His disability won't present a problem and he's ex-military. Yiannis will like that."

Vasso nodded. Neither of them wanted to admit Yiannis had been so unhappy about Zoe's resignation he'd found something wrong with anyone they'd sent for an interview. He'd rather do the extra work himself.

"Will you tell him? I need to get back to the house if only to find out if it's still standing." Since the Sunday Vasso had awakened to a world without Zoe in it, he'd been living at the penthouse when he wasn't out of the city on business. He got up and headed for their private elevator.

"Hey, bro." Akis's concern was written on his face. "Come over for dinner tonight."

"Can I take a rain check?" Akis and Raina had done

everything to help, but there was no help for what was wrong.

"Then promise you'll keep in close touch with me."

"Haven't I always?"

"Not always," Akis reminded him.

No. The Friday night he'd read Zoe's goodbye letter, everything had become a blur until Akis had found him on Sunday morning. By now he'd gotten the message that she had no regrets over leaving him. None.

While he'd waited in the hope that he'd hear from her, he'd gone through every phase of pain and agony. Maybe it would never leave him. Desperate for some relief, he flew to Paxos. When the helicopter dropped him off, he got in his car. After buying some roses in town, he headed for their family church on the summit.

A breeze came up this time of day, filling the air with the scent of vanilla from the yellow broom growing on the hillsides. He pulled off the road and got out. The cemetery was around the back. Sixteen years ago he and Akis had buried their father next to their mother. They'd been young and their grief had been exquisite. In their need they'd clung to each other.

Vasso walked around and placed the tub of roses in front of the headstone. Then he put a knee down and read what was inscribed on the stone until it became a blur. As if it had been yesterday, he still remembered a conversation they'd had with their father before he'd died.

"You're only in your teens and you'll meet a lot of women before you're grown up. When you find *the* one, you must treat her like a queen. Your mother was my queen. I cherished and respected her from the beginning. She deserved that because not only was she going to be my wife, she was going to be the mother of our children."

Tears dripped off Vasso's chin.

"I've found my queen, *Papa,* but her fear of dying early of the same disease as you has made it impossible for us to be together. I don't know how you handled it when our mother died, but somehow you lived through the grief. If you could do it, so can I. I'm the big brother. I *have* to.

"Wouldn't you know Akis is doing much better than I am because he's found the love of his life? They're going to have a baby." His shoulders heaved. "I'm so happy for them. I want to be happy, too. But the real truth of it is…I *have* to find a way for that to happen, *Papa,* otherwise this life no longer makes sense."

Vasso stayed there until he heard the voices of children playing on the slope below him. That meant school was out for the day. He'd been here long enough and wiped the tears with the side of his arm. It was time to drive back to the house and take stock of what he was going to do with his life from here on out.

Something had to change. To go on mourning for something that wasn't meant to be was destructive. He had a business to run. One day soon he'd be an uncle to his brother's child. Vasso intended to love him or her and give all the support he could.

After reaching the car, he drove home with the windows open, taking the lower road that wound along the coastline. As he rounded a curve he saw a cyclist in the far distance. It was a beautiful day. Vasso didn't wonder that someone was out enjoying the sea air.

But when the helmeted figure suddenly disappeared from sight, Vasso was surprised. There was only one turnoff along this particular stretch of road. It led to his beach house. Curious to know if he had a visitor, or if the cyclist was simply a tourist out sightseeing, he stepped on the gas.

When he reached the turnoff, he came close to having a heart attack. Despite the helmet, Vasso could never mistake that well-endowed figure or those shapely legs headed for his house.

It was Zoe on the bike!

He stayed a few yards behind and watched the beautiful sight in front of him, trying to absorb the fact that she was back on the island.

The way she was pedaling, he could tell she was tired. At some point she must have sensed someone was behind her. When she looked over her right shoulder, she let out a cry and lost control of the bike. In the next second it fell over, taking her with it.

Terrified she could be hurt, Vasso stopped on a dime and jumped out of the car. But she'd recovered before he could reach her and was on her feet. His eyes were drawn to the English printed in blue on her white T-shirt with the high V-neck. *I'd rather be in Greece.*

If this was a private message to him, he was receiving it loud and clear. The way she filled it out caused him to tremble.

"Zoe—I'm so sorry. Are you hurt?"

Those shimmering green eyes fastened on him. "Heavens, no. I'm such a klutz."

She looked so adorable in that helmet and those shorts, he could hardly find his voice. "Of course you're not. I should have called out or honked so you'd know I was behind you. But to be honest, I thought maybe I was hallucinating to see you in front of me."

He watched her get back on the bike. "I was coming to visit you."

His heart pounded like thunder. "This has to be perfect timing because I haven't been here for several weeks."

"I probably should have phoned you, but after I got off the ferry earlier, I just decided to come and take my chances." She flashed him one of those brilliant smiles that melted his insides. "Beat you to the house!"

He had a hundred questions to ask, but whatever the reason that had brought Zoe back to Paxos, he didn't care. It was enough to see her again. Something was very different. Her whole body seemed to sparkle with life.

She rode toward the house with more vigor than before, convincing him she hadn't hurt herself. He got back in his car and drove slowly the rest of the way. Zoe reached their destination first and put on the kickstand. She was waiting for him as he parked his car and got out.

"Where are you staying?"

"I don't know yet. Kyria Panos let me leave my luggage with her."

His mind was reeling. "You must be thirsty. Come in the house and we'll both have a soda."

Another smile from her turned his insides to butter. "You're a lifesaver."

They walked to the back door. Using his remote to let them in the house, he said, "The guest bathroom is behind that door at the far end of the kitchen."

"Thanks. I'm a mess."

The most gorgeous mess he'd ever seen. While she disappeared, he took the stairs two at a time to the loft and changed into shorts and a T-shirt. Before she came out, he hurried down to the kitchen in sandals and produced some colas from the fridge for them.

When she emerged she was *sans* the helmet. Her blond hair was attractively disheveled. Vasso wanted to plunge his fingers into it and kiss the very life out of her. Her flushed skin, in fact every single thing about her, was too desirable. But he'd learned a terrible lesson since the day she'd left Greece. He'd pushed her too hard, too soon, and wouldn't be making that mistake again.

He handed her a drink. "Welcome back to Greece." He clicked his can against hers and swallowed half the contents in one long gulp. "I like your T-shirt."

"The second I saw it, I had to have it and bought it from Kyria Panos earlier. She let me change shirts in her bathroom."

"You've made a friend there."

She sipped her drink. "Everyone is a friend on this island. Gus waved to me from the bus while I was riding on the road to your house."

"I take it you haven't seen Yiannis yet."

"No. If I couldn't find you, I was planning to bike to the center."

"You look wonderful in those shorts, Zoe."

She blushed. "Thank you."

"I'm used to seeing you in skirts and dresses."

"I know. They make a nice change. You look wonderful, too."

He didn't know how long he could resist crushing her in his arms, but he needed answers. "Shall we go out on the deck?"

"I'd love it."

They walked over to the sliding doors. She sat on one of the loungers while he pulled a chair around next to her. "Tell me what happened when you went back to New York."

He listened as she gave him an account. They were both circling the giant elephant standing on the deck, but he needed to let her guide this conversation if he wanted to know the reason she'd come back. If she was only here for a few days, he couldn't bear it.

"While I was there, I had to go in for my six-weeks checkup."

This was too much. Vasso broke out in a cold sweat and got up, too restless to sit still. He turned on his heel. "Were you given a death sentence and a date? Is that why you're here? To thank me one more time and say a final goodbye?"

"Vasso—" She paled and shot to her feet.

"Because if you are, I could have done without this visit. You know damn well why I asked you to marry me. Can you possibly understand the pain you've inflicted by turning up here now?" The words had gushed out. He couldn't take them back.

"Do you want to hear the exact quote I got from my doctor?"

"Actually I don't." She seemed determined to tell him, but he couldn't go through this agony again and started for the doorway into the house.

She followed him. "He said, 'There's no recurrence of cancer, Zoe. I'm giving you another clean bill of health. In people like you with none of the other complicating factors, it's possible you'll live a full life.'"

Vasso wheeled around. "But you still don't believe him."

"You didn't let me finish. I told him about you and me."

He closed his eyes tightly. "Go on."

"The doctor said, 'You're a damn fool if you don't fly back there and tell him yes. I don't want to see you in my office again unless you have a wedding ring on your finger'!" Zoe moved closer to him.

"Little did he know he was speaking to the converted. After being the recipient of a miracle, I realized I would be an ungrateful wretch if I didn't embrace life fully. He reminded me that we are all facing a death sentence in life, but most of us don't have a time frame.

"Vasso—I came back because I want to spend the rest of my life with you. You have to know I love you to the depths of my being. I want to have children with you. I want the privilege of being called Kyria Giannopoulos, the wife who has a husband like no other in existence.

"You have no idea how handsome and spectacular you are. I lost my breath the first time I laid eyes on you, and I've never completely recovered. You're probably going to think I'm crazy, but I'm thankful I came down with the disease. It brought me to you. If you'll ask me again to marry you, I promise to make you happy because I'm the happiest woman alive to be loved by you."

He could feel the ice melting around his heart. "So you don't think I want you to be my wife because I feel responsible for you?"

"No, darling. I only said that because I was so afraid you couldn't love me the way I loved you. I know you're not perfect, but you are to me," her voice trembled.

"Then come here to me and show me."

She flew into his arms. When he felt them wind around his neck, he carried her in the house and followed her down on the couch. "*Agape mou*...I'm so in love with you I thought I was going to die when I read your letter.

"You're the woman my father was talking about. You're *the* one. I knew it when you walked in the center's office bringing spring with you. I'll never forget that moment. The fierce beating of my heart almost broke my rib cage. You're so sweet and so funny and so fun and so endearing and so beautiful and so kind and so compassionate all at the same time. I love you," he cried. "*I love you, Zoe.*"

He broke off telling her all the things she meant to him because her mouth got in the way. That luscious mouth that thrilled him in ways he'd never even dreamed possible. They couldn't get enough of each other. Her body melted against him. Their legs entwined and they forgot everything except the joy of loving each other at last.

If it hadn't been for his phone ringing, he didn't know when they would have surfaced. He let it ring because he had to do something else first.

"Maybe you should get that. It could be important," she whispered against his jaw.

"I'm pretty sure it's Akis calling to find out if I'm all right."

A frown marred her lovely features. "He loves you so much."

"I almost lost it when I read your letter. Akis found me here two days later. Just so he won't worry and come flying over here to find out if I'm still alive, just answer me one question, then I'll listen to the message. Will you marry me, Thespinis Zachos? We've already been through the sickness and health part. Will you be my love through life? I adore you."

Her eyes glistened with tears. "You already know my answer. I have a secret. The morning I got off the plane and found you waiting to pick me up at the airport, I wanted to be your wife. I couldn't imagine anything more wonderful." She buried her face in his neck. "You just don't know how much I love you."

He gave her another fierce kiss before getting up to find his phone on the table. "It's from my brother."

"Call him so he won't worry. I'll wait right here for you."

Without listening to the message, he called him back.

"Thanks for returning my call, bro."

"I'm glad you phoned. How would you like to be the best man at my wedding?"

"*What?*"

"She's back and we're getting married as soon as we can."

Akis let out a sound of pure joy then shouted the news to Raina who was in the background and gave her own happy cry. "Tell that Zoe I love her already."

Vasso stared down at her. "I will. She's easy to love."

"I only have one piece of advice. Remember what *Papa* said."

He knew. Treat Zoe like a queen. "I remember."

"Come on over for dinner so we can celebrate."

"You mean now?"

"Now! And you know why." Vasso knew exactly why. "We're expecting you." Akis clicked off.

Vasso hung up and leaned over Zoe. "We're invited for dinner."

"I don't want to move, but considering it's your brother...." She sat up and kissed him passionately. "You two have been through everything together. I get it."

He knew she did. "We'll go in the cruiser. I'll phone Kyria Panos and tell her we'll be by for your luggage later tonight."

CHAPTER TEN

October 16, Paxos Island

"Iris!" Zoe cried out when she saw Akis help her old friend from New York out of the helicopter that had landed on the center's roof. She ran to her and they clung. "This is the best present I could have. You've been like a mother to me. I'm just so thankful you could come for the wedding."

"I wouldn't have missed it. Neither would Father Debakis."

Zoe's eyes lit on the priest who was getting out of the helicopter. The two of them had flown over yesterday and had stayed at the penthouse.

She left Iris long enough to run to the great man she owed her life to. "Oh, Father—I'm so glad you could come to marry us."

He hugged her hard. "It's my privilege. I had a feeling about the two of you a long time ago."

"Nothing gets past you."

Akis walked over to them. "Come on, everyone. Let's get on the elevator. Raina is waiting to help you into your wedding dress. Yiannis will drive you and Raina to the church. I'll drive everyone else in my car.

"Needless to say my older brother is climbing the walls waiting for the ceremony to begin. For his sake, I beg you to hurry, Zoe."

The best man's comment produced laughter from everyone and brought roses to Zoe's cheeks. She had to pinch herself that this was real and that she was getting married to Vasso.

When they reached the main floor, Zoe hurried along the hall to a private room where Raina was waiting.

"They've arrived!"

"Thank heaven! I've had three phone calls from Vasso. If he doesn't see you soon, he's going to have a nervous breakdown."

"Well we can't have that."

Zoe got out of her skirt and blouse and stepped into the white floor-length wedding dress. Raina had dared her to wear the latest fashion. It was strapless, something she would never have picked out on her own. But Raina insisted she was a knockout in it. This was one time she needed to render her soon-to-be husband *speechless*.

"Oh, Raina. It's so fun having you to help me. What I would have given for a sister like you."

"I feel the same way. Today I'm getting her. We're the luckiest women in the world."

"Yup. In a little while I'll be married to a god, too."

"They really are," Raina murmured. "But you've

still got your perfect figure while I'm beginning to get a bump."

"If you ever saw the way Akis looks at you when you're not aware of it, you'd know you and the baby are his whole world."

"Today the focus is on you. I have something for you, Zoe. Vasso asked me to give this to you."

With trembling hands, Zoe opened the satin-lined jewelry box. Inside lay a strand of gleaming pearls. A card sat on top. *"For my queen."*

She looked at Raina in puzzlement. "He thinks of me as his queen?"

Raina nodded. "Akis gave me the same kind of pearls with the same sentiment on his card. When I asked him about it, he told me that his father had told them the women they would choose would be their queens and they needed to treat them like one."

"What a fabulous father he was. Vasso has always treated me like that."

"So has Akis. Now hold still while I put this around your neck."

Zoe's emotions were spilling out all over to feel the pearls against her skin. She'd already done her hair and applied her makeup. She wore pearl studs in her ears.

"Now for the crowning glory." Raina walked over and put the shoulder-length lace mantilla over her head. "When you get to the church, pull it over your face. You know? I think I'd better have an ambulance standing by. After Vasso sees you, anything could happen."

"You're such a tease."

"I'm only speaking the truth." She turned and opened

a long florist's box. Inside was a sheaf of flowers. Raina laid it in the crook of Zoe's arm.

"Aren't they lovely!" Her eyes took in the all-white arrangement: white roses, cymbidium orchids, hydrangeas and stephanotises. "My mother would have planned a bouquet just like this for me. She loved white flowers."

"Don't we all." They both breathed in the heavenly scent.

Zoe eyed her dearest new friend. "You look absolutely stunning in that blue silk suit." Raina wore a gardenia in the lapel.

"Except that I had to undo the zipper to get into it. I think I can get away with it for as long as we're at the church." She smiled at Zoe. "Ready?"

"Yes," she said emotionally.

They left the room and headed for the main entrance. When they walked outside by the fountain Zoe saw Yianni. He looked splendid wearing his former naval uniform. "You're a sight for sore eyes, Zoe."

"So are you. I can see why your wife grabbed you up the second she met you."

"You look radiant today." He kissed her forehead then pulled the edge of the veil down to cover her face.

"Thank you for standing in for my father."

"It's an honor. Now let's get you in the car and be off. Your fiancé is waiting for you. I've had two phone calls from Vasso. He's going to have a coronary if we don't arrive soon."

Zoe laughed and got in the rear of the limo. Raina helped her with her dress. Yianni checked to make sure everything was secure then he drove them through the olive groves and up the steep hillside to the glistening white church at the summit. It made an imposing sight overlooking the sea.

This was the church where Raina and Akis had been married by his family priest. Their parents had been buried in the cemetery behind it. This was the place where history had been made and was still being made today by another Giannopoulos son.

Father Debakis would be doing the honors with the other priest's help. This was right out of a fairy tale.

The closer they got, she could see dozens of cars lining both sides of the road leading to the church. Akis and his best friend Theo had taken care of the invitations. Zoe feared there wouldn't be enough room in the church to accommodate everyone.

Vasso had told her not to worry. The priest would leave the front doors open and set up chairs for those people who couldn't get inside. A real Greek wedding was a high point no one wanted to miss.

When they came around the bend she could see dozens of beautifully dressed guests seated at tables outside with white ribbons on the chairs. But that wasn't all. Behind the chairs were throngs of people willing to stand.

Raina and Theo's wife Chloe had made the arrangements for the food, which would be served on the grounds after the ceremony, followed by singing and dancing. She promised they wouldn't run out of food, but when Zoe saw the amount of people congregated, it shocked her.

Yianni drove past the cars and circled around to the front steps of the church. Suddenly all Zoe could see was Vasso. He stood at the open doors waiting for her in a formal midnight-blue suit with a white rose in the lapel. She couldn't hold back her cry when she saw him. No man was ever created like him.

Once the limo came to a stop, he walked toward her with a loving look in his black eyes that lit up her whole body. Yianni came around the door to help her out. But it was Vasso who grasped her hand and squeezed it.

Raina took the flowers from her and walked behind them with Yianni while Vasso led her into the church. She'd been in here several times in the last few weeks and thought it an exquisite jewel. The smell of incense and flowers greeted them as they moved toward Father Debakis, decked out in his priestly finery. The interior was so full people who hadn't found a seat were lined up against the walls.

Both she and Vasso wanted a traditional wedding to honor their parents. Her heart pounded so hard she knew he could feel its beat through her hand. When they arrived at the altar, he leaned over and lifted the veil. The love pouring from his soul was evident in those gorgeous black eyes.

If ever there was a time to faint, it was now. But she didn't feel light-headed. She felt a spirit of joy wash over her as they grasped hands and entered into this sacred ritual that would make him her husband.

They went through the different stages of the ring

ceremony until it came to the union of the bride and groom with the crowning. This was the part she'd been looking forward to. The priest took two crowns with ribbons from the altar table, blessed them, then put the crowns on their heads.

"Oh, Lord our God, crown them with glory and honor."

The other priest exchanged their crowns over their heads to seal the union. He read from the Gospel account of the wedding in Cana. After a prayer, he passed the common cup for them to take a sip of the wine. This was the part that meant they shared equally in the process of life. Father Debakis then led them around the table three times.

This was where her heart beat wildly as the two of them stared at each other while they made circles. A hint of a smile broke the corners of Vasso's mouth. Zoe felt this part of the wedding ceremony was terribly romantic, but she'd never admit it to anyone but him. He looked so handsome with the crown on she wanted a picture of him just like that.

When they faced the priest again, he removed their crowns. His eyes rested kindly on Vasso. "Be magnified, O Bridegroom, as Abraham." Then he looked at Zoe with such tenderness she was deeply moved. "And you, O Bride, be magnified as was Sarah, and live a long, fruitful life."

He'd added those words meant just for her. Once again she was overcome with gratitude that out of the shadows, she'd emerged into a light greater than the one she could see with the naked eye.

Father Debakis placed a Bible in both their hands and said a final prayer. He smiled at them. "Congratulations, Kyrie and Kyria Giannopoulos. Just think, Vasso," he whispered. "If I hadn't called you..."

"I don't want to think about it, Father," he whispered back. He put his arm around Zoe's waist and they faced the congregation. She'd never seen so many smiling faces in her life, but one stood out above the rest.

It was Akis. He and Vasso exchanged a silent message that was so sweet and said so much Zoe could hardly breathe with the love she could see between the two of them.

Suddenly Vasso lowered his mouth to her ear. "Let the fun begin."

Raina came forward to hand her the sheaf of flowers. After she stepped away, Zoe and Vasso started walking down the aisle. Everyone was here. Olympia and Nestor had come from the center. She smiled at Kyria Lasko, Kyria Panos, Gus the bus driver, Iris, and her doctor from the center in Astoria.

With each step, people said Vasso's name; they were the managers from some of their stores, family friends, their mutual friends, two of the helicopter pilots, the woman called Elpis who'd given the boys free sweets when they were young. The list went on and on. When they reached the rear of the church and stepped outside, there was cheering and music. People rushed to congratulate them.

The paparazzi were out in full measure, but Zoe didn't care. She was too happy to be married to her heart's desire to have a care in the world. They had their own videographer there to record the proceedings of the day.

"Give us a kiss with your husband, Kyria Giannopoulos."

"Gladly!" She turned to Vasso. There was a wild look in his eye before he caught her to him and kissed the life out of her in front of everyone. They were a little drunk with happiness. The taste of his mouth was sweeter than any wine. She would never be able to get enough of it. Anyone could see that.

Part of her felt a fierce pride at the turnout. If she had a megaphone and dared, she'd love to say, "Look at these poor Giannopoulos boys now! Eat your hearts out!" But of course she couldn't say or do that.

The caterers had arrived and had set up more tables to accommodate the huge crowd. With the musicians in place, the dancing began. Yianni grabbed Zoe's other hand and several dozen people joined to form a line. They danced through the tables while everyone threw rice. The excitement had made her heady.

Every time Vasso's fiery eyes met hers, her heart palpitated right out of her chest. She knew what he was thinking. It was all she could think about. Their wedding night.

Zoe had been waiting all her life for the time when she would marry. She actually wanted to call Ms. Kallistos one day and tell her that *she* was the person responsible for the miracle that had come into Zoe's life. But on reflection it wouldn't be a good idea.

Vasso had hired Alexandra and there was no doubt in Zoe's mind the manager had been crazy about him from day one. Through Akis she'd learned that Sofia Peri had left her husband and wanted Vasso back. Zoe couldn't blame her for that. Today she could feel sorry for every woman alive who wasn't married to her Apollo.

Today she'd met so many people who thought the world of Vasso and Akis. If their father were still alive, he would be so proud of them. *And their mother*...Zoe had seen the few pictures they had of her. She'd been a beauty. That's why the two brothers were so gorgeous.

Oh, Vasso. I can't wait until we're alone. Really alone.

The party went on several hours. Toasts were made to the happy couple. As Zoe danced with Akis, Vasso danced with Raina. Then she saw the brothers signal each other. The next thing she knew Akis whirled her toward the limousine where Yianni was parked in front of the church.

Akis opened the rear door and hurried her inside. Vasso came around the other side and slid in next to her. The second his door closed, the limo started moving. Everyone saw them leave and gave out shouts. But Zoe was caught in Vasso's arms. His mouth came down on hers and the world whirled away. When he lifted his lips, she realized the car had come to a stop outside Vasso's beach house.

He opened the door and stepped out. Then he helped her. The second she was on her feet he picked her up and carried her in his arms. "Thank you, Yiannis."

The car drove off, leaving them alone. "I've been dreaming about doing this for weeks, Zoe."

"So have I, darling."

Vasso unlocked the back door with the remote and carried her over the threshold. He didn't stop until he'd gained the loft. "I've never been up here before," she said as he twirled her around.

"That was the plan. Thank heaven the long wait is finally over."

"I love you, my darling Vasso. *I love you.*"

After they'd made love throughout the night, Vasso's beautiful wife fell asleep around five o'clock, but he was still wide awake. Adrenaline rushed through his system like a never-ending fire.

Her wedding dress lay over one of the chairs, her mantilla on the dresser with her wedding flowers. Their scent filled the loft. He'd thrown his wedding suit over another chair. The white rose was still in the lapel.

She was the most unselfish lover he could ever have imagined. For the next little while he lay on his side holding her loosely in his arms so he could study her beautiful features. He still couldn't believe she was his wife, all signed, sealed and delivered to be his, now and forever.

Her mouth was like a half-opened rose, lush with a red tint, like a strawberry. He needed to taste her again and again and never stop. As soon as he started to kiss her in earnest, she made a little moan and her eyes opened.

"Vasso—I dreamed I was kissing you, but I really *am* kissing you."

He laughed deep in his throat. "I wanted to kiss you

good morning. It wasn't nice of me to wake you up, but I'm so in love with you, I don't think I'll ever be able to leave you alone."

"Please don't, or I won't be able to bear it." She rolled over and kissed him so deeply that age-old ritual started again. They didn't come up for breath for several more hours.

Vasso finally lifted his mouth from hers. "Did I tell you yet how gorgeous you looked in that wedding dress? I could hardly breathe when you got out of the limo."

"Raina said I should wear it to give you a jolt."

"You did a lot more than that. Every man at the wedding would have given anything to be in my place. She has the right instincts. Raina's so good for Akis."

"I love her already."

"So do I."

"You kind of stopped traffic yourself. Have I told you yet how good you are for me? You make me thankful to have been born a woman. Seriously, Vasso, I'm so wild about you I think maybe there's something wrong with me."

"I'll never complain." He kissed every feature. "So you don't mind that I'm invading your space?"

"I must have been crazy when I said that."

"It's because you never lived with a man and didn't know it's the only way for a man and woman to experience true joy. These last few years I knew that the most important element in my life was missing. But not anymore." He crushed her body to his, kissing her neck and throat. "Where do you want to go on our honeymoon?"

"Right here with you."

"We could go anywhere," he murmured against her lips.

"I know. What do you say we wait to take a trip after we find out we're going to have a baby."

Vasso smoothed the hair off her forehead. "You want a baby soon?"

"You know I do. I'm so envious of Raina and Akis. There's no reason to wait. You heard what Father Debakis said. Be fruitful."

He rolled her over and looked deep into her eyes. "Maybe he already knows something we don't."

"I know. Exciting, isn't it?"

"In that case we'll just stay here until we get it right."

She cupped his face and pulled him down to press a passionate kiss to his mouth. "I was hoping you'd say that. If you think I'm shameful, I don't care. I need you with every particle of my being."

His expression sobered. He kissed her hands and moved them to either side of her head. "Don't you know you've made me whole? A thrill went through me when you circled the altar with me. I felt your love binding me tighter and tighter."

"I had that same wonderful feeling," she cried softly. "Our ceremony was holy, but it was also very romantic."

He smiled. "Only you could come up with the perfect description. That's because there's only one perfect you. You're the light of my life, *agape mou*. Kiss me again, Kyria Giannopoulos."

Three hours later he heard his cell vibrate. Only one person would be texting him.

Zoe smiled. "That has to be your brother. I love how close you are. Put him out of his misery and tell him we're deliriously happy."

Vasso reached for the phone on the bedside table. "He says to turn on the news. Do you want to watch?"

"No. I don't need to see my beloved husband on TV when I've got him right here in my arms."

"That's just another one of the thousand reasons I love you more than life itself." He buried his face in her neck, crying her name over and over again.

* * * * *

MISS PRIM'S
GREEK ISLAND FLING

MICHELLE DOUGLAS

To Pam, who is always happy to share a bottle of
red and to talk into the wee small hours
of the night.

CHAPTER ONE

IT WAS THE sound of shattering glass that woke her.

Audra shot bolt upright in bed, heart pounding, praying that the sound had been a part of one of her frequent nightmares, but knowing deep down in her bones—in all the places where she knew such things were real—that it wasn't.

A thump followed. Something heavy being dropped to the floor. And then a low, jeering voice. The sound of cupboard doors opening and closing.

She'd locked all the doors and windows downstairs! She'd been hyper-vigilant about such things ever since she'd arrived two days ago. She glanced at her bedroom window, at the curtain moving slowly on a draught of warm night air, and called herself a fool for leaving it open. Anyone could have climbed up onto the first-floor balcony and gained entry.

Slipping out of bed, she grabbed her phone and held it pressed hard against her chest as she crept out into the hallway. As the only person in residence in Rupert's Greek villa, she'd seen no reason to close her bedroom door, which at least meant she didn't have to contend with the sound of it creaking open now.

She'd chosen the bedroom at the top of the stairs and from this vantage point she could see a shadow bounce in and out of view from the downstairs living room. She heard Rupert's liquor cabinet being opened and the sound of a glass bottle being set down. Thieves were stealing her brother's much-loved single malt whisky?

Someone downstairs muttered something in…French? She didn't catch what was said.

Someone answered back in Greek.

She strained her ears, but could catch no other words. So…there were two of them? She refused to contemplate what would happen if they found her here—a lone woman. Swallowing down a hard knot of fear, she made her way silently down the hallway, away from the stairs, to the farthest room along—the master bedroom. The door made the softest of snicks as she eased it closed. In the moonlight she made out the walk-in wardrobe on the other side of the room and headed straight for it, closing that door behind her, fighting to breathe through the panic that weighed her chest down.

She dialled the emergency number. 'Please help me,' she whispered in Greek. 'Please. There are intruders in my house.' She gave her name. She gave the address. The operator promised that someone was on the way and would be there in minutes. She spoke in reassuringly calm tones. She asked Audra where in the house she was, and if there was anywhere she could hide. She told Audra to stay on the line and that helped too.

'I'm hiding in the walk-in wardrobe in the master bedroom.' And that was when it hit her. She was all but locked in a closet. *Again.* It made no difference that this time she'd locked herself in. Panic clawed at her throat as she recalled the suffocating darkness and the way her body had started to cramp after hours spent confined in her tiny hall closet. When Thomas had not only locked her in, but had left and she hadn't known if he would ever return to let her out again. And if he didn't return, how long would it take for anyone to find her? How long before someone raised the alarm? She'd spent hours in a terrified limbo—after screaming herself hoarse for help—where she'd had to fight for every breath. 'I can't stay here.'

'The police are almost there,' the operator assured her.

She closed her eyes. This wasn't her horridly cramped hall closet, but a spacious walk-in robe. It didn't smell of damp leather and fuggy cold. This smelled of…the sea.

And she could stretch out her full length and not touch the other wall if she wanted to. Anger, cold and comforting, streaked through her then. Her eyes flew open. She would *not* be a victim again. Oh, she wasn't going to march downstairs and confront those two villains ransacking her brother's house, but she wasn't going to stay here, a cornered quaking mess either.

Her free hand clenched to a fist. *Think!* If she were a thief, what would she steal?

Electrical equipment—televisions, stereos and computers. Which were all downstairs. She grimaced. Except for the television on the wall in the master bedroom.

She'd bet they'd look for jewellery too. And where was the most likely place to find that? The master bedroom.

She needed to find a better hiding place—one that had an escape route if needed.

And she needed a weapon. Just in case. She didn't rate her chances against two burly men, but she could leave some bruises if they did try to attack her. She reminded herself that the police would be here soon.

For the first time since arriving in this island idyll, Audra cursed the isolation of Rupert's villa. It was the last property on a peninsula surrounded by azure seas. The glorious sea views, the scent of the ocean and gardens, the sound of lapping water combined with the humming of bees and the chattering of the birds had started to ease the burning in her soul. No media, no one hassling her for an interview, no flashing cameras whenever she strode outside her front door. The privacy had seemed like a godsend.

Until now.

Using the torch app on her phone, she scanned the wardrobe for something she could use to defend herself. Her fingers closed about a lacrosse stick. It must've been years since Rupert had played, and she had no idea what he was still doing with a stick now, but at the moment she didn't care.

Cracking open the wardrobe door, she listened for a full minute before edging across the room to the glass sliding door of the balcony. She winced at the click that seemed to echo throughout the room with a *come-and-find-me* din when she unlocked it, but thanked Rupert's maintenance man when it slid open on its tracks as silent as the moon. She paused and listened again for another full minute before easing outside and closing the door behind her. Hugging the shadows of the wall, she moved to the end of the balcony and inserted herself between two giant pot plants. The only way anyone would see her was if they came right out onto the balcony and moved in this direction. She gripped the lacrosse stick so tightly her fingers started to ache.

She closed her eyes and tried to get her breathing under control. The thieves would have no reason to come out onto the balcony. There was nothing to steal out here. And she doubted they'd be interested in admiring the view, regardless of how spectacular it might be. The tight band around her chest eased a fraction.

The flashing lights from the police car that tore into the driveway a moment later eased the tightness even further. She counted as four armed men piled out of the vehicle and headed straight inside. She heard shouts downstairs.

But still she didn't move.

After a moment she lifted the phone to her ear. 'Is it… is it safe to come out yet?' she whispered.

'One of the men has been apprehended. The officers are searching for the second man.' There was a pause. 'The man they have in custody claims he's on his own.'

She'd definitely heard French *and* Greek.

'He also says he's known to your brother.'

'Known?' She choked back a snort. 'I can assure you that my brother doesn't associate with people who break into houses.'

'He says his name is Finn Sullivan.'

Audra closed her eyes. *Scrap that.* Her brother knew *one* person who broke into houses, and his name was Finn Sullivan.

Finn swore in French, and then in Greek for good measure, when he knocked the crystal tumbler from the bench to the kitchen tiles below, making a God-awful racket that reverberated through his head. It served him right for not switching on a light, but he knew Rupert's house as well as he knew his own, and he'd wanted to try to keep the headache stretching behind his eyes from building into a full-blown migraine.

Blowing out a breath, he dropped his rucksack to the floor and, muttering first in French and then in Greek, clicked on a light and retrieved the dustpan and brush to clean up the mess. For pity's sake. Not only hadn't Rupert's last house guest washed, dried and put away the tumbler— leaving it for him to break—but they hadn't taken out the garbage either! Whenever he stayed, Finn always made sure to leave the place exactly as he found it—spotlessly clean and tidy. He hated to think of his friend being taken advantage of.

Helping himself to a glass of Rupert's excellent whisky, Finn lowered himself into an armchair in the living room, more winded than he cared to admit. The cast had come off his arm yesterday and it ached like the blazes now. As did his entire left side and his left knee. Take it easy, the doctor had ordered. But he'd been taking it easy for eight long weeks. And Nice had started to feel like a prison.

Rupert had given him a key to this place a couple of years ago, and had told him to treat it as his own. He'd ring Rupert tomorrow to let him know he was here. He glanced at the clock on the wall. Two thirty-seven a.m. was too late…or early…to call anyone. He rested his head back and closed his eyes, and tried to will the pain coursing through his body away.

He woke with a start to flashing lights, and it took him a moment to realise they weren't due to a migraine. He blinked, but the armed policemen—two of them and each with a gun trained on him—didn't disappear. The clock said two forty-eight.

He raised his hands in the universal gesture of non-aggression. 'My name is Finn Sullivan,' he said in Greek. 'I am a friend of Rupert Russel, the owner of this villa.'

'Where is your accomplice?'

'Accomplice?' He stood then, stung by the fuss and suspicion. 'What accomplice?'

He wished he'd remained seated when he found himself tackled to the floor, pain bursting like red-hot needles all the way down his left side, magnifying the blue-black ache that made him want to roar.

He clamped the howls of pain behind his teeth and nodded towards his backpack as an officer rough-handled him to his feet after handcuffing him. 'My identification is in there.'

His words seemed to have no effect. One of the officers spoke into a phone. He was frogmarched into the grand foyer. Both policemen looked upwards expectantly, so he did too.

'Audra!'

Flanked by two more police officers, she pulled to a dead halt halfway down the stairs, her eyes widening—those too cool and very clear blue eyes. 'Finn?' Delicate nostrils flared. 'What on earth are you doing here?'

The glass on the sink, the litter in the kitchen bin made sudden sense. '*You* called the police?'

'Of course I called the police!'

'Of all the idiotic, overdramatic reactions! How daft can you get?' He all but yelled the words at her, his physical pain needing an outlet. 'Why the hell would you over-react like that?'

'Daft? Daft!' Her voice rose as she flew down the stairs.

'And what do you call breaking and entering my brother's villa at two thirty in the morning?'

It was probably closer to three by now. He didn't say that out loud. 'I didn't break in. I have a key.'

He saw then that she clutched a lacrosse stick. She looked as if she wouldn't mind cracking him over the head with it. With a force of effort he pulled in a breath. A woman alone in a deserted house…the sound of breaking glass… And after everything she'd been through recently…

He bit back a curse. He'd genuinely frightened her.

The pain in his head intensified. 'I'm sorry, Squirt.' The old nickname dropped from his lips. 'If I'd known you were here I'd have rung to let you know I was coming. In the meantime, can you tell these guys who I am and call them off?'

'Where's your friend?'

His shoulder ached like the blazes. He wanted to yell at her to get the police to release him. He bit the angry torrent back. Knowing Audra, she'd make him suffer as long as she could if he yelled at her again.

And he *was* genuinely sorry he'd frightened her.

'I came alone.'

'But I heard two voices—one French, one Greek.'

He shook his head. 'You heard one voice and two languages.' He demonstrated his earlier cussing fit, though he toned it down to make it more palatable for mixed company.

For a moment the knuckles on her right hand whitened where it gripped the lacrosse stick, and then relaxed. She told the police officers in perfect Greek how sorry she was to have raised a false alarm, promised to bake them home-made lemon drizzle cakes and begged them very nicely to let him go as he was an old friend of her brother's. He wasn't sure why, but it made him grind his teeth.

He groaned his relief when he was uncuffed, rubbing his wrists rather than his shoulder, though he was damned if he knew why. Except he didn't want any of them to know how much he hurt. He was sick to death of his injuries.

A part of him would be damned too before it let Audra see him as anything but hearty and hale. Her pity would...

He pressed his lips together. He didn't know. All he knew was that he didn't want to become an object of it.

Standing side by side in the circular drive, they waved the police off. He followed her inside, wincing when she slammed the door shut behind them. The fire in her eyes hadn't subsided. 'You want to yell at me some more?'

He'd love to. It was what he and Audra did—they sniped at each other. They had ever since she'd been a gangly pre-teen. But he hurt too much to snipe properly. It was taking all his strength to control the nausea curdling his stomach. He glanced at her from beneath his shaggy fringe. Besides, it was no fun sniping at someone with the kind of shadows under their eyes that Audra had.

He eased back to survey her properly. She was too pale and too thin. He wasn't used to seeing her vulnerable and frightened.

Frighteningly efficient? *Yes.*

Unsmiling? *Yes.*

Openly disapproving of his lifestyle choices? *Double yes.*

But pale, vulnerable and afraid? *No.*

'That bastard really did a number on you, didn't he, Squirt?'

Her head reared back and he could've bitten his tongue out. 'Not quite as big a number as that mountain did on you, from all reports.'

She glanced pointedly at his shoulder and with a start he realised he'd been massaging it. He waved her words away. 'A temporary setback.'

She pushed out her chin. 'Ditto.'

The fire had receded from her eyes and this time it was he who had to suffer beneath their merciless ice-blue scrutiny. And that was when he realised that all she wore was a pair of thin cotton pyjama bottoms and a singlet top that moulded itself to her form. His tongue stuck to the roof of his mouth.

The problem with Audra was that she was *exactly* the kind of woman he went after. If he had a type it was the buttoned-up, repressed librarian type, and normally Audra embodied that to a tee. But at the moment she was about as far from that as you could get. She was all blonde sleep-tousled temptation and his skin prickled with an awareness that was both familiar and unfamiliar.

He had to remind himself that a guy didn't mess with his best friend's sister.

'Did the police hurt you?'

'Absolutely not.' He was admitting nothing.

She cocked an eyebrow. 'Finn, it's obvious you're in pain.'

He shrugged and then wished he hadn't when pain blazed through his shoulder. 'The cast only came off yesterday.'

Her gaze moved to his left arm. 'And instead of resting it, no doubt as your doctors suggested, you jumped on the first plane for Athens, caught the last ferry to Kyanós, grabbed a late dinner in the village and trekked the eight kilometres to the villa.'

'Bingo.' He'd relished the fresh air and the freedom. For the first two kilometres.

'While carrying a rucksack.'

Eight weeks ago he'd have been able to carry twice the weight for ten kilometres without breaking a sweat.

She picked up his glass of half-finished Scotch and strode into the kitchen. As she reached up into a kitchen cupboard her singlet hiked up to expose a band of perfect pale skin that had his gut clenching. She pulled out a packet of aspirin and sent it flying in a perfect arc towards him—he barely needed to move to catch it. And then she lifted his glass to her lips and drained it and stars burst behind his eyelids. It was the sexiest thing he'd ever seen.

She filled it with tap water and set it in front of him. 'Take two.'

He did as she ordered because it was easier than arguing with her. And because he hurt all over and it seemed too much trouble to find the heavy-duty painkillers his doctor had prescribed for him and which were currently rolling around in the bottom of his backpack somewhere.

'Which room do you usually use?'

'The one at the top of the stairs.'

'You're out of luck, buddy.' She stuck out a hip, and he gulped down more water. 'That's the one I'm using.'

He feigned outrage. 'But that one has the best view!' Which was a lie. All the upstairs bedrooms had spectacular views.

She smirked. 'I know. First in and all that.'

He choked down a laugh. That was one of the things he'd always liked about Audra. She'd play along with him…all in the name of one-upmanship, of course.

'Right, which bedroom do you want? There are another three upstairs to choose from.' She strode around and lifted his bag. She grunted and had to use both hands. 'Yeah, right—light as a feather.'

He glanced at her arms. While the rucksack wasn't exactly light, it wasn't that heavy. She'd never been a weakling. She'd lost condition. He tried to recall the last time he'd seen her.

'Earth to Finn.'

He started. 'I'll take the one on the ground floor.' The one behind the kitchen. The only bedroom in the house that didn't have a sea view. The bedroom furthest away from Audra's. They wouldn't even have to share a bathroom if he stayed down here. Which would be for the best.

He glanced at that singlet top and nodded. *Definitely* for the best.

Especially when her eyes softened with spring-rain warmth. 'Damn, Finn. Do you still hurt that much?'

He realised then that she thought he didn't want to tackle the stairs.

'I—' He pulled in a breath. He *didn't* want to tackle the stairs. He'd overdone it today. He didn't want her to keep looking at him like that either, though. 'It's nothing a good night's sleep won't fix.'

Without another word, she strode to the room behind the kitchen and lifted his bag up onto the desk in there. So he wouldn't have to lift it himself later. Her thoughtfulness touched him. She could be prickly, and she could be mouthy, but she'd never been unkind.

Which was the reason, if he ever ran into Thomas Farquhar, he'd wring the mongrel's neck.

'Do you need anything else?'

The beds in Rupert's villa were always made up. He employed a cleaner to come in once a week so that the Russel siblings or any close friends could land here and fall into bed with a minimum of fuss. But even if the bed hadn't been made pride would've forbidden him from asking her to make it…or to help him make it.

He fell into a chair and slanted her a grin—cocky, assured and full of teasing to hide his pain as he pulled his hiking boots off. 'Well, now, Squirt…' He lifted a foot in her direction. 'I could use some help getting my socks off. And then maybe my jeans.'

As anticipated, her eyes went wide and her cheeks went pink. Without another word, she whirled around and strode from the room.

At that precise moment his phone started to ring. He glanced at the caller ID and grimaced. 'Rupert, mate. Sorry about—'

The phone was summarily taken from him and Finn blinked when Audra lifted it to her ear. Up this close she smelled of coconut and peaches. His mouth watered. Dinner suddenly seemed like hours ago.

'Rupe, Finn looks like death. He needs to rest. He'll call you in the morning and you can give him an ear-bashing then.' She turned the phone off before handing it back to him. 'Goodnight, Finn.'

She was halfway through the kitchen before he managed to call back a goodnight of his own. He stood in the doorway and waited until he heard her ascending the stairs before closing his door and dialling Rupert's number.

'Before you launch into a tirade and tell me what an idiot I am, let me apologise. I'm calling myself far worse names than you ever will. I'd have not scared Audra for the world. I was going to call you in the morning to let you know I was here.' He'd had no notion Audra would be here. It was a little early in the season for any of the Russels to head for the island.

Rupert's long sigh came down the phone, and it made Finn's gut churn. 'What are you doing in Kyanós?' his friend finally asked. 'I thought you were in Nice.'

'The, uh, cast came off yesterday.'

'And you couldn't blow off steam on the French Riviera?'

He scrubbed a hand down his face. 'There's a woman I'm trying to avoid and—'

'You don't need to say any more. I get the picture.'

Actually, Rupert was wrong. This time. It wasn't a romantic liaison he'd tired of and was fleeing. But he kept his mouth shut. He deserved Rupert's derision. 'If you want me to leave, I'll clear out at first light.'

His heart gave a sick kick at the long pause on the other end of the phone. Rupert was considering it! Rupert was the one person who'd shown faith in him when everyone else had written him off, and now—

'Of course I don't want you to leave.'

He closed his eyes and let out a long, slow breath.

'But…'

His eyes crashed open. His heart started to thud. 'But?'

'Don't go letting Audra fall in love with you. She's fragile at the moment, Finn...vulnerable.'

He stiffened. 'Whoa, Rupe! I've no designs on your little sister.'

'She's *exactly* your type.'

'Except she's your sister.' He made a decision then and there to leave in the morning. He didn't want Rupert worrying about this. It was completely unnecessary. He needed to lie low for a few weeks and Kyanós had seemed like the perfect solution, but not at the expense of either Rupert's or Audra's peace of mind.

'That said, I'm glad you're there.'

Finn stilled.

'I'm worried about her being on her own. I've been trying to juggle my timetable, but the earliest I can get away is in a fortnight.'

Finn pursed his lips. 'You want me to keep an eye on her?'

Again there was a long pause. 'She needs a bit of fun. She needs to let her hair down.'

'This *is* Audra we're talking about.' She was the most buttoned-up person he knew.

'You're good at fun.'

His lips twisted. He ought to be. He'd spent a lifetime perfecting it. 'You want me to make sure she has a proper holiday?'

'Minus the holiday romance. Women *like* you, Finn... they fall for you.'

'Pot and kettle,' he grunted back. 'But you're worrying for nothing. Audra has more sense than that.' She had *always* disapproved of him and what she saw as his irresponsible and daredevil lifestyle.

What had happened eight weeks ago proved her point. What if the next time he did kill himself? The thought made his mouth dry and his gut churn. His body was recovering but his mind… There were days when he was a maelstrom of confusion, questioning the choices he was making. He gritted his teeth. It'd pass. After such a close brush with mortality it had to be normal to question one's life. Needless to say, he wasn't bringing anyone into that mess at the moment, especially not one who was his best friend's little sister.

'If she had more sense she'd have not fallen for Farquhar.'

Finn's hands fisted. 'Tell me the guy is toast.'

'I'm working on it.'

Good.

'I've tried to shield her from the worst of the media furore, but…'

'But she has eyes in her head. She can read the headlines for herself.' And those headlines had been everywhere. It'd been smart of Rupert to pack Audra off to the island.

'Exactly.' Rupert paused again. 'None of the Russels have any sense when it comes to love. If we did, Audra wouldn't have been taken in like she was.'

And she was paying for it now. He recalled her pallor, the dark circles beneath her eyes…the effort it'd taken her to lift his backpack. He could help with some of that—get her out into the sun, challenge her to swimming contests… and maybe even get her to run with him. He could make sure she ate three square meals a day.

'If I'd had more sense I'd have not fallen for Brooke Manning.'

'Everyone makes a bad romantic decision at least once in their lives, Rupe.'

He realised he sounded as if he were downplaying what had happened to his friend, and he didn't want to do that. Rupert hadn't looked at women in the same way after Brooke. Finn wasn't sure what had happened between them. He'd been certain they were heading for matrimony, babies and white picket fences. But it had all imploded, and Rupert hadn't been the same since. 'But you're right—not everyone gets their heart shredded.' He rubbed a hand across his chest. 'Has Farquhar shredded her heart?'

'I don't know.'

Even if he hadn't, he'd stolen company secrets from the Russel Corporation while posing as her attentive and very loving boyfriend. That wasn't something a woman like Audra would be able to shrug off as just a bad experience.

Poor Squirt.

He only realised he'd said that out loud when Rupert said with a voice as dry as a good single malt, 'Take a look, Finn. I think you'll find Squirt is all grown up.'

He didn't need to look. The less looking he did, the better. A girl like Audra deserved more than what a guy like him could give her—things like stability, peace of mind, and someone she could depend on.

'It'd be great if you could take her mind off things—make her laugh and have some fun. I just don't want her falling for you. She's bruised and battered enough.'

'You've nothing to worry about on that score, Rupe, I promise you. I've no intention of hurting Audra. Ever.'

'She's special, Finn.'

That made him smile. 'All of the Russel siblings are special.'

'She's more selfless than the rest of us put together.'

Finn blinked. 'That's a big call.'

'It's the truth.'

He hauled in a breath and let it out slowly. 'I'll see what I can do.'

'Thanks, Finn, I knew I could count on you.'

Audra pressed her ringing phone to her ear at exactly eight twenty-three the next morning. She knew the exact time because she was wondering when Finn would emerge. She'd started clock-watching—a sure sign of worry. Not that she had any intention of letting Rupert know she was worried. 'Hey, Rupe.'

He called to check on her every couple of days, which only fed her guilt. Last night's false alarm sent an extra surge of guilt slugging through her now. 'Sorry about last night's fuss. I take it the police rang to let you know what happened.'

'They did. And you've nothing to apologise for. Wasn't your fault. In fact, I'm proud of the way you handled the situation.'

He was? Her shoulders went back.

'Not everyone would've thought that quickly on their feet. You did good.'

'Thanks, I... I'm relieved it was just Finn.' She flashed to the lines of strain that had bracketed Finn's mouth last night. 'Do you know how long he plans to stay?'

'No idea. Do you mind him being there? I can ask him to leave.'

'No, no—don't do that.' She already owed Rupert and the rest of her family too much. She didn't want to cause any further fuss. 'He wasn't looking too crash hot last night. I think he needs to take it easy for a bit.'

'You could be right, Squirt, and I hate to ask this of you...'

'Ask away.' She marvelled how her brother's *Squirt* could sound so different from Finn's. When Finn called her Squirt it made her tingle all over.

'No, forget about it. It doesn't matter. You've enough on your plate.'

She had nothing on her plate at the moment and they both knew it. 'Tell me what you were going to say,' she ordered in her best boardroom voice. 'I insist. You know you'll get no peace now until you do.'

His low chuckle was her reward. Good. She wanted him to stop worrying about her.

'Okay, it's just... I'm a bit worried about him.'

She sat back. 'About Finn?' It made a change from Rupert worrying about her.

'He's never had to take it easy in his life. Going slow is an alien concept to him.'

He could say that again.

'He nearly died up there on that mountain.'

Her heart clenched. 'Died? I mean, I knew he'd banged himself up pretty bad, but…I had no idea.'

'Typical Finn, he's tried to downplay it. While the medical team could patch the broken arm and ribs easily enough, along with the dislocated shoulder and wrenched knee, his ruptured spleen and the internal bleeding nearly did him in.'

She closed her eyes and swallowed. 'You want me to make sure he takes it easy while he's here?'

'That's probably an impossible task.'

'Nothing's impossible,' she said with a confidence she had no right to. After all her brother's support these last few weeks—his lack of blame—she could certainly do this one thing for him. 'Consider it done.'

'And, Audra…?'

'Yes?'

'Don't go falling in love with him.'

She shot to her feet, her back ramrod straight. 'I make one mistake and—'

'This has nothing to do with what happened with Farquhar. It's just that women seem to like Finn. *A lot*. They fall at his feet in embarrassing numbers.'

She snorted and took her seat again. 'That's because he's pretty.' She preferred a man with a bit more substance. *You thought Thomas had substance.*

She pushed the thought away.

'He's in Kyanós partly because he's trying to avoid some woman in Nice.'

Good to know.

'If he hurts you, Squirt, I'll no longer consider him a friend.'

She straightened from her slouch, air whistling between her teeth. Rupert and Finn were best friends, and had been ever since they'd attended their international boarding school in Geneva as fresh-faced twelve-year-olds.

She made herself swallow. 'I've no intention of doing anything so daft.' She'd never do anything to ruin her brother's most important friendship.

'Finn has a brilliant mind, he's built a successful company and is an amazing guy, but...'

'But what?' She frowned, when her brother remained silent. 'What are you worried about?'

'His past holds him back.'

By *his past* she guessed he meant Finn's parents' high-octane lifestyle, followed by their untimely deaths. It had to have had an impact on Finn, had to have left scars and wounds that would never heal.

'I worry he could end up like his father.'

She had to swallow the bile that rose through her.

'I'm not sure he'll ever settle down.'

She'd worked that much out for herself. And she wasn't a masochist. Men like Finn were pretty to look at, but you didn't build a life around them.

Women had flings with men like Finn...and she suspected they enjoyed every moment of them. A squirrel of curiosity wriggled through her, but she ruthlessly cut it off. One disastrous romantic liaison was enough for the year. She wasn't adding another one to the tally. She suppressed a shudder. The very thought made her want to crawl back into bed and pull the covers over her head.

She forced her spine to straighten. She had no intention of falling for Finn, but she could get him to slow down for a bit—just for a week or two, right?

CHAPTER TWO

'YOU HAD BREAKFAST YET, Squirt?'

Audra almost jumped out of her skin at the deep male voice and the hard-muscled body that materialised directly in front of her. She bit back a yelp and pressed a hand to her heart. After sitting here waiting for him to emerge, she couldn't believe she'd been taken off guard.

He chuckled. 'You never used to be jumpy.'

Yeah, well, that was before Thomas Farquhar had locked her in a cupboard. The laughter in his warm brown eyes faded as they narrowed. Not that she had any intention of telling him that. She didn't want his pity. 'Broken sleep never leaves me at my best,' she said in as tart a voice as she could muster. Which was, admittedly, pretty tart.

He just grinned. 'I find it depends on the reasons for the broken sleep.' And then he sent her a broad wink.

She rolled her eyes. 'Glass shattering and having to call the police doesn't fall into the fun category, Finn.'

'Do you want me to apologise again? Do the full grovel?' He waggled his eyebrows. 'I'm very good at a comprehensive grovel.'

'No, thank you.' She pressed her lips together. She bet he was good at a lot of things.

She realised she still held her phone. She recalled the conversation she'd just had with Rupert and set it to the table, heat flushing through her cheeks.

Finn glanced at her and at the phone before cracking eggs into the waiting frying pan. 'So... Rupe rang to warn you off, huh?'

Her jaw dropped. How on earth...? *Ah.* 'He rang you too.'

'You want a couple of these?' He lifted an egg in her direction.

'No…thank you,' she added as a belated afterthought. It struck her that she always found it hard to remember her manners around Finn.

'Technically, I called him.' The frying pan spat and sizzled. 'But he seems to think I have some magic ability to make women swoon at my feet, whereby I pick them off at my leisure and have my wicked way with them before discarding them as is my wont.'

She frowned. Had she imagined the bitterness behind the lightness?

'He read me the Riot Act where you're concerned.' He sent her a mock serious look. 'So, Squirt, while I know it'll be hard for you to contain your disappointment, I'm afraid I'm not allowed to let a single one of my love rays loose in your direction.'

She couldn't help it, his nonsense made her laugh.

With an answering grin, he set a plate of eggs and toast in front of her and slid into the seat opposite.

'But I said I didn't want any.'

Her stomach rumbled, making a liar of her. Rather than tease her, though, he shrugged. 'Sorry, I must've misheard.'

Finn never misheard anything, but the smell of butter on toast made her mouth water. She picked up her knife and fork. It'd be wasteful not to eat it. 'Did Rupert order you to feed me up?' she grumbled.

He shook his head, and shaggy hair—damp from the shower—fell into his eyes and curled about his neck and some pulse inside her flared to life before she brutally strangled it.

'Nope. Rupe's only dictum was to keep my love rays well and truly away from his little sister. All uttered in his most stern of tones.'

She did her best not to choke on her toast and eggs. 'Doesn't Rupert know me at all?' She tossed the words back at him with what she hoped was a matching carelessness.

'See? That's what I told him. I said, Audra's too smart to fall for a guy like me.'

Fall for? Absolutely not. Sleep with…?

What on earth…? She frowned and forced the thought away. She didn't think of Finn in those terms.

Really?

She rolled her shoulders. So what if she'd always thought him too good-looking for his own good? That didn't mean anything. In idle moments she might find herself thinking he'd be an exciting lover. If she were the kind of person who did flings with devil-may-care men. But she wasn't. And *that* didn't mean anything either.

'So…?'

She glanced up at the question in his voice.

'How long have you been down here?'

'Two days.'

'And how long are you here for?'

She didn't really know. 'A fortnight, maybe. I've taken some annual leave.'

He sent her a sharp glance from beneath brows so perfectly shaped they made her the tiniest bit jealous. 'If you took all the leave accrued by you, I bet you could stay here until the middle of next year.'

Which would be heaven—absolute heaven.

'What about you? How long are you staying?'

'I was thinking a week or two. Do some training…get some condition back.'

He was going to overdo it. Well, not on her watch!

'But if my being here is intruding on your privacy, I can shoot off to my uncle's place.'

'No need for that. It'll be nice to have some company.'

His eyes narrowed and she realised she'd overplayed her hand. It wasn't her usual sentiment where Finn was concerned. Normally she acted utterly disdainful and scornful. They sparred. They didn't buddy up.

She lifted her fork and pointed it at him. 'As long as you stop calling me Squirt, stop blathering nonsense about love rays…and cook me breakfast every day.'

He laughed and she let out a slow breath.

'You've got yourself a deal…*Audra*.'

Her name slid off his tongue like warm honey and it was all she could do not to groan. She set her knife and fork down and pushed her plate away.

'I had no idea you didn't like being called Squirt.'

She didn't. Not really.

He stared at her for a moment. 'Don't hold Rupert's protectiveness against him.'

She blinked. 'I don't.' And then grimaced. 'Well, not much. I know I'm lucky to have him…and Cora and Justin.' It was a shame that Finn didn't have a brother or sister. He did have Rupert, though, and the two men were as close as brothers.

'He's a romantic.'

That made her glance up. 'Rupert?'

'Absolutely.'

He nodded and it made his hair do that fall-in-his-eyes thing again and she didn't know why, but it made her stomach clench.

'On the outside he acts as hard as nails, but on the inside…'

'He's a big marshmallow,' she finished.

'He'd go to the ends of the earth for someone he loved.'

That was true. She nodded.

'See? A romantic.'

She'd never thought about it in those terms.

His phone on the table buzzed. She didn't mean to look, but she saw the name Trixie flash up on the screen before Finn reached over and switched it off. *Okay.*

'So…' He dusted off his hands as if ready to take on

the world. 'What were you planning to do while you were here?'

Dear God. *Think of nice, easy, relaxing things.* 'Um… I was going to lie on the beach and catch some rays—' *not love rays* '—float about in the sea for a bit.'

'Sounds good.'

Except he wouldn't be content with lying around and floating, would he? He'd probably challenge himself to fifty laps out to the buoy and back every day. 'Read a book.'

His lip curled. 'Read a book?'

She tried not to wince at the scorn that threaded through his voice.

'You come to one of the most beautiful places on earth to *read a book*?'

She tried to stop her shoulders from inching up to her ears. 'I like reading, and do you know how long it's been since I read a book for pleasure?'

'How long?'

'Over a year,' she mumbled.

He spread his hands. 'If you like to read, why don't you do more of it?'

Because she'd been working too hard. Because she'd let Thomas distract and manipulate her.

'And what else?'

She searched her mind. 'I don't cook.'

He glanced at their now empty plates and one corner of his mouth hooked up. 'So I've noticed.'

'But I want to learn to cook…um…croissants.'

His brow furrowed. 'Why?'

Because they took a long time to make, didn't they? The pastry needed lots of rolling out, didn't it? Which meant, if she could trick him into helping her, he'd be safe from harm while he was rolling out pastry. 'Because I love them.' That was true enough. 'But I've had to be strict with myself.'

'Strict, how?'

'I've made a decision—in the interests of both my waistline and my heart health—that I'm only allowed to eat croissants that I make myself.'

He leaned back and let loose with a long low whistle. 'Wow, Squ— Audra! You really know how to let your hair down and party, huh?'

No one in all her life had ever accused her of being a party animal.

'A holiday with reading and baking at the top of your list.'

His expression left her in no doubt what he thought about that. 'This is supposed to be a holiday—some R & R,' she shot back, stung. 'I'm all go, go, go at work, but here I want time out.'

'Boring,' he sing-songed.

'Relaxing,' she countered.

'You've left the recreation part out of your R & R equation. I mean, look at you. You even look...'

She had to clamp her hands around the seat of her chair to stop from leaping out of it. 'Boring?' she said through gritted teeth.

'Buttoned-up. Tense. The opposite of relaxed.'

'It's the effect you and your love rays always seem to have on me.'

He tsk-tsked and shook his head. 'We're not supposed to mention the love rays, remember?'

Could she scream yet?

'I mean, look at your hair. You have it pulled back *in a bun*.'

She touched a hand to her hair. 'What's wrong with that?'

'A bun is for the boardroom, not the beach.'

She hated wearing her hair down and have it tickle her face.

'Well, speaking of hair, you might want to visit a

hairdresser yourself when you're next in the village,' she shot back.

'But I visited my hairdresser only last week.' He sent her a grin full of wickedness and sin. 'The delectable Monique assured me this look is all the rage at the moment.'

He had a hairdresser called Monique...who was delectable? She managed to roll her eyes. 'The *too-long-for-the-boardroom-just-right-for-the-beach* look?'

'Precisely. She said the same about the stubble.'

She'd been doing her best not to notice that stubble. She was trying to keep the words *dead sexy* from forming in her brain.

'What do you think?' He ran a hand across his jawline, preening. It should've made him look ridiculous. Especially as he was hamming it up and trying to look ridiculous. But she found herself having to jam down on the temptation to reach across and brush her palm across it to see if it was as soft and springy as it looked.

She mentally slapped herself. 'I think it looks...scruffy.' In the best possible way. 'But it probably provides good protection against the sun, which is wise in these climes.'

He simply threw his head back and laughed, not taking the slightest offence. The strain that had deepened the lines around his eyes last night had eased. And when he rose to take their dishes to the sink he moved with an easy fluidity that belied his recent injuries.

He almost died up there on that mountain.

She went cold all over.

'Audra?'

She glanced up to find him staring at her, concern in his eyes. She shook herself. 'What's your definition of a good holiday, then?'

'Here on the island?'

He'd started to wash the dishes so she rose to dry them. 'Uh-huh, here on the island.'

'Water sports,' he said with relish.

'What kind of water sports?' Swimming and kayaking were gentle enough, but—

'On the other side of the island is the most perfect cove for windsurfing and sailing.'

But…but he could hurt himself.

'Throw in some water-skiing and hang-gliding and I'd call that just about the perfect holiday.'

He could kill himself! Lord, try explaining *that* to Rupert. 'No way.'

He glanced at her. 'When did you become such a scaredy-cat, Audra Russel?'

She realised he thought her 'No way' had been in relation to herself, which was just as well because if he realised she'd meant it for him he'd immediately go out and throw himself off the first cliff he came across simply to spite her.

And while it might be satisfying to say I told you so if he did come to grief, she had a feeling that satisfaction would be severely tempered if the words were uttered in a hospital ward…or worse.

'Why don't you let your hair down for once, take a risk? You might even find it's fun.'

She bit back a sigh. Maybe that was what she was afraid of. One risk could lead to another, and before she knew it she could've turned her whole life upside down. And she wasn't talking sex with her brother's best friend here either. Which—*obviously*—wasn't going to happen. She was talking about her job and her whole life. It seemed smarter to keep a tight rein on all her risk-taking impulses. She was sensible, stable and a rock to all her family. That was *who* she was. She repeated the words over and over like a mantra until she'd fixed them firmly in her mind again.

She racked her brain to think of a way to control Finn's risk-taking impulses too. 'There's absolutely nothing wrong with some lazy R & R, Finn Sullivan.' She used his full name in the same way he'd used hers. 'You should try it some time.'

His eyes suddenly gleamed. 'I'll make a deal with you. I'll try your kind of holiday R & R if you'll try mine?'

She bit her lip, her pulse quickening. This could be the perfect solution. 'So you'd be prepared to laze around here with a book if I...if I try windsurfing and stuff?'

'Yep. Quid pro quo.'

'Meaning?'

'One day we do whatever you choose. The next day we do whatever I choose.'

She turned to hang up the tea towel so he couldn't see the self-satisfied smile that stretched across her face. For at least half of his stay she'd be able to keep him out of trouble. As for the other half...she could temper his pace—be so inept he'd have to slow down to let her keep up or have to spend so much time teaching her that there'd been no time for him to be off risking his own neck. *Perfect*.

She swung back. 'Despite what you say, I'm not a scaredy-cat.'

'And despite what you think, I'm not hyperactive.'

Finn held his breath as he watched Audra weigh up his suggestion. She was actually considering it. Which was surprising. He'd expected her to tell him to take a flying leap and stalk off to read her book.

But she was actually considering his suggestion and he didn't know why. He thought he'd need to tease and rile her more, bring her latent competitive streak to the fore, where she'd accept his challenge simply to save face. Still, he *had* tossed out the bait of her proving that her way was better than his. Women were always trying to change him. Maybe Audra found that idea attractive too?

In the next moment he shook his head. That'd only be the case if she were interested in him as a romantic prospect. And she'd made it clear that wasn't the case.

Thank God.

He eyed that tight little bun and swallowed.

'I'll agree to your challenge...'

He tried to hide his surprise. She would? He hadn't even needed to press her.

'On two conditions.'

Ha! He knew it couldn't be that easy. 'Which are?'

'I get to go first.'

He made a low sweeping bow. 'Of course—ladies first, that always went without saying.' It was a minor concession and, given how much he still hurt, one he didn't mind making. They could pick up the pace tomorrow.

'And the challenge doesn't start until tomorrow.'

He opened his mouth to protest, but she forged on. 'We need to go shopping. There's hardly any food in the place. And I'm not wasting my choice of activities on practicalities like grocery shopping, thank you very much.'

'We could get groceries delivered.'

'But it'd be nice to check out the produce at the local market. Rupert likes to support the local businesses.'

And while she was here she'd consider herself Rupert's representative. And it was true—what she did here would reflect on her brother. The Russels had become a bit of a fixture in Kyanós life over the last few years.

'I also want to have a deliciously long browse in the bookstore. And you'll need to select a book too, you know?'

Oh, joy of joys. He was going to make her run two miles for that.

'And...' she shrugged '...consider it a fact-finding mission—we can research what the island has to offer and put an itinerary together.'

Was she really going to let him choose half of her holiday activities for the next week or two? *Excellent.* By the time he was through with her, she'd have colour in her cheeks, skin on her bones—not to mention some muscle tone and a spring in her step. 'You've got yourself a deal... on one condition.'

Her eyebrows lifted.

'That you lose the bun.' He couldn't think straight around that bun. Whenever he glanced at it, he was seized by an unholy impulse to release it. It distracted him beyond anything.

Without another word, she reached up to pull the pins from her bun, and a soft cloud of fair hair fell down around her shoulders. Her eyes narrowed and she thrust out her chin. 'Better?'

It took an effort of will to keep a frown from his face. A tight band clamped around his chest.

'Is it *beachy* enough for you?'

'A hundred per cent better,' he managed, fighting the urge to reach out and touch a strand, just to see if it was as silky and soft as it looked.

She smirked and pulled it back into a ponytail. 'There, the bun is gone.'

But the ponytail didn't ease the tightness growing in his chest, not to mention other places either. It bounced with a perky insolence that had him aching to reach out and give it a gentle tug. For pity's sake, it was just hair!

She stilled, and then her hands went to her hips. 'Are you feeling okay, Finn?'

He shook himself. 'Of course I am. Why?'

'You gave in to my conditions without a fight. That's not like you. Normally you'd bicker with me and angle for more.'

Damn! He had to remember how quick she was, and keep his wits about him.

'If you want a few more days before embarking on our challenge, that's fine with me. I mean, you only just got the cast off your arm.'

He clenched his jaw so hard it started to ache.

'I understand you beat yourself up pretty bad on that mountain.'

She paused as if waiting for him to confirm that, but he had no intention of talking about his accident.

She shrugged. 'And you looked pretty rough last night so...'

'So...what?'

'So if you needed a couple of days to regroup...'

Anger directed solely at himself pooled in his stomach. 'The accident was two month ago, *Squirt*.' He called her Squirt deliberately, to set her teeth on edge. 'I'm perfectly fine.'

She shrugged. 'Whatever you say.' But she didn't look convinced. 'I'm leaving for the village in half an hour if you want to come along. But if you want to stay here and do push-ups and run ten miles on the beach then I'm more than happy to select a book for you.'

'Not a chance.' He shuddered to think what she would make him read as a penance. 'I'll be ready in twenty.'

'Suit yourself.' She moved towards the foyer and the stairs. And the whole time her ponytail swayed in jaunty mockery. She turned when she reached the foyer's archway. 'Finn?'

He hoped to God she hadn't caught him staring. 'What?'

'The name's Audra, not Squirt. That was the deal. Three strikes and you're out. That's Strike One.'

She'd kick him out if he... He stared after her and found himself grinning. She wasn't going to let him push her around and he admired her for it.

'I'll drive,' Finn said, thirty minutes later.

'I have the car keys,' Audra countered, sliding into the driver's seat of the hybrid Rupert kept on the island for running back and forth to the village.

To be perfectly honest, he didn't care who drove. He

just didn't want Audra to think him frail or in need of babying. Besides, it was only ten minutes into the village.

One advantage of being passenger, though, was the unencumbered opportunity to admire the views, and out here on the peninsula the views were spectacular. Olive trees interspersed with the odd cypress and ironwood tree ranged down the slopes, along with small scrubby shrubs bursting with flowers—some white and some pink. And beyond it all was the unbelievable, almost magical blue of the Aegean Sea. The air from the open windows was warm and dry, fragrant with salt and rosemary, and something inside him started to unhitch. He rested his head back and breathed it all in.

'Glorious, isn't it?'

He glanced across at her profile. She didn't drive as if she needed to be anywhere in a hurry. Her fingers held the steering wheel in a loose, relaxed grip, and the skin around her eyes and mouth was smooth and unblemished. The last time he'd seen her she'd been in a rush, her knuckles white around her briefcase and her eyes narrowed—no doubt her mind focussed on the million things on her to-do list.

She glanced across. 'What?'

'I was just thinking how island life suits you.'

Her brows shot up, and she fixed her attention on the road in front again, her lips twitching. 'Wow, you must really hate my bun.'

No, he loved that bun.

Not that he had any intention of telling her that.

She flicked him with another of her cool glances. 'Do you know anyone that this island life wouldn't suit?'

'Me...in the long term. I'd go stir-crazy after a while.' He wasn't interested in holidaying his whole life away.

What are you interested in doing with the rest of your life, then?

He swallowed and shoved the question away, not ready

to face the turmoil it induced, focussed his attention back on Audra.

'And probably you too,' he continued. 'Seems to me you don't like being away from the office for too long.'

Something in her tensed, though her fingers still remained loose and easy on the wheel. He wanted to turn more fully towards her and study her to find out exactly what had changed, but she'd challenge such a stare, and he couldn't think of an excuse that wouldn't put her on the defensive. Getting her to relax and have fun was the remit, not making her tense and edgy. His mention of work had probably just been an unwelcome reminder of Farquhar.

And it was clear she wanted to talk about Farquhar as much as he wanted to talk about his accident.

He cleared his throat. 'But in terms of a short break, I don't think anything can beat this island.'

'Funnily enough, that's one argument you won't get from me.'

He didn't know why, but her words made him laugh.

They descended into the village and her sigh of appreciation burrowed into his chest. 'It's such a pretty harbour.'

She steered the car down the narrow street to the parking area in front of the harbour wall. They sat for a moment to admire the scene spread before them. An old-fashioned ferry chugged out of the cove, taking passengers on the two-hour ride to the mainland. Yachts with brightly coloured sails bobbed on their moorings. The local golden stone of the harbour wall provided the perfect foil for the deep blue of the water. To their left houses in the same golden stone, some of them plastered brilliant white, marched up the hillside, the bright blue of their doors and shutters making the place look deliciously Mediterranean.

Audra finally pushed out of the car and he followed. She pulled her hair free of its band simply to capture it again, including the strand that had worked its way loose, and retied it. 'I was just going to amble along the main shopping strip for a bit.'

She gestured towards the cheerful curve of shops that lined the harbour, the bunting from their awnings fluttering in the breeze. Barrels of gaily coloured flowers stood along the strip at intervals. If there was a more idyllic place on earth, he was yet to find it.

'Sounds good to me.' While she was ambling she'd be getting a dose of sun and fresh air. 'Do you mind if I tag along?' He asked because he'd called her Squirt earlier to deliberately rub her up the wrong way and he regretted it now.

Cool blue eyes surveyed him and he couldn't read them at all. 'I mean to take my time. I won't be rushed. I do enough rushing in my real life and...'

Her words trailed off and he realised she thought he meant to whisk her through the shopping at speed and... and what? Get to the things he wanted to do? What kind of selfish brute did she think he was? 'I'm in no rush.'

'I was going to browse the markets and shops...maybe get some lunch, before buying whatever groceries we needed before heading back.'

'Sounds like an excellent plan.'

The faintest of frowns marred the perfect skin of her forehead. 'It does?'

Something vulnerable passed across her features, but it was gone in a flash. From out of nowhere Rupert's words came back to him: *'She's more selfless than the rest of us put together.'* The Russel family came from a privileged background, but they took the associated social responsibility of that position seriously. Each of them had highly honed social consciences. But it struck him then that Audra put her family's needs before her own. Who put her needs first?

'Audra, a lazy amble along the harbour, while feeling

the sun on my face and breathing in the sea air, sounds pretty darn perfect to me.'

She smiled then—a real smile—and it kicked him in the gut because it was so beautiful. And because he realised he'd so very rarely seen her smile like that.

Why?

He took her arm and led her across the street, releasing her the moment they reached the other side. She still smelled of coconut and peaches, and it made him want to lick her.

Dangerous.

Not to mention totally inappropriate.

He tried to find his equilibrium again, and for once wished he could blame his sense of vertigo, the feeling of the ground shifting beneath his feet, on his recent injuries. Audra had always been able to needle him and then make him laugh, but he had no intention of letting her get under his skin. Not in *that* way. He'd been out of circulation too long, that was all. He'd be fine again once he'd regained his strength and put the accident behind him.

'It's always so cheerful down here,' she said, pausing beside one of the flower-filled barrels, and dragging a deep breath into her lungs.

He glanced down at the flowers to avoid noticing the way her chest lifted, and touched his fingers to a bright pink petal. 'These are...nice.'

'I love petunias,' she said. She touched a scarlet blossom. 'And these geraniums and begonias look beautiful.'

He reached for a delicate spray of tiny white flowers at the same time that she did, and their fingers brushed against each other. It was the briefest of contacts, but it sent electricity charging up his arm and had him sucking in a breath. For one utterly unbalancing moment he thought she meant to repeat the gesture.

'That's alyssum,' she said, pulling her hand away.

He moistened his lips. 'I had no idea you liked gardening.'

She stared at him for a moment and he watched her snap back into herself like a rubber band that had been stretched and then released. But opposite to that because the stretching had seemed to relax her while the snapping back had her all tense again.

'Don't worry, Finn. I'm not going to make you garden while you're here.'

Something sad and hungry, though, lurked in the backs of her eyes, and he didn't understand it at all. He opened his mouth to ask her about it, but closed it again. He didn't get involved with complicated emotions or sensitive issues. He avoided them like the plague. Get her to laugh, get her to loosen up. That was his remit. Nothing more. But that didn't stop the memory of that sad and hungry expression from playing over and over in his mind.

CHAPTER THREE

AUDRA WHEELED AWAY from Finn and the barrel of flowers to survey the length of the village street, and tried to slow the racing of her pulse…to quell the temptation that swept through her like the breeze tugging at her hair. But the sound of the waves splashing against the seawall and the sparkles of light on the water as the sun danced off its surface only fed the yearning and the restlessness.

She couldn't believe that the idea—the temptation—had even occurred to her. She and Finn? The idea was laughable.

For pity's sake, she'd had one romantic disaster this year. Did she really want to follow that up with another?

Absolutely not.

She dragged a trembling hand across her eyes. She must be more shaken by Thomas and his betrayal than she'd realised. She needed to focus on herself and her family, and to make things right again. That was what this break here on Kyanós was all about—that and avoiding the media storm that had surrounded her in Geneva. The one thing she didn't want to do was to make things worse.

The building at the end of the row of shops drew her gaze. Its white walls and blue shutters gleamed in the sun like the quintessential advertisement for a Greek holiday. The For Sale sign made her swallow. She resolutely dragged her gaze away, but the gaily coloured planter pots dotted along the thoroughfare caught her gaze again and that didn't help either. But…

A sigh welled inside her. But if she ever owned a shop, she'd have a tub—or maybe two tubs—of flowers like these outside its door.

You're never going to own a shop.

She made herself straighten. No, she was never going to own a shop. And the sooner she got over it, the better.

The lengthening silence between her and Finn grew more and more fraught.

See what happens when you don't keep a lid on the nonsense? You become tempted to do ridiculous things.

Well, she could annihilate that in one fell swoop.

'If I ever owned a shop, I'd want flowers outside its door too, just like these ones.' And she waited for the raucous laughter to scald her dream with the scorn it deserved.

Rather than laughter a warm chuckle greeted her, a chuckle filled with...affection? 'You used to talk about opening a shop when you were a little girl.'

And everyone had laughed at her—teased her for not wanting to be something more glamorous like an astronaut or ballerina.

Poor poppet, she mocked herself.

'What did you want to be when you were little?'

'A fireman...a knife-thrower at the circus...an explorer...and I went through a phase of wanting to be in a glam-rock band. It was the costumes,' he added when she swung to stare at him. 'I loved the costumes.'

She couldn't help but laugh. 'I'm sure you'd look fetching in purple satin, platform boots and silver glitter.'

He snorted.

'You know what the next challenge is going to be, don't you? The very next fancy dress party you attend, you have to go as a glam rocker.'

'You know there'll be a counter challenge to that?'

'There always is.' And whatever it was, she wouldn't mind honouring it. She'd pay good money to see Finn dressed up like that.

One corner of his mouth had hooked up in a cocky grin, his eyes danced with devilment, and his hair did that 'slide across his forehead perilously close to his eyes' thing and her stomach clenched. Hard. She forced her gaze away, reminded herself who he was. And what he was. 'Well, it might not come with fancy costumes, but playboy adventurer captures the spirit of your childhood aspirations.'

He slanted a glance down at her, the laughter in his eyes turning dark and mocking, though she didn't know if it was directed at her or himself. 'Wow,' he drawled. 'Written off in one simple phrase. You've become a master of the backhanded compliment. Though some might call it character assassination.'

It was her turn to snort. 'While you've perfected drama queen.' But she found herself biting her lip as she stared unseeing at the nearby shop fronts as they walked along. Had she been too hard, too...*dismissive* just then? 'I'm not discounting the fact that you make a lot of money for charity.'

The car races, the mountaineering expeditions, the base jumps were all for terribly worthy causes.

'And yet she can't hide her disapproval at my reckless and irresponsible lifestyle,' he told the sky.

It wasn't disapproval, but envy. Not that she had any intention of telling him so. All right, there was some disapproval too. She didn't understand why he had to risk his neck for charity. There were other ways to fundraise, right? Risking his neck just seemed...stupid.

But whatever else Finn was, she'd never accuse him of being stupid.

She was also officially tired of this conversation. She halted outside the bookshop. 'Our first stop.'

She waited for him to protest but all he did was gesture for her to precede him. 'After you.'

With a big breath she entered, and crossed her fingers and hoped none of the shopkeepers or villagers would mention her recent troubles when they saw her today. She just wanted to forget all about that for a while.

They moved to different sections of the store—him to Non-Fiction, while she started towards Popular Fiction, stopping along the way to pore over the quaint merchandise that lined the front of the shop—cards and pens, bookmarks in every shape and size, some made from paper while others were made from bits of crocheted string with coloured beads dangling from their tails. A large selection of journals and notebooks greeted her too, followed by bookends and paperweights—everything a booklover could need. How she loved this stuff! On her way out she'd buy a gorgeous notebook. Oh, and bookmarks—one for each book she bought.

She lost herself to browsing the row upon row of books then; most were in Greek but some were in English too. She didn't know for how long she scanned titles, admired covers and read back-cover blurbs, but she slowly became aware of Finn watching her from where he sat on one of the low stools that were placed intermittently about the shop for customers' convenience. She surprised a look of affection on his face, and it made her feel bad for sniping at him earlier and dismissing him as a playboy adventurer.

He grinned. 'You look like you're having fun.'

'I am.' This slow browsing, the measured contemplation of the delights offered up on these shelves—the sheer *unrushedness* of it all—filled something inside her. She glanced at his hands, his lap, the floor at his feet. 'You don't have a book yet.'

He nodded at the stack she held. 'Are you getting all of those?'

'I'm getting the French cookbook.' She'd need a recipe for croissants. 'And three of these.'

He took the cookbook from her, and then she handed him two women's fiction titles and a cosy mystery, before putting the others back where they belonged.

'What would you choose for me?' His lip curled as he reached forward to flick a disparaging finger at a blockbuster novel from a big-name writer. 'Something like that?'

'That's a historical saga with lots of period detail. I'd have not thought it was your cup of tea at all.' She suspected the pace would be a bit slow for his taste. 'The object of the exercise isn't to make you suffer.'

Amber eyes darker than the whisky he liked but just as intoxicating swung to her and she saw the surprise in their depths. She recalled the affection she'd surprised in his face a moment ago and swallowed. Had she become a complete and utter shrew somewhere over the last year or two? 'I know that our modus operandi is to tease each other and…and to try to best each other—all in fun, of course.'

He inclined his head. 'Of course.'

'But I want to show you that quieter pursuits can be pleasurable too. If I were choosing a book for you I'd get you—' she strode along to the humour section '—this.' She pulled out a book by a popular comedian that she knew he liked.

He blinked and took it.

She set off down the next row of shelves. 'And to be on the safe side I'd get you this as well…or this.' She pulled out two recent non-fiction releases. One a biography of a well-known sportsman, and the other on World War Two.

He nodded towards the second one and she added it to the growing pile of books in his arms.

She started back the way they'd come. 'If I were on my own I'd get you this one as a joke.' She held up a self-help book with the title *Twelve Rules for Life: An Antidote to Chaos*.

'Put it back.'

The laughter in his voice added a spring to her step. She slotted it back into place. 'I'd get you a wildcard too.'

'A wildcard?'

'A book on spec—something you might not like, but could prove to be something you'd love.'

He pursed his lips for a moment and then nodded. 'I want a wildcard.'

Excellent. But what? She thought back over what he'd said earlier—about wanting to be a fireman, a knife-thrower, an explorer. She returned to the fiction shelves. She'd bet her house on the fact he'd love tales featuring heroic underdogs. She pulled a novel from the shelf—the first book in a fantasy trilogy from an acclaimed writer.

'That's…that's a doorstop!'

'Yes or no?'

He blew out a breath. 'What the hell, add it to the pile.'

She did, and then retrieved her own books from his arms. 'I'm not letting you buy my books.'

'Why not?'

'I like to buy my own books. And I've thrust three books onto you that you may never open.'

He stretched his neck, first one way and then the other. 'Can I buy you lunch?'

'As a thank you for being your bookstore personal shopper? Absolutely. But let's make it a late lunch. I'm still full from breakfast.'

She stopped to select her bookmarks, and added two notebooks to her purchases. Finn chose a bookmark of his own, and then seized a satchel in butter-soft black leather. 'Perfect.'

Perfect for what? She glanced at the selection of leather satchels and calico book bags and bit her lip. Maybe—

With a laugh, Finn propelled her towards the counter. 'Save them for your next visit.'

They paid and while Audra exchanged greetings with Sibyl, the bookshop proprietor, he put all their purchases into the satchel and slung it over his shoulder. 'Where to next?'

She stared at that bag. It'd make his shoulder ache if he wasn't careful. But then she realised it was on his right shoulder, not his left, and let out a breath. 'Wherever the mood takes us,' she said as they moved towards the door.

She paused to read the community announcement board and an advertisement for art classes jumped out at her. Oh, that'd be fun and…

She shook her head. R & R was all very well, but she had to keep herself contained to the beach and her books. Anything else… Well, anything else was just too hard. And she was too tired.

Finn trailed a finger across the flyer. 'Interested?'

She shook her head and led him outside.

He frowned at her. 'But—'

'Ooh, these look like fun.' She shot across to the boutique next door and was grateful when he let himself be distracted.

They flicked through a rack of discounted clothing that stood in blatant invitation out the front. Finn bought a pair of swimming trunks, so she added a sarong to her growing list of purchases. They browsed the markets. Finn bought a pair of silver cufflinks in the shape of fat little aeroplanes. 'My uncle will love these.' He pointed to an oddly shaped silver pendant on a string of black leather. 'That'd look great on you.' So she bought that too. They helped each other choose sunhats.

It felt decadent to be spending like this, not that any of her purchases were particularly pricey. But she so rarely let herself off the leash that she blithely ignored the voice of puritan sternness that tried to reel her in. What was more, it gave her the chance to exchange proper greetings with the villagers she'd known for years now.

Her worries she'd be grilled about Thomas and her reputed broken heart and the upcoming court case dissolved within ten minutes. As always, the people of Kyanós embraced her as if she were one of their own. And she loved them for it. The Russel family had been coming for holidays here for nearly ten years now. Kyanós felt like a home away from home.

'Hungry yet?'

'Famished!' She glanced at her watch and did a double take when she saw it was nearly two o'clock. 'We haven't done the bakery, the butcher, the delicatessen or the wine merchant yet.'

'We have time.'

She lifted her face to the sun and closed her eyes to relish it even more. 'We do.'

They chose a restaurant that had a terrace overlooking the harbour and ordered a shared platter of warm olives, cured meats and local cheeses accompanied with bread warm from the oven and a cold crisp carafe of *retsina*. While they ate they browsed their book purchases.

Audra surreptitiously watched Finn as he sampled the opening page of the fantasy novel...and then the next page...and the one after that.

He glanced up and caught her staring. He hesitated and then shrugged. 'You know, this might bc halfway decent.'

She refrained from saying I told you so. 'Good.'

'If I hadn't seen you choose me those first two books I'd have not given this one a chance. I'd have written it off as a joke like the self-help book. And as I suspect I'll enjoy both these other books...'

If he stayed still long enough to read them.

He frowned.

She folded her arms. 'Why does that make you frown?'

'I'm wishing I'd known about this book when I was laid up in hospital with nothing to do.'

The shadows in his eyes told her how stir-crazy he'd gone. 'What did you do to pass the time?'

'Crosswords. And I watched lots of movies.'

'And chafed.'

'Pretty much.'

'I almost sent you a book, but I thought...'

'You thought I'd misinterpret the gesture? Think you were rubbing salt into the wound?'

Something like that.

He smiled. 'I appreciated the puzzle books.' And then he scowled. 'I didn't appreciate the grapes, though. Grapes are for invalids.'

She stiffened. 'It was supposed to be an entire basket of fruit!' Not just grapes.

'Whatever. I'd have preferred a bottle of tequila. I gave the fruit to the nurses.'

But his eyes danced as he feigned indignation and it was hard to contain a grin. 'I'll keep that in mind for next time.'

He gave a visible shudder and she grimaced in sympathy. 'Don't have a next time.' She raised her glass. 'To no more accidents and a full and speedy recovery.'

'I'll drink to that.'

He lifted his glass to hers and then sipped it with an abandoned enjoyment she envied. 'Who knew you'd be such fun to shop with?'

The words shot out of her impulsively, and she found herself speared on the end of a keen-edged glance. 'You thought I'd chafe?'

'A bit,' she conceded. 'I mean, Rupert and Justin will put up with it when Cora or I want to window-shop, but they don't enjoy it.'

'I wouldn't want to do it every day.'

Neither would she.

'But today has been fun.' He stared at her for a beat too long. 'It was a revelation watching you in the bookstore.'

She swallowed. Revelation, how?

'It's been a long time since I saw you enjoy yourself so much, Squirt, and—' He shot back in his seat. 'Audra! I meant to say Audra. Don't make that Strike Two. I…'

He gazed at her helplessly and she forgave him instantly. He hadn't said it to needle her the way he had with his earlier *Squirt*. She shook herself. 'Sorry, what were you saying? I was miles away.'

He smiled his thanks, but then leaned across the table towards her, and that smile and his closeness made her breath catch. 'You should do things you enjoy more often, Miss Conscientiousness.'

Hmm, she'd preferred Squirt.

'There's more to life than boardrooms and spreadsheets.'

'That's what holidays are for,' she agreed. The boardrooms and spreadsheets would be waiting for her at the end of it, though, and the thought made her feel tired to the soles of her feet.

CHAPTER FOUR

AUDRA GLANCED ACROSS at Finn, who looked utterly content lying on his towel on the sand of this ridiculously beautiful curve of beach, reading his book. It seemed ironic, then, that she couldn't lose herself in her own book.

She blamed it on the half-remembered dreams that'd given her a restless night. Scraps had been playing through her mind all morning—sexy times moving to the surreal and the scary; Finn's and Thomas's faces merging and then separating—leaving her feeling restless and strung tight.

One of those sexy-time moments played through her mind again now and she bit her lip against the warmth that wanted to spread through her. The fact that this beach was so ridiculously private didn't help. She didn't want the words *private* and *Finn*—or *sexy times*—to appear in the same thought with such tempting symmetry. It was *crazy*. She'd always done her best to not look at Finn in *that* way. And she had no intention of letting her guard down now.

This whole preoccupation was just a…a way for her subconscious to avoid focussing on what needed to be dealt with. Which was to regather her resources and refocus her determination to be of service at the Russel Corporation, to be a valuable team member rather than a liability.

'What was that sigh for?'

She blinked to find Finn's beautiful brown eyes surveying her. And they were beautiful—the colour of cinnamon and golden syrup and ginger beer, and fringed with long dark lashes. She didn't know how lashes could look decadent and sinful, but Finn's did.

'You're supposed to be relaxing—enjoying the sun and the sea…your book.'

'I am.'

'Liar.'

He rolled to his side to face her more fully, and she shrugged. 'I had a restless night.' She stifled a yawn. 'That's all.'

'When one works as hard as you do, it can be difficult to switch off.'

'Old habits,' she murmured, reaching for her T-shirt and pulling it over her head and then tying her sarong about her waist, feeling ridiculously naked in her modest one-piece.

Which was crazy because she and Finn and the rest of her family had been on this beach countless times together, and in briefer swimsuits than what either of them were wearing now. 'I don't want to get too much sun all at once,' she said by way of explanation, although Finn hadn't indicated by so much as a blink of his gorgeous eyelashes that he'd wanted or needed one. She glanced at him. 'You've been incapacitated for a couple of months and yet I'm paler than you.'

'Yeah, but my incapacitation meant spending a lot of time on the rooftop terrace of my apartment on the French Riviera, so…not exactly doing it tough.'

Fair point.

'You ever tried meditation?'

'You're talking to me, Audra, remember?'

His slow grin raised all the tiny hairs on her arms. 'Lie on your back in a comfortable position and close your eyes.'

'Finn…' She could barely keep the whine out of her voice. 'Meditation makes me feel like a failure.' And there was more than enough of that in her life at the moment as it was, thank you very much. 'I know you're supposed to *clear your mind*, but…it's impossible!'

'Would you be so critical and hard on someone else? Cut yourself some slack.' He rolled onto his back. 'Work on quietening your mind rather than clearing it. When a thought appears, as it will, simply acknowledge it before focussing on your breathing again.'

He closed his eyes and waited. With another sigh, Audra rolled onto her back and settled her hat over her face. It was spring and the sun wasn't fierce, but she wasn't taking any chances. 'Okay,' she grumbled. 'I'm ready. What am I supposed to do?'

Finn led her through a guided meditation where she counted breaths, where she tensed and then relaxed different muscle groups. The deep timbre of his voice, unhurried and undemanding, soothed her in a way she'd have never guessed possible. Her mind wandered, as he'd said it would, but she brought her attention back to his voice and her breathing each time, and by the time he finished she felt weightless and light.

She heard no movement from him, so she stayed exactly where she was—on a cloud of euphoric relaxation.

And promptly fell asleep.

Finn didn't move until Audra's deep rhythmic breaths informed him that she was asleep. Not a light and sweet little nap, but fully and deeply asleep.

He rolled onto his tummy and rested his chin on his arms. When had she forgotten how to relax? He'd spent a large portion of every Christmas vacation from the age of twelve onwards with the Russel family.

She'd been a sweet, sparky little kid, fiercely determined to keep up with her older siblings and not be left behind. As a teenager she'd been curious, engaged...and a bit more of a dreamer than the others, not as driven in a particular direction as they'd been either. But then he'd figured that'd made her more of an all-rounder.

When had she lost her zest, her joy for life? During her final years of school? At university? He swallowed. When her mother had died?

Karen Russel had died suddenly of a cerebral aneurysm

ten years ago. It'd shattered the entire family. Audra had only been seventeen.

Was it then that Audra had exchanged her joy in life for...? For what? To become a workaholic managing the charitable arm of her family's corporation? In her grief, had she turned away from the things that had given her joy? Had it become a habit?

He recalled the odd defiance in her eyes when she'd spoken about owning a shop—the way she'd mocked the idea...and the way the mockery and defiance had been at odds. He turned to stare at her. 'Hell, sweetheart,' he whispered. 'What are you doing to yourself?'

She slept for an hour, and Finn was careful to pretend not to notice when she woke, even though his every sense was honed to her every movement. He kept his nose buried in his book and feigned oblivion, which wasn't that hard because the book was pretty gripping.

'Hey,' she said in sleepy greeting.

'Hey, yourself, you lazy slob.' Only then did he allow himself to turn towards her. 'I didn't know napping was included on the agenda today.'

'If I remember correctly, the order for the day was lazing about in the sun on the beach, reading books and a bit of swimming.' She flicked out a finger. 'My nap included lying on the beach *and*—' she flicked out a second finger '—lazing in the sun. So I'm following the remit to the letter, thank you very much.'

The rest had brightened her eyes. And when she stretched her arms back over her head, he noted that her shoulders had lost their hard edge. He noted other things—things that would have Rupert taking a swing at him if he knew—so he did his best to remove those from his mind.

In one fluid motion, she rose. 'I'm going in for a dip.'

That sounded like an excellent plan. He definitely needed to cool off. Her glance flicked to the scar of his splenectomy when he rose too, and it took an effort to not turn away and hide it from her gaze.

And then she untied her sarong and pulled her T-shirt over her head and it was all he could do to think straight at all.

She nodded at the scar. 'Does it still hurt?'

He touched the indentations and shook his head. 'It didn't really hurt much after it was done either.' At her raised eyebrows he winked. 'Wish I could say the same about the broken ribs.'

She huffed out a laugh, and he was grateful when she moved towards the water's edge without asking any further questions about his accident. Its aftershocks continued to reverberate through him, leaving him at a loss. He didn't know how much longer he'd have to put up with it. He didn't know how much longer he *could* put up with it.

The cold dread that had invaded the pit of his stomach in the moments after his fall invaded him again now, and he broke out in an icy sweat. He'd known in that moment—his skis flying one way and the rest of him going another—that he'd hurt himself badly. He'd understood in a way he never had before that he could die; he had realised he might not make it off the mountain alive.

And every instinct he'd had had screamed a protest against that fate. He hadn't wanted to die, not yet. There were things he wanted—*yearned*—to do. If he'd had breath to spare he'd have begged the medical team to save him. But there'd been no breath to spare, and he'd started spiralling in and out of consciousness.

When he'd awoken from surgery…the relief and gratitude…there were no words to describe it. But for the life of him, now that he was all but recovered, he couldn't remember the things he'd so yearned to do—the reasons why staying alive had seemed so urgent.

All of it had left him with an utter lack of enthusiasm for any of the previous high-octane sports that had once sung to his soul. Had he lost his nerve? He didn't think so. He didn't feel afraid. He just—

A jet of water hit him full in the face and shook him immediately out of his thoughts. 'Lighten up, Finn. I'd have not mentioned the scar if I'd known it'd make you so grim. Don't worry. I'm sure the girls will still fall at your feet with the same old regularity. The odd scar will probably add to your mystique.'

She thought he was brooding for reasons of...*vanity*?

She laughed outright at whatever she saw in his face. 'You're going to pay for that,' he promised, scooping water up in his hands.

They were both soaked at the end of their water fight. Audra simply laughed and called him a bully when he picked her up and threw her into the sea.

He let go of her quick smart, though, because she was an armful of delicious woman...and he couldn't go there. Not with her. 'Race you out to the buoy.'

'Not a chance.' She caressed the surface of the water with an unconscious sensuality that had his gut clenching. 'I'm feeling too Zen after that meditation. And, if you'll kindly remember, there's no racing on today's agenda, thank you very much.'

'Wait until tomorrow.'

She stuck her nose in the air. 'Please don't disturb me while I'm living in the moment.'

With a laugh, he turned and swam out to the buoy. He didn't rush, but simply relished the way his body slid through the water, relished how good it felt to be rid of the cast. He did five laps there and back before his left arm started up a dull ache...and before he could resist finding out what Audra was up to.

He glanced across at where she floated on her back, her face lifted to the sky. He couldn't tell from here whether she had her eyes open or closed. She looked relaxed—now. And while *now* she might also be all grown up, during their water fight she'd laughed and squealed as she had when a girl.

He had a feeling, though, that when her short holiday was over all that tension would descend on her again, pulling her tight. Because…?

Because she wasn't doing the things that gave her joy, wasn't living the life that she should be living. And he had a growing conviction that this wasn't a new development, but an old one he'd never picked up on before. He had no idea how to broach the topic either. She could be undeniably prickly, and she valued her privacy. *Just like you do.* She'd tell him to take a flying leap and mind his own business. And that'd be that.

Walk away. He didn't do encouraging confidences. He didn't do complicated. And it didn't matter which way he looked at it—Audra had always been complicated. Fun and laughter, those were his forte.

He glided through the water towards her until he was just a couple of feet away. 'Boo.'

He didn't shout the word, just said it in a normal tone, but she started so violently he immediately felt sick to his gut. She spun around, the colour leaching from her face, and he wanted to kick himself—hard. 'Damn, Audra, I didn't mean to scare the living daylights out of you.'

She never used to startle this easily. What the hell had happened to change that?

None of the scenarios that played in his mind gave him the slightest bit of comfort.

'Glad I didn't grab you round the waist to tug you under, which had been my first thought.' He said it to try to lighten the moment. When they were kids they all used to dunk each other mercilessly.

If possible she went even paler. And then she ducked under the water, resurfacing a moment later to slick her hair back from her face. 'Note to self,' she said with remarkable self-possession, though he noted the way her hands shook. 'Don't practise meditation in the sea when Finn is around.'

He wanted to apologise again, but it'd be making too big a deal out of it and he instinctively knew that would make her defensive.

'I might head in.' She started a lazy breaststroke back towards the shore. 'How many laps did you do?'

'Just a couple.' Had she been watching him?

'How does the arm feel?'

He bit back a snap response. *It's fine. And can we just forget about my accident already?* She didn't deserve that. She had to know he didn't like talking about his injuries, but if this was the punishment she'd chosen for his ill-timed *Boo* then he'd take it like a man. 'Dishearteningly weak.'

Her gaze softened. 'You'll get your fitness back, Finn. Just don't push it too hard in these early days.'

He'd had every intention of getting to Kyanós and then swimming and running every day without mercy until he'd proven to himself that he was as fit as he'd been prior to his accident. And yet he found himself more than content at the moment to keep pace beside her. He rolled his shoulders. He'd only been here a couple of days. That old fire would return to his belly soon enough.

He pounced on the cooler bag as soon as he'd towelled off. 'I'm famished.'

He tossed her a peach, which she juggled, nearly dropped and finally caught. He grinned and bit into a second peach. The fragrant flesh and sweet juice hitting the back of his throat tasted better than anything he'd eaten in the last eight weeks. He groaned his pleasure, closing his eyes to savour it all the more. When he opened his eyes again, he found her staring at him as if she'd never seen him before.

Hell, no! Don't look at me like that, Audra.

Like a woman who looked at a man and considered his...um...finer points. It made his skin go hot and tight.

It made him want to reach out, slide a hand behind the back of her head and pull her close and—

He glanced out to sea, his pulse racing. He wanted to put colour back into her cheeks, but not like that. The two of them were like oil and water. If he did something stupid now, it'd impact on his relationship with her entire family, and the Russels and his uncle Ned were the only family he had.

He dragged in a gulp of air. Given his current state of mind, he had to be hyper-vigilant that he didn't mess all this up. He had a history of bringing trouble to the doors of those he cared about—Rupert all those years ago, and now Joachim. Rupert was right—Audra had been through enough. He had no intention of bringing more trouble down on her head.

He forced his stance to remain relaxed. 'Wanna go for a run?'

'A run?' She snapped away and then stared at him as if he'd lost his mind. Which was better. Much *much* better. 'Do you not know me at all?'

He shrugged. 'It was worth a shot.'

'No running, no rushing, no racing.' She ticked the items off her fingers. 'Those are the rules for today. I'm going to explore the rock pools.'

He followed because he couldn't help it. Because a question burned through him and he knew he'd explode if he didn't ask it.

They explored in silence for ten or fifteen minutes. 'Audra?' He worked hard to keep his voice casual.

'Hmm?'

'What the hell did that bastard Farquhar do to you?'

She froze, and then very slowly turned. 'Wow, excellent tactic, Sullivan. Don't get your way over going for a run so hit a girl with an awkward question instead.'

A question he noted she hadn't answered. He rolled with it. 'I work with what I've got.'

Her hands went to her waist. She wore her T-shirt again but not her sarong, and her legs… Her legs went on and on…and on. Where had she been hiding them? 'Who's this woman in Nice you're trying to avoid?'

Oho! So Rupert had told her about that. 'You answer my question, and I'll answer any question you want.'

Her brows rose. '*Any* question?'

'Any time you want to ask it.'

CHAPTER FIVE

ANY TIME SHE wanted to ask it?

That meant… Audra's mind raced. That meant if Finn were running hell for leather, doing laps as if training for a triathlon, risking his neck as if there were no tomorrow, then…then she could ask a question and he'd have to stop and answer her?

Oh, she'd try other stalling tactics first. She wasn't wasting a perfectly good question if she could get him to slow down in other ways, but…

She tried to stop her internal glee from showing. 'You have yourself a deal.'

Finn readjusted his stance. 'So what's the story with Farquhar? The bit that didn't make the papers.'

She hiked herself up to sit on a large rock, its top worn smooth, but its sides pitted with the effects of wind and sand. It was warm beneath her hands and thighs.

He settled himself beside her. 'Is it hard to talk about?'

She sent him what she hoped was a wry glance. 'It's never fun to own up to being a fool…or to having made such a big mistake.'

'Audra—'

She waved him silent. 'I'm surprised you don't know the story.' She'd have thought Rupert would've filled him in.

'I know what was in the paper but not, I suspect, the whole story.'

Dear Rupert. He'd kept his word.

Oddly, though, she didn't mind Finn knowing the story in its entirety. While they might've been friendly adversaries all these years, he was practically family. He'd have her best interests at heart, just as she did his.

'Right.' She slapped her hands to her thighs and he glanced down at them. His face went oddly tight and he immediately stared out to sea. A pulse started up in her throat and her heart danced an irregular pattern in her chest.

Stop it. Don't think of Finn in that way.

But...he's hot.

And he thinks you're hot.

Nonsense! He's just... He just found it hard to not flirt with every woman in his orbit.

She forced herself to bring Thomas's face to mind and the pulse-jerking and heart-hammering came to a screeching halt. 'So the part that everyone knows—' the part that had made the papers '—is that Thomas Farquhar and I had been dating for over seven months.'

Wary brown eyes met hers and he gave a nod. 'What made you fall for him?'

She shrugged. 'He seemed so...*nice*. He went out of his way to spend time with me, and do nice things for me. It was just...nice,' she finished lamely. He'd been so earnest about all the things she was earnest about. He'd made her feel as if she were doing exactly what she ought to be doing with her life. She'd fallen for all of that intoxicating attention and validation hook, line and sinker.

'But it's clear now that he was only dating me to steal company secrets.' A fact the entire world now knew thanks to the tabloids. She shrivelled up a little more inside every time she thought about it.

The Russel Corporation, established by her Swiss grandfather sixty years ago, had originally been founded on a watchmaking dynasty but was now made up of a variety of concerns, including a large charitable arm. Her father was the CEO, though Rupert had been groomed to take over and, to all intents and purposes, was running the day-to-day operations of the corporation.

Her siblings were champions of social justice, each in

their own way, just as her parents and grandparents had been in their younger days. Their humanitarian activities were administered by the Russel Corporation, and, as one of the corporation's chief operation managers, Audra had the role of overseeing a variety of projects—from hiring the expertise needed on different jobs and organising the delivery of necessary equipment and goods, to wrangling with various licences and permissions that needed to be secured, and filling in endless government grant forms. And in her spare time she fundraised. It was hectic, high-powered and high-stakes.

For the last five years her sister, Cora, a scientist, had been working on developing a new breakthrough vaccine for the Ebola virus. While such a vaccine would help untold sufferers of the illness, it also had the potential to make pharmaceutical companies vast sums of money.

She tried to slow the churning of her stomach. 'Thomas was after Cora's formulae and research. We know now that he was working for a rival pharmaceutical company. We suspect he deliberately targeted me, and that our meeting at a fundraising dinner wasn't accidental.'

From the corner of her eye she saw Finn nod. She couldn't look at him. Instead she twisted her hands together in her lap and watched the progress of a small crab as it moved from one rock pool to another. 'He obviously worked out my computer password. There were times when we were in bed, when I thought he was asleep, and I'd grab my laptop to log in quickly just to check on something.'

She watched in fascination as his hand clenched and then unclenched. 'You'd have had to have more than one password to get anywhere near Cora's data.'

'Oh, I have multiple passwords. I have one for my laptop, different ones for my desktop computers at home and work. There's the password for my Russel Corporation account. And each of the projects has its own password.'

There'd been industrial espionage attempts before. She'd been briefed on internet and computer security. 'But it appears he'd had covert cameras placed around my apartment.'

'How…?'

How did he get access? 'I gave him a key.' She kept her voice flat and unemotional. She'd given an industrial spy unhampered access to her flat—what an idiot! 'I can tell you now, though, that all those romantic dinners he made for us—' his pretext for needing a key '—have taken on an entirely different complexion.' It'd seemed mean-spirited not to give him a key at the time, especially as he'd given her one to his flat.

He swore. 'Did he have cameras in the bedroom?'

'No.' He'd not sunk that low. But it didn't leave her feeling any less violated. 'But…but he must've seen me do some stupid, ugly, unfeminine things on those cameras. And I know it's nothing on the grand scale, but… it *irks* me!'

'What kind of things?'

She slashed a hand through the air. 'Oh, I don't know. Like picking my teeth or hiking my knickers out from uncomfortable places, or… Have you ever seen a woman put on a pair of brand-new sixty-denier opaque tights?'

He shook his head.

'Well, it's not sexy. It looks ludicrous and contortionist and it probably looks hilarious and… And I feel like enough of a laughing stock without him having footage of that too.'

A strong arm came about her shoulder and pulled her in close. Just for a moment she let herself sink against him to soak up the warmth and the comfort. 'He played me to perfection,' she whispered. 'I didn't suspect a damn thing. I thought—' She faltered. 'I thought he liked me.'

His arm tightened about her. 'He was a damn fool. The

man has to be a certifiable idiot to choose money over you, sweetheart.'

He pressed his lips to her hair and she felt an unaccountable urge to cry.

She didn't want to cry!

'Stop it.' She pushed him away and leapt down from the rock. 'Don't be nice to me. My stupidity nearly cost Cora all of the hard work she's put in for the last five years.'

'But it didn't.'

No, it hadn't. And it was hard to work up an outraged stomp in flip-flops, and with the Aegean spread before her in twinkling blue perfection and the sun shining down as if the world was full of good things. The files Thomas had stolen were old, and, while to an outsider the formulae and hypotheses looked impressive, the work was neither new nor ground-breaking. Audra didn't have access to the information Thomas had been so anxious to get his hands on for the simple fact that she didn't need it. The results of Cora's research had nothing to do with Audra's role at work.

But Thomas didn't know that yet. And there was a court case pending. 'So...' She squinted into the sun at him. 'Rupert told you that much, huh?'

'I didn't know about the hidden cameras, but as for the rest...' He nodded.

'You know that's all classified, right?'

He nodded again. 'What hasn't Rupert told me?' He dragged in a breath, his hands clenching. 'Did Farquhar break your heart?'

She huffed out a laugh. 'Which of those questions do you want me to answer first?' When he didn't answer, she moved back to lean against the rock. 'I'll answer the second first because that'll move us on nicely to the first.' She winced at the bitterness that laced her *nicely.* 'No, he didn't break my heart. In fact I was starting to feel smothered by him so I...uh...'

'You...?'

'I told him I wanted to break up.'

He stared at her for a long moment. The muscles in his jaw tensed. 'What did he do?'

She swallowed. 'He pushed me into the hall closet and locked me in.'

He swore and the ferocity of his curse made her blink. He landed beside her, his expression black.

'I...I think he panicked when I demanded my key back. So he locked me in, stole my computer and high-tailed it out of there.'

'How long were you in there?'

'All night.' And it'd been the longest night of her life.

'How...?'

He clenched his fists so hard he started to shake. In a weird way his outrage helped.

'How did you get out?'

'He made the mistake of using my access code to get into the office early the next morning. Very early when he didn't think anyone else would be around. But Rupert, who had jet lag, had decided to put in a few hours. He saw the light on in my office, and came to drag me off to break-fast.' She shrugged. 'He found Thomas rifling through my filing cabinets instead. The first thing he did was to call Security. The second was to call my home phone and then my mobile. Neither of which I could answer. He has a key to my flat, so...'

'So he raced over and let you out.'

'Yep.'

She'd never been happier to see her older brother in her life. Her lips twisted. 'It was only then, though, that I learned of the extent of Thomas's double-dealing. And all I wanted to do was crawl back in the closet and hide from the world.'

'Sweetheart—'

She waved him quiet again. 'I know all the things you're

going to say, Finn, but don't. Rupert's already said them. *None of this is my fault. Anyone can be taken in by a conman... Blah-blah-blah.*'

She moved to the edge of the rock shelf and stared out at the sea, but its beauty couldn't soothe her. She'd been taken in by a man whose interest and undivided attention had turned her head—a man who'd seemed not only interested but invested in hearing about her hopes and dreams…and supporting her in those dreams. She hadn't felt the focus of somebody's world like that since her mother had died.

She folded her arms, gripped her elbows tight. But it'd all been a lie, and in her hunger for that attention she'd let her guard down. It'd had the potential to cause untold damage to Cora's career, not to mention the Russel Corporation's reputation. She'd been such an idiot!

And to add insult to injury she'd spent the best part of six weeks trying to talk herself out of breaking up with him because he'd seemed so darn perfect.

Idiot! Idiot! Idiot!

'So now you feel like a gullible fool who's let the family down, and you look at every new person you meet through the tainted lens of suspicion—wondering if they can be trusted or if they're just out for whatever they can get.'

Exactly. She wanted to dive into the sea and power through the water until she was too tired to think about any of this any more. It was a decent swim from here back to the beach, but one that was within her powers. Only… if she did that Finn would follow and five laps out to the buoy and back was enough for him for one day.

She swung around to meet his gaze. 'That sounds like the voice of experience.'

He shrugged and moved to stand beside her, his lips tightening as he viewed the horizon. 'It's how I'd feel in your shoes.'

'Except you'd never be so stupid.' She turned and

started to pick her way back along the rock pools towards the beach.

'I've done stupider things with far less cause.'

He had? She turned to find him staring at her with eyes as turbulent as the Aegean in a storm. She didn't press him, but filed the information away. She might ask him about that some day.

'And even Rupert isn't mistake free. Getting his heart broken by Brooke Manning didn't show a great deal of foresight.'

'He was young,' she immediately defended. 'And we all thought she was as into him as he was into her.'

He raised an eyebrow, and she lifted her hands. 'Okay, okay. I know. It's just… Rupert's mistake didn't hurt anyone but himself. My mistake had the potential to ruin Cora's life's work to date and impact on the entire Russel Corporation, and—'

Warm hands descended to her shoulders. 'But it didn't. Stop focussing on what could have happened and deal with what actually did happen. And the positives that can be found there.'

'Positives?' she spluttered.

'Sure.'

'Oh, I can't wait to hear this. C'mon, wise guy, name me one positive.'

He rubbed his chin. 'Well, for starters, you'd worked out Farquhar was a jerk and had kicked his sorry butt to the kerb.'

Not exactly true. She'd just been feeling suffocated, and hadn't been able to hide from that fact any more.

'And don't forget that's been caught on camera too.'

She stared up at him. And a slow smile built through her. 'Oh, my God.'

He cocked an eyebrow.

'He argued about us breaking up. He wanted me to reconsider and give him another chance.'

'Not an unusual reaction.'

'I told him we could still see each other as friends.'

Finn clutched his chest as if he'd been shot through the heart. 'Ouch!'

'And then he ranted and paced for a bit, and when he had his back to me a few times I, uh, rolled my eyes and...'

'And?'

'Checked my watch because there was a programme on television I was hoping to catch.'

He barked out a laugh.

'And this is embarrassing, for him, so I shouldn't tell it.'

'Yes, you should. You *really* should.'

'Well, he cried. Obviously they were crocodile tears, but I wasn't to know that at the time. I went to fetch the box of tissues, and while my back was to him I pulled this horrible kind of "God help me" face at the wall.'

She gave him a demonstration and he bent at the waist and roared. 'Crocodile tears or not, that's going to leave his ego in shreds. I'm sorry, sweetheart, but getting caught picking your nose suddenly doesn't seem like such a bad thing.'

'I do *not* pick my nose.' She stuck that particular appendage in the air. But Finn was right. She found she didn't care quite so much if Thomas had seen her pigging out on chocolate or dancing to pop music in her knickers. Now whenever she thought about any of those things she'd recall her hilarious grimace—probably straight at some hidden camera—and would feel partially vindicated.

She swung to Finn. 'Thank you.'

'You're welcome.'

They reached the beach and shook sand off their towels, started the five-minute climb back up the hill to the villa. 'Audra?'

'Hmm?'

'I'm sorry I scared you when I arrived the other night.

I'm sorry I scared you with my *boo* out there.' He waved towards the water.

She shrugged. 'You didn't mean to.'

'No, I didn't mean to.'

And his voice told her he'd be careful it wouldn't happen again. Rather than being irked at being treated with kid gloves, she felt strangely cared for.

'I guess I owe you an answer now to your question about the woman in Nice who I'm avoiding.'

'No, thank you very much. I mean, you *do* owe me an answer to a question—that was the deal. But I'm not wasting it getting the skinny on some love affair gone wrong.'

He didn't say anything for a long moment. 'What's your question, then?'

'I don't know yet. When I do know I'll ask it.' And then he'd have to stop whatever he was doing and take a time-out to answer it. *Perfect.*

Finn studied Audra across the breakfast table the next morning. Actually, their breakfast table had become the picnic table that sat on the stone terrace outside, where they could drink in the glorious view. She'd turned down the bacon and eggs, choosing cereal instead. He made a mental note to buy croissants the next time they were in the village.

'What are you staring at, Finn?'

He wanted to make sure she was eating enough. But he knew exactly how well that'd go down if he admitted as much. 'I'm just trying to decide if that puny body of yours is up to today's challenge, Russel.'

A spark lit the ice-blue depths of her eyes, but then she shook her head as if realising he was trying to goad her into some kind of reaction. 'This puny body is up for a whole lot more lazing on a beach and a little bobbing about in the sea.'

'Nice try, sweetheart.'

She rolled her eyes. 'What horrors do you have planned?'

'You'll see.' He was determined that by the time she left the island she'd feel fitter, healthier and more empowered than she had when she'd arrived.

She harrumphed and slouched over her muesli, but her gaze wandered out towards the light gleaming on the water and it made her lips lift and her eyes dance. Being here—taking a break—had already been good for her.

But he wanted her to have fun too. A workout this morning followed by play this afternoon. That seemed like a decent balance.

'You want us to what?'

An hour later Audra stared at him with such undisguised horror it was all he could do not to laugh. If he laughed, though, it'd rile her and he didn't want her riled. Unless it was the only way to win her cooperation.

'I want us to jog the length of the beach.'

Her mouth opened and closed. 'But...why? How can this be fun?'

'Exercise improves my mood.' It always had. As a teenager it'd also been a way to exorcise his demons. Now it just helped to keep him fit and strong. He *liked* feeling fit and strong.

He waited for her to make some crack about being in favour of anything that improved his mood. Instead she planted her hands on her hips and stared at him. She wore a silky caftan thing over her swimsuit and the action made it ride higher on her thighs. He tried not to notice.

'Your mood has been fine since you've been here. Apart from your foul temper when you first arrived.'

'You mean when the police had me in handcuffs?'

She nodded.

'I'd like to see how silver-tongued you'd be in that situation!'

She smirked and he realised she'd got the rise out of

him that she'd wanted, and he silently cursed himself. He fell for it every single time.

'But apart from that blip your mood has been fine.'

She was right. It had been. Which was strange because he'd been an absolute bear in Nice. He'd been a bear since the accident.

He shook that thought off. 'And we want to keep it that way.'

'But—' she gestured '—that has to be nearly a mile.'

'Yep.' He stared at her downturned mouth, imagined *again* that mongrel Farquhar shoving her in a cupboard, and wanted to smash something. He didn't want to bully her. If she really hated the idea... 'Is there any medical reason why you shouldn't run?'

She eyed him over the top of her sunglasses. 'No. You?'

'None. Running ten miles is out of the question, but one mile at a gentle pace will be fine.' He'd checked with his doctors.

'I haven't run since I was a kid. I work in an office... sit behind a desk all day. I'm not sure I can run that far.'

He realised then that her resistance came from a sense of inadequacy.

'I mean, even banged up you're probably super fit and—'

'We'll take it slow. And if you can't jog all the way, we'll walk the last part of it.'

'And you won't get grumpy at me for holding you back?'

'I promise.'

'No snark?'

He snorted. 'I'm not promising that.'

That spark flashed in her eyes again. 'Slow, you said?'

'Slow,' he promised.

She hauled in a breath. 'Well, here goes nothing...'

He started them slowly as promised. It felt good to be running again, even if it was at half his usual pace. Audra started a bit awkwardly, a trifle stiffly, as if the action were unfamiliar, but within two minutes she'd found a steady rhythm and he couldn't help but admire her poise and balance.

That damn ponytail, though, threatened his balance every time he glanced her way, bobbing with a cheeky nonchalance that made things inside him clench up…made him lose his tempo and stray from his course and have to check himself and readjust his line.

At the five-minute mark she was covered in a fine sheen of perspiration, and he suddenly flashed to a forbidden image of what she might look like during an athletic session of lovemaking. He stumbled and broke out into a cold sweat.

Audra seemed to lose her rhythm then too. Her elbows came in tight at her sides…she started to grimace…

And then her hands lifted to her breasts and he nearly fell over. She pulled to a halt and he did too. He glanced at her hands. She reefed them back to her sides and shot him a dark glare. 'Look, you didn't warn me that this is what we'd be doing before we hit the beach.'

Because he hadn't wanted her sniping at him the entire time they descended the hill.

'But they created exercise gear for a reason, you know? If I'm going to jog I need to wear a sports bra.'

He stared at her, not comprehending.

'It hurts to run without one,' she said through gritted teeth.

He blinked. *Hell.* He hadn't thought about that. She wasn't exactly big-breasted, but she was curvy where it mattered and…

'And while we're at it,' she ground out, 'I'd prefer to wear jogging shoes than run barefoot. This is darn hard on the ankles.' Her hands went to her hips. 'For heaven's sake, Finn, you have to give a girl some warning so she can prepare the appropriate outfit.'

He felt like an idiot. 'Well, let's just walk the rest of the way.'

It was hell walking beside her. Every breath he took was scented with peaches and coconut. And from the corner of his eye he couldn't help but track the perky progress of her ponytail. In his mind's eye all he could see was the way she'd cupped her breasts, to help take their weight while running, and things inside him twisted and grew hot.

When they reached the tall cliff at the beach's far end, Audra slapped a hand to it in a 'we made it' gesture. 'My mood doesn't feel improved.'

She sounded peeved, which made him want to laugh. But those lips…that ponytail… He needed a timeout, a little distance. *Now.*

She straightened and gave him the once-over. 'You're not even sweating the tiniest little bit!'

Not where she could see, at least. For which he gave thanks. But he needed to get waist-deep in water soon before she saw the effect she was having on him.

He gestured back the way they'd come. 'We're going to swim back.' Cold water suddenly seemed like an excellent plan.

Her face fell. 'Why didn't you say so before? I don't want to get my caftan wet. I could've left it behind.'

He was glad she hadn't. The less on show where she was concerned, the better.

'It'll take no time at all to dry off at the other end.'

'It's not designed to be swum in. It'll fall off my shoulder and probably get tangled in my legs.'

He clenched his jaw tight. *Not* an image he needed in his mind.

'I won't be able to swim properly.'

He couldn't utter a damn word.

Her chin shot up. 'You think I'm trying to wriggle my way out, don't you? You think I'm just making up excuses.'

It was probably wiser to let her misinterpret his silence than tell her the truth.

'Well, fine, I'll show you!'

She pulled the caftan over her head and tossed it to him. He did his best not to notice the flare of her hips, the long length of her legs, or the gentle swell of her breasts.

'I'll swim while you keep my caftan dry, cabana boy.'

Her, in the water way over there? Him, on the beach way over here? Worked for him.

'But when we reach the other end it's nothing but lazing on the beach and reading books till lunchtime.'

'Deal.' He was looking forward to another session with his book.

He kept pace with her on the shore, just in case she got a cramp or into some kind of trouble. She alternated freestyle with breaststroke and backstroke. And the slow easy pace suited him. It helped him find his equilibrium again. It gave him the time to remind himself in detail of all the ways he owed Rupert.

He nodded. He owed Rupert big-time—and that meant Audra was off limits and out of bounds. It might be different if Finn were looking to settle down, but settling down and Finn were barely on terms of acquaintance. And while he might feel as if he were at a crossroads in his life, that didn't mean anything. The after-effects of his accident would disappear soon enough. When they did, life would return to normal. He'd be looking for his next adrenaline rush and…and he'd be content again.

'Jetskiing?'

Audra stared at him with… Well, it wasn't horror at least. Consternation maybe? 'We had a laze on the beach, read our books, had a slow leisurely lunch…and now it's time for some fun.'

She rolled her bottom lip between her teeth. 'But aren't jetskis like motorbikes? And motorbikes are dangerous.'

He shook his head. 'Unlike a motorbike, it doesn't hurt if you fall off a jetski.' At least, not at the speeds they'd be going. 'They're only dangerous if we don't use them right...if we're stupid.'

'But we're going to be smart and use them right?'

He nodded. 'We're even going to have a lesson first.' He could teach her all she needed to know, but he'd come to the conclusion it might be *wiser* to not be so hands-on where Audra was concerned.

She stared at the jetskiers who were currently buzzing about on the bay. 'A lesson?' She pursed her lips. 'And...and it doesn't look as if it involves an awful lot of strength or stamina,' she said, almost to herself. And then she started and jutted her chin. 'Call me a wimp if you want, but I have a feeling I'm going to be sore enough tomorrow as it is.'

'If you are, the best remedy will be a run along the beach followed by another swim.'

She tossed her head. 'In your dreams, cabana boy.'

He grinned. It was good to see her old spark return. 'This is for fun, Audra, and no other reason. Just fun.'

He saw something in her mind still and then click. 'I guess I haven't been doing a whole lot of that recently.'

She could say that again.

'Okay, well...where do we sign up?'

There were seven of them who took the lesson, and while Finn expected to chafe during the hour-long session, he didn't. It was too much fun watching Audra and her cheeky ponytail as she concentrated on learning how to manoeuvre her jetski. They had a further hour to putter around the bay afterwards to test out her new-found skills. He didn't go racing off on his own. He didn't want her trying to copy him and coming to grief. They'd practised what to do in case of capsizing, but he didn't want them to have to put it into practice. Besides, her laughter and the way her eyes sparkled were too much fun to miss out on.

'Oh, my God!' She practically danced on the dock when they returned their jetskis. 'That was the best fun ever. I'm definitely doing that again. Soon!'

He tried to stop staring at her, tried to drag his gaze from admiring the shape of her lips, the length of her legs, the bounce of her hair. An evening spent alone with her in Rupert's enormous villa rose in his mind, making him sweat. 'Beer?' Hanging out in a crowd for as long as they could suddenly struck him as a sound strategy.

'Yes, please.'

They strode along the wooden dock and he glanced at her from the corner of his eye. The transformation from two days ago was amazing. She looked full of energy and so...*alive*.

He scrubbed both hands back through his hair. Why *was* she hell-bent on keeping herself on such a tight leash? Why didn't she let her hair down once in a while? Why...?

The questions pounded at him. He pressed both hands to the crown of his head in an effort to tamp them down, to counter the impulse to ask her outright. The thing was, even if he did break his protocol on asking personal questions and getting dragged into complicated emotional dilemmas, there was no guarantee Audra would confide in him. She'd never seen him as that kind of guy.

What if she needs to talk? What if she has no one else to confide in?

He wanted to swear.

He wanted to run.

He also wanted to see her filled with vitality and enthusiasm and joy, as she was now.

They ordered beers from a beachside bar and sat at a table in the shade of a jasmine vine to drink them.

'Today has been a really good day, Finn. Thank you.'

Audra wasn't like the women he dated. If she needed someone to confide in, he could be there for her, couldn't he? He took a long pull on his beer. 'Even the running?'

'Ugh, no, the running was awful.' She sipped her drink. 'I can't see I'm ever going to enjoy that, even with the right gear. Though I didn't mind the swimming. There's bound to be a local gym at home that has a pool.'

She was going to keep up the exercise when she returned home? Excellent.

He leaned back, a plan solidifying in his gut. 'You haven't asked your question yet.'

'I already told you—I don't want to hear about your woman in Nice. If you want to brag or grumble about her go right ahead. But I'm not wasting a perfectly good question on it.'

He wondered if he should just tell her about Trixie, but dismissed the idea. Trixie had no idea where he was. She wouldn't be able to cause any trouble here for him, for Joachim or for Audra. And he wanted to keep the smile, the sense of exhilaration, on Audra's face.

He stretched back, practically daring Audra to ask him a question. 'Isn't there anything personal you want to ask me?'

CHAPTER SIX

DID FINN HAVE any clue how utterly mouth-wateringly gorgeous he looked stretched out like that, as if for her express delectation? Audra knew he didn't mean anything by it. Flirting was as natural to him as breathing. If he thought for a moment she'd taken him seriously, he'd backtrack so fast it'd almost be funny.

Almost.

And she wasn't an idiot. Yet she couldn't get out of her mind the idea of striding around the table and—

No, not striding, *sashaying* around the table to plant herself in his lap, gently because she couldn't forget his injuries, and running her hand across the stubble of his jaw before drawing his lips down to hers.

Her mouth went dry and her heart pounded so hard she felt winded…dizzy. Maybe she was an idiot after all.

It was the romance of this idyllic Greek island combined with the euphoria of having whizzed across the water on a jetski. It'd left her feeling wild and reckless. She folded her hands together in her lap. She didn't do wild and reckless. If she went down that path it'd lead to things she couldn't undo. She'd let her family down enough as it was.

Finn folded himself up to hunch over his beer. 'Scrap that. Don't ask your question. I don't like the look on your face. You went from curiously speculative to prim and disapproving.'

She stiffened. 'Prim?'

'Prim,' he repeated, not budging.

'I am *not* prim.'

'Sweetheart, nobody does prim like you.'

His laugh set her teeth on edge. She forced herself to

settle back in her chair and to at least appear relaxed. 'I see what you're doing.'

'What am I doing?'

'Reverse psychology. Tell me not to ask a question in the hope I'll do the exact opposite.'

'Is it working?'

'Why are you so fixated on me asking you my owed question?'

A slow grin hooked up one side of his mouth and looking at it was like staring into the sun. She couldn't look away.

'Is that your question?'

Strive for casual.

'Don't be ridiculous.' If Rupert hadn't put the darn notion in her head—*Don't fall for Finn*—she wouldn't be wondering what it'd be like to kiss him.

She sipped her beer. As long as speculation didn't become anything more. She did what she could to ignore the ache that rose through her; to ignore the way her mouth dried and her stomach lurched.

She wasn't starting something with Finn. Even if he proved willing—which he wouldn't in a million years—there was too much at stake to risk it, and not enough to be won. She was *determined* there wouldn't be any more black marks against her name this year. There wouldn't be any more *ever* if she could help it.

If only she could stop thinking about him…*inappropriately*!

For heaven's sake, she was the one in her family who kept things steady, regulated, trouble-free. If there were choppy waters, she was the one who smoothed them. She didn't go rocking the boat and causing drama. That wasn't who she was. She ground her teeth together. And she wasn't going to change now.

She stared out at the harbour and gulped her beer. This was what happened when she let her hair down and indulged in a bit of impulsive wildness. It was so hard to get her wayward self back under wraps.

Finn might call her prim, but she preferred the terms self-controlled and disciplined. She needed to get things back on a normal grounding with him again, but when she went to open her mouth, he spoke first. 'I guess it's a throwback to the old game of Truth or Dare. I'm not up for too much daredevilry at the moment, but your question—the truth part of the game—is a different form of dangerousness.'

He stared up at the sky, lips pursed, and just like that he was familiar Finn again—family friend. Their session of jetskiing must've seemed pretty tame to him. He'd kept himself reined in for her sake, had focussed on her enjoyment rather than his own. Which meant that dark thread of restlessness would be pulsing through him now, goading him into taking unnecessary risks. She needed to dispel it if she could, to prevent him from doing something daft and dangerous.

'The truth can be ugly, Finn. Admitting the truth can be unwelcome and…' she settled for the word he'd used '…dangerous.'

Liquid brown eyes locked with hers as he drank his beer. He set his glass down on the table and wiped the back of his hand across his mouth. 'I know.'

'And yet you still want me to ask you a possibly dangerous question?'

'I'm game if you are.'

Was there a particular question he wanted her to ask? He stared at her and waited. She moistened her lips again and asked the question that had been rattling around in her mind ever since Rupert's phone call. 'Why do you avoid long-term romantic commitment?'

He blinked. '*That's* what you want to know?'

She shrugged. 'I'm curious. You've never once brought a date to a Russel family dinner. The rest of us have, multiple times. I want to know how you got to avoid the youthful mistakes the rest of us made. Besides…'

'What?'

'When Rupe was warning me off, he made some comment about you not being long-term material. Now we're going to ignore the fact that Rupert obviously thinks women only want long-term relationships when we all know that's simply not true. He obviously doesn't want to think of his little sister in those terms, bless him. But it made me think there's a story there. Hence, my question.'

He nodded, but he didn't speak.

She glanced at his now empty glass. 'If you want another beer, I'm happy to drive us home.'

He called the waiter over and ordered a lime and soda. She did the same. He speared her with a glare. 'I don't need Dutch courage to tell you the truth.'

'And yet that doesn't hide the fact that you don't want to talk about it.' Whatever *it* was. She shrugged and drained the rest of her beer too. 'That's okay, you can simply fob me off with an "I just haven't met the right girl yet" and be done with it.'

'But that would be lying, and lying is against the rules.'

'Ah, so you have met the right girl?' Was it Trixie who'd texted him?

He wagged a finger at her, and just for a moment his eyes danced, shifting the darkness her question had triggered. 'That's an altogether different question. If you'd rather I answer that one…?'

It made her laugh. 'I'll stick with my original question, thank you very much.'

The waiter brought their drinks and Finn took the straw from his glass and set it on the table. His eyes turned sombre again. 'You know the circumstances surrounding my father's death?'

'He died in a caving accident when you were eight.'

'He liked extreme sports. He was an adrenaline junkie. I seem to have inherited that trait.'

She frowned and sat back.

His eyes narrowed. 'What?'

She took a sip of her drink, wondering at his sharp tone. 'Can one inherit risk-taking the same way they can brown eyes and tawny hair?'

'Intelligence is inherited, isn't it? And a bad temper and... Why?'

He glared and she wished she'd kept her mouth shut. 'Just wondering,' she murmured.

'No, you weren't.'

Fine. She huffed out a breath. 'I always thought your adventuring was a way of keeping your father's memory alive, a way to pay homage to him.'

He blinked.

She tried to gauge the impact her words had on him. 'There isn't any judgement attached to that statement, Finn. I'm not suggesting it's either good or bad.'

He shook himself, but she noted the belligerent thrust to his jaw. 'Does it matter whether my risk-taking is inherited or not?'

'Of course it does. If it's some gene you inherently possess then that means it's always going to be a part of you, a...a natural urge like eating and sleeping. If it's the latter then one day you can simply decide you've paid enough homage. One means you can't change, the other means you can.'

He shoved his chair back, physically moving further away from her, his eyes flashing. She raised her hands. 'But that's not for me to decide. Your call. Like I said, no judgement here. It was just, umm...idle speculation.' She tried not to wince as she said it.

The space between them pulsed with Finn's...outrage? Shock? Disorientation? Audra wasn't sure, but she wanted to get them back on an even keel again. 'What does this have to do with avoiding romantic commitment?'

He gave a low laugh and stretched his legs out in front of him. 'You warned me this could be dangerous.'

It had certainly sent a sick wave of adrenaline coursing through her. 'We don't have to continue with this conversation if you don't want to.'

He skewered her with a glance. 'You don't want to know?'

She ran a finger through the condensation on her glass. He was being honest with her. He deserved the same in return. 'I want to know.'

'Then the rules demand that you get your answer.'

Was he laughing at her?

He grew serious again. 'My father's death was very difficult for my mother.'

Jeremy Sullivan had been an Australian sportsman who for a brief moment had held the world record for the men's four-hundred-metre butterfly. Claudette Dupont, Finn's mother, had been working at the French embassy in Canberra. They'd met, fallen in love and had moved to Europe where Jeremy had pursued a life of adventure and daring. Both of Finn's grandfathers came from old money. They, along with the lucrative sponsorship deals Jeremy received, had funded his and Claudette's lifestyle.

And from the outside it had been an enviable lifestyle— jetting around the world from one extreme sporting event to another—Jeremy taking part in whatever event was on offer while Claudette cheered him from the sidelines. And there'd apparently been everything from cliff diving to ice climbing, bobsledding to waterfall kayaking, and more.

But it had ended in tragedy with the caving accident that had claimed Jeremy's life. Audra dragged in a breath. 'She was too young to be a widow.' And Finn had been too young to be left fatherless.

'She gave up everything to follow him on his adventures—her job, a stable network of friends…a home. She was an only child and there weren't many close relatives apart from her parents.'

Audra wondered how she'd cope in that same situation. 'She had you.'

He shook his head. 'I wasn't enough.'

The pain in his eyes raked through her chest, thickened her throat. 'What happened?' She knew his mother had died, but nobody ever spoke of it.

'She just…faded away. She developed a lot of mystery illnesses—spent a lot of time in hospital. When she was home she spent a lot of time in bed.'

'That's when your uncle Ned came to look after you?' His father's brother was still a big part of Finn's life. He'd relocated to Europe to be with Finn and Claudette.

'He moved in and looked after the both of us. I was eleven when my mother died, and the official verdict was an accidental overdose of painkillers.' He met her gaze. 'Nobody thought she did it deliberately.'

That was something at least. But it was so sad. Such a waste.

'My uncle's verdict was that she'd died of a broken heart.'

Audra's verdict was that Claudette Sullivan had let her son down. Badly. But she kept that to herself. Her heart ached for the little boy she'd left behind and for all the loss he'd suffered.

'Ned blamed my father.'

Wow. 'It must've been hard for Ned,' she offered. 'I don't know what I'd do if I lost one of my siblings. And to then watch as your mother became sicker… He must've felt helpless.'

'He claimed my father should never have married if he wasn't going to settle down to raise a family properly.'

Finn's face had become wooden and she tried not to

wince. 'Families aren't one-size-fits-all entities. They don't come in pretty cookie-cutter shapes.'

He remained silent. She moistened her lips. 'What happened after your mother died?'

He straightened in his chair and took a long gulp of lime and soda. 'That's when Ned boarded me at the international school in Geneva. It was full of noisy, rowdy boys and activities specifically designed to keep us busy and out of mischief.'

It was an effort, but she laughed as he'd meant her to. 'I've heard stories about some of the mischief you got up to. I think they need to redesign some of those activities.'

He grinned. 'It was full of life. Ned came to every open day, took me somewhere every weekend we had leave. I didn't feel abandoned.'

Not by Ned, no. But what about his mother? She swallowed. 'And you met Rupert there.'

His grin widened. 'And soon after found myself adopted by the entire Russel clan.'

'For your sins.' She smiled back, but none of it eased the throb in her heart.

'I always found myself drawn to the riskier pastimes the school offered…and that only grew as I got older. There's nothing like the thrill of paragliding down a mountain or surfing thirty-foot waves.'

'Or throwing oneself off a ski jump with gay abandon,' she added wryly, referencing his recent accident.

'Accidents happen.'

But in the pastimes Finn pursued, such accidents could have fatal consequences. Didn't that bother him? 'Did Ned never try and clip your wings or divert your interests elsewhere?' He'd lost a brother. He wouldn't have wanted to lose a nephew as well.

'He's too smart for that. He knew it wouldn't work, not once he realised how determined I was. Before I was of age, when I still needed a guardian's signature, he just made sure I had the very best training available in whatever activity had taken my fancy before he'd sign the permission forms.'

'It must've taken an enormous amount of courage on his behalf.'

'Perhaps. But he'd seen the effect my grandfather's refusals and vetoes had had on my father. He said it resulted in my father taking too many unnecessary chances. In his own way, Ned did his best to keep me safe.'

She nodded.

'The way I live my life, the risks I take, they're not conducive to family life, Audra. When I turned eighteen I promised my uncle to never take an unnecessary risk—to make sure I was always fully trained to perform whatever task I was attempting.'

Thinking about the risks he took made her temples ache.

'I made a promise to myself at the same time.' His eyes burned into hers. 'I swore I'd never become involved in a long-term relationship until I'd given up extreme sports. It's not fair to put any woman through what my father put my mother through.'

It was evident he thought hell had a better chance of freezing over than him ever giving up extreme sports. She eyed him for a moment. 'Have you ever been tempted to break that contract with yourself?'

'I don't break my promises.'

It wasn't an answer. It was also an oblique reminder of the promise he'd made to Rupert. As if that were something she was likely to forget.

'But wouldn't you like a long-term relationship some day? Can't you ever see a time when you'd give up extreme sports?'

His eyes suddenly gleamed. 'Those are altogether separate questions. I believe I've answered your original one.'

Dammit! He had to know that only whetted her appetite for more.

None of your business.

It really wasn't, but then wasn't that the beauty, the temptation, of this game of 'truth or dare' questions—the danger?

Finn wanted to laugh at the quickened curiosity, the look of pique, in Audra's face. He shouldn't play this game. He should leave it all well enough alone, but…

He leaned towards her. 'I'll make a tit-for-tat deal with you.'

Ice-blue eyes shouldn't leave a path of fire on his skin, but beneath her gaze he started to burn. She cocked her head to one side. 'You mean a question-for-question, quid pro quo bargain?'

'Yep.'

She leaned in and searched his face as if trying to decipher his agenda. He did his best to keep his face clear. Finally she eased back and he could breathe again.

'You must be *really* bored.'

He wasn't bored. Her company didn't bore him. It never had. He didn't want to examine that thought too closely, though. He didn't want to admit it out loud either. 'Life has been…quieter of late than usual.'

'And you're finding that a challenge?'

He had in Nice, but now…not really. Which didn't make sense.

Can you inherit a risk-taking gene? He shied away from that question, from the deeper implications that lay beneath its surface. So what if some of his former pursuits had lost their glitter? That didn't mean anything.

He set his jaw. 'Let's call it a new experience.'

Her lips pressed together into a prim line he wanted to mess up. He'd like to kiss those lips until they were plump and swollen and— *Hell!*

'Are you up for my question challenge?' He made his voice deliberately mocking in a way he knew would gall her.

'I don't know. I'll think about it.'

He kinked an eyebrow, deliberately trying to inflame her competitive spirit. 'What are you afraid of?'

She pushed her sunglasses further up her nose and re-adjusted her sunhat. 'Funny, isn't it, how every question now seems to take on a double edge?'

He didn't pursue it. In all honesty letting sleeping dogs lie would probably be for the best.

Really?

He thrust out his jaw. And if not, then there was more than one way to find out what was troubling her. He just needed to turn his mind to it. Find another way.

Finn laughed when Audra pulled the two trays of crois-sants from the oven. Those tiny hard-looking lumps were supposed to be croissants? Her face, comical in its indig-nation, made him laugh harder.

'How can you laugh about this? We spent hours on these and…and *this* is our reward?'

'French pastry has a reputation for being notoriously difficult, hasn't it?' He poked a finger at the nearest hard lump and it disintegrated to ash beneath his touch. 'Wow, I think we just took French cooking to a new all-time low.'

'But…but you're half French! That should've given us a head start.'

'And you're half Australian but I don't see any particu-lar evidence of that making you handy with either a cricket bat or a barbecue.'

Like Finn's father, Audra's mother had been Austra-lian. Audra merely glowered at him, slammed the cook-book back to the bench top and studied its instructions once again. He hoped she wasn't going to put him through the torture of working so closely beside her in the kitchen again. There'd been too much accidental brushing of arms, too much…heat. Try as he might, he couldn't blame it all on the oven. Even over the smell of flour, yeast and milk, the scent of peaches and coconut had pounded at him, making him hungry.

But not for food.

He opened a cupboard and took out a plate, unwrapped the bakery bag he'd stowed in the pantry earlier and placed half a dozen croissants onto it. He slid the plate towards Audra.

She took a croissant without looking, bit into it and then pointed at the cookbook. 'Here's where we went wrong. We—'

She broke off to stare at the croissant in her hand, and then at the plate. 'If you dare tell me here are some croissants you prepared earlier, I'll—'

'Here are some croissants I *bought* at the village bakery earlier.'

'When earlier?'

'Dawn. Before you were up.'

The croissant hurtled back to the plate and her hands slammed to her hips. He backed up a step. 'I wasn't casting aspersions on your croissant-making abilities. But I wanted a back-up plan because…because I wanted to eat croissants.' Because she'd seemed so set on them.

Her glare didn't abate. 'What else have you been doing at the crack of dawn each morning?'

He shook his head, at a loss. 'Nothing, why?'

'Have you been running into the village and back every morning?'

He frowned. 'I took the car.' Anyway, he wasn't up to running that distance yet. And he hadn't felt like walking. Every day he felt a little stronger, but… It hadn't occurred to him to run into the village. Or to run anywhere for that matter. Except with her on the beach, when it was his turn to choose their daily activities. Only then he didn't make her jog anyway. They usually walked the length of the beach and then swam back.

'Or…or throwing yourself off cliffs or…or kite surfing or—'

He crowded in close then, his own temper rising, and it made her eyes widen…and darken. 'That wouldn't be in the spirit of the deal we made, would it?'

She visibly swallowed. 'Absolutely not.'

'And I'm a man of my word.'

Her gaze momentarily lowered to his lips before lifting again. 'You're also a self-professed adrenaline junkie.'

Except the adrenaline flooding his body at the moment had nothing to do with extreme sports. It had to do with the perfect shape of Audra's mouth and the burning need to know what she'd taste like. Would she taste of peaches and coconut? Coffee and croissant? Salty or sweet? His skin tightened, stretching itself across his frame in torturous tautness.

Her breathing grew shallow and a light flared to life in her eyes and he knew she'd recognised his hunger, his need, but she didn't move away, didn't retreat. Instead her gaze roved across his face and lingered for a beat too long on his mouth, and her lips parted with an answering hunger.

'A man of his word?' she murmured, swaying towards him.

Her words penetrated the fog surrounding his brain. *What are you doing? You can't kiss her!*

He snapped away, his breathing harsh. Silence echoed off the walls for three heart-rending beats and then he heard her fussing around behind him…dumping the failed croissants in the bin, rinsing the oven trays. 'Thank you for buying backup croissants, Finn.'

He closed his eyes and counted to three, before turning around. He found her surveying him, her tone nonchalant and untroubled—as if she hadn't been about to reach up on her tiptoes and kiss him. He'd seen the temptation in her eyes, but somehow she'd bundled up her needs and desires and hidden them behind a prim wall of control and restraint. It had his back molars grinding together.

He didn't know how he knew, but this was all related— her tight rein on her desires and needs, her refusal to let her hair down and have fun, the dogged determination to repress it all because…?

He had no idea! He had no answer for why she didn't simply reach out and take what she wanted from life.

She bit into her croissant and it was all he could do then not to groan.

'I have a "truth or dare" question for you, Finn.'

He tried to match her coolness and composure. 'So you've decided to take me up on the quid pro quo bargain?'

She nodded and stuck out a hip. If he'd been wearing a tie he'd have had to loosen it. 'If you're still game,' she purred.

In normal circumstances her snark would've had him fighting a grin. But nothing about today and this kitchen and Audra felt the least bit normal. Or the least bit familiar. 'Ask your question.'

She eyed him for a moment, her eyes stormy. 'Don't you want something more out of life?'

'More?' He felt his eyes narrow. 'Like what?'

'I mean, you flit from adventure to adventure, but…' That beautiful brow of hers creased. 'Don't you want something more worthwhile, more…*lasting*?'

His lips twisted. A man showed no interest in settling down—

'I'm not talking about marriage and babies!' she snapped as if reading his mind. 'I'm talking about doing something good with your life, making a mark, leaving a legacy.'

Her innate and too familiar disapproval stung him in

ways it never had before. Normally he'd have laughed it off, but…

He found himself leaning towards her. He had to fight the urge to loom. He wasn't Thomas-blasted-Farquhar. He didn't go in for physical intimidation. 'Do you seriously think I *just* live off my trust fund while I go trekking through the Amazon and train for the London marathon, and—'

'Look, I know you raise a lot of money for charity, but there doesn't seem to be any rhyme or reason to your methods—no proper organisation. You simply bounce from one thing to the next.'

'And what about my design company?'

Her hands went to her hips. 'You don't seem to spend a lot of time in the office.'

His mouth worked. 'You think I treat my company like a…a toy?'

'Well, don't you? I mean, you never talk about it!'

'You never ask me about it!'

She blinked. 'From where I'm standing—'

'With all the other workaholics,' he shot back.

'It simply looks as if you're skiving off from the day job to have exciting adventures. Obviously that's your prerogative, as you're the boss, but—'

He raised his arms. 'Okay, we're going to play a game.'

She stared at him. Her eyes throbbed, and he knew that some of this anger came from what had almost happened between them—the physical frustration and emotional confusion. He wanted to lean across and pull her into his arms and hug her until they both felt better. But he had a feeling that solution would simply lead to more danger.

Her chin lifted. 'And what about my question?'

'By the end of the game you'll have your answer. I promise.' And in the process he meant to challenge her to explore the dreams she seemed so doggedly determined to bury.

Her eyes narrowed and she folded her arms. 'What does this game involve?'

'Sitting in the garden with a plate of croissants and my computer.'

She raised her eyebrows. 'Sitting?'

'And eating…and talking.'

She unfolded her arms. 'Fine. That I can do.'

What was it his uncle used to say? *There's more than one way to crack an egg.* He might never discover the reasons Audra held herself back, but the one thing he could do was whet her appetite for the options life held, give her the push she perhaps needed to reach for her dreams. After all, temptation and adventure were his forte. He frowned as he went to retrieve his laptop. At least, they had been once. And he'd find his fire for them again soon enough.

And he couldn't forget that once he'd answered her question, he'd have one of his own in the kitty. He might never use it—she was right, these questions could be dangerous—but it'd be there waiting just in case.

CHAPTER SEVEN

AUDRA BLINKED WHEN Finn handed her a large notepad and a set of pencils. She opened her mouth to ask what they were for, but when he sat opposite and opened his laptop she figured she'd find out soon enough.

For the moment she was simply content to stare at him and wonder what that stubble would feel like against her palms and admire the breadth of his shoulders and—

No, no. *No!*

For the moment she was content to…to congratulate herself for keeping Finn quiet for another day. And she'd… *admire the view.* The brilliant blue of the sea contrasted with the soft blue of the sky, making her appreciate all the different hues on display. A yacht with a pink and blue sail had anchored just offshore and she imagined a honeymooning couple rowing into one of the many deserted coves that lay along this side of the island, and enjoying…

Her mind flashed with forbidden images, and she shook herself. *Enjoying a picnic.*

'Audra?'

She glanced up to find Finn staring at her, one eyebrow raised. She envied that. She'd always wanted to do it. She tried it now, and he laughed. 'What are you doing?'

'I love the "one eyebrow raised" thing. It looks great and you do it really well. I've always wanted to do it, but…' She tried again and he convulsed. Laughter was good. She needed to dispel the fraught atmosphere that had developed between them in the kitchen. She needed to forget about kissing him. He'd been looking grim and serious in odd moments these last few days too…sad, after telling her about the promise he'd made to himself when he'd turned eighteen.

She didn't want him sad. In the past she'd often wanted to get the better of him, but she didn't want that now either. She just wanted to see him fit and healthy. Happy. And she wanted to see him the way she used to see him—as Rupert's best friend. If she focussed hard enough, she could get that back, right?

She gave a mock sigh. 'That's not the effect I was aiming for.'

'There's a trick.'

She leaned towards him. 'Really?'

He nodded.

'Will you tell it to me?'

'If you'll tell me what you were thinking about when you were staring out to sea.' He gestured behind him at the view. 'You were a million miles away.'

Heat flushed her cheeks. She wasn't going to tell him about her imaginary honeymoon couple, but... 'It's so beautiful here. *So* beautiful. It does something to me—fills me up...makes me feel more...'

He frowned. 'More what?'

She lifted her hands only to let them drop again. 'I'm not sure how to explain it. It just makes me feel more... myself.'

He sat back as if her words had punched the air from his lungs. 'If that's true then you should move here.'

'Impossible.' Her laugh, even to her own ears, sounded strained.

'Nothing's impossible.'

She couldn't transplant her work here. She didn't even want to try. It'd simply suck the colour and life from this place for her anyway, so she shook her head. 'It's just a timely reminder that I should be taking my holidays more often.' She had a ridiculous amount of leave accrued. She had a ridiculous amount of money saved too. Maybe even enough for a deposit on a little cottage in the village? And then, maybe, she could own her own bit of paradise—a bit that was just hers.

And maybe having that would help counter the grey monotony her life in Geneva held for her.

Finn stared at her as if he wanted to argue the point further. No more. Some pipe dreams made her chest ache, and not in a good way. 'Fair's fair. Share your eyebrow-raising tip.'

So he walked her through it. 'But you'll need to practise. You can do an internet search if you want to.'

Really? Who'd have thought?

He rubbed his hands together. 'Now we're going to play my game.'

'And the name of the game…?'

'Designing Audra's favourite…'

'Holiday cottage?' she supplied helpfully.

His grin widened and he clapped his hands. 'Designing Audra's favourite shop.'

Her heart started to pound.

'How old were you when you decided shopkeeping sang to your soul?'

She made herself laugh because it was quite clearly what he intended. 'I don't know. I guess I must've been about six.' And then eleven…fifteen…seventeen. But her owning a shop—it was a crazy idea. It was so *indulgent*.

But this was just a game. Her heart thumped. It wouldn't hurt to play along for an hour or so. Finn obviously wanted to show off some hidden talent he had and who was she to rain on his parade? The lines of strain around his eyes had eased and the grooves bracketing his mouth no longer bit into his flesh so deeply. Each day had him moving more easily and fluidly. Coming here had been good for him. Taking it easy was good for him. She wanted all that goodness to continue in the same vein.

She made herself sit up straighter. 'Right, the name of the game is Designing Audra's Dream Shop.'

He grinned and it sent a breathless kind of energy zinging through her.

'We're going to let our minds go wild. The sky's the limit. Got it?'

'Got it.'

He held her gaze. 'I mean it. The point of the game is to not be held back by practicalities or mundane humdrummery. That comes later. For this specific point in time we're aiming for best of the best, top of the pops, no compromises, just pure unadulterated dream vision.'

She had a feeling she should make some sort of effort to check the enthusiasm suddenly firing through her veins, but Finn's enthusiasm was infectious. And she was in the Greek islands on holiday. She was allowed to play. She nodded once, hard. 'Right.'

'First question…' his fingers were poised over the keyboard of his computer '…and experience tells me that the first answer that pops into your mind is usually the right one.'

'Okay, hit me with Question One.'

'Where is your ideal location for your shop?'

'Here on Kyanós…in the village's main street, overlooking the harbour. There's a place down there that's for sale and…' she hesitated '…it has a nice view.'

His fingers flew over the keyboard. 'What does your ideal shop sell?'

'Beautiful things,' she answered without hesitation.

'Specifics, please.'

So she described in detail the beautiful things she'd love to sell in her dream shop. 'Handicrafts made by local artisans—things like jade pendants and elegant bracelets, beautiful scented candles and colourful scarves.' She pulled in a breath. 'Wooden boxes ornamented with beaten silver, silver boxes ornamented with coloured beads.' She described gorgeous leather handbags, scented soaps and journals made from handcrafted paper.

She rested her chin on her hands and let her mind drift
into her dream shop—a pastime she'd refused to indulge in
for…well, years now. 'There'd be beautiful prints for sale
on the walls. There'd be wind chimes and pretty vases…
glassware.'

She pulled back, suddenly self-conscious, heat bursting across her cheeks. 'Is that…uh…specific enough?'

'It's perfect.'

He kept tap-tapping away, staring at the computer
screen rather than at her, and the heat slowly faded from
her face. He looked utterly engrossed and she wondered
if he'd worn the same expression when he'd set off on his
ill-fated ski jump.

He glanced at her and she could feel herself colour again
at being caught out staring. Luckily, he didn't seem to notice. He just started shooting questions at her again. How
big was her shop? Was it square or rectangle? Where did
she want to locate the point of sale? What colour scheme
would she choose? What shelving arrangements and display options did she have in mind?

Her head started to whirl at the sheer number of questions, but she found she could answer them all without
dithering or wavering, even when she didn't have the correct terminology for what she was trying to describe. Finn
had a knack for asking her things and then reframing her
answers in a way that captured exactly what she meant.
She wasn't sure how he did it.

'Okay, you need to give me about fifteen minutes.'

'I'll get us some drinks.' She made up a fruit and cheese
platter to supplement their lunch of croissants, added some
dried fruits and nuts before taking the tray outside.

Finn rose and took the tray from her. 'Sit. I'll show you
what I've done.'

She did as he bid. He turned the computer to face her.

She gasped. She couldn't help it. She pulled the computer towards her. She couldn't help that either. If she

could've she'd have stepped right inside his computer because staring out at her from the screen was the interior of the shop she'd dreamed about ever since she was a little girl—a dream she'd perfected as she'd grown older and her tastes had changed. 'How...?' She could barely push the word past the lump in her throat. 'How did you do this?'

'Design software.'

He went to press a button, but she batted his hand away. 'Don't touch a thing! This is *perfect*.' It was amazing. The interior of her fantasy shop lived and breathed there on the screen like a dream come true and it made everything inside her throb and come alive.

'Not perfect.' He placed a slice of feta on a cracker and passed it across to her. 'It'd take me another couple of days to refine it for true perfection. But it gives a pretty good indication of your vision.'

It did. And she wanted this vision. She wanted it so bad it tasted like raspberries on her tongue. Instead of raspberries she bit into feta, which was pretty delicious too.

'If you push the arrow key there're another two pictures of your shop's interior from different angles.'

She popped the rest of the cracker into her mouth and pressed the arrow key...and marvelled anew at the additional two pictures that appeared—one from the back of the shop, and one from behind the sales counter, both of which afforded a glorious view of a harbour. There was a tub of colourful flowers just outside the door and her eyes filled. She reached out and touched them. 'You remembered.'

'I did.'

She pored over every single detail in the pictures. She could barely look away from the screen, but she had to. This dream could never be hers. She dragged in a breath, gathered her resources to meet Finn's gaze and to pretend that this hadn't been anything more than a game, an interesting exercise, when her gaze caught on the logo in the bottom right corner of the screen. The breath left her lungs in a rush. She knew that logo!

Her gaze speared to his. '*You're* Aspiration Designs?'

'Along with my two partners.'

He nodded a confirmation and she couldn't read the expression in his eyes. 'How did I not know about this?'

He shrugged. 'It's not a secret.'

'But…your company was called Sullivan Brand Consultants.'

'Until I merged with my partners.'

She forced her mind back to the family dinners and the few other times in recent years that she'd seen Finn, and tried to recall a conversation—any conversation—about him expanding his company or going into partnership. There'd been some vague rumblings about some changes, but…she'd not paid a whole lot of attention. She wanted to hide her face in her hands. Had she really been so uninterested…so set in her picture of who Finn was?

She moistened her lips. Aspiration Designs was a boutique design business in high demand. 'You created the foyer designs for the new global business centre in Geneva.'

He lifted a shoulder in a silent shrug.

Those designs had won awards.

She closed the lid of the laptop, sagging in her seat. 'I've had you pegged all wrong. For all these years you haven't been flitting from one daredevil adventure to another. You've been—' she gestured to the computer '—making people's dreams come true.'

'I don't make people's dreams come true. They make their own dreams come true through sheer hard work and dedication. I just show them what their dream can look like.'

In the same way he'd burned the vision of her dream shop onto her brain.

'And another thing—' he handed her another cracker

laden with cheese '—Aspirations isn't a one-man band. My partners are in charge of the day-to-day running. Also, I've built an amazing design team and one of my superpowers is delegation. Which means I can go flitting off on any adventure that takes my fancy, almost at a moment's notice.'

She didn't believe that for a moment. She bet he timed his adventures to fit in with his work demands.

'And in hindsight it's probably not all that surprising that you don't know about my company. How often have we seen each other in the last four or five years? Just a handful of times.'

He had a point. 'Christmas…and occasionally when you're in Geneva I'll catch you when you're seeing Rupert.' But that was often for just a quick drink. They were on the periphery of each other's lives, not inside them.

'And when you do see me you always ask me what my latest adventure has been and where I'm off to next.'

Her stomach churned. Never once had she asked him about his work. She hadn't thought he did much. Instead, she'd vicariously lived adventure and excitement through him. But the same disapproval she directed at herself— to keep herself in check—she'd also aimed at him. How unfair was that!

She'd taken a secret delight in his exploits while maintaining a sense of moral superiority by dismissing them as trivial. She swallowed. 'I owe you an apology. I'm really sorry, Finn. I've been a pompous ass.'

He blinked. 'Garbage. You just didn't know.'

She hadn't wanted to know. She'd wanted to dismiss him as an irresponsible lightweight. Her mouth dried. And in thinking of him as a self-indulgent pleasure-seeker it had been easier to battle the attraction she'd always felt simmering beneath the surface of her consciousness for him.

God! That couldn't be true.

Couldn't it?

She didn't know what to do with such an epiphany, so she forced a smile to uncooperative lips. 'You have your adventures *and* you do good and interesting work. Finn...' she spread her hands '...you're living the dream.'

He laughed but it didn't reach his eyes. She recalled what he'd told her—about the promise he'd made to himself when he'd come of age—and a protest rose through her. 'I think you're wrong, Finn—both you and Ned. I think you *can* have a long-term relationship *and* still enjoy the extreme sports you love.' The words blurted out of her with no rhyme or reason. Finn's head snapped back. She winced and gulped and wished she could call them back.

'Talk about a change of topic.' He eased away, eyed her for a moment. 'Wrong how?'

She shouldn't have started this. But now that she had... She forced herself to straighten. 'I just don't think you can define your own circumstances based on what happened to your parents. And I'm far from convinced Ned should blame your father for everything that happened afterwards.' She raised her hands in a conciliatory gesture. 'I know! I know! He has your best interests at heart. And, look, I love your uncle Ned.' He came to their Christmas dinners and had become as much a part of the extended family as Finn had. 'But surely it's up to you and your prospective life partner to decide what kind of marriage will work for you.'

'But my mother—'

Frustration shot through her. 'Not every woman deals with tragedy in the same way your mother did!'

'Whoa!' He stared at her.

Heck!

'Sorry. Gosh, I...' She bit her lip.

What had she been thinking?

'Sorry,' she said again, swallowing. 'That came out harsher than I meant it to—*way* harsher. I just meant, people react to tragedy in different ways. People react to broken hearts in different ways. I'm not trying to trivialise it; I'm not saying it's easy. It's just…not everyone falls into a decline. If you live by those kinds of rules then—'

He leaned towards her and she almost lost her train of thought. 'Um, then…it follows that *you'd* better never marry a woman who's into extreme sports or…or has a dangerous job because if she dies then you wouldn't be able to survive it.'

His jaw dropped.

'And from the look on your face, it's clear you don't think of yourself as that kind of person.'

He didn't.

Finn stared at Audra, not sure why his heart pounded so hard, or why something chained inside him wanted to suddenly break free.

She retied her ponytail, not quite meeting his eyes. 'I mean, not everyone wants to marry and that's fine. Not everyone wants to have kids, and that's fine too. Maybe you're one of those people.'

'But?'

She bit her bottom lip and when she finally released it, it was plump from where she'd worried at it. She shrugged. 'But maybe you're not.'

'You think I want to marry and have kids?'

Blue eyes met his, and they had him clenching up in strange ways. 'I have no idea.' She leaned towards him the tiniest fraction. 'Wouldn't you eventually like to have children?'

'I don't know.' He'd never allowed himself to think about it before. 'You?'

'I'd love to be a mother one day.'

'Would you marry someone obsessed with extreme sports?'

'I wouldn't marry someone obsessed with anything,

thank you very much. I don't want my life partner spending all his leisure time away from me—whether it's for rock climbing, stamp collecting or golf. I'd want him to want to spend time with me.'

Any guy lucky enough to catch Audra's eye would be a fool not to spend time with her. *Lots* of time. As much as he could.

'I don't want *all* of his leisure time, though.' She glared as if Finn had accused her of exactly that. 'There are girlfriends to catch up with over coffee and cake…or cocktails. And books to read.'

Speaking of books, he hoped she had reading down on today's agenda. He wouldn't mind getting back to his book. 'But you'd be okay with him doing some rock climbing, hang-gliding or golf?'

'As long as he doesn't expect me to take up the sport too. I mean, me dangling from a thin rope off a sheer cliff or hurtling off a sheer cliff in a glorified paper plane—what could possibly go wrong?'

A bark of laughter shot out of him. 'We're going to assume that this hypothetical life partner of yours would insist on you getting full training before attempting anything dangerous.'

She wrinkled her nose. 'Doesn't change the fact I'm not the slightest bit interested in rock climbing, hang-gliding or golf. I wouldn't want to go out with someone who wanted to change me.'

He sagged back on the wooden bench, air leaving his lungs. 'Which is why you wouldn't change him.' It didn't mean she wouldn't worry when her partner embarked on some risky activity, but she'd accept them for who they were. She'd want them to be happy.

Things inside him clenched up again. So what if laps around a racetrack had started to feel just plain boring—round and round in endless monotonous laps? *Yawn.* And so what if he couldn't remember why he'd thought hurtling off that ski jump had been a good idea. It didn't mean he wanted to change his entire lifestyle. It didn't mean anything. Yet…

He'd never let himself think about the possibility of having children before. He moistened suddenly dry lips. He wasn't sure he should start now either.

And yet he couldn't let the matter drop. 'Do you think about having children a lot?'

Her brow wrinkled. 'Where are you going with this? It's not like I'm obsessed or anything. It's not like it's constantly on my mind. But I am twenty-seven. Ideally, if I were going to start a family, I'd want that to happen in the next ten years. And I wouldn't want to get married and launch immediately into parenthood. I'd want to enjoy married life for a bit first.'

She frowned then. 'What?' he demanded, curious to see inside this world of hers—unsure if it attracted or repelled him.

'I was just thinking about this hypothetical partner you've landed me with. I hope he understands that things change when babies come along.'

Obviously, but…um. 'How?'

She selected a brazil nut before holding the bowl out to him. 'Suddenly you have way less time for yourself. Cocktail nights with the girls become fewer and farther between.'

He took a handful of nuts. 'As do opportunities to throw yourself off a cliff, I suppose?'

'Exactly.'

Except having Finn hadn't slowed his father down. And his mother certainly hadn't insisted on having a stable home base. She'd simply towed Finn and his nanny along with them wherever they went. And when he was old enough, she hired tutors to homeschool him.

And everything inside him rebelled at blaming his parents for that.

'A baby's needs have to be taken into consideration and—'

She broke off when she glanced into his face. 'I'm not criticising your parents, Finn. I'm not saying they did it wrong or anything. I'm describing how *I'd* want to do it. Each couple works out what's best for them.'

'But you'd want to be hands-on. I have a feeling that nannies and boarding schools and in-home tutors aren't your idea of good parenting. You'd want a house in the suburbs, to host Christmas dinner—'

'It doesn't have to be in the burbs. It could be an apartment in the city or a house overlooking a Greek beach. And if I can afford a nanny I'll have one of those too, thank you very much. I'd want to keep working.'

His parents had chosen to not work. At all.

'But when I get home from work, I'd want to have my family around me. That's all.' Their eyes locked. 'It's not how my parents did it…and I'm not saying I hated boarding school, because I didn't. I know how lucky I've been. I'm not saying my way is better than anybody else's. I'm just saying that's the way that'd make *me* happy.'

She'd just described everything he'd wanted when he was a child, and it made the secret places inside him ache. It also brought something into stark relief. She knew what would make her happy in her personal life—she knew the kind of home life and family that she wanted, and it was clear she wasn't going to settle for less. So why was she settling for less in her work life?

The question hovered on his tongue. He had a 'truth or dare' question owing to him, but something held him back, warned him the time wasn't right. Audra was looking more relaxed with each day they spent here. Her appetite had returned, as had the colour in her cheeks. But he recalled the expression in her eyes when he'd first turned his computer around to show her that shop, and things inside him knotted up. It was too new, and too fragile. She needed more time to pore over those pictures…to dream.

He wanted her hunger to build until she could deny it no longer.

He loaded two crackers with cheese and handed her one, before lifting the lid of his computer. 'I'll email those designs through to you.'

'Oh, um…thank you. That'll be fun.'

Fun? Those walls had just gone back up in her eyes. That strange restraint pulled back into place around her. He didn't understand it, but he wasn't going to let her file those pictures away in a place where she could forget about them. He'd use Rupert's office later to print hard copies off as well. She might ignore her email, but she'd find the physical copies much harder to ignore.

'What's on the agenda for the rest of the day?'

She sent him a cat-that-got-the-cream grin. 'Nothing. Absolutely nothing.'

Excellent. 'Books on the beach?'

'You're getting the hang of this, Sullivan.' She rose and collected what was left of the food, and started back towards the house. 'Careful,' she shot over her shoulder, 'you might just find yourself enjoying it.'

He was enjoying it. He just wasn't sure what that meant.

He shook himself. It didn't mean anything, other than relief at being out of hospital and not being confined to quarters. He'd be an ingrate—not to mention made of marble—not to enjoy all this glorious Greek sun and scenery.

And whatever else he was, he wasn't made of marble. With Audra proving so intriguing, this enforced slower pace suited him fine for the moment. Once he got to the bottom of her strange restraint his restlessness would return. And then he'd be eager to embark on his next adventure—in need of a shot of pure adrenaline.

His hunger for adventure would return and consume him, and all strange conversations about children would be forgotten. He rose; his hands clenched. This was about Audra, not him.

Audra stared at the ticket Finn had handed her and then at the large barn-like structure in front of them. She stared down at the paper in her hand again. 'You…you enrolled us in an art class?'

If Finn had been waiting for her to jump up and down in excitement and delight, he'd have been disappointed.

Which meant… Yeah, he was disappointed.

How had he got this wrong? 'When you saw the flyer in the bookshop window you looked…'

'I looked what?'

Her eyes turned wary with that same damn restraint that was there when she talked about her shop. Frustration rattled through him. Why did she do that?

'Looked what?' she demanded.

'Interested,' he shot back.

Wistful, full of yearning…hungry.

'I can't draw.'

'Which is why it says *"Beginners"*—' he pointed '—right here.'

She blew out a breath.

'What's more I think you were interested, but for some reason it intimidated you, so you chickened out.'

Her chin shot up, but her cheeks had reddened. 'I just didn't think it'd be your cup of tea.'

'You didn't think lying on a beach reading a book would float my boat either, but that didn't stop you. And I've submitted with grace. I haven't made a single complaint about your agendas. Unlike you with mine.'

'Oh!' She took a step back. 'You make me sound mean-spirited.'

She *wasn't* mean-spirited. But she *was* the most frustrating woman on earth!

'I'm sorry, Finn. Truly.' She seemed to gird her loins.

'You've chosen this specifically with me in mind. And I'm touched. Especially as I know you'd rather be off paragliding or aqua boarding or something.'

He ran a finger around the collar of his T-shirt. That wasn't one hundred per cent true. It wasn't even ten per cent true. Not that he had any intention of saying so. 'But?' he countered, refusing to let her off the hook. 'You don't want to do it?'

'It's not that.'

He folded his arms. 'Then what is it?'

'Forget it. You just took me by surprise, is all.' She snapped away from him. 'Let's just go in and enjoy the class and—'

He reached out and curled his hand around hers and her words stuttered to a halt. 'Audra?' He raised an eyebrow and waited.

Her chin shot up again. 'You won't understand.'

'Try me.'

A storm raged in her eyes. He watched it in fascination. 'Do you ever have rebellious impulses, Finn?'

He raised both eyebrows. 'My entire life is one big rebellion, surely?'

'Nonsense! You're living your life exactly as you think your parents would want you to.'

She snatched her hand back and he felt suddenly cast adrift.

'You've not rebelled any more than I have.'

That wasn't true, but... He glanced at the studio behind her. 'Art class is a rebellion?'

'In a way.'

'How?'

She folded her arms and stared up at the sky. He had a feeling she was counting to ten. 'Look, I can see the sense in taking a break, in having a holiday. Lying on a beach and soaking up some Vitamin D, getting some gentle exercise via a little swimming and walking, reading a book—I see the sense in those things. They lead to a rested body and mind.'

'How is an art class different from any of those things?'

'It just is! It feels…self-indulgent. It's doing something for the sake of doing it, rather than because it's good for you or…or…'

'What about fun?'

She stared at him. 'What's *fun* got to do with it?'

He couldn't believe what he was hearing. 'Evidently nothing.' Was she really that afraid of letting her hair down?

'When I start doing one thing just for the sake of it— *for fun*,' she spat, 'I'll start doing others.'

He lifted his arms and let them drop. 'And the problem with that would be…?'

Her eyes widened as if he were talking crazy talk and a hard, heavy ball dropped into the pit of his stomach. It was all he could do not to bare his teeth and growl.

'I knew you wouldn't understand.'

'I'll tell you what I understand. That you're the most uptight, repressed person I have *ever* met.'

'Repressed?' Her mouth opened and closed. 'I— What are you doing?'

He'd seized her hand again and was towing her towards a copse of Aleppo pine and carob trees. 'What's that?' He flung an arm out at the vista spread below them.

She glared. 'The Aegean. It's beautiful.'

'And that?' He pointed upwards.

She followed his gaze. Frowned and shrugged, evidently not following where he was going with this. 'The… sky?'

'The sun,' he snapped out. 'And it's shining in full force in case you hadn't noticed. And where are we?'

She swallowed. 'On a Greek island.'

He crowded her in against a tree, his arms going either side of her to block her in. 'If there was ever a time to let your hair down and rebel against your prim and proper strictures, Audra, now's the time to do it.'

She stared up at him with wide eyes, and he relished the moment—her stupefaction…her bewilderment…her undeniable hunger when her gaze lowered to his lips. This moment had seemed inevitable from when she'd appeared on the stairs a week ago to peer at him with those icy blue eyes, surveyed him in handcuffs, and told him it served him right.

His heart thudded against his ribs, he relished the adrenaline that surged through his body, before he swooped down to capture her lips in a kiss designed to shake up her safe little world. And he poured all his wildness and adventurous temptation into it in a devil-may-care invitation to dance.

CHAPTER EIGHT

THE ASSAULT ON Audra's senses the moment Finn's lips touched hers was devastating. She hadn't realised she could feel a kiss in so many ways, that its impact would spread through her in ever-widening circles that went deeper and deeper.

Finn's warmth beat at her like the warmth of the sun after a dip in the sea. It melted things that had been frozen for a very long time.

His scent mingled with the warm tang of the trees and sun-kissed grasses, and with just the tiniest hint of salt on the air it was exactly what a holiday should smell like. It dared her to play, it tempted her to reckless fun… and…and to a youthful joy she'd never allowed herself to feel before.

And she was powerless to resist. She had no defences against a kiss like this. It didn't feel as if defences were necessary. A kiss like this…it should be embraced and relished…welcomed.

Finn had been angry with her, but he didn't kiss angry. He kissed her as though he couldn't help it—as though he'd been fighting a losing battle and had finally flung himself wholeheartedly into surrender. It was *intoxicating*.

Totally heady and wholly seductive.

She lifted her hands, but didn't know what to do with them so rested them on his shoulders, but they moved, restless, to the heated skin of his neck, and the skin-on-skin contact sent electricity coursing through both of them. He shuddered, she gasped…tongues tangled.

And then his arms were around her, hauling her against his body, her arms were around his neck as she plastered herself to him, and she stopped thinking as desire and the moment consumed her.

It was the raucous cry of a rose-ringed parakeet that penetrated her senses—and the need for air that had them easing apart. She stared into his face and wondered if her lips looked as well kissed as his, and if her eyes were just as dazed.

And then he swore, and a sick feeling crawled through the pit of her stomach. He let her go so fast she had to brace herself against the trunk of the tree behind her. She ached in places both familiar and unfamiliar and…and despite the myriad emotions chasing across his face—and none of them were positive—she wished with all her might that they were somewhere private, and that she were back in his arms so those aches could be assuaged.

And to hell with the consequences.

'I shouldn't have done that,' he bit out. 'I'm sorry.'

'I don't want an apology.'

The words left her without forethought, and with a brutal honesty that made her cringe. But they both knew what she *did* want couldn't happen. Every instinct she had told her he was hanging by a thread. His chest rose and fell as if he'd been running. The pulse at the base of his throat pounded like a mad thing. He wanted her with the same savage fury that she wanted him. And everything inside her urged her to snap his thread of control, and the consequences be damned.

It was *crazy*! Her hands clenched. She couldn't go on making romantic mistakes like this. Oh, he was nothing like Thomas. He'd never lie to her or betray her, but…but if she had an affair with Finn, it'd hurt her family. They'd see her as just another in a long line of Finn's *women*. It wasn't fair, but it was the reality all the same. She wouldn't hurt her family for the world; especially after all they'd been through with Thomas. She couldn't let them down so badly.

If she and Finn started something, when it ended—and that was the inevitable trajectory to all of Finn's relationships—he'd have lost her family's good opinion. They'd shun him. She knew how much that'd hurt him, and she'd do anything to prevent that from happening too.

And yet if he kissed her again she'd be lost.

'I'm not the person I thought I was,' she blurted out.

He frowned. 'What do you mean?'

Anger came to her rescue then. 'You wanted me to lose control. You succeeded in making that happen.' She moved in close until the heat from their bodies mingled again. 'And now you want me to just what…? Put it all back under wraps? To forget about it? What kind of game are you playing, Finn?'

The pulse in his jaw jumped and jerked. 'I just wanted you to loosen up a bit. Live in the moment instead of over-thinking and over-analysing everything and…'

She slammed her hands to her hips. 'And?' She wasn't sure what she wanted from him—what she wanted him to admit—but it was more than this. That kiss had changed *everything*. But she wasn't even sure what that meant. Or what to do about it.

'And I'm an idiot! It was a stupid thing to do.' His eyes snapped fire as if *he* were angry with *her*. 'I do flings, Audra. Nothing more.' Panic lit his face. 'But I don't do them with Rupert's little sister.'

The car keys sailed through the air. She caught them automatically.

'I'll see you back at the villa.'

She watched as he stormed down the hill. He was running scared. From her? From fear of destroying his friendship with Rupert? Or was it something else…like thoughts of babies and marriage?

Was that what he thought she wanted from him?

Her stomach did a crazy twirl and she had to sit on a

nearby rock to catch her breath. She'd be crazy to pin those kinds of hopes on him. And while she might be crazy with lust, she hadn't lost her mind completely.

She touched her fingers to her lips. *Oh, my, but the man could kiss.*

Audra glanced up from her spot on the sofa when Finn finally came in. She'd had dinner a couple of hours ago. She'd started to wonder if Finn meant to stay out all night.

And then she hadn't wanted to follow that thought any further, hadn't wanted to know where he might be and with whom…and what they might be doing.

He halted when he saw her. The light from the doorway framed him in exquisite detail—outlining the broad width of his shoulders and the lean strength of his thighs. Every lusty, heady impulse that had fired through her body when they'd kissed earlier fired back to life now, making her itch and yearn.

'I want to tell you something.'

He moved into the room, his face set and the lines bracketing his mouth deep. She searched him for signs of exhaustion, over-exertion, a limp, as he moved towards an armchair, but his body, while held tight, seemed hale and whole. Whatever else he'd done—or hadn't done—today, he clearly hadn't aggravated his recent injuries.

She let out a breath she hadn't even known she'd been holding. 'Okay.' She closed her book and set her feet to the floor. Here it came—the 'it's not you it's me' speech, the 'I care about you, but…' justifications. She tried to stop her lips from twisting. She'd toyed with a lot of scenarios since their kiss…and this was one of them. She had no enthusiasm for it. Perhaps it served her right for losing her head so completely earlier. A penance. She bit back a sigh. 'What do you want to tell me?'

'I want to explain why it's so important to me that I don't break Rupert's trust.'

That was easy. 'He's your best friend.' He cared more for Rupert than he did for her. It made perfect sense, so she couldn't explain why the knowledge chafed at her.

'I want you to understand how much I actually owe him.'

'How you *owe* him?' Would it be rude to get up, wish him goodnight and go to bed?

Of course it'd be rude.

Not as rude as sashaying over to where he sat, planting herself in his lap, and kissing him.

She tried to close her mind to the pictures that exploded behind her eyelids. How many times did she have to tell herself that he was off limits?

'I haven't told another living soul about this and I suspect Rupert hasn't either.'

Her eyes sprang open. 'Okay. I'm listening.'

His eyes throbbed, but he stared at the wall behind her rather than at her directly. It made her chest clench. 'Finn?'

His nostrils flared. 'I went off the rails for a while when we were at school. I don't know if you know that or not.'

She shook her head.

'I was seventeen—full of hormones and angry at the world. I took to drinking and smoking and…and partying hard.'

With girls? She said nothing.

'I was caught breaking curfew twice…and one of those times I was drunk.'

She winced. 'That wouldn't have gone down well. Your boarding school was pretty strict.'

'With an excellent reputation to uphold. I was told in no uncertain terms that one more strike and I was out.'

She waited. 'So…? Rupert helped you clean up your act?'

'Audra, Audra, Audra.' His lips twisted into a mockery of a smile. 'You should know better than that.'

Her stomach started to churn, though she wasn't sure why. 'You kept pushing against the boundaries and testing the limits.'

He nodded.

'And were you caught?'

'Contraband was found in my possession.'

'What kind of contraband?'

'The type that should've had me automatically expelled.'

She opened her mouth and then closed it. It might be better not to know. 'But you weren't expelled.' Or had he been and somehow it'd all been kept a secret?

'No.'

The word dropped from him, heavy and dull, and all of the fine hairs on her arms lifted. 'How…?'

'Remember the Fallonfield Prize?'

She snorted. 'How could I not? Rupert was supposed to have been the third generation of Russel men to win that prize. I swear to God it was the gravest disappointment of both my father's and grandfather's lives when he didn't.'

Nobody had been able to understand it, because Rupert had been top of his class, and that, combined with his extra-curricular community service activities and demonstrated leadership skills…

Her throat suddenly felt dry. 'He was on track to win it.'

Finn nodded.

Audra couldn't look away. The Fallonfield Prize was a prestigious award that opened doors. It practically guaranteed the winner a place at their university of choice, and it included a year-long mentorship with a business leader and feted humanitarian. As a result of winning the prize, her grandfather had gone to Chile for a year. Her father had gone to South Africa, which was where he'd met Audra's mother, who'd been doing aid work there.

The Russel family's legacy of social justice and responsibility continued to this very day. Rupert had planned to go to Nicaragua.

'What happened?' she whispered, even though she could see the answer clear and plain for herself.

'Rupert took the blame. He said the stuff belonged to him, and that he'd stowed it among my things for safe-keeping—so his parents wouldn't see it when they'd come for a recent visit.'

She moistened her lips. 'He had to know it'd cost him the scholarship.'

Finn nodded. He'd turned pale in the telling of the story and her heart burned for him. He'd lost his father when he was far too young, and then he'd watched his mother die. Who could blame him for being angry?

But… 'I'm amazed you—' She snapped her mouth closed. *Shut up!*

His lips twisted. 'You're amazed I let him take the rap?'

She swallowed and didn't say a word.

'I wasn't going to. When I'd found out what he'd done I started for the head's office to set him straight.'

'What happened?'

'Your brother punched me.'

'Rupert…' Her jaw dropped. Rupert had punched Finn?

'We had a set-to like I've never had before or since.'

She wanted to close her eyes.

'We were both bloody and bruised by the end of it, and when I was finally in a state to listen he grabbed me by the throat and told me I couldn't disappoint my uncle or your parents by getting myself kicked out of school— that I owed it to everyone and that I'd be a hundred different kinds of a weasel if I let you all down. He told me I wasn't leaving him there to cope with the fallout on his own. He told me I wasn't abandoning him to a life of stolid respectability. And…'

'And?' she whispered.

'And I started to cry like a goddamn baby.'

Her heart thumped and her chest ached.

'I'd felt so alone until that moment, and Rupert hugged me and called me his brother.'

Audra tried to check the tears that burned her eyes.

'He gave me a second chance. And make no mistake, if he hadn't won me that second chance I'd probably be dead now.'

Even through the haze of her tears, the ferocity of his gaze pierced her.

'He made me feel a part of something—a family, a community—where what I did mattered. And that made me turn my life around, made me realise that what I did had an impact on the people around me, that it mattered to somebody…that what I did with my life mattered.'

'Of course it matters.' He just hadn't been able to see that then.

'So I let him take the rap for me, knowing what it would cost him.'

She nodded, swiped her fingers beneath her eyes. 'I'm glad he did what he did. I'm glad you let him do it.' She understood now how much he must feel he owed Rupert.

'So when Rupert asks me to…to take care with his little sister, I listen.'

She stilled. Her heart gave a sick thump.

'I promised him that I wouldn't mess with you and your emotions. And I mean to keep my word.'

She stiffened. Nobody—not Rupert, not Finn—had any right to make such decisions on her behalf.

His eyes flashed. 'You owe me a "truth or dare" question.'

She blinked, taken off guard by the snap and crackle of his voice, by the way his lips had thinned. 'Fine. Ask your question.'

'Knowing what you know now, would you choose to destroy my friendship with Rupert for a quick roll in the hay, Squirt?'

He knew he was being deliberately crude and deliberately brutal, but he had to create some serious distance between him and Audra before he did something he'd regret for the rest of his life.

She rose, as regal as a queen, her face cold and her eyes chips of ice. 'I'd never do anything to hurt your friendship with Rupert. Whether I'd heard that story or not.'

And yet they'd both been tempted to earlier.

'So, Finn, you don't need to worry your pretty little head over that any longer.'

He had to grind his teeth together at her deliberately patronising tone.

She spun away. 'I'm going to bed.'

She turned in the doorway. 'Also, the name is Audra— not Squirt. Strike Two.'

With that she swept from the room. Finn fell back into his chair and dragged both hands through his hair. He should never have kissed her. He hadn't known that a kiss could rock the very foundations of his world in the way his kiss with Audra had. Talk about pride coming before a fall. The gods punished hubris, didn't they? He'd really thought he could kiss her and remain unmarked... unmoved...untouched.

The idea seemed laughable now.

He'd wanted to fling her out of herself and force her to act on impulse. He hadn't known he'd lose control. He hadn't known that kiss would fling him out of himself... and then return him as a virtual stranger.

If it'd been any other woman, he'd have not been able to resist following that kiss through to its natural conclusion, the consequences be damned. His mouth dried. Whatever else they were, he knew those consequences would've been significant. Maybe he and Audra had dodged a bullet.

Or maybe they'd—

Maybe nothing! He didn't do long term. He didn't do family and babies. He did fun and adventure and he kept things uncomplicated and simple. Because that was the foundation his life had been built on. It was innate, in-born…intrinsic to who he was. There were some things in this world you couldn't change. Leopards couldn't change their spots and Finn Sullivan couldn't change his free-wheeling ways.

Finn heard Audra moving about in the kitchen the next morning, but he couldn't look up from the final pages of his book.

He read the final page…closed the cover.

Damn!

He stormed out into the kitchen and slammed the book to the counter. The split second after he'd done it, he winced and waited for her to jump out of her skin—waited for his stomach to curdle with self-loathing. He was such an idiot. He should've taken more care, but she simply looked at him, one eyebrow almost raised.

He nodded. 'Keep practising, it's almost there.'

She ignored that to glance at the book. 'Finished?'

He pointed at her and then slammed his finger to the book. 'That was a dirty, rotten, low-down trick. It's not finished!'

'My understanding is that particular story arc con-cludes.'

'Yeah, but I don't know if he gets his kingdom back. I don't know if she saves the world and defeats the bad guy. And…and I don't know if they end up together!'

Both her eyebrows rose.

'You…you tricked me!'

She leaned across and pointed. 'It says it's a trilogy here… And it says that it's Book One here. I wasn't keeping anything from you.'

Hot damn. So it did. He just… He hadn't paid any attention to the stuff on the cover. He rocked back on his heels, hands on hips. 'Didn't see that,' he murmured. 'And I really want to know how it ends.'

'And you feel cheated because you have to read another two books to find that out?'

Actually, the idea should appal him. But… 'I, uh…just guess I'm impatient to know how it all works out.'

'That's easily fixed. The bookshop in the village has the other two books in stock.'

He shoved his hands into his back pockets. 'Sorry, I shouldn't have gone off like that. Just didn't know what I was signing up for when I started the book.'

'God, Finn!' She took a plate of sliced fruit to the table and sat. 'That's taking commitment phobia to a whole new level.'

He indicated her plate. 'I'm supposed to do breakfast. That was part of the deal.'

'Part of the deal was calling me Audra too.'

She lifted a piece of melon to her lips. He tried to keep his face smooth, tried to keep his pulse under control as her mouth closed about the succulent fruit. 'So…what's on the agenda today?'

She ate another slice of melon before meeting his gaze. 'I want a Finn-free day.'

He fought the automatic urge to protest. An urge he knew was crazy because a day spent not in each other's company would probably be a wise move. 'Okay.'

'I bags the beach this morning.'

It took all his strength to stop from pointing out it was a long beach with room enough for both of them.

'Why don't you take the car and go buy your books, and then go do something you'd consider fun?'

Lying on a beach, swimming and reading a book, those things were fun. He rolled his shoulders. So were jetskiing and waterskiing and stuff. 'Okay.' He thrust out his jaw. 'Sounds great.'

She rose and rinsed her plate. 'And you'll have the house to yourself this evening.'

Her words jolted him up to his full height. 'Why?'

'Because I'm going into the village for a meal, and maybe some dancing. *Not* that it's any of your business.'

She wanted to go dancing? 'I'll take you out if that's what you want.'

'No, thank you, Finn.'

'But—'

Her eyes sparked. 'I don't want to go out to dinner or dancing with you.'

'Why not?' The words shot out of him and he immediately wished them back.

She folded her arms and peered down her nose at him. 'Do you really want me to answer that?'

He raised his hands and shook his head, but the anger in her eyes had his mind racing. 'You're annoyed with me. Because I kissed you?' Or because he wouldn't kiss her again?

Stop thinking about kissing her.

'Oh, I'm livid with you.'

He swallowed.

'And with Rupert.'

He stiffened. 'What's Rupert done? He's not even here.'

'And with myself.' She folded her arms, her expression more bewildered than angry now. 'You really don't see it, do you?'

See what?

'Between you, you and Rupert decided what was in my best interests. And—' the furrow in her brow deepened '—I let you. I went along with it instead of pointing out how patronising and controlling it was.' She lifted her chin. 'I'm a grown-up who has the right to make her own choices and decisions, be they wise or unwise. I'm not a child. I don't need looking after, and I do *not* have to consult with either of you if I want to kiss someone or… or start a relationship. And that's why I'm going into the village this evening on my own without an escort—to remind myself that I'm an adult.'

She swept up her beach bag and her sunhat and stalked out of the door.

I do not *have to consult…if I want to kiss someone…*

Was she planning on kissing someone tonight? But… but she couldn't.

Why not?

Scowling, he slammed the frying pan on a hot plate, turned it up to high before throwing in a couple of rashers of bacon. He cracked in two eggs as well. Oops—fine, he'd have scrambled eggs. He ground his teeth together. He *loved* scrambled eggs.

He gathered up the litter to throw into the bin, pushed open the lid…and then stilled. Setting the litter down on the counter again, he pulled out three A4 sheets of paper from the bottom of the bin, wiped off the fruit skins and let forth a very rude word. These were his designs for Audra's shop. He glared out of the glass sliding doors, but Audra had disappeared from view. 'That's not going to work, Princess.'

He pulled the frying pan from the heat, went to his room to grab his laptop and then strode into Rupert's office, heading straight for the printer.

He placed one set of printouts on the coffee table. The next set he placed on the tiny hall table outside her bedroom door. The third set he put in a kitchen drawer. The next time she reached for the plastic wrap, they'd greet her. The rest he kept in a pile in his bedroom to replace any of the ones she threw away.

* * *

'You're not taking the car?'

Audra didn't deign to answer him.

He glanced at his watch. 'Six thirty is a bit early for dinner, isn't it?'

She still didn't answer him. She simply peered at her reflection in the foyer mirror, and slicked on another coat of ruby-red lipstick. Utter perfection. She wore a sundress that made his mouth water too—the bodice hugged her curves, showing off a delectable expanse of golden skin at her shoulders and throat while the skirt fell in a floaty swirl of aqua and scarlet to swish about her calves. His heart pounded.

Don't think about messing up that lipstick.

He shoved his hands into his pockets. 'Why aren't you taking the car?'

She finally turned. 'Because I plan to have a couple of drinks. And I don't drink and drive.'

'But how will you get home?'

She raised an eyebrow.

He raised one back at her. 'You've almost got that down pat.'

She waved a hand in front of her face. 'Stop it, Finn.'

'What? It was a compliment and—'

'Stop it with the twenty questions. I know what time I want to eat. I know how to get home at the end of an evening out. Or—' she smiled, but it didn't reach eyes that flashed and sparked '—how to get home the morning after an evening out if that's the way the evening rocks.'

She…she might not be coming home? But—

And then she was gone in a swirl of perfume and red and aqua skirt as the village taxi pulled up in the driveway and tooted its horn.

Finn spent the evening pacing. Audra might be a grown woman, but she'd had fire in her eyes as she'd left. He knew she was angry with him and Rupert, but what if that anger led her to do something stupid…something she'd later regret? What the hell would he tell Rupert if something happened to her?

He lasted until nine p.m. Jumping in the car, it felt like a relief to finally be doing something, to be setting off after her. Not that he knew what he was going to do once he did find her.

She was in the first place he looked—Petra's Taverna. The music pouring from its open windows and doors was lively and cheerful. Tables spilled onto the courtyard outside and down to a tiny beach. Finn chose a table on the edge of the scene in the shadows of a cypress with an excellent view, via two enormous windows, inside the taverna.

Audra drew his eyes like a magnet. She sat on a stool framed in one of the windows and threw her head back at something her companion said, though Finn's view of her companion was blocked. She nodded and her companion came into view—a handsome young local—as they moved to the dance floor.

Beneath the table, Finn's hands clenched. When a waiter came he ordered a lemon squash. Someone had to keep their wits about them this evening! As the night wore on, Finn's scowl only grew and it deterred anyone who might've been tempted from coming across and trying to engage him in conversation.

And the more morose he grew, the merrier the tabloid inside became. As if those two things were related.

Audra was the life of the party. He lost track of the number of dance partners she had. She laughed and talked with just about every person in the taverna. She alternated glasses of white wine with big glasses of soda water. She snacked on olives and crisps and even played a hand of cards. She charmed everyone. And everything charmed her. He frowned. He'd not realised before how popular she was here in Kyanós. His frown deepened. It struck him that she was more alive here than he could ever remember seeing her.

And at a little after midnight, and after many pecks on cheeks were exchanged, she caught the taxi—presumably back to the villa—on her own.

He sat there feeling like an idiot. She'd had an evening out—had let her hair down and had some fun. She hadn't drunk too much. She hadn't flirted outrageously and hadn't needed to fight off inappropriate advances. She hadn't done anything foolish or reckless or ill-considered. She hadn't needed him to come to her rescue.

I'm a grown-up who has the right to make her own choices.

And what was he? Not just a fool, but some kind of creep—a sneak spying on a woman because he'd been feeling left out and unnecessary. And as far as Audra was concerned, he *was* unnecessary. *Completely* unnecessary. She didn't need him.

He could try to dress it up any way he liked—that he'd been worried about her, that he wanted to make sure she stayed safe—but what he'd done was spy on her and invade her privacy.

Why the hell had he done that? What right did he think he had?

Earlier she'd accused him and Rupert of being patronising and controlling, and she was right.

She deserved better from him. Much better.

CHAPTER NINE

WHEN AUDRA REACHED in the fridge for the milk for her morning coffee and found yet another set of printouts—in a plastic sleeve, no less, that would presumably protect them from moisture and condensation—it was all she could do not to scream.

She and Finn had spent the last three days avoiding each other. She'd tried telling herself that suited her just fine, but...

It *should* suit her just fine. She had the beach to herself in the mornings, while Finn took the car and presumably headed into the village. And then he had the beach in the afternoons while she commandeered the car. In terms of avoiding each other, it worked *perfectly*. It was just...

She blew out a breath. She wished avoidance tactics weren't necessary. She wished they could go back to laughing and having fun and teasing each other as they had before that stupid kiss.

And before she'd got all indignant about Rupert's overprotectiveness, and galled that Finn had unquestioningly fallen into line with it...and angry with herself for not having challenged it earlier. Where once her brother's protectiveness had made her feel cared for, now it left her feeling as if she was a family liability who needed safeguarding against her own foolishness.

Because of Thomas?

Or because if she could no longer hold tight to the label of being responsible and stable then...then what could she hold onto?

Stop it! Of course she was still responsible and stable. Thomas had been a mistake, and everyone was entitled to one mistake, right? Just as long as she didn't compound that by doing something stupid with Finn; just as long as she maintained a sense of responsibility and calm and balance, and remembered who *he* was and remembered who *she* was.

Sloshing milk into her coffee, she went to throw the printouts in the bin when her gaze snagged on some subtle changes to the pictures. Curiosity warred with self-denial. Curiosity won. Grabbing a croissant—Finn always made sure there was a fresh supply—she slipped outside to the picnic table to pore over the designs of this achingly and heart-wrenchingly beautiful shop.

Letting her hair down and doing things she wanted to do just for the sake of it—for fun—hadn't helped the burning in her soul whenever she was confronted with these pictures. They were snapshots of a life she could never have. And with each fresh reminder—and for some reason Finn seemed hell-bent on reminding her—that burn scorched itself into her deeper and deeper.

She bit into the croissant, she sipped coffee, but she tasted nothing.

Ever since Finn had kissed her she'd...*wanted*.

She'd *wanted* to kiss him again. She wanted *more*. She'd not known that a kiss could fill you with such a physical need. That it could make you crave so hard. She was twenty-seven years old. She'd thought she knew about attraction. She'd had good sex before. But that kiss had blown her preconceptions out of the stratosphere. And it had left her floundering. Because there was no way on God's green earth that she and Finn could go *there*. She didn't doubt that in the short term it'd be incredible, but ultimately it'd be destructive. She wasn't going to be responsible for that kind of pain—for wounding friendships and devastating family ties and connections.

She couldn't do that to Rupert.

She wouldn't do that to Finn.

But the kiss had left her wanting *more* from life too.

And she didn't know how to make that restlessness and sense of dissatisfaction go away.

So she'd tried a different strategy in the hope it would help. Instead of reining in all her emotions and desires, she'd let a few of them loose. Finn was right: if there was ever a time to rebel it was now when she was on holiday. She'd hoped a mini-rebellion would help her deal with her attraction for Finn. She'd hoped it would help her deal with the dreary thought of returning home to her job.

She'd gone dancing. It'd been fun.

She'd taken an art class and had learned about form and perspective. Her drawing had been terrible, but moving a pencil across paper had soothed her. The focus of next week's class was going to be composition. Her shoulders sagged. Except she wouldn't be here next week.

She'd even gone jetskiing again. It'd felt great to be zipping across the water. But no sooner had she returned the jetski than her restlessness had returned.

She pressed her hands to her face and then pulled them back through her hair. She'd hoped those things would help ease the ache in her soul, but they hadn't. They'd only fed it. It had been a mistake to come here.

And she wished to God Finn had never kissed her!

'Morning, Audra.'

As if her thoughts had conjured him, Finn appeared. His wide grin and the loose easy way he settled on the seat opposite with a bowl of cereal balanced in one hand inflamed her, though she couldn't have said why. She flicked the offending printouts towards him. 'Why are you leaving these all over the house?'

He ate a spoonful of cereal before gesturing to them. 'Do you like the changes I've made?'

'I—'

'Market research suggests that locating the point of sale over here provides for "a more comfortable retail experience"—' he made quotation marks in the air with one hand '—for the customer.'

She had to physically refrain from reaching across and shaking him. Drawing in a breath, she tried to channel responsible, calm balance. 'Why does any of this matter?'

'Because it needs to be perfect.'

Her chest clenched. Her eyes burned. Balance fled. 'Why?'

He shrugged and ate more cereal. 'Because that's what I do. I create designs as near perfect as possible.'

Didn't he know what these pictures and the constant reminders were doing to her?

He pulled the sheets from their plastic sleeve. 'What do you think about this shelving arrangement? It's neither better nor more functional than the ones you've already chosen, but apparently this design is all the range in Scandinavia at the moment, so I thought I'd throw it into the mix just to see what you thought?'

She couldn't help it; she had to look. The sleek lines were lovely, but these didn't fit in with the overall feel she was trying to achieve at all.

You're not trying to achieve an overall feel, remember? Pipe dream!

With a growl she slapped the picture facedown.

'No?' He raised one eyebrow—perfectly—which set her teeth even further on edge. 'Fair enough.'

'Enough already,' she countered through gritted teeth. 'Stop plastering these designs all over the house. I've had enough. I can see you do good work—excellent work. I'm sorry I misjudged you, but I believe I've already apologised. I'll apologise again if you need me to. But stop with the pictures. *Please.*'

He abandoned his breakfast to lean back and stare at her. She couldn't help wondering what he saw—a repressed woman he'd like to muss up?

It was what she wanted to believe. If it were true it'd

provide her with a form of protection. But it wasn't true. She knew that kiss had shaken him as much as it'd shaken her. It was why he'd avoided her for these last few days as assiduously as she had him.

'I'll stop with the pictures of the shop if you answer one question for me.'

'Oh, here we go again.' She glared. She didn't raise an eyebrow. She needed more practice before she tried that again. She folded her arms instead. 'Ask your question.'

He leaned towards her. The perfect shape of his mouth had a sigh rising up through her. 'Why are you working as an operations manager instead of opening up your dream shop here on this island and living a life that makes you happy?'

She flinched. His words were like an axe to her soul. How did he know? When Rupert, Cora and Justin had no idea? When she'd been so careful that none of them should know?

He held up the printouts and shook them at her. 'Your face when you described this shop, Audra… You came alive. It was…'

Her heart thumped so hard she could barely breathe.

'Magnificent,' he finally decided. 'And catching.'

She blinked. 'Catching…how?'

'Contagious! Your enthusiasm was contagious. I've not felt that enthusiastic about anything—'

He broke off with a frown. '—for a long time,' he finished. He stared at each of the three pictures. 'I want you to have this shop. I want you to have this life. I don't understand why you're punishing yourself.'

Her head reared back. 'I'm not punishing myself.'

'I'm sorry, Princess, but that's not what it looks like from where I'm sitting.'

'I do worthy work!' She shot to her feet, unable to sit for the agitation roiling through her. 'The work the Russel Corporation does is important.' She strode across to the bluff to stare out at the turquoise water spread below.

'I'm not disputing that.' His voice came from just behind her. 'But...so what?'

She spun to face him. 'How can you say that? Look at the amazing things Rupert, Cora and Justin are doing.'

His jaw dropped. 'This is about sibling rivalry? Come on, Audra, you're twenty-seven years old. I know you always wanted to keep up with the others when you were younger, but—' He scanned her face, rocked back on his heels. 'It's not about sibling rivalry.'

'No,' she said. It was about sibling loyalty. *Family* loyalty.

He remained silent, just...waiting.

She pressed her fingers to her temples for a moment before letting her arms drop back to her sides. 'When our mother died it felt like the end of the world.'

He reached out and closed his hand around hers and she suddenly felt less alone, less...diminished. She gripped his hand and stared doggedly out to sea. She couldn't look at him. If she looked at him she might cry. 'She was the lynchpin that kept all our worlds turning. The crazy thing was I never realised that until she was gone.' She hauled in a breath. 'And the work she did at the Russel Corporation was crucial.'

Karen Russel had been the administrator of the Russel Corporation's charity arm, and Audra's father had valued her in that role without reservation. Humanitarian endeavours formed a key component of the corporation's mission statement and it wasn't one he was comfortable trusting to anyone outside the family.

'But her influence was so much wider than that.' She blinked against the sting in her eyes. 'She worked out a strategy for Rupert to evolve into the role of CEO; she researched laboratories that would attract the most funding and would therefore provide Cora with the most promising opportunities. If she'd lived long enough she'd have found excellent funding for Justin's efforts in South-East Asia.' Justin was implementing a dental-health programme to the impoverished populations in Cambodia. He had ambitions to take his programme to all communities in need throughout South-East Asia.

She felt him turn towards her. 'Instead you found those funding opportunities for him. You should be proud of yourself.'

No sooner were the words out of his mouth than he stilled. She couldn't look at him. He swore softly. 'Audra—'

'When our mother died, I'd never seen the rest of my family so devastated.' She shook her hand free. 'I wanted to make things better for them. You should've seen my father's relief when I said I'd take over my mother's role in the corporation after I'd finished university. Justin floundered towards the end of his last year of study. He had exams coming up but started panicking about the licences and paperwork he needed to file to work in Cambodia, and finding contacts there. The laboratory Cora worked for wanted sponsorship from business and expected her to approach the family corporation. And Rupert... well, he missed the others so having me around to boss helped.'

She'd stepped into the breach because Karen was no longer there to do it. And someone had to. It'd broken her heart to see her siblings hurting so badly.

Finn had turned grey. He braced his hands on his knees, and she couldn't explain why, but she had to swallow the lump that did everything it could to lodge in her throat. 'You've been what they've all needed you to be.'

'I'm not a martyr, Finn. I *love* my family. I'm proud I've been able to help.' Helping them had helped her to heal. It'd given her a focus, when her world had felt as if it were spinning out of control.

He straightened, his eyes dark. 'She wouldn't want this for you.'

'You don't know that.' She lifted her chin. 'I think she'd be proud of me.'

He chewed on his bottom lip, his brows lowering over his eyes. 'Have you noticed how each of you have coped with your mother's death in different ways?'

She blinked.

'Rupert became super-protective of you all.'

Rupert had always been protective, but… She nodded. He'd become excessively so since their mother's death.

'Cora threw herself into study. She wanted to top every class she took.'

Cora had found solace in her science textbooks.

'Justin started living more in the moment.'

She hadn't thought about it in those terms, but she supposed he had.

One corner of Finn's mouth lifted. 'Which means he leaves things to the last minute and relies on his little sister to help make them right.'

Her lips lifted too.

'While you, Princess…' He sobered. 'You've tried to fill the hole your mother has left behind.'

She shook her head. 'Only the practical day-to-day stuff.' Nobody could fill the emotional hole she'd left behind.

'Your siblings have a genuine passion for what they do, though. They're following their dreams.'

And in a small way she'd been able to facilitate that. She didn't regret that for a moment.

'You won't be letting your mother down if you follow your own dreams and open a shop here on Kyanós.'

'That's not what it feels like.' She watched a seabird circle and then dive into the water below. 'If I leave the Russel Corporation it'll feel as if I'm betraying them all.'

'You'll be the only who feels that way.'

The certainty in his tone had her swinging to him.

He lifted his hands to his head, before dropping them back to his sides. 'Audra, they're all doing work they love!'

'Good!' She stared at his fists and then into his face. He was getting really het-up about this. 'I want them to love what they do.'

'Then why don't you extend yourself that same courtesy?'

He bellowed the words, and her mouth opened and closed but no sound came out. He made it sound so easy. But it wasn't! She loved being there for her brothers and sister. She loved that she could help them.

'How would you feel if you discovered Rupert or Cora or Justin were doing their jobs just to keep you feeling comfortable and emotionally secure?'

Oh, that'd be awful! It'd—

She took a step away from him, swallowed. Her every muscle scrunched up tight. That scenario, it wasn't synonymous with hers.

Why not?

She pressed her hands to her cheeks, trying to cool them. Her siblings were each brilliant in their own way— fiercely intelligent, politically savvy and driven. She wasn't. Her dreams were so ordinary in comparison, so lacking in ambition. A part of her had always been afraid that her family would think she wasn't measuring up to her potential.

Her heart started to pound. Had she been using her role in the family corporation as an excuse to hide behind? Stretching her own wings required taking risks, and those risks frightened her.

'I hate to say this, Princess, but when you get right down to brass tacks you're just a glorified administrator, a pen-pusher, and anyone can do the job that you do.'

* * *

'Why don't you tell me what you really think, Finn?'

The stricken expression in Audra's eyes pierced straight through the centre of him. He didn't want to hurt her. But telling her what he really thought was wiser than doing what he really wanted to do, which was kiss her.

He had to remind himself again of all the reasons kissing her was a bad idea.

He pulled in a breath. He didn't want to hurt her. He wanted to see her happy. He wanted to see her happy the way she'd been happy when describing her shop…when she'd been learning to ride a jetski…and when she'd been dancing. Did she truly think those things were frivolous and self-indulgent?

He tapped a fist against his lips as he stared out at the glorious view spread in front of them. The morning sun tinged everything gold, not so much as a breeze ruffled the air and it made the water look otherworldly still, and soft, like silk and mercury.

He pulled his hand back to his side. *Right*. 'It's my day.'

From the corner of his eye he saw her turn towards him. 'Pardon?'

'To choose our activities. It's my day.'

She folded her arms and stuck out a hip. She was going to tell him to go to blazes—that she was spending the day *on her own*. She opened her mouth, but he rushed on before she could speak. 'There's something I want to show you.'

She snapped her mouth shut, but her gaze slid over him as if it couldn't help it, and the way she swallowed and spun seawards again, her lips parted as if to draw much-needed air into her lungs, had his skin drawing tight. She was right. It'd be much wiser to continue to avoid each other.

But…

But he might never get this opportunity again. He

wanted to prove to her that she had a right to be happy, to urge her to take that chance.

'The yacht with the pink and blue sail is back.'

She pointed but he didn't bother looking. 'Please,' he said quietly.

She met his gaze, her eyes searching his, before she blew out a breath and shrugged. 'Okay. Fine.'

'Dress code is casual and comfortable. We're not hiking for miles or doing anything gruelling. I just… I've been exploring and I think I've found some things that will interest you.'

'Sunhat and sandals…?'

'Perfect. How soon can you be ready?'

One slim shoulder lifted. 'Half an hour.'

'Excellent.' He gathered up his breakfast things and headed back towards the house before he did something stupid like kiss her.

Their first port of call was Angelo's workshop. Angelo was a carpenter who lived on the far side of the village. He made and sold furniture from his renovated garage. Most of the pieces he made were too large for Audra's hypothetical shop—chest of drawers, tables and chairs, bedheads and bookcases—but there were some smaller items Finn knew she'd like, like the pretty trinket boxes and old-fashioned writing desks that were designed to sit on one's lap.

As he'd guessed, Audra was enchanted. She ran a finger along a pair of bookends. 'The workmanship is exquisite.'

Finn nodded. 'He says that each individual piece of wood that he works with tells him what it wants to be.'

'You've spoken to him?'

'Finn!' Angelo rushed into the garage. 'I thought that was your car out front. Come, you and Audra must have coffee with the family. Maria has just made *baklava*.'

'Angelo!' Audra gestured around the room. 'I didn't know you made such beautiful things.'

Finn stared at her. 'You know Angelo?'

'Of course! His brother Petros is Rupert's gardener. And Maria used to work in the bakery.'

They stayed an hour.

Next Finn took Audra to Anastasia's studio, which sat solitary on a windswept hill. He rolled his eyes. 'Now you're going to tell me you know Anastasia.'

She shook her head. 'I've not had that pleasure.'

Anastasia took Audra for a tour of her photography studio while Finn trailed along behind. If the expression on Audra's face was anything to go by, Anastasia's photographs transfixed her. They'd transfixed him too. It was all he could do to drag her back to the car when the tour was finished.

Then it was back into the village to visit Eleni's workshop, where she demonstrated how she made not only scented soap from products sourced locally, but a range of skincare and cosmetic products as well. Audra lifted a set of soaps in a tulle drawstring bag, the satin ribbon entwined with lavender and some other herbs Finn couldn't identify. 'These are packaged so prettily I can't resist.' She bought some candles too.

They visited a further two tradespeople—a leather worker who made wallets and purses, belts and ornately worked book jackets, and a jeweller. Audra came away with gifts for her entire family.

'Hungry?' he asked as he started the car. He'd walked this hill over the last three days, searching for distraction, but today, for the sake of efficiency, he'd driven.

'Starved.'

They headed back down the hill to the harbour, and ate a late lunch of *marida* and *spanakorizo* at a taverna that had become a favourite. They dined beneath a bougainvillea-covered pergola and watched as the water lapped onto the pebbled beach just a few metres away.

Audra broke the silence first. 'Anastasia's work should hang in galleries. It's amazing. Her photographs reveal a Greece so different from the tourist brochures.'

'She's seventy. She does everything the old way. She doesn't even have the internet.'

She nodded and sipped her wine, before setting her wine glass down with a click. 'I'd love for Isolde, one of my friends from school—she's an interior decorator and stager, furnishes houses and apartments so they look their absolute best for selling—to see some of Angelo's bigger pieces. She'd go into raptures over them.' She started to rise. 'We need to go back and take some photos so I can send her—'

'My *loukoumades* haven't come yet.' He waved her back to her seat. 'There's time. We can go back tomorrow.' He topped up her wine. 'What about Eleni's pretty smelly things? They'd look great in a shop.'

Audra shook her head and then nodded, as if holding a conversation with herself. 'I should put her in touch with Cora's old lab partner, Elise. Remember her? She moved into the cosmetic industry. Last I heard she was making a big push for eco-friendly products. I bet she'd love Eleni's recipes.'

She was still putting everyone else's needs before her own. The *loukoumades* came and a preoccupied Audra helped him eat them. While her attention was elsewhere, he couldn't help but feast his eyes on her. She'd put on a little weight over the last eleven days. She had colour in her cheeks and her eyes sparked with interest and vitality. An ache grew inside him until he could barely breathe.

He tried to shake it off. Under his breath he called himself every bad name he could think of. Did he really find the allure of the forbidden so hard to resist?

He clenched his jaw. He *would* resist. He'd cut off his

right hand rather than let Rupert down. He'd cut off his entire arm rather than ever hurt Audra.

But when she came alive like this, he couldn't look away.

She slapped her hands lightly to the table. 'I wonder how the villagers would feel about an annual festival.'

'What kind of festival?'

'One that showcases the local arts and crafts scene, plus all the fresh produce available here—the cured meats, the cheeses, the olive oils and…and…'

'The *loukoumades*?'

'Definitely the *loukoumades*!'

She laughed. She hadn't laughed, not with him, since he'd kissed her…and the loss of that earlier intimacy had been an ache in his soul.

The thought that he might be able to recapture their earlier ease made his heart beat faster.

'What?' she said, touching her face, and he realised he was staring.

He forced himself backwards in his seat. 'You're amazing, you know that?'

Her eyes widened. 'Me?'

'Absolutely. Can't you see how well you'd fit in here, and what a difference you could make? You've connections, energy and vision…passion.'

She visibly swallowed at that last word, and he had to force his gaze from the line of her throat. He couldn't let it linger there or he'd be lost.

Her face clouded over. 'I can't just walk away from the Russel Corporation.'

'Why not?' He paused and then nodded. 'Okay, you can't leave *just like that*.' He snapped his fingers. 'You'd have to hang around long enough to train up your replacement…or recruit a replacement.'

He could see her overdeveloped sense of duty begin to overshadow her excitement at the possibilities life held for her. He refused to let it win. 'Can you imagine how much your mother would've enjoyed the festival you just described?'

Her eyes filled.

'I remember how much she used to enjoy the local market days on Corfu, back when the family used to holiday there…when we were all children,' he said. Karen Russel had been driven and focussed, but she'd relished her downtime too.

'I know. I just…' Audra glanced skywards and blinked hard. 'I'd just want her to be proud of me.'

Something twisted in Finn's chest. Karen had died at a crucial stage in Audra's life—when Audra had been on the brink of adulthood. She'd been tentatively working her way towards a path that would give her life purpose and meaning, and searching for approval and support from the woman she'd looked up to. Her siblings had all had that encouragement and validation, but it'd been cruelly taken from Audra. No wonder she'd lost her way. 'Princess, I can't see how she could be anything else.'

Blue eyes, swimming with uncertainty and remembered grief, met his.

'Audra, you're kind and you work hard. You love your family and are there for them whenever they need you. She valued those things. And I think she'd thank you from the bottom of her heart for stepping into the breach when she was gone and doing all the things that needed doing.'

A single tear spilled onto her cheek, and he had to blink hard himself.

'The thing is,' he forced himself to continue, 'nobody needs you to do those things any more. And I'd lay everything on the bet that your mother would have loved the shop you described to me. Look at the way she lived her life—with passion and with zeal. She'd want you to do the same.'

Audra swiped her fingers beneath her eyes and pulled in a giant breath. 'Can…can we walk for a bit?'

They walked along the harbour and Audra hooked her arm through his. The accidental brushing of their bodies as they walked was a sweet torture that made him prickle and itch and want, but she'd done it without thinking or forethought—as if she needed to be somehow grounded while her mind galloped at a million miles an hour. So he left it there and didn't pull away, and fought against the growing need that pounded through him.

She eventually released him to sit on the low harbour wall, and he immediately wanted to drag her hand back into the crook of his arm and press his hand over it to keep it there.

'So,' she started. 'You're saying it wouldn't be selfish of me to move here and open my shop?'

'That's exactly what I'm saying. I know you can't see it, but you don't have a selfish bone in your body.'

Sceptical eyes lifted to meet his. 'You really don't think I'd be letting my family down if I did that?'

'Absolutely not. I think they'd be delighted for you.' He fell down beside her. 'But don't take my word for it. Ask them.'

She pondered his words and then frowned. 'Do you honestly think I could fit in and become a permanent part of the community here on Kyanós?'

He did, but… 'Don't you?' Because at the end of the day it wasn't about what he thought. It was what she thought and believed that mattered.

'I want to believe it,' she whispered, 'because I want so badly for it to be true. I'm afraid that's colouring my judgement.'

He remained silent.

'I don't have half the talents of the artisans we visited today.' She drummed her fingers against her thigh. 'But

I do have pretty good admin and organisational skills. I know how to run a business. I have my savings.'

She pressed her hands to her stomach. 'And it'd be so exciting to showcase local arts and crafts in my shop—nobody else is doing that so I'd not be going into competition with another business on the island. I'd be careful not to stock anything that was in direct competition with the bookshop or the clothing boutiques. And I could bring in some gorgeous bits and bobs that aren't available here.'

Her face started to glow. 'And if everyone else here thought it was a good idea, it'd be really fun to help organise a festival. All my friends would come. And maybe my family could take time off from their busy schedules.'

She leapt to her feet, paced up and down in front of him. 'I could do this.'

'You could. But the question is…'

She halted and leaned towards him. 'What's the question?'

He rested back on his hands. 'The question is, are you going to?'

Fire streaked through her eyes, making them sparkle more brilliantly than the water in the harbour. 'Uh-huh.' She thrust out her chin, and then a grin as wide as the sky itself spread across her face. And Finn felt as if he were scudding along on an air current, sailing through the sky on some euphoric cloud of warmth and possibility.

'I'm going to do it.'

She did a little dance on the spot. She grinned at him as if she didn't know what else to do. And then she leaned forward and, resting her hands on his shoulders, kissed him. Her lips touched his, just for a moment. It was a kiss of elation and excitement—a kiss of thanks, a kiss between friends. And it was pure and magical, and it shifted the axis of Finn's world.

She eased away, her lips parted, her breath coming fast and her eyes dazed, the shock in her face no doubt reflecting the shock in his. She snatched her hands away, smoothed them down the sides of her skirt and it was as if the moment had never been.

Except he had a feeling it was branded on his brain for all time. Such a small contact shouldn't leave such an indelible impression.

'Thank you, Finn.'

He shook himself. 'I didn't do anything.'

She raised an eyebrow and then shook her head and collapsed back down beside him on the sea wall. 'Don't say anything. I know it needs more practice. And you did do something—something big. You helped me see things differently. You gave me the nudge I needed and...' She turned and met his gaze, her smile full of excitement. 'I'm going to change my life. I'm going to turn it upside down. And I can't wait.'

Something strange and at odds like satisfaction and loss settled in the pit of his stomach, warring with each other for pre-eminence. He stoutly ignored it to grin back and clap his hands. 'Right! This calls for champagne.'

CHAPTER TEN

AUDRA WOKE EARLY, and the moment her eyes opened she found herself grinning. She drummed her heels against the mattress with a silent squeal as her mind sparked and shimmered with plans and purpose.

She threw on some clothes and her running shoes, before picking her way down to the beach and starting to run. *To run.*

Unlike the previous three mornings—when she and Finn had been avoiding each other—she didn't time herself. She ran because she had an excess of energy and it seemed a good idea to get rid of some of it. The decisions she was about to make would impact the rest of her life and, while joy and excitement might be driving her, she needed to make decisions based on sound business logic. She wanted this dream to last forever—not just until her money ran out and she'd bankrupted herself.

She reached the sheer wall of cliff at the beach's far end and leaned against it, bracing her hands on her knees, her breath coming hard and fast. Who'd have thought she could run all this way? She let out a whoop. Who knew running could feel so *freeing*?

She pulled off her shoes and socks and ambled back along the shoreline, relishing the wash of cool water against her toes as she made her way back towards the villa.

When she walked in, Finn glanced up from where he slouched against the breakfast bar, mug of coffee clasped in one hand. His eyes widened as they roved over her. He straightened. 'Have you been for a run?'

Heat mounted her cheeks. 'I, uh…'

One side of his mouth hooked up in that grin, and her

blood started to pound harder than when she'd been running. 'That's not a "truth or dare" question, Audra. A simple yes or no will suffice.'

She dropped her shoes to the floor and helped herself to coffee. 'You got me kind of curious when you wanted us to run that day.' He'd made her feel like a lazy slob, but she didn't say that out loud because she didn't want him to feel bad about that. Not after everything he'd done for her yesterday. 'Made me wonder if I *could* run the length of the beach.'

'I bet you rocked it in.'

His faith warmed her. 'Not *rocked* it in,' she confessed, planting herself at the table. 'But I did it. And it gets a bit easier every day.'

He moved to sit opposite. 'You've been for more than one run? How many?'

She rolled her shoulders. 'Only four.'

'And you don't hate it?'

'It's not like my new favourite thing or anything.' But she didn't *hate* it. Sometimes it felt good to be pounding along the sand. It made her feel…powerful. 'I like having done it. It makes me feel suitably virtuous.'

He laughed and pointed to a spot above her head. 'That's one very shiny halo.'

He leaned back and drained his coffee. 'Who'd have thought it? You find you don't hate running, and I find I don't hate lying on a beach reading a book.'

He hadn't seemed restless for any of his usual hard and fast sports. She opened her mouth to ask him about it, but closed it again. She didn't want to put ideas into his head.

He rose. 'I had a couple of new thoughts about some designs for your shop. Wanna see them after breakfast?'

That caught her attention. 'Yes, please!'

An hour later she sat at the outdoor picnic table with Finn, soaking up the sun, the views and the incredible designs he kept creating. 'These are amazing.' She pulled his laptop closer towards her. 'You've gone into so much detail.'

'You gave me good material to work with.'

She flicked through the images he'd created, loving everything that she saw. 'You said—that first day when you showed me what you did—that the first step was the "dreaming big with no holds barred" step.'

He nodded.

She pulled in a breath. 'What's the next step?'

'Ah.' His lips twisted. 'The next step consists of the far less sexy concept of compromise.'

'Compromise?'

He pointed towards his computer. 'These are the dream, but what are the exact physical dimensions of your shop going to be? We won't know that until you find premises and either buy them or sign a lease. So these designs would have to be modified to fit in with that.'

Right.

'You'll also need to take into account any building works that may need doing on these new premises. And if so, what kind of council approvals you might need. Does the building have any covenants in place prohibiting certain work?'

Okay.

'What's your budget for kitting out your shop? See this shelving system here? It costs twice as much as that one. Is it worth twice as much to you? If it's not, which other shelving system do you settle on?'

'So…fitting the dream to the reality?'

'Exactly. Deciding on the nitty-gritty detail.'

He swung the computer back his way, his fingers flying across the keyboard, his brow furrowed in concentration and his lips pursed. As she stared at him something inside Audra's chest cracked open and she felt herself falling and falling and falling. Not 'scream and grab onto something' falling, but flying falling.

Like anything was possible falling.

Like falling in love falling.

Her heart stopped. The air in front of her eyes shimmered. Finn? She'd…she'd fallen in love with Finn? Her heart gave a giant kick and started beating in triple time. She swallowed. No, no, that was nonsense. She wasn't stupid enough to fall for Finn. He didn't do serious. He treated women as toys. He was a playboy!

And yet… He *did* do serious because they'd had several very serious discussions while they'd been here. She'd discovered depths to him she'd never known. He wasn't just an adrenaline junkie, but a talented designer and canny businessman. The playboy thing… Well, he hadn't been out carousing every night. And he hadn't treated her like a toy. Even when she'd wanted him to. So it was more than possible that she had him pegged all wrong about that too.

In the next moment she shook her head. Rupert had warned her against Finn, and Rupert would know.

But…

She didn't want to kill the hope trickling through her. Was it really so stupid?

'Okay, here's a budget version of your shop.'

Finn turned the laptop back towards her. She forced herself to focus on his designs rather than the chaos of her mind. And immediately lost herself in the world he'd created.

'What do you think?'

'This is still beautiful.'

He grinned and her heart kicked against the walls of her chest. She brushed her fingers across the picture of the barrel of flowers standing by the front door. 'You have such a talent for this. Don't you miss it when you're off adventuring?'

Very slowly he reached across and closed the lid of his laptop. 'That's a "truth or dare" question, Audra. And the answer is yes.'

Her heart stuttered. So did her breath.

'I've been fighting it. Not wanting to acknowledge it.'

'Why not?'

'Because I want to be more than a boring, driven businessman.'

'That's not boring!' She pointed to his computer. 'That…it shows what an artist you are.'

Hooded eyes met hers. 'I lead this exciting life—living the dream. It should be enough.'

But she could see that it wasn't. 'Dreams can change,' she whispered.

He stared down at his hands. 'I've had a lot of time to think over the last fortnight…and our discussions have made me realise a few things.'

Her mouth went dry. In a part of her that she refused to acknowledge, she wanted him to tell her that he loved her and wanted to build a life and family with her. 'Like?' she whispered.

'Like how much the way I live my life has to do with my parents.'

'In what way?' She held her breath and waited to see if he would answer.

He shrugged, but she sensed the emotion beneath the casual gesture. 'I hated not having a home base when I was growing up. I hated the way we were constantly on the move. I hated that I didn't have any friends my own age. But when my parents died…' He dragged a hand down his face. 'I'd have done anything to have them back. But at the same time—' the breath he drew in was ragged '—I didn't want to give up the life Uncle Ned had created for me. I liked that life a hundred times better.'

Her heart squeezed at the darkness swirling in his eyes—the remembered grief and pain, the confusion and strange sense of relief. She understood how all those things could bewilder and baffle a person, making it impossible to see things clearly.

'And that made me feel guilty. So I've tried to mould my life on a balance between the kind of life they lived and the kind of life Ned lived. I wanted to make them all proud. Similar to the way you wanted to make your mother proud, I guess. I thought I could have the best of both worlds and be happy.'

'But you're not happy.'

He wanted it to be enough. She could see that. But the simple fact was it wasn't. And him wishing otherwise wouldn't change that fact.

She swallowed. 'Have you ever loved a song so much that you played it over and over and over, but eventually you play it too much and you wreck it somehow? And then you don't want to listen to it any more, and when you do unexpectedly hear it somewhere it doesn't give you the same thrill it once did?'

Hooded eyes lifted. 'I know what you mean.'

'Well, maybe that's what you've done with all of your adrenaline-junkie sports. Maybe you're all adrenalined out and now you need to find a new song that sings to your soul.'

He stared at her, scepticism alive in his eyes. 'This is more than that. This is the entire way I live my life. Walking away from it feels as if I'm criticising the choices my parents made.'

'I don't see it as a criticism. You're just…just forging your own path.'

He shrugged, but the darkness in his eyes belied the casual gesture. 'The thing is I can no longer hide from the fact that racing down a black ski run no longer gives me the thrill it once did, or that performing endless laps in a sports car is anything other than monotonous, and that trekking to base camp at Everest is just damned cold and uncomfortable.'

But she could see it left him feeling like a bad person—an ingrate.

He speared her with a glance. 'I can't hassle and lecture you about living your dreams and then hide from it when it applies to my own life. That'd make me a hypocrite on top of everything else.'

Her heart burned. She wanted to help him the way he'd helped her—give him the same clarity. 'How old was your father when he died?'

'Thirty-five.'

'So only a couple of years older than you are now?' She gave what she hoped was an expressive shrug. 'Who knows what he might've chosen to do if he'd lived longer?'

'Give up extreme sports, my father?' Finn snorted. 'You can't be serious.'

'Is it any crazier than me opening a shop?'

He smiled. 'That's not crazy. It's what you have a passion for. It's *exciting*.'

Her heart chugged with so much love she had to lower her gaze in case he saw it shining there. 'We can never know what the future might've held for your father, but he could've had a mid-life crisis and decided to go back to Australia and...and start a hobby farm.'

A bark of laughter shot out of him.

'I know a lot of people have criticised the way your parents lived, wrote them off as irresponsible and frivolous.' And she guessed she was one of them. 'But they didn't hurt anyone living like they did; they paid their bills. They were...free spirits. And free spirits, Finn, would tell you to follow your heart and do the things that make you happy. And to not care what other people think.'

His head snapped up.

'If they were true free spirits they'd include themselves amongst those whose opinions didn't matter.'

She watched his mind race. 'What are you going to do?' she asked when she couldn't hold the question back any longer.

He shook his head. 'I've no idea.'

She swallowed. He needed time to work it out.

When his gaze returned to hers, though, it was full of warmth and…and something she couldn't quite define. Affection…laughter…wonder? 'It's been a hell of a holiday, Audra.'

Her name sounded like gold on his tongue. All she could do was nod.

A warm breeze ruffled her hair, loose tendrils tickling her cheek. She pulled it back into a tighter ponytail, trying to gather up all the loose strands. For some reason her actions made Finn smile. 'I'm going to get it cut,' she announced, not realising her intention until the words had left her.

His eyebrows shot up.

'Short. *Really* short. A pixie cut, perhaps. I hate it dangling about my face. I always have.'

'So how come you haven't cut it before now?'

She had no idea. 'Just stuck in the old ways of doing things, I guess. Walking a line I thought I should and presenting the image I thought I should, and not deviating from it. But now…'

'Now?'

'Now anything seems possible.' Even her and Finn didn't seem outside the realms of possibility. He cared for her, she knew that much. And look at everything they'd shared this last fortnight. Look how much he'd done for her. Look how much of an impact they'd had on each other. It had to mean something, right?

'I'm going to ask Anna in the village if she'll cut it for me.'

'When?'

'Maybe…maybe this afternoon.' If she could get an appointment.

He stared at her for a long moment and she had to fight the urge to fidget. 'What?'

'I did something.'

There was something in his tone—something uncertain, and a little defiant, and…a bit embarrassed, maybe? She didn't know what it meant. 'What did you do?'

He scratched a hand through his hair, his gaze skidding away. 'It might be best if I simply show you.'

'Okay. Now?'

He nodded.

'Where are we going? What's the dress code?'

'Into the village.' His gaze wandered over her and it left her burning and achy, prickly and full of need. 'And what you're wearing is just fine.'

They stopped at the hairdresser's first, because Finn insisted. When Anna said she could cut Audra's hair immediately Finn accepted the appointment on her behalf before she could say anything. Audra surveyed him, bemused and not a little curious.

'It'll give me some time to get set up properly,' he explained when he caught her stare.

She shook her head. 'I've no idea what you're talking about.'

'I know.' He leaned forward and pressed a kiss to her brow. 'All will be revealed soon. I'll be back in an hour.'

He was gone before the fresh, heady scent of him had invaded her senses, before she could grab him by the collar of his shirt and kiss him properly. Dear God, what did she do with her feelings for him? She had no idea! Should she try to bury them…or did she dare hope that, given time, he could return them?

Don't do anything rash.

She swallowed and nodded. She couldn't afford to make another mistake. She and Thomas had only broken up six weeks ago. This could be a rebound thing. Except… She'd not been in love with Thomas. She'd wanted to be, but she could see now it'd been nothing but a pale imitation—a combination of loneliness and feeling flattered by his attentions. She pressed her hands to her stomach as it started to churn.

Don't forget Rupert warned you against falling in love with Finn.

Yeah, but Rupert was overprotective and—

'Audra, would you like to take a seat?'

Audra shook herself, and tried to quiet her mind as she gave herself over to Anna's ministrations.

As promised, Finn returned an hour later. Audra's hair had been cut, shampooed and blow-dried and it felt…*wonderful*! She loved what Anna had done—short at the back and sides but still thick and tousled on top. She ran her fingers through it, and the excitement she'd woken with this morning vibrated through her again now.

She and Anna were sharing a cup of tea and gossip when Finn returned, and the way his eyes widened when he saw her, the light that flared in his eyes, and the low whistle that left his lips, did the strangest things to her insides.

'It looks…' He gestured. 'I mean, you look…' He swallowed. 'It's great. You look great.'

Something inside her started to soar. He wanted her. He tried to hide it, but he wanted her in the same way she wanted him. It wasn't enough. But it was something, right? She could build on that, and… Her heart dipped. Except their holiday was almost over and there was so little time left—

He frowned. 'You're not regretting it, are you?'

She tried to clear her face. 'No! I love it.' She touched a self-conscious hand to her new do. 'It feels so liberating.' She did what she could to put her disturbing thoughts from her mind. 'Now put me out of my misery and show me whatever it is you've done. I'm dying here, Finn!'

'Come on, then.' He grinned and took her arm, but

dropped it the moment they were outside. She knew why—because the pull between them was so intense.

What if she were to seduce him? Maybe…

That could be a really bad idea.

Or an inspired one.

Her heart picked up speed. She had to force herself to focus on where they were going.

Finn led her along the village's main street. She made herself glance into the windows of the fashion boutiques with their colourful displays, dragged in an appreciative breath as they passed the bakery that sold those decadent croissants. She slowed when they reached the bookshop, but with a low laugh Finn urged her past it.

At the end of the row stood the beautiful whitewashed building with freshly painted shutters the colour of a blue summer day that had silently sat at the centre of herÁ dreams. The moment she'd seen the For Sale sign when she'd clambered off the ferry a fortnight ago, she'd wanted to buy it. Her heart pounded. This place was…*perfect*.

'I remember you saying there was a place for sale in the village that would be the ideal location for your shop, and I guessed this was the place you meant.'

She spun to him, her eyes wide.

'So I asked around and found it belongs to the Veros family.'

'The Veros family who own the deli?'

'One and the same. I asked if we could have a look inside.' He brandished a key. 'And they said yes.'

Excitement gathered beneath her breastbone until she thought she might burst.

'Shall we?'

'Yes, please!'

He unlocked the door. 'Do you want the shutters open?' He gestured to the shutters at the front window. She could barely speak so she simply nodded. She wanted to see the interior bathed in the blues and golds of the late morning light. 'You go on ahead, then, while I open them.'

Pressing one hand to her chest, she reached out with the other to push the door open. Her heart beat hard against her palm. Could this be the place where she could make her dreams come true? Was this the place where she could start the rest of her life? She tried to rein in her excitement. This was the next step—making the dream fit the reality. She needed to keep her feet on the ground.

Inside it was dim and shadowy. She closed her eyes and made a wish, and when she opened her eyes again, light burst through the spotlessly clear front window as Finn flung the shutters back. Her heart stuttered. The world tilted on its axis. She had to reach out and brace herself against a wall to stop from falling.

Her heart soared...stopped...pounded.

She couldn't make sense of what she was seeing, but in front of her the designs Finn had created for her shop had taken shape and form in this magical place. She squished her eyes shut, but when she opened them again nothing had changed.

She spun around to find Finn wrestling a tub of colourful flowers into place just outside the front door. Her eyes filled. He'd done all of this for her?

He came inside then and grinned, but she saw the uncertainty behind the smile. 'What do you think?'

'I think this is amazing! How on earth did you manage to do this in such a short space of time?'

One shoulder lifted. 'I asked Angelo to whip up a couple of simple display arrangements—don't look too closely because they're not finished.'

'But...but there's stock on the shelves!'

'I borrowed some bits and pieces from Angelo, Eleni, Kostas and Christina. They were more than happy to help me out when I told them what it was for. You're very well thought of in these parts. They consider you one of their own, you know?'

It was how she'd always felt here.

'So you'll see it gets a little more rough and ready the further inside we go.'

He took her arm and led her deeper into the shop and she saw that he'd tacked pictures of all the things she meant to sell on temporary shelves. It brought her dream to magical life, however—helped her see how it could all look in reality. The layout and design, the colours and the light flooding in, the view of the harbour, it was all so very, *very* perfect. 'I love it.'

'Wait until you see upstairs.' Reaching for her hand, he towed her to the back of the shop. 'There's a kitchenette and bathroom through here and storeroom there.' He swung a door open and clicked on the light, barely giving her time to glance inside before leading her up a narrow set of stairs to a lovely apartment with a cosy living room, compact but adequate kitchen, and two bedrooms. The living room and the master bedroom, which was tucked beneath the eaves on the third floor, had exceptional views of the harbour. It was all *utterly* perfect.

'I can't believe you did this!'

'So you like it?'

'I couldn't love it any better.'

His grin was full of delight and…affection.

Her mind raced. He was attracted to her, and he cared for her. He'd done all of this for her. It had to *mean* something.

'I made enquiries and the price they're asking seems reasonable.'

He named a price that made her gulp, but was within her means. She pulled in a breath. 'I'm going to get a building inspection done and…and then put in an offer.'

He spun back to her. 'You mean it?'

She nodded. She wanted to throw herself at him and hug him. But if she did that it'd make his guard go back up. And before that happened she needed to work through the mass of confusion and turbulence racing through her mind.

She followed him back down the stairs silently. His gaze narrowed when they reached the ground floor. 'Is everything okay?'

'My mind is racing at a hundred miles a minute. I'm feeling a little overwhelmed.'

His eyes gentled. 'That's understandable.'

She gestured around. 'Why did you do this for me, Finn? I'm not complaining. I love it. But…it must've taken a lot of effort on your part.'

'I just want you to have your dream, Princess. You deserve it.'

She stared at him, wishing she could read his mind. 'You've spent a lot of time thinking about my future, and I'm grateful. But don't you think you should've been spending that time focussing on some new directions for yourself?'

His gaze dropped. He straightened a nearby shelf, wiped dust from another. 'I've been giving some thought to that too.'

The admission made her blink. He had?

'Kyanós, it seems, encourages soul-searching.' He shoved his hands into the back pockets of his cargo shorts and eyed her for a long moment. 'I've been toying with a plan. I don't know. It could be a stupid idea.' He pulled his hands free, his fingers opening and closing at his sides. 'Do you want to see?'

Fear and hope warred in her chest. All she could do was nod.

'Come on, then. We'll return the key and then I'll show you.'

The car bounced along an unsealed road that was little more than a gravel track. Audra glanced at the forest of olive and pine trees that lined both sides. She'd thought he'd meant to take them back to the villa. 'I've not been on this road before.'

'I've spent some time exploring the island's hidden places these last few days.'

Along with exploring all the ways she could make her dream a reality. He'd been busy.

'It brings us out on the bluff at the other end of the beach from Rupert's place.'

The view when they emerged into a clearing five minutes later stole her breath. Finn parked and cut the engine. She pushed out of the car and just stared.

He shoved his hands into his pockets, keeping the car between them. 'It's a pretty amazing view.'

Understatement much? 'I'm not sure I've ever seen a more spectacular view. This is...*amazing*.' Water surrounded the headland on three sides. From this height she could only make out a tiny strip of beach to her left and then Rupert's villa gleaming in amongst its pines in the distance.

Directly out in front was the Aegean reflecting the most glorious shade of blue that beguiled like a siren's call, the horizon tinted a fiery gold, the outlines of other islands in the distance adding depth and interest. It'd be a spectacular sight when the sun set.

To her right the land fell in gentle undulations, golden grasses rippling down to a small but perfectly formed beach. A third of the way down was a collection of run-down outbuildings.

'This plot—thirty acres in total—is for sale.' He pointed to the outbuildings. 'The farmer who owns it used those to store olives from his groves...and goats, among other things apparently. They haven't been used for almost fifteen years. The moment I clapped eyes on them I knew exactly how to go about transforming them into an amazing house.'

It was the perfect site for a home—sheltered and sunny, and with that beautiful view. Audra swallowed. 'That sounds lovely.'

'I even came up with a name for the house—the Villa Óneira.'

Óneira was the Greek word for dreams. The House of Dreams. He...he wanted to live here on Kyanós? Her heart leapt. *That* had to mean something.

She tried to keep her voice casual. 'What would you do with the rest of the plot?' Because no matter how hard she tried, she couldn't see Finn as an olive farmer or a goat herder.

He gestured to the crest of the headland. 'Do you remember once asking me what activities I couldn't live without?'

She'd been thinking of the rally-car racing, the rock climbing, the skydiving. 'What's the answer?'

'Hang-gliding.'

She blinked. 'Hang-gliding?'

'It's the best feeling in the world. Sailing above it all on air currents—weightless, free...exhilarating.'

Her heart burned as she stared at him. He looked so *alive*.

'That was a great question to ask, Audra, because it made me think hard about my life.'

It had?

'And when I stumbled upon this plot of land and saw that headland, I knew what I could do here.'

She found it suddenly hard to breathe.

'I've been fighting it and telling myself it's a stupid pipe dream.' He swung to her, his face more animated than she'd ever seen it. 'But after our talk this morning, maybe it's not so daft after all.'

'What do you want to do?'

'I want to open a hang-gliding school. I'm a fully qualified instructor.'

He was?

'And I've had a lot of experience.'

He had?

'The school would only run in the summer.' He shrugged. 'For the rest of the time I'd like to focus on the work I do for Aspiration Designs. But I want to work off the grid.' He flung out an arm. 'And here seems as good a place to do it as any. Kyanós has a great community vibe, and I'd love to become a part of it.'

He stopped then as if embarrassed, shoved his hands in his pockets and scuffed a tussock of grass with the toe of his sneaker.

She stared at him. His dream... It was lovely. Beautiful. 'Your plan sounds glorious, Finn.'

He glanced up. 'But?'

She shook her head. 'No buts. It's just... I remember you saying island life wouldn't suit you.'

'I was wrong. Being on a permanent holiday wouldn't suit me. But being in an office all day wouldn't suit me either. I'd want to leave the day-to-day running of Aspirations to my partners—they're better at that than me. Design is my forte. But the thought of sharing my love of hang-gliding with others and teaching them how to do it safely in this amazing place answers a different need.'

'Wow.' She couldn't contain a grin. 'Looks like we're going to be neighbours.'

He grinned back and it nearly dazzled her. 'Looks like it. Who'd have thought?'

This had to mean something—something big! Even if he wasn't aware of it yet.

He tossed the car keys in the air and caught them. 'Hungry?'

'Starved.'

CHAPTER ELEVEN

'LOOKS LIKE YOUR sailboat is coming in again, Audra.'

They were eating a late lunch of crusty bread, cheese and olives, and Audra's mind was buzzing with Finn's plans for the future. If they were both going to be living on Kyanós, then…

Her heart pounded. It was possible that things could happen. Romantic things. She knew he hadn't considered settling down, falling in love—marrying and babies. Not yet. But who knew how that might change once he settled into a new life here? Given time, who knew what he might choose to do?

She tried to control the racing of her pulse. She had no intention of rushing him. *She* was in no rush. She meant to enjoy their friendship, and to relish the changes she was making in her life. And—she swallowed—they would wait and see what happened.

He'd risen to survey the beach below. She moved to stand beside him, and was greeted with the now familiar pink and blue sail. 'It looks like they're coming ashore.'

Heat burned her cheeks when she recalled her earlier musings about the honeymooners who might be on board. She hoped they weren't planning to have hot sex on her beach. Not that it was *hers* per se, but… She turned her back on the view, careful not to look at Finn. 'Do you want any more of these olives or cheese?'

He swung back and planted himself at the table again. 'Don't take the olives! They're the best I've ever eaten.'

She tried to laugh, rather than sigh, at the way he savoured one.

He helped himself to another slice of a Greek hard

cheese called *kefalotiri*. 'Whose turn is it to choose the activities for the day?'

She helped herself to a tiny bunch of grapes. 'I've no idea.' She'd lost count. Besides, the day was half over.

'Then I vote that a long lazy lunch is the order of the day.'

She laughed for real this time. 'It's already been long and lazy.'

'We could make it longer and lazier.'

Sounded good to her.

'We could open a bottle of wine…grab our books…'

Okay, it sounded perfect. 'Count me in.'

'We could head down to the beach if you want…'

She shook her head. 'Let the visitors enjoy it in privacy. I'm stuffed too full of good food to swim.'

He grinned. 'I'll grab the wine.'

'I'll grab our books.'

But before either of them could move, the sound of voices and crackling undergrowth had them looking towards the track. Audra blinked when Rupert, accompanied by a woman she didn't know, emerged.

A smile swept through her—he should've let them know he was coming! Before she could leap up, however, Finn's low, savage curse had her senses immediately going on high alert. She glanced at him, and her stomach nosedived at the expression on his face.

Finn rose.

Rupert and the woman halted when they saw him. The air grew thick with a tension Audra didn't understand. Nobody spoke.

She forced herself to stand too. 'What's going on, Finn?'

He glanced down at her and she recognised regret and guilt swirling in his eyes, and something else she couldn't decipher. 'I really should've told you about that woman in Nice I'd been trying to avoid. I'm sorry, Princess.'

Audra stared at the woman standing beside Rupert— a tall, leggy brunette whose eyes were hidden behind a large pair of sunglasses—and her mouth went dry. That gorgeous woman was Finn's latest girlfriend? Her stomach shrivelled to the size of a small hard pebble. *Why* had Rupert brought her to the island? She recalled his warnings about Finn and closed her eyes.

'Trust me!'

Her eyes flew open at Finn's words. She wasn't sure if they were a command or a plea.

His eyes burned into hers. 'I promise I will not allow anything she does to hurt you.'

What on earth…?

'You're going to make damn sure of it,' Rupert snarled, striding forwards. He kissed her cheek with a clipped, 'Squirt.' But the glare he shot Finn filled her stomach with foreboding. And it turned Finn grey. 'Audra, this is Trixie McGraw.'

The woman held out her hand. Audra shook it. Trixie? She *hated* that name. It took all her strength to stop her lips from twisting.

'What Rupert has left out of his introduction,' Finn drawled, 'is that Ms McGraw here is an investigative journalist. *Not* an ex-girlfriend, *not* an ex-lover.'

She wasn't…

She was a journalist!

Audra swung to Rupert, aghast. 'You've brought the press to the island?'

Rupert opened his mouth, but Finn cut in. 'She's not here for you, Audra. She wants to interview me.'

'Why?'

If possible, Finn turned even greyer and she wanted to take his hand and offer him whatever silent support she could, but Rupert watched them both with such intensity she didn't want to do anything he could misinterpret. She didn't want to do anything that would damage their friendship.

'My recent accident—the ski-jump disaster—it happened on a resort owned by a friend, Joachim Firrelli. Trixie here was Joachim's girlfriend before they had an ugly bust-up. She's now trying to prove that his facilities are substandard—that he's to blame for my accident. Except I'm not interested in being a pawn in her little game of revenge.'

'It doesn't sound *little* to me. It sounds bitter and a lot twisted.'

Trixie didn't bat so much as an eyelid. Rupert's mouth tightened.

'As I've repeatedly told Ms McGraw, the accident was nobody's fault but my own. I lost concentration. End of story. And I'm not going to let a friend of mine pay the price for my own recklessness.'

His guilt made sudden and sickening sense. He felt guilty that his actions could cause trouble for his friend. And he felt guilty that he'd unwittingly attracted a member of the press to the island when she was doing all that she could to avoid them. *Oh, Finn.*

Finn had crossed his arms and his mouth was set. Her heart pounded, torn between two competing impulses. One was the nausea-inducing reminder that Finn wasn't the kind of man to settle down with just one woman and that to love him would leave her with nothing but a broken heart.

The other…well, it continued to hope. After all, he'd wasted no time in telling her who this Trixie McGraw was, and what she wanted from him. He hadn't wanted her to think this woman was a girlfriend or lover, and that had to mean something, right?

She glared at Rupert. 'Why on earth…? Did you *know* this woman was on a witch hunt?'

Rupert's hands fisted. He turned to Trixie. 'Is what Finn said true?'

One shoulder lifted. 'Pretty much. Except for the "witch hunt" part.'

The woman had the most beautiful speaking voice Audra had ever heard.

'Your sister seems to think I'm motivated by revenge, though I can assure you that is not the case. I believe it's in the public interest to know when the safety standards on a prominent ski resort have deteriorated.'

It was all Audra could do not to snort. 'I can't believe you've brought the media to the island.' Not when he'd done everything he could to protect her from the attention of the press before she'd arrived here.

'I didn't *bring* her. She was already here. I received an email from her yesterday. That's why I'm here now. I left Geneva this morning. I'm not this woman's friend.'

She took a moment to digest that.

So... None of them wanted to talk to this woman?

The press had made her life hell back in Geneva. She wasn't going to let that happen again here on the island. She wasn't going to let them turn Finn and his friend Joachim into their next victims either. She folded her arms. 'Rupert, you have a choice to make.'

He blinked. 'What choice?'

She met his gaze. It was sombre and focussed. 'This is your house. You can invite whomever you want. But you either choose me or you choose her, because one of us has to leave. And if you do choose her, there will be repercussions. There won't be any family dinners in the foreseeable future, and you can kiss a family Christmas goodbye.'

Rupert's nostrils flared.

'Audra,' Finn started, but she waved him quiet.

'I don't trust her, Rupe, but I do trust Finn.' Something in Rupert's eyes darkened and it made her blink. *Wow.* He didn't? When had that happened? She swallowed. 'And you trust me, so—'

'Forgive me, Ms Russel,' the beautiful voice inserted. 'I understand your current aversion to the press given the circus surrounding your relationship with Thomas Farquhar but I'm not here to discuss that. Your privacy is assured.'

Maybe, but Finn's wasn't. She ignored her. 'I want her off this property. Choose, Rupert.'

'It's no competition, Squirt. You'd win in a heartbeat. But I need your help with something first. We won't go inside the house, I promise. But bear with me here. This will take ten minutes. Less. If you still want Trixie to leave after that, I'll escort her off the premises.'

It didn't seem too much to ask. And in the face of Rupert's sheer reasonableness she found her outrage diminishing. 'Ten minutes.' She pulled out her phone and set a timer.

Rupert motioned to Trixie and she pulled a large A4 manila envelope from her backpack and placed it on the table. Rupert gestured for her and Finn to take a look at the contents. His glance, when it clashed with Finn's, was full of barely contained violence that made Finn's gaze narrow and his shoulders stiffen. Wasting no further time, she reached inside the envelope and pulled out…photographs.

She inhaled sharply, and her heart plummeted. Pictures of her and Finn.

The first captured the moment yesterday when she'd leant forward and in the excitement of the moment had kissed Finn. The next showed the moment after when they'd stared at each other—yearning and heat palpable in both their faces. She could feel the heat of need rising through her again now. She flipped to the next one. It was of her and Finn drinking champagne in a harbourside tavern afterwards. They were both smiling and laughing. And she couldn't help it, her lips curved upwards again now. This dreadful woman had captured one of the happiest moments of Audra's life.

'This is what you do?' she asked the other woman. 'You spy on people?'

Trixie, probably wisely, remained silent.

She glanced at Rupert. 'You're upset about this? I know you warned Finn off, but *I* kissed *him*, not the other way around. I took him off guard. He didn't stand a chance.' Behind her Finn snorted. 'Besides, it was a friendly kiss… a thank-you kiss. And it lasted for less than two seconds.'

Without a word, Rupert leaned across and pulled that photo away to reveal the one beneath. She stared at it and everything inside her clenched up tight. It was of her and Finn outside the art studio that day, and they were… She fought the urge to fan her face. They were oblivious to everything. They were wrapped so tightly in each other's arms it was impossible to tell where one began and the other ended. It had, quite simply, been the best kiss of her life.

She lifted her head and shrugged. 'I'm not sure she got my best side.'

Nobody laughed.

'Trixie has informed me that unless she gets an interview with Finn, she'll sell these photos to the tabloids.' Rupert speared Finn with a glare that made all the hairs on her arms lift. 'Finn *will* give her that interview and make sure *you* aren't subjected to any more grubby media attention.'

A fortnight ago she might've agreed with Rupert, but now… She drew in a breath, then lifted her chin. 'I'm not ashamed of these photos.'

'It's okay, Princess. I don't mind. I don't have anything incriminating to tell our fair crusader here, so an interview won't take long at all.'

She wanted to stamp her feet in her sudden frustration. 'No, you're not hearing me. *I'm not ashamed of these photographs.*'

He met her gaze, stilled, and then rocked back on his heels. 'I—'

She held up a hand and shook her head. Pursing his lips, he stared at her for what seemed like forever, and then eventually nodded, and she knew he was allowing her to choose how they'd progress from here. She swung back to Rupert and Trixie. 'In fact, I'm so *not* ashamed of these photographs, if Ms McGraw doesn't mind, I'm going to keep them.'

'I have the digital files saved in several different locations. Your keeping that set won't prevent them from being made public.'

'I didn't doubt that for a moment.' Audra's phone buzzed. 'Time's up, Rupert.'

'You still want her to leave?'

'Absolutely! I'd much rather these pictures appear in the papers than any more gratuitous speculation about me and Thomas.' The situation with Thomas had left her feeling like a fool, not to mention helpless and a victim. The pictures of her and Finn, however… Well, they didn't.

'Besides, we all know how the press can twist innocent words to suit their own purposes. It sounds to me as if Joachim doesn't deserve to become the next target in a media scandal that has no substance.'

'You're mistaken. There's substance,' Trixie said.

'Then go find your evidence elsewhere, because you're not going to hit the jackpot here,' Audra shot back.

Rupert's eyes flashed as he turned to Finn. 'So you refuse to do the honourable thing?'

Rupert's words felt like a knife to his chest. Finn refused to let his head drop. 'I'm going to do whatever Audra wants us to do.' He'd known how disempowered Farquhar had left her feeling. He wasn't going to let Trixie McGraw make her feel the exact same way. *He* wasn't going to make her feel that same way.

He'd sensed that the photographs had both amused and empowered her, though he wasn't sure why. She'd been amazing to watch as she'd dealt with the situation—strong and capable, invulnerable. He wasn't raining on her parade now.

Rupert's hands clenched. 'You promised you wouldn't mess with her!'

Finn braced himself for the impact of Rupert's fist against his jaw, but Audra inserted herself between them. 'Not in front of Lois Lane here, please, Rupe.' She pointed back down the path. 'I believe you mentioned something about escorting her from the premises.'

A muscle in Rupert's jaw worked. 'You sure about this?'

'Positive.'

Trixie shook her head. 'You're making a mistake.'

'And you're scum,' Audra shot back.

Amazingly, Trixie laughed. As Rupert led her to the top of the path, she said, 'I like your sister.'

'I'm afraid she doesn't return the favour. I'll meet you back on the boat later.'

Without another word, Trixie started back down to the beach. She waved to them all when she reached the bottom.

'I think we should take this inside,' Audra said, when Rupert turned to stare at Finn.

Finn's heart slugged like a sick thing in his chest. He'd kissed Audra, and Rupert's sense of betrayal speared into him in a thousand points of pain.

Rupert hadn't been joking when he'd said he'd no longer consider Finn a friend if Finn messed about with Audra. Finn had to brace his hands against his knees at the sense of loss that pounded through him. He'd destroyed the most important friendship of his life. This was his fault, no one else's. The blame was all his. He forced himself to straighten. 'I think we'll do less damage out here, Audra.'

'The two of you are *not* fighting.'

He met the other man's gaze head-on. 'I'm not going to fight, Princess.' But if Rupert wanted to pound him into the middle of next week, he'd let him. Rupert's eyes narrowed and Finn saw that he'd taken his meaning.

'*Rupe,*' Audra warned.

Rupert made for the house. 'You're not worth the bruised knuckles.'

The barb hit every dark place in Finn's soul. He'd never been worth the sacrifice Rupert had made for him. He'd never been worth the sacrifices he'd always wanted his parents to make for him.

Hell! A fortnight on this island with Audra and he'd laid his soul bare. He lifted his arms and let them drop. He didn't know what any of it meant. What he did know was that this Greek island idyll was well and truly over. He wanted to roar and rage at that, but he had no right.

No right at all. So he followed Rupert and Audra into the house, and it was all he could do to walk upright rather than crawl.

They went into the living room. Audra glanced from Rupert to Finn and back again. 'I think we need to talk about that kiss.'

Finn fell into an armchair. Was it too early for a whisky? 'It won't help.' He'd broken his word and that was that. He'd blown it.

Rupert settled on the sofa, stretched his legs out. 'I'm interested in what you have to say, Squirt.' He ignored Finn.

'The kiss—the steamy one—it wasn't calculated, you know?'

She twisted her hands together and more than anything Finn wanted to take them and kiss every finger. He hated the thought of anything he'd done causing her distress. *You should've thought about that before kissing her!*

For a moment he felt the weight of Rupert's stare, but he didn't meet it. The thought of confronting the other man's disgust left him exhausted.

'It was Finn who ended the kiss. I wanted to take it to its natural conclusion, but Finn held back because of how much he feels he owes you.'

He sensed the subtle shift in Rupert's posture. 'You know about that?'

She nodded. 'I'm glad you did what you did when you were sixteen, Rupe. It was a good thing to do.' She folded her arms. 'But it doesn't change the fact that I'm furious with you at the moment.'

Rupert stiffened. 'With me?'

She leaned forward and poked a finger at him. 'You have no right to interfere in my love life. I can kiss whoever I want, and you don't get to have any say in that.'

Finn dragged a hand down his face, trying to stop her words from burrowing in beneath his flesh. Rupert knew Finn wasn't good enough for his sister. Finn knew it too.

'I understand the kiss,' Rupert growled. 'I get the spur-of-the-moment nature of being overwhelmed before coming to your senses. I understand attraction and desire. None of those things worry me, Squirt.' He reached for the photos she'd set on the coffee table, rifled through them and then held one up. '*This* is what worries me.'

Audra stilled, and then glanced away, rubbing a hand across her chest.

Finn glanced at it. What the hell...? It was the second photo—the one after the kiss. Okay, there was some heat in the way they looked at each other, but that picture was innocent. 'What the hell is wrong with that?'

Rupert threw him a withering glare before turning his attention back to his sister. 'Have you fallen in love with him?'

Every cell in Finn's body stiffened. His breathing grew ragged and uneven. What the hell was Rupert talking about?

'Princess?' He barely recognised the croak that was his voice.

Her face fell as if something inside her had crumbled. 'Your timing sucks, big brother.'

'You're family. You matter to me. I don't want to see you hurt. Have you fallen in love with Finn?'

Her chin lifted and her eyes sparked. 'Yes, I have. What's more I don't regret it. I think you're wrong about him.'

Finn shot to his feet. 'You can't have! That's not possible!' He pointed a finger at her. 'We talked about this.'

Audra's chin remained defiant. 'We talked about a lot of things.'

They had and—

He shook himself. 'None of what I said means I'm ready to settle down.'

Her hands went to her hips, but the shadows in her eyes made his throat burn. 'I think that's *exactly* what it means. I just think you're too afraid to admit it to yourself.'

He might be ready to put his freewheeling, adrenaline-loving days behind him, but it didn't mean he'd ever be ready for a white picket fence.

Even as he thought it, though, a deep yearning welled inside him.

He ignored it. Happy families weren't for him. They hadn't worked out when he was a child and he had no faith they'd work out for him as a man. 'Look, Audra, what you're feeling at the moment is just a by-product of your excitement…for all the changes you're going to make in your life, and—'

From the corner of his eyes he saw Rupert lean forward.

'And the romance of the Greek islands.' If he called her Squirt now, she'd tell him that was Strike Three and… and it'd all be over. He opened his mouth, but the word refused to come.

Audra drew herself up to her full height, her eyes snapping blue fire. 'Don't you dare presume to tell me what I'm feeling. I know exactly what I'm feeling. *I love you, Finn.*' She dragged in a shaky breath. 'And I know this feels too soon for you to admit, but you either love me too.

Or you don't. But I'm not letting you off the hook with platitudes like that.'

He flinched.

Her eyes filled and he hated himself. He glanced at Rupert. The other man stared back, his gaze inscrutable. Finn wished he'd shoot off that sofa and beat him to a pulp. Rupert turned back to Audra. 'When did he start calling you Princess?'

He could see her mentally go back over their previous conversations. 'After that kiss—the steamy one.'

Rupert pursed his lips. 'He doesn't do endearments. He never has.'

What the hell...? That didn't mean anything!

Audra moved a step closer then as if Rupert's observation had given her heart. 'You might want to look a little more closely, a little more deeply, at the reasons it's been so important to you to look after me this last fortnight.'

'I haven't looked after you!' He didn't do nurturing.

'What do you call it, then?' She started counting things off on her fingers. 'You've fed me up. You forced me to exercise. And you made sure I got plenty of sun and R & R.'

He rolled his shoulders. 'You were too skinny.' And she'd needed to get moving—stop moping. Exercise was a proven mood enhancer. As for the sun and the R & R... 'We're on a Greek island!' He lifted his hands. 'When in Rome...'

Her eyes narrowed. 'You read a book on the beach, Finn. If that's not going above and beyond...'

Rupert's head snapped up. 'He read a book? *Finn* read a book?' Audra glared at him and he held his hands out. 'Sorry, staying quiet again now.'

So what? He'd read a book. He'd *liked* the book.

'And that's before we get to the really important stuff like you challenging me to follow a path that will make me happy—truly happy.' She swallowed. 'And don't you think it's revealing that you sensed that dream when no one else ever has?'

His mouth went dry. 'That's…that's just because of how much time we've been spending together recently—a by-product of forced proximity.'

She snorted. 'There was nothing forced about it. We spent three days avoiding each other, Finn. We never had to spend as much time together as we did.' She folded her arms and held his gaze. 'And I know you spent those three days thinking about me.'

His head reared back.

'You spent that time bringing my dream to full Technicolor life.'

He scowled. 'Nonsense. I just showed you what it could look like.' He'd wanted to convince her she could do it.

'And while you're analysing your motives for why you did all those things for me, you might also want to consider why it is you've enjoyed being looked after by me so much too.'

She hadn't—

He stared at her. 'That ridiculous nonsense of yours when we went running… And then making sure I didn't overdo it when we went jetskiing.' Enticing him to read not just a book, but a trilogy that had hooked him totally. 'You wanted me to take it easy after my accident.'

She'd been clever and fun, and she'd made him laugh. He hadn't realised what she'd been up to. She'd challenged him in ways that had kept his mind, not just active, but doing loop-the-loops, while his body had been recuperating and recovering its strength. *Clever.*

'You haven't chafed the slightest little bit at the slower pace.'

Because it hadn't felt slow. It'd felt perfect. Everything inside him stilled. *Perfect?* Being here with Audra…? She made him feel… He swallowed. She made him feel as if he were hang-gliding.

She was perfect.

Things inside him clenched up. She said that she loved him.

'You're planning to move to the island too. Don't you think that means something?'

It felt as if a giant fist had punched him in the stomach. He saw now exactly what it did mean. He loved her. He wasn't sure at what point in the last fortnight that'd happened, but it had. *She said she loved him.* His heart pounded. With everything he had he wanted to reach out and take it, but…

He glanced at Rupert. Rupert stared back, his dark eyes inscrutable, and a cold, dank truth swamped Finn in darkness. Acid burned hot in his gut. Rupert *knew* Finn wasn't good enough for his sister. Rupert knew Finn couldn't make Audra happy…he knew Finn would let her down.

A dull roar sounded in his ears; a throbbing pounded at his temples.

'I have a "truth or dare" question for you, Finn.'

He forced himself to meet her gaze.

'Do you or don't you love me?'

The question should've made him flinch, but it didn't. He loved her more than life itself. And if he denied it, he knew exactly how much pain that'd inflict on her. He knew exactly how it'd devastate her.

He glanced at Rupert. He glanced back at her. She filled his vision. He'd helped her find her dream, had helped her find the courage to pursue it. That was no small thing. She would lead a happier life because of it. And he—

He swung to Rupert, his hands forming fists. 'Look, I know you don't think I'm good enough for your little sister, and you're probably right! But you don't know how amazing she is. If I have to fight you over this I will, but—'

Rupert launched himself out of his seat. 'What the hell! I *never* said you weren't good enough for Audra. When have I ever given you the impression that you weren't good enough?'

Finn's mouth opened and closed, but no sound came out.

'When have I ever belittled you, made light of your achievements, or treated you like you weren't my equal?'

Rupert's fists lifted and Finn kept a careful eye on them, ready to dodge if the need arose. He'd rarely seen Rupert so riled.

'That's just garbage!' Rupert slashed a hand through the air. 'Garbage talk from your own mind, because you still feel so damn guilty about me giving up that stupid prize all those years ago.'

Rupert glared at him, daring him to deny it. Finn's mind whirled. He'd carried the guilt of what Rupe had sacrificed for him for seventeen years. He'd used that guilt to keep him on the straight and narrow, but in the process had it skewed his thinking?

'But you ordered me to keep my distance from Audra. *Why?*'

'Because I always sensed you could break her heart. And with you so hell-bent on avoiding commitment I—'

'Because of the promise he made to himself when he was eighteen,' Audra inserted.

'What promise?' Rupert stared from one to the other. He shook himself. 'It doesn't matter. The thing is, I never realised Audra had the potential to break your heart too.'

Finn couldn't say anything. He could feel the weight of Audra's stare, but he wasn't ready to turn and meet it. 'You saved my life, Rupe.' Rupert went to wave it away, but Finn held a hand up to forestall him. 'But Audra is the one who's made me realise I need to live that life properly.'

Rupert dragged a hand down his face. 'I should never have interfered. It wasn't fair. I should've kept my nose well and truly out, and I hope the two of you can forgive me.' He looked at Audra. 'You're right to be furious with me. It's just…'

'You've got used to looking out for me. I know that. But, Rupe, I've got this.'

He nodded. 'I'm going to make myself scarce.'

She nodded. 'That would be appreciated.'

He leaned forward to kiss the top of her head. 'I love you, Squirt.' And then he reached forward and clapped Finn on the shoulder. 'I'll be back tomorrow.' And then he was gone.

Finn turned towards Audra. She stared at him, her eyes huge in her face. 'You haven't answered my question yet,' she whispered.

He nodded. 'All my life I've thought I've not been worthy of family...or commitment. I never once thought I was worth the sacrifice Rupert made for me seventeen years ago.'

'Finn.'

She moved towards him, but he held up a hand. 'I can see now that my parents left me with a hell of a chip on my shoulder, and a mountain-sized inferiority complex. All of my racing around choosing one extreme sport after another was just a way to try to feel good about myself.'

She nodded.

'It even worked for a while. Until I started wanting more.'

Her gaze held his. 'How much more?'

He moved across to cup her face. 'Princess, you've made me realise that I can have it *all*.'

A tear slipped down her cheek. She sent him a watery smile. 'Of course you can.'

A smile built through him. 'I want the whole dream, Audra. Here on Kyanós with you.'

Her chin wobbled. 'The whole dream?'

She gasped when he went down on one knee in front of her. 'At the heart of all this is you, Princess. It's you and your love that makes me complete. I love you.' He willed her to believe every word, willed her to feel how intensely he meant them. 'I didn't know I could ever love anyone the way I love you. The rest of it doesn't matter. If you hate the idea of me opening up a hang-gliding school I'll do something different. If you'd prefer to live in the village rather than on the plot of land I'm going to buy, then that's fine with me too. I'll make any sacrifice necessary to make you happy.'

Her eyes shimmered and he could feel his throat thicken.

He took her hands in his and kissed them. 'I'm sorry it took me so long to work it out. But I realise now that I'm not my father...and I'm not my mother. I'm in charge of my own life, and I mean to make it a good life. And it's a life I want to share with you, if you'll let me.'

Tears spilled down her cheeks.

'Audra Russel, will you do me the very great honour of marrying me and becoming my wife?'

And then he held his breath and waited. She'd said she loved him. But had he just screwed up here? Had he rushed her before she was ready? Had—?

She dropped to her knees in front of him, took his face in her hands and pulled his head down to hers. Heat and hunger swept through him at the first contact, spreading like an inferno until he found himself sprawled on the floor with her, both of them straining to get closer and closer to each other. Eventually she pulled back, pushed upwards and rolled until she straddled him. 'That was a yes, by the way.' She traced her fingers across his broad chest. 'I love your dream, Finn. I love you.'

He stroked her cheek, his heart filled with warmth and wonder. 'I don't know how I got so lucky. I'm going to make sure you never regret this decision. I'm going to spend the rest of my life making you happy.'

She bit her lip. 'Can...can you take me back to your plot of land?'

'What, now?' Right this minute?

She nodded, but looked as if she was afraid he'd say no.

He pulled his baser instincts back into line and hauled them both upright. Without another word, he moved her in the direction of the car. From now on he had every intention of making her every wish come true.

Audra stared at the amazing view and then at the man who stood beside her. She pointed towards the little bay. 'Do you think we could have a jetski?'

'Will that make you happy?'

'Yes.'

'Then we can have two.'

She turned and wrapped her arms around his neck. He pulled her in close; the possessiveness of the gesture and the way his eyes darkened thrilled her to the soles of her feet. 'I want you to teach me to hang-glide.'

His eyes widened. Very slowly he nodded. 'I can do that.'

She stared deep into his eyes and all the love she felt for him welled inside her. She felt euphoric that she no longer had to hide it. 'Do you know why I wanted to come here this afternoon?'

'Why?'

'Because I want *this* to be the place where we start our life together.' She swallowed. 'I love your vision of our future. And this…'

He raised an eyebrow. 'This…?'

She raised an eyebrow too and he laughed. 'Spot on,' he told her. 'The practice has paid off.'

Heat streaked through her cheeks then. His eyebrow lifted a little higher. 'Is that a blush, Princess?' His grin was as warm as a summer breeze. 'I'm intrigued.'

Suddenly embarrassed, she tried to ease away from him, but his hands trailed down her back to her hips, moulding her to him and making her gasp and ache and move against him restlessly instead. 'Tell me what you want, Audra.'

'You,' she whispered, meeting his gaze. He was right. There was no need for secrets or coyness or awkwardness. Not now. She loved him. And the fact that he loved her gave her wings. 'I wanted to come here because this is where I want our first time to be.' She lifted her chin. 'And I want that first time to happen this afternoon.'

His eyes darkened even further. His nostrils flared, and he lifted a hand to toy with a button on her blouse, a question in his eyes.

She shook her head, her breath coming a little too fast. 'No more kisses out in the open, thank you very much. I bet Lois Lane is still lurking around here somewhere. And one set of photographs in circulation is more than enough.'

He laughed.

She glanced down the hill at the outbuildings. 'Why don't you walk me through your plans for our home?'

He grinned a slow grin that sent her pulse skyrocketing, before sliding an arm about her waist and drawing her close as they walked down the slope. 'What an excellent plan. I hope you don't have anywhere you need to be for the next few hours, Princess. My plans are…big.' He waggled his eyebrows. 'And it'd be remiss of me to not show them to you in comprehensive detail.'

'That,' she agreed, barely able to contain her laughter and her joy, 'would be *very* remiss of you.'

When they reached the threshold of what looked as if it were once a barn, he swung her up into his arms. 'Welcome home, Princess.'

She wrapped her arms about his neck. *He* was her home. Gazing into his eyes, she whispered, 'It's a beautiful home, Finn. The best. I love it.'

His head blocked out the setting sun as it descended towards her, and she welcomed his kiss with everything inside her as they both started living the rest of their lives *right now*.

EPILOGUE

'Go! Go, *PAIDI MOU*!'

Audra laughed as Maria shooed her in the direction of Finn, who was waiting beside a nearby barrel of flowers in full bloom. The town square was still full of happy holidaymakers and *very* satisfied vendors.

'You listen to my wife, Audra,' Angelo said with a wide grin. 'Your husband wants to spend some time with his beautiful wife. Go and drink some wine and eat some olives, and bask in the satisfaction of what you've achieved over the last three days.'

'What *we've* achieved,' she corrected. 'And there's still things to—'

'We have it under control,' Maria told her with a firm nod. 'You work too hard. Go play now.'

Audra submitted with a laugh, and affectionate pecks to the cheeks of the older couple who'd become so very dear to both her and Finn during the last fourteen months since they'd moved to the island.

As if afraid she'd change her mind and head back to work, Finn sauntered across to take her hand. As always, it sent a thrill racing through her. *Her husband.* A sigh of pure appreciation rose through her.

'You make her put her feet up, Finn,' Maria ordered.

He saluted the older woman, and, sliding an arm around Audra's shoulders, led her down towards the harbour. Audra slipped her arm around his waist, leaning against him and relishing his strength. They'd been married for eight whole months, but she still had to pinch herself every day.

Standing on tiptoe, she kissed him. 'I think we can safely say the festival went well.'

'It didn't just *go well*, Princess.' He grinned down at her. 'It's been a resounding success. The festival committee has pulled off the event of the year.'

She stuck her nose in the air. 'The event of the year was our wedding, thank you very much.' They'd been married here on the island in the tiny church, and it had been perfect.

His grin widened. 'Okay, it was the second biggest event of the year. And there are plans afoot for next year already.'

He found a vacant table at Thea Laskari's harbourside taverna. 'I promised Thea you'd be across for her *kataifi*.'

They'd no sooner sat than a plate of the sweet nutty pastry was placed in front of them, along with a carafe of sparkling water. 'Yum!' She'd become addicted to these in recent weeks.

'On the house,' Ami, the waitress, said with a smile. 'Thea insists. If we weren't so busy she'd be out here herself telling everyone how fabulous the festival has been for business.' Ami glanced around the crowded seating area with a grin. 'I think we can safely predict that the festival cheer will continue well into the night. Thea sends her love and her gratitude.'

'And give her mine,' Audra said.

She did a happy dance when Ami left to wait on another table. 'Everyone has worked so hard. And it's all paid off.' She gestured at the main street and the town square, all festooned in gaily coloured bunting and stall upon stall of wares and produce. Satisfaction rolled through her. It'd been a lot of work and it'd taken a lot of vision, but they'd created something here they could all be proud of.

'*You've* worked so hard.' Finn lifted her hand to his mouth and kissed it, and just like that the blood heated up in her veins.

'I heard Giorgos tell Spiros that next year the committee needs to market Kyanós as an authentic Greek getaway.

With so many of the young people leaving the island, most families have a spare room they can rent out—so people can come here to get a bona fide taste of genuine Greek island life.'

She laughed. 'Everyone has been so enthusiastic.'

'This is all your doing, you know?'

'Nonsense!'

'You were the one that suggested the idea and had everyone rallying behind it. You've been the driving force.'

'*Everyone* has worked hard.'

He stared at her for a long moment. 'You're amazing, you know that? I don't know how I got to be so lucky. I love you, Audra Sullivan.'

Her throat thickened at the love in his eyes. She blinked hard. 'And I love you, Finn Sullivan.' This was the perfect time to tell him her news—with the sun setting behind them, and the air warm and fragrant with the scent of jasmine.

She opened her mouth but he spoke first. 'I had a word with Rupert earlier.'

She could tell from the careful way he spoke that Rupert had told him the outcome of the court case against Thomas Farquhar. She nodded. 'I had a quiet word with Trixie.'

Finn shook his head. 'I can't believe you're becoming best friends with a reporter.'

'I believe it might be Rupert who's her best friend.' Something was going on with her brother and the beautiful journalist, but neither of them was currently giving anything away. 'She told me the pharmaceutical company Thomas was working for have paid an exorbitant amount of money to settle out of court.'

'Are you disappointed?'

'Not at all. Especially as I have it on rather good authority that Rupert means for me to administer those funds in any way I see fit.'

He started to laugh. 'And you're going to give it all to charity?'

'Of course I am. I want that money to do some good. I suspect Thomas and his cronies will think twice before they try something like that again.'

They ate and drank in silence for a bit. 'Everyone is meeting at Rupert's for a celebratory dinner tonight,' Finn finally said.

'Excellent. It's so nice to have the whole family together.' She'd like to share her news with all of them tonight. But she had to tell Finn first. 'Do you ever regret moving to Kyanós, Finn?'

His brow furrowed. 'Not once. Never. Why?'

She shrugged. 'I just wanted to make sure you weren't pining for a faster pace of life.'

'I don't miss it at all. I have you.' His grin took on a teasing edge. '*And* I get to hang-glide.' He raised an eyebrow. 'We could sneak off to continue your training right now if you wanted.'

She'd love to, but... Her pulse started to skip. 'I'm afraid my training is going to have to go on hold for a bit.'

He leaned towards her. 'Why? You've been doing so well and...and you love it.' Uncertainty flashed across his face. 'You do love it, don't you? You're not just saying that because it's what you think I want to hear?'

'I totally love it.' She reached out to grip his hand, a smile bursting through her. 'But I'm just not confident enough in my abilities to risk it for the next nine months.'

He stared at her. She saw the exact moment the meaning of her words hit him. His jaw dropped. 'We're...we're having a baby?'

She scanned his face for any signs of uncertainty... for any consternation or dismay. Instead what she found mirrored back at her were her own excitement and love. Her joy.

He reached out to touch her face. His hands gentle and full of reverence. 'We're having a baby, Princess?'

She nodded. He drew her out of her seat to pull her into his lap. 'I—'

She could feel her own tears spill onto her cheeks at the moisture shining in his eyes. 'Amazing, isn't it?'

He nodded, his arms tightening protectively around her.

'And exciting,' she whispered, her heart full.

He nodded again. 'I don't deserve—'

She reached up and pressed her fingers to his mouth. 'You deserve every good thing, Finn Sullivan, and don't you forget it.' She pulled his head down for a kiss and it was a long time before he lifted it again. 'And they lived happily ever after,' she whispered.

He smiled, and Audra swore she could stay here in his arms forever. 'Sounds perfect.'

She had to agree that it did.

* * * * *

THE GREEK'S
NINE-MONTH
SURPRISE

JENNIFER FAYE

For Lois.

To an amazing lady who always makes me smile.

Thanks for your support.

PROLOGUE

THE WEDDING BOUQUET tumbled through the air.

The breath caught in Sofia Moore's throat as she watched the flowers sail end over end. They were headed her way. She raised her hands high in the air. With a firm grasp on the bouquet, she smiled triumphantly, thankful her friend had chosen flowers that didn't bother her allergies. Sofia lowered her arms, taking a moment to admire the beautiful white lilies and the delicate blue orchids.

As a round of applause went up, she lifted her head. Her gaze immediately met a set of piercing blue-gray eyes. Only one person had such mesmerizing eyes. Niko Stravos.

Her heart pounded in her chest. He quickly averted his gaze, but the connection had been long enough for her stomach to quiver with excitement. He liked her. Of that she was certain.

In turn, she was drawn to him like a honeybee to a sun-warmed daisy. How could she not be? He was drop-dead gorgeous in the tall, dark and dreamy sort of way. But there was something more—something she couldn't quite put her finger on.

She moved to where he was standing. His stance was a bit stiff, and a frown marred his handsome face. What had caused him to look so uncomfortable? Just moments ago, they'd been enjoying their time together. Their conversation had been light and entertaining. She wasn't ready for it to end.

"Care to dance again?" She hoped to cajole him back into a good mood.

Niko's hesitant gaze zeroed in on the bouquet before

returning to her face. "Perhaps we should rest. Aren't you tired?"

"Tired? Not a chance. I love weddings." This was the first time since she'd called off her engagement that she'd truly enjoyed herself. She didn't want this magical evening to end. "Don't you?"

"What?" Lines creased between his dark brows.

"Don't you enjoy weddings?"

His gaze moved to the colorful lilies again. "Not so much. I'm usually too busy at the office to attend them."

"In that case, you should make the most of the occasion. I'm sure Kyra's glad you made an exception today." She noticed how his attention kept straying back to the flowers. She turned and placed the arrangement on the bridal table. But still the pensive look on his face remained. "I love this song. Let's go dance."

He shook his head. "I don't think so."

"But why?"

He glanced around as though trying to avoid her pointed stare. "You should dance with someone else. I...I don't want to take up your entire evening. I should go."

"But we were having fun. Don't say goodbye. Not yet." She needed this—she needed to feel alive again after beating herself up for letting herself stay in a dead-end relationship for too long. "Please."

Niko hesitated. Then he held out his arm to her. "Shall we?"

A smile pulled at her lips. "I thought you'd never ask."

He escorted her onto the crowded dance floor that had been erected on the beach of the Blue Tide Resort beneath a giant tent supported by white columns. Everyone around them was smiling and laughing. The tables were adorned with white linens, floral centerpieces and votive candles. It was so easy to get swept up in the joyful celebration of her best friend's wedding.

A smile lifted the corners of his mouth. "You are unlike anyone I've ever known. I never know what to expect from you."

"I like to keep you guessing." She stepped into his very capable arms.

"You enjoy being different, don't you?"

"Yes." There was no hesitation in her response. None whatsoever. "I tried living up to someone's expectations. I turned myself inside out, and it still wasn't enough. In fact, it was an utter disaster. Since then, I've decided to march to my own drum."

"And how's that working for you?"

"Quite well." After all, she was dancing the night away with the most eligible bachelor at this wedding. "Quite well indeed. You should try it."

His eyes widened. "And what makes you think I don't march to my own drum?"

"Just a feeling."

He struck her as the conservative type, from his restrained emotions to his proper hold on her as they danced; not standing too close and his hands always remained in a respectable place. But then there was his longer, wavy dark hair. And the way he stared at her when he didn't think she noticed. Perhaps there was an impulsive side to him just longing to get out. She relished the idea.

Wanting to push him out of his safety zone, she moved closer to him. Her curves brushed up against his muscular chest. Immediately he sucked in a deep breath as his body stiffened.

"Relax," she murmured, feeling exceedingly daring. Perhaps it was the dim lighting. Or maybe it was the sparkling wine. Whatever it was, she decided not to fight it. She was having too much fun. "Don't worry—I won't bite."

A deep, rich chuckle rumbled from his chest. They began to move to the music again. He leaned in close—

real close. His breath lightly brushed over her neck, sending goose bumps down her arms. "Why do I get the feeling you're trying to take advantage of me?"

She swallowed hard, trying to ignore the way he had her pulse racing. "Would that be so bad?"

"I never let anyone have the advantage."

"Maybe you should—think of all you're missing out on." She wasn't one for flings, but Niko was different. The push and pull of her common sense versus her desires raged war within her. Should she? Or shouldn't she? In the end, she threw caution to the wind and decided that for Niko, she just might make an exception.

"Sofia? Did you hear me?"

He'd been talking? Between the loud voices and the strums of the eight-piece band, not to mention her own riotous thoughts, she'd missed what he'd said. And that was a shame because she loved his voice that was heavily laden with a Greek accent.

"I'm sorry. I'm having trouble hearing you."

"Perhaps you'd care to stop by my suite. We could continue our conversation. It's much quieter there. Unless of course you'd care to dance the night away."

He was inviting her to his suite? Her immediate response was no. But, then again, after tonight he'd be gone. And tomorrow she'd be like Cinderella, trading in her royal blue chiffon gown and satin heels for a black-and-white maid's uniform complete with no-nonsense black shoes with rubber soles.

The way Niko implored her with his eyes eroded any lingering doubts. Tonight would be her fairy tale—something she'd remember for years to come.

"Lead the way."

CHAPTER ONE

Twelve weeks later...

HE WAS LATE.

He was never late. Nikolas Stravos III expelled a disgruntled sigh as he stood in the shower. There was something about being at the Blue Tide Resort that always seemed to have him acting out of character. His previous stay had included the most fascinating evening with the most incredible woman. He smiled at the memory.

He turned away from the spray of water, letting the soapsuds slide down his body. He leaned forward, pressing his palms against the cold tiles. The jets of water beat against the backs of his shoulders. Hundreds of droplets of water came together and trickled down his spine. He longed for the pulsating rhythm to ease away the ache in his tense muscles.

A lot had happened since he'd last been to the Blue Tide. He now had a solo voice in the operation and direction of the Stravos Trust, a position he'd been groomed to ascend to since childhood. But no one had warned him the promotion would cost him dearly.

It'd all started here at the resort, at Cristo Kiriakas's wedding to Kyra, Niko's newfound cousin. The memories unfolded in his mind like a promo to a blockbuster movie, hitting all the highlights.

Some of the recollections were amazing, like getting to know Sofia, the maid of honor. And spending a glorious night together, an evening he hadn't been able to banish from his mind. But as good as that brief period had been, what had followed was horrific—losing his grandfather suddenly to a heart attack. The memory still sliced through him. There had been no time for goodbyes—no final words. It was all over before Niko had time to react.

He cursed under his breath as he turned off the water. Life could be so cruel sometimes. If he'd learned one thing, it was that everything could change at the drop of a hat. No notice. No nothing. And then you were all alone in this big, cold world. It was the story of his life.

Niko reached for the towel waiting for him just outside the shower stall. Instead of thinking about his upcoming business meeting with Cristo to finalize the terms of the sale of the Stravos Star Hotels, Niko found his thoughts spiraling back to Sofia. He ran the plush towel over his face. He made a mental note to inquire about her. He hadn't even gotten a chance to learn where she lived. By the time he'd awoken on that not-so-long-ago morning, she was gone. Like a dream, she'd vanished—

Thunk!

The startling noise drew his thoughts up short. *What was that?* It sure sounded like something had fallen over. But how was that possible? He didn't recall leaving a window open for the breeze to wreak havoc. But he conceded that, in his exhausted state after working day and night, anything was possible. And he had opened the windows last night when he'd first arrived. Perhaps he'd forgotten to close one of them.

Not bothering to dry himself off, he draped the towel around his waist, anxious to find out what damage had been done. His feet moved soundlessly over the cool ceramic tile floor.

He stepped into the outer room when he heard, "Ghuahh!"

He stopped in his tracks. He scanned the room, at last

settling on a most beautiful woman. Her eyes were round with alarm as she straightened, holding a lamp that belonged on the end table. Who was this woman? And what was she doing in his bungalow uninvited?

His gaze moved back to her face. It took a second before he realized he knew her—in fact, he knew her quite well, in a manner of speaking. Sofia. She'd come back. And this time, she wasn't a figment of his dreams. She was standing before him with those tempting lips and all her curvy goodness.

He noticed how her gaze slipped down to his towel before quickly returning to his face. Her cheeks were suffused with color. *Really?* How could she be so innocent after the night they'd spent together?

Still, at the sight of her embarrassment, he felt as though the towel had shrunk to half its size. He should have excused himself to go throw on some clothes, but his mind wasn't exactly working right. "Sofia? What are you doing here?"

Her mouth opened, but nothing came out. She turned and bolted for the door.

"Hey, wait!" He hadn't meant to scare her off. Perhaps his tone hadn't exactly been welcoming, but she was in his bungalow without an invitation—oh, who was he kidding? He was frustrated with himself for being so excited to see her.

And he just couldn't let her get away without finding out why she'd sought him out. He started after her, but when he reached the covered porch of his exclusive bungalow, a breeze rushed past him, reminding him that he was dressed in nothing more than a bath towel.

He stopped and stared at Sofia's back as she moved away from him as quickly as her legs would carry her.

What puzzled him the most was why she kept leaving him without so much as a word.

Usually he had the opposite problem with women. They were too clingy for his comfort. Sofia was different. She intrigued him. He'd have to work harder at making a good impression the next time they met.

He pressed his hand to the wooden rail as he watched her make her way along the path surrounded by lush, colorful vegetation. All too soon, she disappeared from sight. The part that stuck with him was the fact she'd been wearing a maid's uniform. *She works here?*

A whistle drew his attention. He turned to find a pretty brunette in a red bikini sunbathing not far from his bungalow. She flashed him a toothy smile and waved, but he didn't return the gesture, not wanting to encourage her attention.

His phone chimed with a reminder that he had a meeting in fifteen minutes. With a shake of his head, he turned and headed inside the thatched-roof bungalow. Thoughts of Sofia persisted. Had she, too, been unable to forget about their time together? Was that why she'd shown up at his bungalow? But if so, why had she run away? Surely it wasn't his lack of clothing. It had to be more than that. But what?

He inwardly groaned as he removed the first suit he came across in the wardrobe. His knowledge of women wouldn't even fill up a shot glass. And he had no intention of learning more—at least not anytime soon. And when he did decide to settle down, it would be a marriage of convenience.

He'd experienced enough loss in his life. He wasn't about to risk his heart on romance. A strategically planned marriage would be best for all concerned. It's what made the most sense. From what he'd observed, emotions were too fickle. Sometimes he wondered if romantic love truly existed or if people only imagined it. He sighed. Even if it did exist, he was better off without such an entanglement. It just made life more complicated than it needed to be.

If he were smart, he'd forget Sofia. That was the best thing he could do for both of them, because he had nothing to offer her except a moment here or a moment there. Certainly nothing consistent—nothing lasting.

In fact, tomorrow he would be jetting off, far from the Blue Tide Resort. His grandfather had given him one last mission to complete. And that had to be Niko's focus—not a beautiful woman with eyes full of mystery.

Her heart pounded.

Sofia pressed a hand to her chest as she eased open the door to the employee area in the lower level of the resort. With it being midmorning, the locker area was deserted. Everyone was busy trying to get their assigned tasks completed while the guests soaked up rays on the beach, golfed or toured the picturesque seaside.

She moved to the far corner of the room, anxious to be alone. Her mind had been racing ever since she ran into Mr. Dreamy, as she'd dubbed him during her best friend's wedding. What was he doing back here? And why hadn't Kyra mentioned his visit?

Sofia leaned against the cool tiled wall. She slid down to the floor and pulled out her phone. She could really use a sounding board. It wasn't until then that she realized her hands were trembling.

She didn't know what she'd been expecting for their reunion, but it certainly wasn't the suspicion in Niko's eyes. And when he spoke, his voice had been laced with agitation.

The backs of her eyes stung, and her stomach churned. This couldn't be happening. She hadn't meant to catch him by surprise. There had been no privacy notice on the door, and she'd knocked several times without getting a response. She hadn't even known that he'd returned to the Blue Tide.

Her fingers moved over the keyboard as she messaged Kyra.

MaidintheShade347 (Sofia): He's here!

Seconds passed and nothing. She willed Kyra to message her back. Of all the times she needed her best friend... Sofia's hand moved protectively over her still-flat midsection.

"It's okay, little one. I'll get this all sorted out. I promise." Impatiently her fingers moved over the keypad again.

MaidintheShade347 (Sofia): I need you.

Mop&Glow007 (Kyra): I'm here. Who's here?

MaidintheShade347 (Sofia): Niko. What do I do?

Mop&Glow007 (Kyra): Do you want to see him?

Sofia hadn't told Kyra the steamy bits that had transpired between her and Niko. It felt strange to hold back from her best friend, who until this point in her life had known all her secrets and insecurities. But this was different. She'd had a one-night stand with Niko—Kyra's long-lost cousin. That totally changed the rules of the game.

There was something else Sofia hadn't told Kyra—she was pregnant. Sofia had just found out earlier that week. She would tell Kyra everything just as soon as she figured out how best to deal with Niko.

MaidintheShade347 (Sofia): No. Yes. I don't know.

Mop&Glow007 (Kyra): Do you want me to say something to him for you?

MaidintheShade347 (Sofia): No!

Mop&Glow007 (Kyra): Are you sure?

MaidintheShade347 (Sofia): I'll handle it.

Mop&Glow007 (Kyra): LMK if you change your mind. I'll help.

The offer was generous, so typical of Kyra. Her friend had already pulled strings and gotten Sofia enrolled in an in-house managerial training program. Sofia was immensely grateful for the opportunity, but she was seriously considering returning to the States to earn an accounting degree. She'd always had a knack for numbers.

Though Kyra's offer to help smooth over things with Niko was tempting, Sofia would have to face Niko on her own. She couldn't even imagine how he'd react to her news.

CHAPTER TWO

NIKO YANKED AT his necktie, loosening it. He took the steps leading up to his bungalow two at a time while holding firmly to the notes he'd taken during his meeting with Cristo. He released the top buttons on his dress shirt. Whatever made him think wearing a suit at the Blue Tide was a good idea?

Because it was a habit. He felt in control in a suit and tie. His grandfather had drilled this message into him since he was just a boy. Without his father around to assume his rightful place as the Stravos heir, the role had fallen to Niko. He'd vowed at an early age to be the type of man that would have made his father and grandfather proud. That role included dressing the part.

However, Cristo hadn't felt the need for business attire, even though they were dealing with a very big contract that involved the sale of Niko's international hotel chain to Cristo. Thankfully the meeting had gone quite well. The changes to the terms of the contract were minor. So why was he so uptight? So out of sorts?

The answer immediately came to him in the vision of Sofia. He strode into the bungalow, where he uncharacteristically tossed his tie over the back of the couch, followed by his suit jacket. Why had she looked at him as if he were the Big Bad Wolf and she were Little Red Riding Hood? Had he really been that gruff?

He gave himself a mental shake as he sat down at the spacious desk and turned on his laptop. He'd be lost without it. Immediately his email software popped up on the screen. Forty-three new emails since that morning. All appeared to be business related. He inwardly groaned. They'd have to wait a little longer.

Niko opened a new email and started typing a note to his legal team. Sofia's panic-stricken face as she'd rushed out the door came to him. He shoved the image to the back of his mind as he transcribed his hasty notes into something more understandable.

When he'd finished proofreading the rather lengthy email, he pressed Send. He soon found three more emails had landed in his inbox. He leaned back in his chair as the memory of Sofia continued to plague him.

What had she wanted? Why had she looked so upset? He couldn't fully focus on his work until he had answers.

Niko strode over to the phone and was quickly connected with the front desk. He couldn't come straight out and request they send over Sofia. It would raise too many questions. Instead he requested the maid who'd cleaned his room to stop by, as he'd misplaced some papers and needed to know if she'd seen them. He assured the desk clerk that no crime had been committed. He just needed a bit of help.

Not more than five minutes later, there was a knock at the door. Niko opened it to find Sofia holding a stack of plush white towels as though they were a shield. "Hi. Thanks for coming back."

Her gaze didn't quite meet his. "I...I didn't see any papers."

He arched a brow. "And you would know this how? You took off so fast this morning that you didn't have time to look around."

"I'm sorry about that. I didn't know you were in the bungalow."

After being up late into the night working, he'd slept in. He'd forgotten to put out the do-not-disturb placard. That answered some of his questions but not all of them.

"I understand about the mix-up this morning, but we still need to talk."

Panic reflected in her brown eyes. "We...we do."

He got the feeling from her awkward stance and the way her gaze didn't quite meet his that whatever she had to say he wasn't going to like it. Not one little bit. It was like he'd walked in on the middle of a play and he had absolutely no idea what was going on.

If he was smart, he'd just make a quick excuse to disentangle himself from Sofia right here and now. But what came out of his mouth was something entirely different. "Come inside."

She hesitated before moving past him, taking great pains to keep some distance between them. This was not the way he'd expected her to act after their amazing night together. In fact, it was exactly the opposite.

When she stood in the middle of the living room, clenching and unclenching her hands, he said, "You can have a seat."

She perched on the edge of the couch. She laced her fingers together and rested them in her lap. The awkward silence stretched out.

"What did you want to discuss?" Surely it couldn't be as serious as her body language indicated. Perhaps she regretted running out on him the morning after the wedding and she wanted to know if they could start over.

The thought of letting her down weighed on him. He'd really enjoyed getting to know her. She'd been so easy to be around. But as amazing as he found her, he wasn't at a place in his life where he could even think about a serious relationship. Maybe it wasn't right—wasn't fair—but neither would lying to her. In the end, it would hurt her more.

His gaze met hers. There was a vulnerability in her eyes that evoked a protective side of him he hadn't been aware of before that moment. Her eyes grew shiny as though she were about to burst into tears at any moment.

No. Please. Not that.

Niko sat down on an adjacent armchair, uncomfortable with the thought of dealing with an emotional woman. He had absolutely no experience in that area. He wasn't a love-'em-and-leave-'em kinda guy. But on the rare occasions he spent the evening in a woman's company, whether for a fund-raiser or a business dinner, he made sure she knew up front that there would never be anything serious between them.

Had he told Sofia that? His memory was a bit fuzzy. He remembered when he'd first approached her at the wedding reception. She'd been sitting all alone at the bridal table. He'd been drawn to her, unable to resist talking to her.

Her smile had been the first thing he noticed. It had lit up her whole face, and it was infectious. The evening had been full of dancing and sparkling wine. Then more dancing, more laughing and more wine. He honestly hadn't wanted the night to end.

The woman sitting before him didn't resemble the engaging, bubbly woman at his cousin's wedding—she may look the same, but it was obvious something major had changed. What could it be? Why did she look as though she had the weight of the world on her delicate shoulders?

He drew his thoughts up short. Whatever was bothering her, he wasn't the one to resolve it. As much as he wanted to ride to her rescue, he was only in town for the night. There simply wasn't enough time—or so he tried to tell himself.

Sofia had no idea why Niko had requested her presence. Obviously, it wasn't to locate any missing papers or to restock his towels. Realizing she was still holding the fresh linens, she placed them on the couch next to her. She knew for a fact he had more than enough fresh towels because once he'd departed the bungalow that morning, she'd rushed back in. She'd done her fastest, most thorough cleaning job to date. So whatever he wanted had absolutely nothing to do with housekeeping.

And by the serious look on his face, he wasn't anxious to pick up where they'd left off. So where did that leave them? Was he just upset about finding her in his room? Or did he know about her pregnancy? No, impossible. She hadn't told a soul.

The best course of action was to get it all out there in the open, but her mouth refused to cooperate. She could feel Niko's gaze on her, and she averted her eyes to the pattern on the rug. Her stomach quivered.

Why was she letting herself get all twisted up in knots? It wasn't as if she wanted anything from him. Quite the contrary. She planned to take care of the baby on her own.

Niko cleared his throat. "Listen, I know you probably came here expecting us to pick up where we left off—"

"What? No, I didn't." Was that what he was expecting? Another clandestine hookup before he left?

His eyes widened. "You didn't?"

"What do you take me for?" Sofia pressed her lips together, holding back a stinging comment. Just because he was sexy and rich didn't mean she was going to throw herself at him. Was that how little he thought of her?

"I apologize if I jumped to the wrong conclusion." The look in his eyes said he didn't quite believe her. "Then why did you agree that we needed to talk?"

"I...I..." Her stomach lurched nauseously.

She jumped to her feet, not about to get sick in front of him. It was time to make a hasty exit. She would admit to her pregnancy later, when she wasn't so nervous. She rushed to the door. She could hear Niko curse under his breath as he hurried after her.

"Sofia, wait!"

She stopped at the edge of the porch. She inhaled a couple of deep breaths. Her stomach settled a bit. Her hands gripped the wood and squeezed tight, willing herself to remain calm enough to utter words.

"I need to tell you something." So far so good. Now if only she could get the rest out. "It's about the night of the wedding."

"It's okay." He stopped just behind her. His voice was much softer than it had been just moments before. "I understand. I haven't been able to forget that night, either."

"You haven't?" She turned, finding him much closer than she'd expected. That was not what she was expecting him to say.

His voice lowered and vibrated with emotion. "No, I haven't. It was special." He stared deep into her eyes. "You are special. But after you disappeared without a word, I thought you regretted it."

Her heart leaped into her throat. Was this really happening? Was it possible she'd totally misjudged him? "You really mean it? About the special part?"

His head dipped, and his lips claimed hers. There was no room for doubt in his kiss. This was how she remembered things from that one magical night. Maybe it'd been the sparkling wine or the romantic ballads, but Niko had swept her off her feet…just like now.

His lips moved over hers, brushing aside the rush of turbulent emotions and replacing them with pure, undiluted passion. She suddenly remembered how on that not-so-long-ago night she'd momentarily disengaged from her common sense and followed her heart. Their time together wasn't supposed to be anything serious, but sometimes actions have consequences. And in her—well, their—case, it was a life-altering consequence.

But as his hands moved over her back, her stiff muscles eased. Her body leaned into his. Her hands wrapped around the back of his neck as her fingertips played with the longer strands of his dark hair. She could easily get used to this—quite easy indeed.

Thunk!

Sofia jumped back as though the bungalow had been struck by lightning. She glanced around. Her gaze came to rest on a volleyball. A couple of teenage girls came rushing up to the bungalow and apologized. Niko smiled, flashing his white teeth, and assured them it wasn't a problem. Just as if nothing had happened.

Sofia tried to wrap her mind around how things had gotten so far off course. Her hand moved to her lips, her fingers gently swiping over her now-sensitive lips. Though her heart fluttered at the memory of their kiss, she knew she had to show more self-restraint. Giving in to her desires had succeeded only in complicating matters even more.

Her attention moved to the steps. She wanted to flee—wanted to avoid the inevitable questions—

"Don't even think about escaping. I'm dressed this time. I'll follow you."

CHAPTER THREE

"THAT KISS...IT CAN'T happen again." Sofia met his confused gaze.

Best to get this over with.

The sooner, the better.

Her palms moistened, and her mouth grew dry. She had no idea how much longer she could stand to be so close to him and yet so far away. Because she knew her secret would drive a permanent wedge between them. Nothing would ever be the same.

His expression hardened. "Then what exactly did you want to talk about?"

The time had come. Her stomach took another nervous lurch. And the words that she'd rehearsed over and over again utterly fled her mind.

"Sofia?"

It wasn't as if she'd gotten into this position by herself. And though it was the truth, it didn't settle her nerves. Why did this have to be so hard? Because he'd blame her. His eyes would grow dark and cold, shutting her out.

Niko made a point of glancing at his Rolex watch. "I don't have much time. Maybe we should talk later—"

"No!" When he frowned, she realized her response had been a bit too exuberant.

He arched a dark brow. "It's that important?"

She nodded, not trusting her mouth.

"Then come back inside."

She did as he asked. It was just two words—*I'm pregnant*. Why did she have to make such a production of this?

Just say the words and leave. Easy. Peasy. Not!

He moved to the minibar. "Can I get you something to drink? A mimosa?"

She shook her head. She couldn't drink in her condition. Instead of taking advantage of the opening, she said, "I can't. I'm still working. Some water would be nice."

In no time at all, he was handing her a glass of ice water. "Now, what did you need to talk about?"

She sipped at the water, needing it to wet her dry mouth. Once she set it aside, she clenched her hands and faced him. "I'm pregnant."

For a moment, nothing moved. It was as if time were suspended. As the seconds ticked by, the color leached from Niko's face.

At last he spoke in a strangled voice. "It…it's mine?"

"Of course it's yours. You surely don't think I have sex with every man I meet."

He raked his fingers through his hair. "How should I know?"

She glared at him. "That doesn't say much for you."

"You're right. I'm sorry. I'm not thinking clearly." He started to pace back and forth. "I just never thought." He stopped and stared at her as though expecting an answer. "But how could this happen?"

She frowned at him. Was their night so forgettable? Her face warmed at the memory. Did she really have to recount the evening in detail for him?

He shook his head. "Never mind. It was a stupid question. I… I'm just shocked. We took precaution."

"And it failed somewhere along the way. But analyzing the how of it isn't going to change the fact. What is done is done."

His face grew even paler. "Things did get pretty out of hand that night."

That was the understatement of the century. She'd never thought she'd ever have a one-night stand in her life, but that was before she met Niko. He was a mixture of hotness, sweetness and power wrapped up in a really cute package.

Funnily enough, telling him the news of the baby had a calming effect on her. She had not been expecting that. Perhaps it was because she was no longer harboring a huge, life-changing secret. With the truth out in the open, they could make whatever decisions were necessary.

"You're sure about this?" He gazed at her with one last bit of hope glimmering in his eyes.

She nodded. "I went to the doctor this week. He confirmed what I suspected."

Niko's shoulders slumped. "Oh."

She felt bad for him. He obviously wasn't looking to start a family anytime soon, and she had blindsided him with this news. She hadn't known any other way to tell him. She knew it wouldn't be unreasonable to expect him to step up and take responsibility. But that wasn't why she'd told him. As the father he had a right to know.

"Listen, I know this isn't what you want."

His head snapped around to face her. His dark brows rose high as his gaze searched hers. "And it's what you want?"

She wasn't about to get into what she did and didn't want. Ideally she wanted to be in love with the father of her baby, and even though they'd shared an incredibly intense attraction, she refused to let herself believe in love at first sight. Whatever she'd felt for Niko at the wedding had been an intense attraction. Nothing more.

She stared deep into his eyes and swallowed hard. "I'm keeping the baby if that's what you mean."

His expression didn't give away his thoughts. "I'll need some time to digest this."

"That's fair." There was one more thing she hadn't told him. "How much time are we talking?"

He raked his fingers through his hair. "I don't know. Why?"

"I'm leaving in two weeks."

"Leaving?"

She nodded. "I'd appreciate it if you didn't tell anyone, as I haven't turned in my notice yet."

"Leaving and going where?"

"Home. Back to New York. I want my baby—"

"Our baby."

She sighed. "Our baby to grow up around family."

His mouth opened, but before he could utter a word, her phone chimed. It was the ringtone she'd assigned to her boss. Although this was a bad time for a phone call, she couldn't ignore it, either.

Her gaze met Niko's. "It's my supervisor."

Niko's lips pressed together as he waved at her to go ahead and answer it. Was it her imagination or was he relieved by the distraction? There was no time for her to contemplate it as the phone chimed again.

She pressed the button, knowing her absence had been noticed and she didn't have a good excuse. Or at least not one that she was willing to share.

She moved to the porch for some privacy. "Hello."

This can't be happening.

Alone now, Niko paced back and forth. Sofia had appeared more than relieved to be summoned back to work. He glanced down at the scrap of paper where she'd jotted down her phone number and told him to call her when he was ready to talk.

Talk? He couldn't think straight much less string together a bunch of coherent sentences. Not so long ago, he'd had his life planned out. But in a matter of weeks, twelve to be exact, it'd all gone off course.

First, his grandfather unexpectedly passed away and

now he was about to become a father. *A father.* The words sounded so off to him. He wasn't ready to be a father. What did he even know about being a parent? *Nothing. Zip. Zilch. And nada.*

And to think that not so long ago this news would have been the answer to so many of his problems with his grandfather. The thought of not being able to share this news with him sent a fresh wave of sorrow washing over Niko. His hands balled up at his sides as he struggled to control his rising emotions.

His cell phone rang, but he ignored it—something he rarely did. He wasn't in any frame of mind to talk business. He wasn't sure how it felt to be in shock, but he'd hazard a guess it was what he was experiencing now.

The truth was he wasn't ready to be a family man.

He had too much to do…like restructuring the numerous divisions to eliminate overlap of personnel and continuing to overhaul his outdated company with new human resources policies. Even though he'd faced employee pushback in the face of change, he refused to let that stop him. He wasn't the boss in order to win friends. He'd been groomed to lead the company into the future. To do that, change must be a part of his plan.

But how was he supposed to fit a baby into that plan?

He accepted that someday he'd need an heir or two to hand down the family business. That was in his plan—his long-range plan. But a family didn't fit in his agenda now.

Still, there was a baby on the way. That couldn't be changed. Nor could he turn his back on his own flesh and blood. For the first time in his life, he didn't know which way to turn. The stakes were just too high.

His grandfather's solution would have been to have a wedding—quick and simple. He imagined how his grandfather would pat him on the back, pleased that he was carrying on the Stravos line. But would his parents have been just as pleased? Or would they have been disappointed in him? The thought weighed heavily on him. He missed them, especially at a time like this.

So what options did that leave him? To marry Sofia? But was it the right decision? Could Sofia be his convenient bride? Would she accept an unconventional marriage?

He recalled her contagious laughter at the wedding—the way she'd turned his head. She'd been like a breath of fresh air, and he'd been unable to get enough of her.

Could they ever get back to that happy place? He'd like to think once the shock wore away that they could smile and laugh again—together. So maybe the idea of marriage had come much sooner than he expected. He and Sofia had hit it off. He may not want a romantic entanglement, but he would like them to be on friendly terms when they wed. And the fact they were compatible in bed was a definite bonus.

Would Sofia jump at the offer? Or would she rebuff his proposal? The one thing he'd learned about Sofia was that she could be unpredictable, which made her quite intriguing. But it also left him uncertain when it came to his proposition of a marriage in name only.

Certain that he was on to something, he called Cristo. Luckily, his friend had just wrapped up a meeting. He was available to have coffee and a chat. Though Cristo asked him repeatedly if there was a problem, Niko was reluctant to get into it over the phone. This delicate conversation needed to be handled in person. And even then Niko was hesitant to share the full details—only what was necessary to bring his quickly evolving plan to fruition.

CHAPTER FOUR

THIS PLAN JUST had to work.

Niko stepped inside Cristo's luxury suite. Not so long ago they'd met here to discuss business, but this time his agenda was a bit more personal. Over the months, he and Cristo had become not only family, but also close friends. It was interesting to both of them how much they had in common—powerful families with unrealistic expectations.

Niko joined Cristo on his private balcony overlooking the beach littered with sunbathers soaking up the sunshine while others enjoyed the warm water of the resort's private cove. They all looked so relaxed and happy. Right now, Niko couldn't remember what it was like to be either of those two things.

His gut knotted up. If he made the wrong decision, he knew it would impact not only his life but Sofia's and their unborn baby's. The decision to make Sofia his bride didn't have to be made overnight. If he cut his trip short, Sofia would still be at the Blue Tide when he returned.

Cristo cleared his throat. "Sorry about the delay. Some staffing issues were just brought to my attention."

"You really take a hands-on approach with this place, don't you?"

Cristo poured them each a cup of coffee. "Yes. This resort is special to me. It was my idea. I've seen it through the planning, building and opening. And now that Kyra and I married here, it's our home."

"Even more so than New York?"

"My home is wherever my wife is, and right now, she's enjoying her time here." Cristo sipped his coffee. "So tell me what's on your mind."

Niko wasn't sure how much of what he was thinking he should vocalize. "I wanted to ask you about Sofia."

A knowing smile came across Cristo's face. "I saw the way you two hit it off at the wedding. Kyra wanted to do some matchmaking, but I told her not to get involved. It's better when things work out on their own. So you and Sofia, are you getting serious?"

Now how exactly did he answer that? The pregnancy was serious. The rest of it had yet to be determined. "We might be."

"And that's why you're here? You want to know if there's any reason you shouldn't get involved?"

Niko inclined his head. "Something like that."

Cristo took another sip of his coffee. "I don't know if I'm the person you should consult."

"Why's that?"

"Because I know nothing about romance and relationships."

"But how can that be? You're happily married."

"And that's due to my amazing wife. She's the one who believed in us and helped me to get past some rough spots. If it wasn't for her, I'd still be miserable and alone."

That last comment really caught Niko's attention. "You were miserable when you were single?"

Cristo shrugged his shoulders. "I just didn't want to admit it to myself. I thought I knew what would make me happy. And I was completely wrong. Lucky for me, Kyra opened my eyes. Your cousin is very smart, but if you tell her I said any of this, I'll totally deny it."

A smile pulled at Niko's lips. "Don't worry. I don't think I have to tell my cousin a thing. Anyone can see the happiness radiating from you two."

"It's easy when you have the right person in your life. Do you think Sofia is the right person for you?"

The smile slipped from Niko's face. "I think so."

"Why do you look so worried?"

"I'm not sure Sofia feels the same way."

"Ah, I understand. Women are tough to read."

Niko cleared his throat. "Speaking of Sofia, have you known her long?"

"Depends on how you look at it. I've known her as long as I've known Kyra. And that was long enough for me to realize I wasn't going to let Kyra get away. From what I've witnessed, Sofia is loyal and trustworthy."

"Thanks for the insight."

"But if you're curious about Sofia, why aren't you talking to her?"

Cristo was right. He just wanted to make sure there wasn't something he was missing about Sofia before he enacted his plan. "It's just that... Oh, never mind. I need to focus on my trip so we can finalize our deal. I'll worry about this stuff later."

"How long will you be gone?"

"Not long." While away, he intended to give his idea of marriage to Sofia some serious thought. "A few weeks."

"That fast?"

"You sound surprised." To him, being away from the Stravos Trust during this pivotal transition seemed like an eternity.

"I don't know. I just thought you might want to take some downtime after everything that has happened."

He was referring to the death of Niko's grandfather. "I did take a little time off, but I found the work helps. It's therapeutic for me."

Cristo nodded in understanding. "Maybe the trip will be good for you, too."

"Honestly, I'm not thrilled about this trip. It couldn't have come at a worse time."

"Then why not delay it?"

"Trust me—the thought has crossed my mind more than

once. But the sale of the hotel chain can't be delayed. I have plans for the money, and I'm sure you're anxious to get on with the merger of the two hotel chains."

"When are you leaving?"

"Tomorrow."

"And what about Sofia? You don't want to miss this opportunity. You might never get it back."

Cristo's warning made Niko hesitate. Had he somehow found out about Sofia's plans to return to New York? She'd said she hadn't turned her resignation in yet, but after their discussion perhaps she'd changed her mind. "Is there a particular reason you say that?"

Cristo rubbed his clean-shaven jaw. "I really shouldn't say anything—"

"This is important. If it's about Sofia, I really need to know."

Cristo's brows rose. "Fine. The phone call I was on when you arrived was from my manager. Sofia has tendered her resignation at the Blue Tide Resort. She's transferring back to the New York hotel."

"How soon?"

"Immediately."

"Immediately?" This was news.

"I haven't spoken to her myself, but from what I can gather, she's planning to hop on the next plane to New York. You wouldn't know anything about that, would you?"

"Let's just say I might have some idea about what's going on." When Cristo sent him an *I knew it* look, Niko continued, "The thing is I, um, need her help. Would it be possible to give her some time off?"

"What sort of time are we talking? A day? Or two?"

"At least a few weeks."

Cristo's eyes widened. "I see. Well, I think we could make that work. But is Sofia willing to go along with whatever you have in mind?"

"I don't know, but I'm about to find out."

"Are you sure—"

"I am." Niko jumped to his feet. "Thanks. I have to go."

He didn't have a specific plan in mind to delay her departure, but he'd think of something. He didn't have a choice. He couldn't let Sofia disappear before they settled things. He was good at coming up with spontaneous plans. He had to come up with something good, something irresistible.

With a sigh, Sofia settled on the couch in her efficiency apartment. It had been a long, stressful day, and all she wanted now was to stay put, eat some leftover pizza and watch a romantic comedy. It might cheer her up. Then again, an adventure movie might be better.

Her meeting with Niko hadn't gone terribly wrong, but it hadn't been good, either. Was it so far-fetched that she'd secretly envisioned his happy acceptance of the news? Instead, Niko looked as though he'd been diagnosed with a month to live.

Sofia glanced down at the uneaten slice of pepperoni pizza in her hand. Her stomach lurched. She slipped the food back on the plate. Maybe she'd finish it later—much later. After her stomach stopped feeling as if it was on the high seas. She hadn't experienced morning sickness until this week. Perhaps it was her nerves. Whatever it was, she wanted it to go away.

When her phone chimed, she welcomed the distraction. She snatched it from the coffee table, expecting to find a text from Kyra. Sofia had messaged her best friend earlier, telling her they needed to talk ASAP.

She'd been best friends with Kyra since junior high. Sofia thought they complemented each other well. She liked to take risks while Kyra liked to toe the line. Between the two of them, they'd kept out of trouble—or at least were never caught, as Kyra had reminded her over the years. But still, having a baby with a man that Kyra was just getting to know as family might put a strain on their friendship. Sofia hoped she was worried for nothing, but she'd learned the hard way that things don't always work out the way you imagine.

When she glanced at her phone, she saw the message wasn't from Kyra, after all. It was Niko. Her heart pounded, and her palms grew clammy. She immediately clicked on the text, anxious to find out what he wanted.

NikoStravosIII: Can we meet?

MaidintheShade347 (Sofia): When?

NikoStravosIII: Now.

She glanced down at her gray sweat shorts and faded pink T-shirt. She definitely wasn't in any condition to run out the door and meet up with a billionaire. She wondered if he ever had a hair out of place or dressed in anything but designer clothes. She highly doubted it.

MaidintheShade347 (Sofia): Now isn't a good time.

NikoStravosIII: It has to be tonight.

MaidintheShade347 (Sofia): I don't know.

NikoStravosIII: We must talk before you leave tomorrow.

He knew? At least it saved her from having to tell him. And as much as she hated to admit it, he was right. They had to finish their discussion, and perhaps it'd be easier in person. But he wouldn't change her mind—she was going home. She'd just heard about an opening at the hotel in New York, and she'd jumped on it. It would make it possible for her to make a future for her and the baby near her family.

MaidintheShade347 (Sofia): Can you give me a little time?

NikoStravosIII: Hurry.

MaidintheShade347 (Sofia): I will.

Sofia leaped up from the couch. After tossing her leftover pizza back in the fridge, she hurried to her small bedroom. A glance in the mirror told her that she would benefit from jumping in the shower and starting all over again, but she knew Niko wouldn't have the patience to wait that long. So she'd have to do her best to quickly paste herself back together.

At last she settled for a short summer dress that had a sleeveless denim blouse that tied at the waist and a white flowered skirt. It looked good on her without letting on that she'd tried too hard. After all, this wasn't a date or anything.

She texted Niko when she was ready. He wanted to meet on the beach. It was evening now, and the resort's guests would be having dinner. For the most part, they'd have the beach to themselves.

She rushed out the door, all the while wondering what he'd decided. As she rode down the elevator by herself, she pressed a protective hand to her abdomen and whispered, "Don't worry, little one. Everything will be all right." If only she could convince herself of that. "Your daddy will see that I'm doing what's best for all concerned."

Sofia made her way from the small employee complex on the outskirts of the resort to the hotel. It wasn't until then that she realized Niko hadn't been explicit in his instructions. The beach was huge. But she didn't have to wonder for long as he waved to her.

She joined him on the overlook that gave a stunning view of the private cove. The setting sun splashed streaks of pink and purple over the darkening water. But it wasn't the horizon that made the breath catch in Sofia's throat.

Her gaze settled on Niko. His wavy hair was finger-combed back off his face. Talk about hitting the jackpot in the gene department. If their baby took after him, it'd be adorable.

Niko was wearing dark slacks and a blue dress shirt. Didn't the man ever go casual? She was starting to wonder if his wardrobe contained anything but designer suits. Although tonight he'd dispensed with his jacket and tie. The sleeves of his shirt were rolled up, and the top buttons were undone, giving a hint of the few dark curls on his chest. Her fingers longed to reach out to him as she had on that unforgettable night.

Her gaze rose, meeting his. A frown pulled at his lips as he glanced down at himself. "Is there something wrong with my clothes?"

Realizing that she'd been caught staring, she shook her head. "Um…no."

"Are you sure? Did I spill something on myself?"

She shook her head again. "I was just wondering if you ever wear anything but suits."

"Really? That's what you were thinking?" When she nodded, he added, "And what's wrong with a suit?"

She waved her hand around at the beach. "You do realize this is a resort. People come here to relax and unwind. You look like you're ready to close a billion-dollar deal."

"Ah, but in my case I came to the Blue Tide Resort to do exactly that." He smiled, sending her stomach dipping.

"Well, not the billion-dollar part, but it's a substantial deal. Therefore, my attire is quite appropriate."

"Are you always so uptight? Do you ever kick back? Relax?"

"Of course."

She didn't believe him. "I think you focus on business 24/7."

"Did you ever consider I might find it relaxing?"

"And the suits?"

"To quote my grandfather, a man must dress properly to do business. But if you hadn't noticed, I did dispense with my jacket and tie."

She shook her head in disbelief. Inside, her stomach shivered with nervous tension. Critiquing his attire wasn't why he'd invited her here, but she welcomed the diversion. "How about some jean shorts and a T-shirt? Or in your case, perhaps dress shorts and a polo shirt?"

He glanced away. "I'm more comfortable like this."

"Do you even own any casual clothes?"

"Of course." He responded much too quickly, making her wonder whether he really did own anything she would classify as casual. "But I just returned from a meeting."

Was it really his clothes that bothered her? Or was it the thought that if she dressed him down, then his attitude might not be so serious? She wasn't quite sure. "Did you pack any of these casual clothes?"

"As a matter of fact, I did."

"Good. I'll wait here while you go change."

"Change? Why would I do that?"

"So we can go for a walk on the beach."

His hesitant gaze moved to the deserted beach and then back at her. "Wouldn't you be more comfortable talking here? We could order dinner and eat on the terrace."

He wanted to talk and eat? Her stomach lurched. There was no way. Walking and talking was much more appealing. "I'm not hungry." She didn't even want to smell food at this point. "I'd really like to walk."

He looked at her closely. "Are you feeling all right?"

She nodded.

"You're sure? You look a little pale."

She frowned. "Well, thank you. That's always what a woman wants to hear."

"I didn't mean it like that. I just meant... Oh, never mind. Wait here. I'll be right back."

She nodded, but still he hesitated. "I'll wait. I promise."

His eyes said that he didn't trust her. At all. "Good. We have important issues to discuss."

She couldn't tell by the tone of his voice if she was going to like what he had to say or not. At this point, she wasn't even sure what she wanted him to say. The push and pull of her conflicting emotions made her temples start to throb.

It will all work out. It will all work out.

She turned back to the view of the cove. All the while, she kept repeating those five words like some sort of mantra. It helped calm her nerves. Or so she wanted to believe.

She took in the colorful sky and the gentle lapping of the water. This was the kind of setting for a romantic movie where the hero and heroine walk off into the sunset. She inwardly groaned. That would never be her and Niko.

About to admit her mistake, she spun around to tell Niko that she'd changed her mind, but he was already gone. Whatever she did this evening, she had to keep her wits about her. Nothing good would come of repeating that toe-curling kiss. Nothing at all.

Still, her mind dwelled on that moment at his bunga-low when he'd held her in his arms. Her heart picked up its pace. She'd never been kissed with such passion. No one had ever made her feel as if she was the only woman in the world for him—

No! No! No! she scolded herself. It didn't help when she recalled how delicious it was having his lips pressed to hers. She had to resist the temptation. She had to. Somehow...

CHAPTER FIVE

SINCE WHEN DID he take orders?

He was the boss. He handed out the orders.

Niko glanced at Sofia. What was it about her that had him continually making exceptions to the rules?

The shorts and polo shirt he now wore were the only casual clothes he'd brought with him. To be honest, he wasn't quite sure what had possessed him to toss them into his suitcase. It must have been the fact that he liked to be prepared for any occasion. Although there was nothing in his suitcase to prepare him for a discussion about his baby—his baby—the words echoed in his mind.

"Niko?" Sofia's voice drew him from his thoughts.

Had she been speaking? He hadn't heard a word she'd said. That wasn't like him. He was good at multitasking, especially at business meetings. He could respond to emails on his phone while listening to a presentation and never lose a beat. But when he was around Sofia, he had problems staying on task.

"What did you say?"

"I asked if your business meeting went well."

He nodded. "It would have gone better if I'd been able to close the deal then and there."

"Why couldn't you?"

He didn't want to get into any of that now. They had other things to discuss. "That's not important." He stopped walking and turned to her. "We need to talk about your situation."

"You mean my pregnancy."

"Yes. That." She said it so easily, as if she'd already come to terms with it all. Was it possible she was happy about it? Could that be? "What are you planning to do? Because if you need—"

"I don't need anything. I already told you—I'm keeping it."

He frowned. "I don't know what you thought I was about to say. And I don't want to know. However, if you had let me finish, I was going to ask if I could help with your medical expenses."

He wanted only the best for her and their baby. Her vehement devotion to keeping their baby struck him. How had she become so attached and protective in such a short amount of time? It must be different for mothers, because he was still struggling to wrap his mind around the whole baby issue. A baby. His baby. It still didn't feel real.

Curious about her acceptance of the situation, he asked, "How long have you known that you are pregnant?"

"I told you—I found out this week." She turned and started walking again, farther from the resort.

That's right. He vaguely remembered her mentioning it earlier that day, but he'd been too shocked for it to stick. "If it's all new to you, how can you be so certain you want this baby? It's going to change your entire world. Nothing will be the same."

"The timing might not be the best, but I always hoped that someday I'd be a mother." Her hand moved to her abdomen. Then, as though she realized what she was doing, she lowered her hand to her side. "But I understand that just because I feel this way doesn't mean you feel the same way. And…and I'm okay with that. We can say our goodbyes and—"

"Hold on. I didn't say anything about saying goodbye." She was the mother of his baby—the Stravos heir. Like it or not, their lives were intricately entwined.

She turned to him, her eyes flashing with surprise. "So

this means that you, um…want to be involved with the baby?"

That's what surprised her? "It is my baby—"

"Our baby."

He was going to have to work on that. He wasn't used to sharing anything with anyone. As an only child, he hadn't had the luxury of a sibling. As an adult, he'd never ventured into a committed relationship. So sharing was a new concept to him, but he would excel at it just like he did with everything he tackled in the boardroom. And by the stubborn look on Sofia's face, he didn't have any choice in the matter.

"How can you be so sure that being a mother at this stage in your life is the right thing to do?"

She glanced at him. "You really want to know?"

There was so much about her he wanted to know, but this was a good starting point. "Is it wrong for me to be curious?"

"No. But I'll warn you, it isn't what you're thinking. I don't want the baby because of who its father is. I want this baby for itself."

The conviction in her voice had him wanting to believe her. But could he trust her? "You still didn't answer the question."

She sighed. "It all started when I met who I thought was the most wonderful guy. He was cute and charming. In fact, he ticked all of the boxes in what I thought I wanted in a man. He was a hard worker with a bright future in his uncle's construction firm."

"I take it he wasn't all you thought he'd be?"

She shook her head. "At the time, I worked as a housekeeper at the Glamour Hotel in New York. A lot of times our schedules didn't line up, so we'd go long stretches without seeing each other. As time went on, he seemed to work longer and longer hours."

Niko could relate with her ex. It was easy to get caught up in one's work. He did it all the time. But something told him there was more to Sofia's story than she'd revealed so far.

"My family immediately loved Bobby. My mother was anxious to plan a wedding, and at the time I thought it was what I wanted, as well."

"Families sometimes have the best of intentions, but they aren't always right."

"Are you referring to your grandfather?"

Niko nodded. "He sounds a lot like your mother, except for the part about planning a wedding. That would have never happened."

"Because he believed it's women's work?"

"No. Because it would have taken time away from his work."

"Anyway, when Bobby was home, he was too tired to spend quality time with me. My mother, with her eye on the wedding ring, assured me all was fine. Couples got busy, and we just had to work extra hard to find time to spend together. So I gave up my apartment and moved in with him."

Not that Niko wasn't interested in her background, but he suddenly felt as though this conversation was going much deeper than he'd ever anticipated. The more she opened up to him, the closer they became and the harder it would be for him to keep his distance. "But what does any of this have to do with you wanting a baby at this stage?"

She frowned at him. "I'm getting to it if you'll just give me a minute."

"Sorry." He wasn't. He didn't want to get caught up in her sticky details. He didn't want to empathize with her. He didn't want any entanglements, but he supposed with a baby on the way they would be forever entangled.

"I was certain moving in together would fix things. And it did. At first. Then things fell back into a busy routine.

He started working all hours of the day and night, including weekends. It was ridiculous."

"Well, business isn't always conducted between nine and five, you know."

She stopped and planted her hands on her hips. "Who's telling this story?"

Had she really just admonished him? He wasn't used to this. At the office, people cowered in his presence. Not that he'd done anything to warrant such a reaction. He supposed it was the legacy his grandfather had left him. That man had been a force to be reckoned with. His grandfather had made grown men quake in their boots with just a look.

"I was just trying to explain." When Sofia sent him an *Are you done yet?* look, he added, "Okay. Continue."

"Bobby promised it would get better. He said we'd have the rest of our lives together. He just needed some time to work on his career while I cooked, cleaned and did his laundry. He was too busy for those things." She sighed. "This went on for a while, and then I got pregnant. Bobby was excited. We got engaged. He started spending more time at home, and he expected me to be there. He wanted me to quit my job because he thought my place was in the home." Frown lines marred her pretty face. "I refused to quit. I liked getting out of the apartment every day and having my own financial independence."

None of this surprised Niko. Since the first time he met Sofia, she had struck him as fiercely independent. Obviously this story didn't have a happy ending. His gut told him not to push her, that she'd say it when she was ready.

They continued walking. The sea washed up on the shore, ever closer to their feet. The curiosity to know the rest of Sofia's story grew with each roll of the tide.

"And then I lost the baby." A poignant note of pain threaded through her voice. "Bobby didn't say he blamed me, but it was there in his eyes every time he looked at me."

"Don't." Niko stopped her with a gentle hand on her arm. "I don't know anything about pregnancy, but I do know that sometimes in life things happen that are way beyond our control. I'm sure you didn't do anything wrong."

Her gaze met his. "You barely even know me—"

"I know enough."

"And what is it that you think you know about me?"

"That you're an honest person with a good heart who would do anything to protect your child."

Sofia sniffled and blinked repeatedly. "You see a lot."

"Only the truth."

No wonder she was eager to turn her life upside down. He believed she would love their child the way children were supposed to be loved. He was so thankful for that part.

"And your boyfriend, what happened to him? Did he leave you because you wouldn't cave in to his demands?"

"No. But that would have been so much easier."

"Easier than what?"

She shook her head. "Never mind. I shouldn't have rattled on so much."

Just when she was getting to the interesting part, she decided to clam up. Frustration churned in his gut. He wasn't sure if he was more upset with her for stringing him along with her story only to leave him wondering how the jerk had broken her heart, or if he was upset with himself for letting his guard down and caring about her. Maybe it was a bit of both.

"I take that to mean you've sworn off men."

"Yes. And now that I'm pregnant, I don't have time to date. I've got other priorities."

Well, that would make what he had in mind even harder. But he was never one to back down from a challenge. Although the stakes had never been this high.

"Shouldn't you take it easy? You know, after what

happened before?" She didn't have to work. He had the resources to keep her comfortable and well cared for throughout her pregnancy.

"I'm fine." She smiled. "I had all of the appropriate tests done, and the doctor doesn't see any reason for the past to repeat itself."

Only then realizing he'd been holding his breath in anticipation of her response, he exhaled. They turned around and started back toward the resort.

Knowing for a fact that she'd oppose any talk of marriage at this point, he was more certain than ever that his plan would work...if only he could convince Sofia to go along with it.

"I have a proposition for you." He didn't know how else to phrase it.

"What sort of proposition?"

"I'd like to hire your services."

She stopped walking and sent him a puzzled stare. "You want to hire me? For what?"

"I'd like you to do some cleaning. I can make it worth your time."

Confusion reflected in her eyes. "Here at the Blue Tide? But I already cleaned your bungalow."

"Let me explain. Tomorrow I leave on a round-the-world trip. The Stravos family over the years has accumulated numerous private residences at a number of the Stravos Star Hotels. It's my job to see they are emptied and cleaned for the new owner."

"I'd like to help you, but I have plans to return to New York."

"I'll take you there at the conclusion of the trip."

She shook her head. "I don't have time for an extended trip. I have to find a home for myself and the baby."

"It'll only be for a few weeks, and I can help you find a

place to live." *With me on my private island in Greece*, but he decided to keep that part to himself for now.

"I didn't tell you about the baby so you'd come riding to my rescue. I don't need a knight in shining armor."

"So what are your plans when you return to New York?"

"I'm planning to go back to school."

"School? Really?" By the deepening frown on her face, he'd utterly failed to keep the surprise from his voice.

"It just so happens that I always did well in school."

"So why didn't you get your secondary education?"

She shrugged. "I met my ex just before I graduated high school. And I let myself get distracted, thinking I was in love and trying to make him happy. I always planned to go back someday."

"And this is someday?"

"Yes. I have a knack with numbers, and I intend to get my accounting degree."

"And something tells me you'll do exactly that."

Her admission made him all the more intent on helping her. He couldn't imagine being a single parent would be easy for anyone, especially when the pregnancy was a surprise. And then to go back to school on top of it all.

Luckily he was fast and could think on his feet. He was, after all, a Stravos—his family hadn't amassed a fortune over the years without being quick thinkers and following their guts. He could remedy this by meeting both of their needs.

He turned to her. "Come with me on this trip, and I'll pay the tuition to the school of your choice."

CHAPTER SIX

FOUR YEARS' WORTH of tuition earned in just a few weeks?

Was he for real?

Sofia studied Niko's face, finding a very serious expression there. "Why are you working so hard to get me to agree to this trip?"

"Why not? It's a win-win for both of us. I get help making the suites presentable, and you get money to follow your dreams."

She had to admit that it was tempting—very tempting. But her grandmother had taught her to be suspicious of offers that were too good to be true.

Sofia recalled his earlier admission about not being able to forget their night together. Was he interested in picking up where they'd left off at the wedding? That wasn't going to happen. She wasn't interested in a relationship. She'd been there and done that. Her heart still held the scars. And now with a baby coming, there was no way she was going to risk her heart. Not for Niko. Not for anyone.

"Why me? You can afford to hire anyone."

"Ah…but see, I don't want to spend the next couple of weeks globe-trotting with just anyone. My jet is big but not that big. You and I hit it off. You're entertaining. I like talking to you. And we already know we get along well—"

"That was one night—a night with wine flowing freely. You can't base any decisions on that evening."

"But you do have to admit it was unforgettable."

She glanced away, not about to let him read the truth in her eyes. That night had been amazing—he'd been amazing. But like with all dreams, eventually you woke up and reality settled in. "If I agree, and I'm not saying that I have, but if I did, it'd be purely business."

He inwardly sighed. He'd never had this hard of a time convincing a woman to travel with him. Not about to let her slip through his fingers, he said, "Yes, it'll be business only, if that's what you want."

"It is." And then her eyes twinkled as though a thought had just dawned on her. "And I'd have one other stipulation."

He knew he wasn't going to like this. "And that would be?"

"Your wardrobe."

"What about it?"

"It's not the most practical attire for cleaning out suites. I'm assuming you'll be helping to box up mementos and such." He nodded and she continued, "Then you'll want some more casual clothes. After all, who would do manual labor in a designer suit? Each one probably cost more than a month's rent."

She had a point, and by the frown forming on his face, he couldn't argue. She wondered if he'd ever cleaned and packed up an apartment in his life. His background was so different than hers.

"What are you thinking?"

She shook her head, not about to upset her potential employer. "It's nothing."

"You know you didn't have a problem opening up to me the night of the reception."

"That night was different."

"It'll be a very long trip if we must censor everything we say to each other."

She had to agree. "Fine. I was wondering if you've ever done any cleaning and packing, or if you always had a staff to do it for you."

"It might surprise you to know that at boarding school I

was responsible for my half of the dorm room. We learned to do laundry, mop floors, make up our beds and dust. Inspection was every Friday afternoon with some surprise inspections in between."

She struggled to keep her mouth from falling open. Niko Stravos knew how to do laundry? That was more than Bobby ever cared to know. Her ex had expected hot food on the table and clean clothes in the closet without having to lift a helping hand. Niko was way ahead of him.

"I see I've caught you by surprise." His shoulders straightened. "And at the beginning of each semester we were charged with the task of unpacking. When classes concluded, we had to repack all of our belongings. So in answer to your question, yes, I can clean and pack. But I'll need help if I'm going to make good time. And I'm sure you'll do a much better job than me."

Not trusting her judgment after her disastrous relationship with Bobby, she was unsure if Niko was being on the level with her. Not that it mattered. She had a lead on some apartments that would open up in the next month. Her inside source had told her that once they were posted in the paper they'd be snapped up in a New York minute.

"I'm sure you can find someone else to help you." Sofia wasn't giving up her chance to obtain semi-affordable housing, not when her baby was counting on her.

"You're right, I could. But I want you." Niko's tone was firm but not threatening. "And if you know anything about me, you'll know that I generally get what I want. I've already cleared your time off with Cristo—"

"You did what? How could you?" She crossed her arms and glared at him. "You had no right." He'd jeopardized her plans to care for the baby.

"Cristo hinted around that you might not take my butting in well. But he doesn't know the circumstances." Niko combed his fingers through his dark hair, scattering the wavy strands. "I…I thought—"

"You thought wrong. Just because you're richer than Midas and used to getting your way in the boardroom doesn't mean you can bulldoze right over me, my wants and my needs."

"That wasn't what I meant to do."

She lifted her chin. "If you're even considering coparenting with me, you have to learn that I won't be dictated to. I can make my own decisions, even if they don't always line up with what you want. Is that understood?"

His eyes widened at her outburst, but then he relented and nodded his head. "I understand. Can I at least explain why I made the request on your behalf?"

She'd made her point. Something told her Niko wasn't one to repeat his mistakes. "Go ahead."

"I'm leaving first thing in the morning, and I won't be back for a while. I want you to come with me. I really want your help."

She shook her head. "I can't."

"Is it the baby? Is there something you haven't told me?"

It'd be so easy to tell him that was the case. She gazed up at his face. His forehead was creased with lines, and his eyes had grown dark with worry. She couldn't let him get worked up over a problem that didn't exist—even if it'd make her life easier. No one deserved to needlessly worry about their unborn child.

"The baby is strong and healthy. And there's no reason I can't travel."

"You're sure? Because I don't want to do anything that will jeopardize you or the baby."

Her heart squeezed with his display of concern. No man had ever worried about her like that before—not even her ex when she'd miscarried. Bobby hadn't even made it to the hospital to visit her. And now here was Niko, not even her boyfriend, worried about her.

She quickly tamped down the rush of gratitude because Niko was only worried about the baby—his child—his heir. She meant nothing to him. And it was best that things remained that way. Her heart was already a patchwork of scars. She refused to make it worse.

She swallowed hard. "Yes, I'm sure. The reason I need to get back to New York is that there's an apartment opening up and I want to apply for it."

"I see. Perhaps I could have my PA search for some other apartments and schedule some walk-throughs for you."

"It's more than just the apartment. I have colleges to apply to and day care to line up. Furniture to pick out. Diapers to buy—and the list goes on."

He frowned. "I had no idea. So that's why Cristo didn't think you'd be receptive to my idea."

She shrugged. "Kyra has been cheering me on to go back to school. I wouldn't be surprised if she mentioned it to him."

"So this is something you've been planning, even before you knew about the baby?"

"Yes. I never came to Greece intending to stay forever. The visit was what I needed at the time to get my head back on straight. And now that it is, it's time I go home. I have a list of potential apartments that are in close proximity to my parents, who will most likely volunteer to help with the baby and to lighten my day care expenses. I also need to make a doctor's appointment to get my records up-to-date with the pregnancy."

"You've really done a lot of planning in such a short amount of time. But what about us?"

"Us? There is no us."

The frown lines on his face deepened. "But you're carrying my baby. In my book that makes you and me an us."

"Well, it doesn't to me. We're coparents, nothing more." Wow, was she lying. Even to herself. This baby had forged an unbreakable bond between herself and Niko where one hadn't existed before. Nothing she said was going to erase that. And by the disbelief reflected in Niko's eyes, he wasn't buying what she was saying, either.

Niko's gaze dipped before meeting hers again. "I apologize for overstepping with Cristo and I promise not to do it again so long as you give my proposal due consideration."

"If you really want me to take your offer seriously, you're going to have to be honest with me about why you want me to accompany you on this trip. And, please, don't mention the cleaning thing again. You want something else—I can tell."

Though she wouldn't admit it to him, the college tuition money was truly tempting, especially with a surprise baby on the way. Her savings were rather lacking when she started to think of everything she would need for this new part of her life.

So just how badly did he want her to go on this trip with him?

Was he ready to take the risk and open up to her?

Why did this woman have to question everything he said?

Niko sighed heavily. Something told him that Sofia would stand her ground until she had all the answers. A part of him respected that stubborn streak in her— the trait had just happened to reveal itself at exactly the wrong time.

He thought it over for a moment beneath Sofia's close scrutiny. She wasn't going to rush him. Let her wait and wonder.

What would it hurt to be perfectly honest with her? After all, she'd been totally up front with him about the baby and why it was so important to her. He really respected her for her honesty and for the fact that she didn't play games with him, which he knew other women might have done to work the situation to their advantage.

"Okay. Here's the deal. I'd like a chance to get to know you better. And with a baby on the way, it seems like the sooner we do that, the better."

She shook her head. "If you have it in your head that you're going to marry me, forget it. I told you before that's not going to happen. I don't need a husband. I can get by on my own."

She may not be interested now, but if he convinced her to go with him, he'd have a couple of weeks to change her mind. He could be persuasive when he set his mind to it. "Are you really prepared to do this all alone, including the three a.m. feedings? The no sleep? The colic? And going to work the next day sleep deprived? I mean, I may not be a parent, but I have plenty of them working for me. And I hear things—sometimes things I'd rather not hear."

After all her bold statements, worry now reflected in her eyes. "You make parenthood sound awful."

And then her eyes grew shiny. She wasn't going to cry, was she? Oh, man, that wasn't what he'd meant to have happen. He was just voicing his concerns out loud. In the future, he'd have to be careful what he said. But for now, he had no clue what to do.

Her eyes shimmered as they met his. There was something about her that got to him more than any other person he'd ever known. She was complicated with the way she was so strong one minute and yet so vulnerable the next. In that moment, he wanted nothing more than to comfort her—to reignite the flame that normally burned so bright in her.

He reached out, brushing the backs of his fingers along her cheek. "Don't worry. We'll figure this all out."

"Are you sure?"

He nodded and hoped he sounded more certain than he felt. "We're in this together."

Her hand reached up and squeezed his. The heat of lingering attraction warmed his veins. With every fiber of his being, he wanted to pull her close and kiss away her fears. His body started to sway toward hers. Just a little farther and they'd be chest to chest. His gaze moved to her glossy lips.

The part of his brain that warned him against such an action was getting drowned out by the pounding of his heart. He knew why they'd had the most amazing night together, and it had absolutely nothing to do with the sparkling wine. It was Sofia. She was simply enchanting with her sunny smile and witty comments that kept him on his toes. He wanted that fun part of her back.

His thumb traced her jawline before brushing over her full bottom lip. There was a rush of intense desire mingled with the excitement of the unknown that had the adrenaline pumping through his veins. He hadn't been this nervous about kissing a girl since high school.

How would she react? The look in her eyes said that she wanted him, too. Or was he just seeing what he wanted to? He glanced down at her very inviting lips. If he were just to lean in and kiss her, he'd wipe away any doubts she might have about them doing what was right for their child. He could make their marriage work for both of them, if only she'd give him a chance.

Questions reflected in her eyes, putting a halt to his actions. He inwardly groaned as logic wedged its way into his fantasy. As much as he wanted to shove it aside and deal with it later, he couldn't shut off his mind.

The voice of logic said a kiss would be a mistake. He was trying to talk her into taking this trip with him. Where did he think kissing her would lead them? She'd probably turn him down flat, thinking all he wanted was to get lucky.

He couldn't let her get the wrong idea about him. He had to show her that he was man enough to keep his hands to himself—for now. Once they were married, well, maybe they could explore their options.

With great reluctance, he pulled his hand away. He took a step back and cleared his throat. "I promise to make this trip as short as possible. And if you're unable to find a suitable apartment, I'll buy a building and become your landlord."

Her mouth gaped. "You're serious, aren't you?"

He nodded. He'd never been more serious in his life. "Come with me. You won't regret it. Besides, it isn't every day you're offered a trip around the world, is it?"

She shook her head. "You promise you'll drop me in New York?"

"You have my word. New York just happens to be on the travel itinerary."

CHAPTER SEVEN

THIS REQUIRED MORE than a text message.

Sofia had arranged to meet Kyra in person to tell her all that had transpired between her and Niko. As the words tumbled from Sofia's mouth one after the other, Kyra's eyes grew round. Sofia hoped her friend would be able to somehow understand that sometimes life happens when you least expect it.

In many ways, Sofia was still coming to terms with all the changes in her life and the knowledge that Niko still made her heart race. She'd have to get over him now that she'd agreed to accompany him on this trip. Their mission was to close the family residences while figuring out how to be good coparents. Anything beyond that would just complicate matters. And right now, they had more than enough complications.

"You're pregnant?" Disbelief echoed in Kyra's voice.

"It might not be the best time or the ideal set of circumstances, but, yes, I'm pregnant."

"And my cousin is the father?"

Sofia nodded as Kyra's mouth gaped. "I think you're in as much shock as he is at the moment."

Kyra didn't say anything for a second. The seconds stretched into a minute and then two. Sofia laced her fingers together to keep from fidgeting. *Please don't be mad.*

Unable to take the extended silence, Sofia asked, "What are you thinking?"

"Do you really want to know?"

Oh, no. Perhaps she didn't want to know. The air caught in Sofia's lungs. Then again, she couldn't stand the suspense. "Just tell me."

"That this makes us officially family." Kyra's face lit up with a smile.

A pent-up breath rushed from Sofia's straining lungs. "Really?"

Kyra nodded as tears of happiness gathered in her eyes before splashing onto her cheeks. "I always thought of us as family, and now it's official."

"Even if I don't marry your cousin? Because you know about me and men. The two do not mix, at least not for any extended period of time."

"No matter what, you and I are family." They hugged. Kyra pulled back and gave her a serious look. "Now shouldn't you go pack? You have some globe-trotting to do."

For a second there, Sofia had been so wrapped up in worrying about Kyra's reaction that she'd forgotten that come the next morning, she was due to set off on an adventure of a lifetime. "Oh, yes, I should get going."

They hugged again. Her friend pulled back and looked her in the eyes. "Give the guy a chance. You never know what might happen. And I'm not saying that just because he's my cousin."

"Don't get your hopes up." She really hated to disappoint Kyra.

"I won't. But remember what I said."

"I will." Sofia walked away, certain she would keep her guard up around Niko. She couldn't—she wouldn't—be hurt again. Because when the shock of the baby wore off, so would Niko's fascination with her. He would go back to his billionaire lifestyle, and she would return to her conservative life on the Upper East Side. It was the way it had to be.

This was really happening...

A giddy feeling sent Sofia's stomach fluttering. She was in Tokyo. *Wow!* And here she thought that flying from New

York to Greece had been a big deal, but it was nothing compared to a round-the-world trip on a private jet with one of the world's most eligible bachelors. Her heart beat a little faster as the image of Niko came to mind. Right now, he was in the study of the luxury suite dealing with yet another business call.

Sofia took a break from cleaning to stand by a large window that gave an impressive view of the city as the colorful lights dotted the night sky. Talk about being on top of the world. They were fifty floors up in the penthouse suite.

Niko claimed this building was one of the first Stravos Star Hotels, which meant it had been around for quite a while, but you couldn't tell. The lobby of the hotel consisted of glass, white marble and lush potted greenery. It had a graceful elegance that made Sofia feel as though she'd stepped into another world—Niko's world.

She'd observed how he'd moved with ease through the building as though it were a second home for him. It certainly didn't strike her as homey. Everything was updated and modern, from the Oriental artwork adorning the white walls to the computer kiosks off to the side of the lobby. A key card accessed all the hotel's amenities, and there were many, including the very tempting five-star spa. She'd hoped to visit it yesterday after she had finished cleaning for the day, but it was long closed by the time she quit. If only Sofia had a little spare time...

"Sorry about that." Niko returned to the living room, slipping his phone into his pocket. "It was my office in Athens."

She merely nodded, having heard that numerous times already on their trip. She began taping cardboard around a family photo. She had no idea what it was like to be that important, but something told her it wasn't a lot of fun, at least not going by the frown lines that formed on Niko's face every time he pulled the phone out of his pocket.

Needing to finish up the cleaning and packing of the suite, she said, "This is the last of the family portraits. I just need you to tell me if you want any of the artwork on the walls."

"I'm really sorry about leaving you to do the bulk of the work. Yesterday's meetings couldn't be avoided. And today, well, some things cropped up." His lips lowered into a frown. "Why don't you go put up your feet and let me finish?"

She stopped and straightened to look at him. He wanted to do her work? By the look on his face, he was serious. There was no humor to be found in his bottomless gaze. Well, no matter, she didn't shirk her responsibilities.

"You're going to clean in those clothes?" She indicated his blue trousers and light blue dress shirt with the rolled-up sleeves. "You're kidding, right?"

His dark brows furrowed as he glanced down at his clothes. "No worries. I'll be careful."

"Easier said than done. Besides, this is what you hired me to do."

"But I thought we would do everything together."

"Everything?" At the sound of her voice, Niko's eyes glittered with intrigue. Why did she have to vocalize her thoughts?

"Yes. I thought this would be a team effort."

He moved toward her and held out his hand. "Here, let me take that for you."

If he was that insistent, why should she argue? She handed over the scissors and packing tape, then grabbed a fresh rag and dust spray. "Did you spend much time here?"

"Oh, yes. When I was a kid, being this high up was like being on top of the world. But I'm sure you don't want to hear any of that."

"I do." She glanced over her shoulder, pleading with him to continue.

"My grandfather was a busy man. When I was young, he did quite a bit of traveling. If I wasn't away at school, he'd take me with him. In fact, my bedroom is the first one on the right. It's just the way I left it."

"Surely you must have changed it as you grew up." It wasn't until she saw his slightly bemused expression that she realized she'd misspoken.

"Why would I do that?"

Sofia swallowed down her disbelief. "Um, no reason."

Seriously? That was supposed to be his room when he was young? There had been no baseballs or footballs. No posters. No mementos. Nothing like her brothers' rooms had been when they were growing up. Even now, there were still random pieces of their past in their rooms. Their mother never had the heart to remove everything.

But Niko's room was no different than the guest rooms. No personal mementos. It was so mature. So formal. She couldn't help but wonder if it was indicative of his childhood—proper and stifling.

Niko snipped a piece of tape. "While I waited for my grandfather to get done with his business meetings, I'd read a lot. I had a big imagination."

"I bet that has come in handy."

He ran another strip of tape around the package. "You mean so I could entertain myself? Because you don't have to worry. I always came up with something to do."

"No, that wasn't what I meant." The sad image of him as a little boy in this big suite with no other kids around filled her mind. Her heart went out to him for having to find ways to constantly entertain himself. She'd never had that problem with all her brothers and cousins around. "I meant now that you are the boss, you can use your imagination to envision a big, bright future for the company."

He nodded in understanding. "I have lots of plans for

the Stravos Trust. I just wish my ideas didn't meet so much resistance."

"Well, you did just take over, didn't you?"

"I've been working there in one manner or another most of my life."

"Really?" She stopped dusting a gold Oriental table with hand painted bamboo, pink flowers and hummingbirds on the front. "You worked there as a kid."

Niko moved the now-packaged portrait and leaned it against the wall with the others that were being shipped back to Greece. "I didn't have a full-time position, if that's what you mean. But I was being groomed to assume control of the company one day."

"Wouldn't you have rather been outside playing with your friends?"

He shrugged. "I didn't have many friends, just a few I made at boarding school. I didn't have time to hang out. I had my studies to concentrate on."

"So you were always an overachiever?"

He shrugged. "There were expectations I had to meet. As a Stravos, I was expected to live up to my father's memory. I had to be the best in my class. Second best wasn't good enough for a Stravos."

"Niko, I'm so sorry. That must have been so difficult for you."

He shrugged. "It was no different from how my father and grandfather were raised."

"Oh." She wasn't sure what to say at that point, not wanting to upset him.

"You have to understand that the Stravos Trust has far-reaching interests. It's not a job one can just step into. It takes years to learn how it all comes together. And without my father to take his rightful place at the helm, it has become my responsibility."

That was such a big burden to place on such young

shoulders. She wondered if Niko ever got to be a kid. Surely he wouldn't want the same thing for their child. Without thinking, she gently touched her stomach.

"What's the matter?" Concern laced Niko's voice. "Are you feeling all right?"

Sofia jerked her hand away from her midsection. She wasn't about to admit the direction of her thoughts. Not at this point. Niko hadn't even discussed custody with her. "I'm fine."

"Maybe you should rest." He moved to her side, and, without giving her a chance to protest, he took the rag from her hand.

"Hey!"

He held the cloth out of her reach. Considering he had quite a few inches on her, it didn't take much. "Go rest. I've got this."

With this being the last room that needed to be dusted and vacuumed, she wasn't going to fight with him. Her knees were sore from kneeling, and her back ached from bending over. But the suite was clean and had the fresh scent she always enjoyed.

She admired the way he got to work. When his phone rang, he ignored it. She could hardly believe her eyes as he forwarded it to voice mail. "If you need to take that, I can finish."

"I told you I've got this. I'll return the call later."

A few minutes of awkward silence passed before Sofia spoke. "How soon are we leaving?"

"We're staying here tonight, and tomorrow we'll take off."

"Oh." She had to admit that she was bummed they wouldn't be sticking around Tokyo long enough for her to go exploring. She'd seen a bit of it on their way to the Stravos Star Hotel, but not nearly enough. She hoped Niko would slow down at some of their stops for her to do some sightseeing. "You were able to take care of all your business here so quickly?"

He nodded. "Mission accomplished, and I found the first piece of the puzzle."

"Puzzle? You make it sound like you're on some sort of scavenger hunt."

"I am, in a manner of speaking."

"That sounds awfully intriguing. If you don't mind me asking, what are you searching for?"

He hesitated. "It's nothing. I shouldn't have mentioned it."

"I'm glad you did. After all, I thought part of the reason you invited me along on this trip was so we could get to know each other better since we're going to be coparenting."

"Yes, you're right." He left the room and quickly returned carrying a folder. He withdrew a paper from the manila folder and handed it to her. "Here. This will explain things better than I ever could."

Her questioning gaze moved from his drawn face to the paper in his hand. There was handwriting all over it as though it were a letter. She was reluctant at first to take it. She had the distinct feeling Niko wouldn't have so readily shared his motives if it weren't for her prodding. Words of refusal teetered on her tongue.

"Go ahead. Take it." He continued holding the paper out to her.

She accepted it, even though she wasn't comfortable with the situation. She'd just wanted him to open up a bit and let her in. She didn't mean to make him feel obligated to her. This getting-to-know-each-other stuff was going to be much harder than she'd ever imagined.

She glanced down at the distinct handwriting with strong strokes. Niko's name was at the top. Her questioning gaze met Niko's once more to see if he'd changed his mind before she went further. When he nodded, she turned back to the letter, quite unsure what she would learn.

Niko,

I know that I was not the replacement father you deserved. By the time you knew me, I was an old man who was quite set in my ways. It wasn't always this way. Perhaps you were too young to remember the adventures your father would lead us on. And that is my fault. Instead of keeping those memories alive for you, it was easier and less painful not to speak of them. And so before this deal is finalized with Cristo Kiriakas, I am sending you on a very important mission. You are to visit and close the family's apartments in each of the following hotels: Tokyo, Honolulu, New Orleans, the Caribbean and New York City.

Most of what you'll find will be of no value to you and can be disposed of quickly. But in each apartment is a safe. In them, you will find pieces of your past. Things I should have given you years ago. Forgive this old man for his procrastination.

If I should die before you complete the mission, the Stravos Trust will be yours to do with as you see fit. But I beg you to do as I ask. Though I taught you everything I know about business, there are other life lessons that I failed to impart to you. This is my attempt to set things right.

Now go with an open mind and heart. And know that I love you.

Bon Voyage

She wasn't sure what to say to Niko now. He was truly on a sort of real-life scavenger hunt. She glanced over at him. They were so close and yet so far away. She was beginning to see him with new eyes—a lonely little boy who'd lost his parents and was forgotten by a driven grandfather. Her heart went out to him.

When Niko glanced up, catching her gaze, she knew she had to say something—anything to make this moment less awkward. "So our next stop is Hawaii?"

"It is. How does that sound to you?"

"Wonderful." A smile tugged at her lips. "I've always wanted to go there."

"Then your wish is my command."

If only...

Her mind skidded off in a totally inappropriate direction... Niko would sweep her into his arms. His lips would claim hers. The daydream sent her heart racing. Her gaze landed on the man of her dreams, admiring his broad shoulders, narrow waist and firm backside. He was definitely worthy of a dream or two.

A sigh passed by her lips. Too bad that's all it'd ever be.

CHAPTER EIGHT

AT LAST THE jet began a slow descent as they neared the Hawaiian Islands. Niko glanced over to find Sofia napping in her seat. He wished she had taken him up on his earlier suggestion for her to go curl up in the bed at the rear of the plane. She'd have been so much more comfortable.

As it was, her head lolled to the side and her arms were wrapped tightly about her as though she was cold. He supposed that was possible because he liked to keep the thermostat on the cooler side. He grabbed his suit jacket and got to his feet.

With the utmost care, he draped it over her. She murmured something he couldn't make out, but she never fully woke up. He wouldn't rouse her until he absolutely had to. It was obvious she'd worn herself out cleaning the suite in Tokyo. He admonished himself once again for not doing more to help her.

As he stood in front of her, he couldn't help but notice her unique beauty. He longed to reach out and stroke her creamy complexion. If their baby took after her, it would be aces in the looks department. It was still so unreal to him that she was carrying his baby.

Quietly he made it back to his seat and picked up his computer, but he couldn't stop thinking of Sofia and their baby. In what? Six months or so, there'd be a new Stravos in this world. And long before then he intended to take Sofia as his bride. The more time he spent with her, the more certain he became that this was the right decision for all three of them.

He forced himself to stare at the computer monitor, but he found himself unable to concentrate on analyzing the figures on his screen. His gaze blurred. He rubbed his tired eyes. With a sigh, he closed the computer. These long hours working were starting to catch up to him.

A green folder sticking out of his briefcase drew his attention. It was what he'd retrieved from the wall safe in the Tokyo penthouse. He'd been distracted by helping Sofia move furniture in order to clean and had put off investigating the file's contents. What could be so important that his grandfather had sent him on this round-the-world journey?

Niko withdrew the expandable folder from his briefcase. He reached inside and pulled out a stack of black-and-white photos.

"What in the world?"

He hadn't meant to speak the words out loud. His surprised reaction had Sofia shifting in her seat. He pressed his lips together, waiting and hoping she'd doze off again. When he didn't hear anything further, he continued his search.

One by one he examined the photos for a sign of someone he recognized. But none of the faces looked familiar. When he turned the photos over, he found names and dates. These people—these strangers—were his family.

Sofia yawned and stretched her arms above her head, letting his jacket slide down over her gentle curves and gather in her lap. "Whatcha doing?"

He glanced over at her. Her short dark hair was mussed, and her cheeks were rosy from her nap. Her smile made her eyes sparkle like gemstones. She looked absolutely adorable. An unfamiliar sensation swirled within him and settled in his chest, filling him with warmth.

"Niko? Is everything all right?"

"Hmm? Oh, yes. I was just looking at some old photos."

"Is that what your grandfather left you in the safe in Tokyo?"

Niko nodded. "Except I don't know any of these people. I mean, I know that I'm somehow related to them, but they don't mean anything to me." Frustrated with whatever lesson his grandfather was trying to teach him, he tossed them back in the folder. "I knew this trip was going to be one big waste of time. And this just proves it."

"May I see the photos?"

"Sure." He handed over the folder and got to his feet. "They're of no value to me."

"Of no value? How can you say that? These people are your family."

He shook his head. "They are people I never met, never knew. They mean nothing to me."

A frown flickered across her face, but she didn't say anything as she removed one photo after the next. "How can this not mean anything to you? Most people want to know about their past. Look at your cousin, Kyra. She traveled half the globe in the hopes of finding some part of her past."

"I'm not like that. I'm fine just the way I am. I don't need some old photos to make me feel whole."

"But don't you ever wonder where you got your dark, wavy hair? Or perhaps your blue-gray eyes?"

He shook his head. "I look like my grandfather. But who cares?"

"Perhaps your son or daughter will care? Won't you want to be able to tell them about their family?"

He hadn't considered that. "I don't know what I'd tell them."

"Perhaps that's what your grandfather is trying to do for you—give you some answers. Maybe there are questions you never thought of asking. And maybe right now these photos don't mean anything to you, but once you're a father, the past and the future will collide. It will mean something to you then."

"Perhaps you're right."

His gut told him his grandfather would have approved of Sofia. She might like to have a good time now and then, but she had a level head on her shoulders. And perhaps she would have understood his grandfather in ways that Niko was never able to grasp.

If Sofia was right, at least this trip wouldn't be a total waste of time. He still couldn't help but wonder why he had to travel from country to country collecting these photos. It made no sense to him when his grandfather could have gathered it all and left everything in a box at the house on their private island.

But what puzzled Niko the most was the fact that his grandfather wasn't one to send him on a fool's errand. There had to be more to this trip than he'd figured out so far. What could it be?

Niko got to his feet and moved about the plane, stretching his aching muscles. Some people may think that a round-the-world trip was something dreams were made of, but not him—not with the frantic pace that he planned to complete this trip. The sooner it was done, the sooner he'd have a clear conscience—having fulfilled his grandfather's final wish.

And then Niko could concentrate fully on his plans to expand the shipping segment of the Stravos Trust. He already had the construction of his first megacargo carrier under way.

When his phone buzzed, he answered it. After he hung up, he turned to Sofia. "That was the pilot. He said to buckle up. We're getting ready to land in Honolulu."

She set aside his jacket and strapped in. "I've never been to Hawaii. Will we be here long?"

"Long enough to close up the suite."

"Oh." She didn't expand on her disappointment, but it was quite evident in her tone.

He hadn't thought about her expectations when he'd invited her on this trip. Perhaps he should have done a better job of explaining his aggressive agenda. She was probably imagining a leisurely trip where she'd get to relax and take in the sights.

He inwardly groaned. The last thing in the world he wanted to do now was play tourist. But it wasn't fair of him to keep her prisoner on this jet as it spanned the world. "Would you like to do some sightseeing?"

"Yes." Her answer came quickly, but then she pressed her lips together as though realizing she shouldn't have shown her eagerness so readily. "I mean, it's okay if you're too busy and don't have time. I'd understand."

He didn't want to, but he would make time to spend one day sightseeing. After all, there was no reason they couldn't fly at night. "Then it's decided. We'll go sightseeing. Anything special you want to see?"

"Um…everything." Her eyes lit up like his employees' when Christmas bonuses were hand delivered by him.

"That's a lot. I'm not sure we have time to squeeze in everything. But if you make a list, we'll work on it."

"Okay."

"Why don't you hand me those?" He gestured to the photos. "They aren't much to look at."

She glanced down at the stack of photos all in different shapes and sizes. "I'm surprised you never saw any of these before. You mean you didn't have any copies at your house in Greece?" When he shook his head, she added, "How strange."

"Not necessarily." He didn't want to admit it, but he had given the photos some consideration. "Can I see a few of them?"

She scooped up half the stack and handed them to him. He started flipping through them one at a time. But this time, instead of focusing on the people, he studied the background. And in almost every photo he was able to identify a location in Tokyo. "I think all of these were taken someplace in Tokyo. The penthouse must have been open to the extended family's use. So it's only natural that some photos would gather there over time."

"You should have them put in a scrapbook."

"Why would I do that?"

"To keep them nice and make it easy for you to look over them from time to time."

She obviously had much stronger family ties than he'd ever had in his life. "Is that what you do with your photos, place them in scrapbooks?"

She nodded. "My mother loves to make them. She took a class at a local craft store and now she makes fancy scrapbooks with colorful paper and stickers. She uses all sorts of things. They're so popular that family members are always asking her to make one for them for various occasions like weddings, baby showers and graduations."

He'd never had anyone care enough about the details of his life to want to paste them in a book. He didn't even have a clue if his grandfather had any snapshots of him as a kid other than the formal portraits that hung in the living room. "That must be a very special gift."

"It is. I'm sure when I return to New York that my mother will be following me around with her camera. She's going to be so excited about her first grandchild."

"Is that what you truly want—to return to New York?"

Sofia nodded. "I want to be with my family when the baby is born."

And he wasn't family. She didn't say it, but she didn't have to. He could hear the unspoken words loud and clear. Once again he was on the outside looking in. His grandfather did the best he could for him, but he was older and had no patience for an overactive young boy.

And now once again, Niko should be a part of a family, but instead he was left on the fringes. He clenched his hands. Why did he feel as if he had to work for a place in this new family? Weren't those sorts of things supposed to come naturally without so much effort?

No matter what, he wasn't giving up. He didn't want his son or daughter growing up like he had, wondering about his parents and what they'd been like.

Niko looked down at the photos. His problem was that he was thinking about Sofia and this baby too much. Everything would work out just as it should. He always got what he went after—some things just took more patience than others.

His gaze strayed back to Sofia. He was going to need lots of patience. His attention zeroed in on her glossy lips. And lots of restraint—until they said, *I do*.

So this was Hawaii?

Sofia smiled as she glanced around from the balcony of their penthouse suite in Honolulu. A warm breeze rushed over her skin. She couldn't imagine why Niko would ever want to part with such an amazing view. Blue skies overhead were dotted by small puffy white clouds. She looked down at Waikiki Beach. This place was like heaven on earth with the white sand and clear water. So much like the Blue Tide Resort and yet so different.

Niko had been gone by the time she woke up that morning. Her nap on the plane just hadn't been relaxing, and she had been wiped out by the time they reached Niko's penthouse suite in the Stravos Star Hotel.

They'd agreed to a good night's sleep before sightseeing the next day. So when she awoke and found herself alone in the suite, she was surprised. On the kitchen counter, she found a note with her name on it.

I'll be back by noon. There's food in the refrigerator or feel free to ring room service. See you soon, Niko

She glanced at her watch. It was half past twelve, and she was anxious to get out and enjoy her one day in Hawaii. She was already frustrated that she'd slept so late. Time was ticking away.

Just then her phone buzzed. She rushed over to the table by the wall of windows, hoping it was Niko. Which she knew was crazy. It wasn't as if they were here on vacation or anything. But she couldn't help missing him just a little.

When she clicked on her phone, there was a text message from Kyra.

Mop&Glow007 (Kyra): Just thinking about you. What part of the world are you in now?

MaidintheShade347 (Sofia): Hawaii. It's gorgeous.

Mop&Glow007 (Kyra): Am totally jealous.

MaidintheShade347 (Sofia): You're in sunny Greece. You can't be jealous.

Mop&Glow007 (Kyra): Says who? A trip around the world sounds amazing.

It would be if the situation was different. Niko hadn't invited her along because he was interested in picking up where they'd left off. No, he was busy trying to decide what he wanted to do about the baby. She knew he had enough money and influence to cause problems for her regarding custody. She couldn't give him any reason to think the baby wouldn't be well cared for with her.

Her phone chimed again, drawing her from her thoughts. She glanced down to find another message from Kyra.

Mop&Glow007 (Kyra): Am I to assume you and Niko have hit it off?

Seconds turned to minutes as Sofia contemplated the question. She knew what Kyra meant—that they'd hooked up romantically. That ship had sailed. Right now, they were concentrating on becoming friends. And she'd give Niko credit, when he wasn't on the phone or computer, he made conversation. The problem was sometimes she wished they'd do more than just talk—

Chime. Chime. Chime.

Mop&Glow007 (Kyra): Sofia? You still there?

MaidintheShade347 (Sofia): Sorry. I'm here. We're okay.

Mop&Glow007 (Kyra): Okay? That's not very encouraging.

Sofia didn't know what to say to that. Perhaps Kyra wasn't the best person to confide in about her complicated relationship with Niko. After all, he was Kyra's cousin and they'd just been recently united. Sofia didn't want to do anything to hamper that new relationship.

MaidintheShade347 (Sofia): Everything is good. No worries. I'm just heading out now.

Mop&Glow007 (Kyra): Oh, good. I was starting to worry.

MaidintheShade347 (Sofia): Well, stop. I'll message later.

Mop&Glow007 (Kyra): Hugs.

MaidintheShade347 (Sofia): Hugs back.

Sofia really missed her best friend. But this was one situation where she would have to work through it on her own. The truth was even if Kyra were here in Hawaii with her, there was no way she'd tell her about the kisses she'd shared with Kyra's cousin or the looks that had passed between herself and Niko. Kyra would jump to the wrong conclusion, thinking there was hope for a happily-ever-after.

The truth of the matter was that aside from chemistry, they had nothing in common…except the baby. Once she showed him she was fully capable of taking care of herself, he'd stop worrying and go back to his business, letting her raise the baby in peace. Or at least she hoped so.

And she'd start by getting out of this suite and showing herself around Honolulu. She didn't need Niko to play tour guide. She would do fine on her own.

She grabbed her phone and bag. After jotting a note to Niko, she headed out the door. She rushed to the elevator, taking it down to the ground floor. The lobby of the Stravos Star Hotel was congested. Sofia glanced around, hoping to catch sight of Niko, but she didn't see anyone that even remotely resembled his tall, dark good looks.

With a shrug, she refused to be disappointed. After all, she had an adventure awaiting her. And photos to take as she'd promised to send some to her mother and Kyra. She would have a good time…and for just a little bit, she'd stop worrying about the future.

She stepped outside and immediately squinted in the bright sunshine. She slipped on her sunglasses and started off toward the beach. A stroll along the shore with the water washing over her feet would be just what she needed to soothe away the tension that had the muscles in her body stiff and sore.

She paused at the edge of the patio area and gazed out at the crowd of people littering the beach. There were older people, younger people, little kids and lifeguards. But what caught and held her attention was the large number of couples. Some were sitting side by side reading. Others were playing and laughing. And then others were walking hand in hand.

It was at that particular moment that Sofia felt a poignant stab of loneliness. She would never have that closeness because she refused to accept anything less than true love. The kind that came with promises of devotion, undying love and forever. The kind of relationship her parents and grandparents had found. And that sort of love seemed impossible for her to find.

Her thoughts tripped back to Bobby and how he'd said all the right words. Then when things got serious, he expected her to be the little lady waiting on him hand and foot. He didn't respect her work outside the home and that hurt—a lot.

When she'd become pregnant that seemed to help for a bit. Everything was the baby this or the baby that...until she'd miscarried. Bobby had soon become uninterested in her. She wouldn't let the same thing happen with Niko. If she let another man into her life, it'd be because he cared about her and not the fact that she was carrying his child. She needed to be loved for herself.

She approached the concrete steps leading to the sandy beach and started down them. And then she heard something. Was someone calling her name? Niko? Her heart picked up its pace. Had he taken time out of his busy day to be with her?

When she went to turn around, her foot missed the step. She reached out for the rail, but she was too far away. A scream tore from her lungs. Her body lurched forward.

Panic had her mind freezing up. Her body smacked the concrete. In a blur, she tumbled down the set of steps. She landed at the bottom in a heap.

CHAPTER NINE

"SOFIA!"

Niko sprinted toward her. His dress shoes pounded the stone patio. He dodged tables, chairs and loitering people. *Please. No. Let her be okay.*

But he'd been too far away. He could do nothing more than watch her lose her balance and topple down the steps. His chest tightened. By the time he reached the top of the steps, she was lying at the bottom.

He took the steps two at a time. When he reached her side, she was attempting to sit up. There was blood smudged from her lip onto her chin. Angry brush burns marred her beautiful complexion.

"Sofia, it's okay. I'm here."

"I…I'm fine. I, um, just need to get up."

He pressed a gentle hand to her shoulder. "Don't move. You aren't fine. You're bleeding."

"I am?" She moved her hand in front of her and stared at the blood on her palm. Her voice rose to an eerie, shrill level. "The baby." Her hand pressed to her abdomen, smearing blood over her top.

Niko swallowed hard. *Please don't let her lose the baby.* He slipped out his phone and with shaky fingers dialed 9-1-1. He gave the operator the necessary information, including the fact Sofia was pregnant.

"Niko, do you think that's necessary?" Sofia's eyes widened with worry.

Though he was fully concerned as she'd taken quite a tumble, he couldn't let on to her that he was anything but calm and positive. "It's just a precaution. Where's the pain?"

"I...I don't know. It hurts all over."

He wasn't a doctor, but he'd hazard a guess she was experiencing a bit of shock. "Don't worry. The hospital will get you all checked out and cleaned up."

A few tense moments passed as a rather large crowd of curious onlookers had formed around them. Sofia glanced up hesitantly. And then she tried once again to get to her feet. "I need to move. Everyone's staring."

Niko again placed his hand on her shoulder. "What you need to do is stay still. You and the baby had quite a fall. Just rest." He got to his feet, but he didn't move from her side. He assumed his boardroom demeanor, hoping these people would take him as seriously as the board did when he used his no-nonsense tone. "Thank you for your concern. We have everything under control. Please move on and give the young woman some space."

Thankfully most of the people walked away, leaving just a few looky-loos here and there. At least they weren't breathing down their necks. Niko kneeled down next to Sofia. Her face was pale, and her eyes were filled with unshed tears. *Not a good sign. Not good at all. Where's that ambulance?*

"Hey there, how are you doing?"

"I...I'm scared. What if—"

"Shh...don't think about what-ifs. Just think positive. This will all work out."

"But if—"

"You and the baby will be fine." He hoped he sounded more certain than he felt at the moment. A commotion at the top of the steps had Niko glancing up to find the paramedics rushing toward them. "See. Help is here. You'll be all fixed up in no time."

"And the baby?"

Niko squeezed her hand. "The baby will be fine." He glanced up at the paramedic. "She's pregnant."

The man nodded in understanding. "How far along?"

Niko thought back to the wedding and how beautiful Sofia had looked. "It'll be fourteen weeks on Saturday."

Surprise flickered in the paramedic's eyes, but he didn't ask how Niko could be so exact about the date of conception, and Niko was relieved. He didn't want to delve into his very complicated relationship with Sofia. He wouldn't know what to say or how to explain the flurry of emotions she created within him.

He stepped back just enough for the two paramedics to treat her. But Niko didn't go far. He would be right there making sure Sofia got the treatment she needed. And in case she called out for him, he wanted to be there for her.

After all, this was all his fault. If he hadn't been so anxious to catch up to her—if he hadn't called out her name—she wouldn't have turned around, and her foot wouldn't have missed the step. He cursed his own stupidity. What had he done?

All morning the meetings with the hotel staff had dragged on. One after the other with no end in sight, and all he could think about was Sofia. He'd wanted to slip away and head straight for the penthouse, but questions from his staff kept cropping up.

Never in his life had he been torn between his private life and that of his business. It had to be the news of the baby—that had to be it. Because he was immune to love. Niko was smarter than to get caught up in something that wouldn't last.

But if he was so smart, then why had he put the mother of his child in such peril? He thanked his lucky stars that Sofia appeared to be all right, but questions still remained where the baby was concerned. And that was all on him.

He continued to stare at Sofia, seeing the fear reflected

in her eyes. And he knew she wasn't worried about herself. She was scared of losing her baby—their baby.

In that moment, he knew he'd sacrifice anything to make this right for her.

Poked, prodded and bandaged.

Sofia lay on the hospital gurney. She fidgeted with the edge of the bleached white sheet. They'd been anxiously awaiting the doctor for what felt like forever. What was taking so long? She glanced at Niko as he paced back and forth within the small exam room as though he were a caged animal. He was probably thinking she was totally irresponsible. And he'd be right. She had only one important job to do right now—take care of their baby. And she'd failed miserably.

The baby just had to be okay. Sofia would never be able to forgive herself if her carelessness had hurt her child. The memory of her miscarriage and that sense of emptiness plagued her. She couldn't go through that again. She'd do anything to keep the baby safe. She sent up a silent prayer.

She blinked repeatedly, willing her emotions to remain under wraps. The only thing that could make this situation worse was for her to break down in tears. She glanced over at Niko. His head was lowered and his shoulders drooped as he paced the length of the private room.

She should say something to make him feel better, but no words would come. All she could think about was the baby and willing it to be okay. Did that make her selfish? Thoughtless?

And then, unable to stand the sound of his dress shoes clicking over the tiled floor, she uttered, "You don't have to stay."

Niko stopped pacing and turned to her. His handsome

face was creased with lines. "I'm not going anywhere, not until I know that you and the baby are all right."

"What if…" Her shaky voice trailed away. She squeezed her eyes shut. How could she have been so clumsy?

Niko sat on the edge of her bed and stared deep into her eyes. "Think positive."

"But what if—"

"Everything will be fine." He reached out, running his hand down over her hair and stroking her cheek.

His fingers moved over a tender spot on her jaw, but she didn't say anything. Right now every part of her was sore. She definitely wouldn't recommend tumbling down steps to anyone. But somehow with Niko sitting there next to her, her aches lessened to some extent.

Was it wrong that she took comfort in his touch when her own child was at risk? And why should his soothing words bring her such peace? There was definitely something special about Niko that went so much deeper than his good looks. There was a tender, caring side of him that she was just getting to see, and she'd like to see so much more of it.

"Maybe you're right." She tried to send him a reassuring smile, but she just couldn't muster the expression. Though she was no longer on the verge of tears, she was still a ball of nerves. "I haven't had any cramping in a while now. Not since the nurse was here." Sitting in this small room with no clock and no window made it impossible for her to tell how much time had passed. "How long has that been?"

Niko consulted his Rolex watch. "I'd say at least thirty minutes."

"Seems more like forever. But the lack of cramping must be a good sign." She rubbed her hand over her abdomen. "You just stay in there, little one. It's not time for you to make an appearance yet."

"See, there you go. Thinking positive is always helpful."

And then out of the blue, a worrisome thought struck her. Would Niko think that if she couldn't take care of herself, she couldn't take care of the baby? She studied him as though by staring at him long enough and hard enough, she'd gain insight into his thoughts. Maybe if she explained—apologized—he wouldn't make a big deal of this.

"Niko, it was an accident. I didn't mean to—"

The door swung open, and the doctor strode in wearing a white lab coat. She'd previously examined Sofia and had decided that a sonogram was in order. "How are you feeling? Is the cramping decreasing?"

Sofia gave her answer some thought, trying to remember what the cramps had felt like when she'd first arrived at the ER. "Yes."

"But you're still experiencing some cramping?"

"Not for a while now. At least a half hour."

"Good. Let's have a look at your baby. Would you like that?"

"Yes." But it wasn't Sofia that responded. It was Niko.

The doctor glanced over at Niko. "Are you the baby's father?"

"Yes. I'm Niko Stravos." He shook hands with the doctor. "I can step outside."

He started for the door. Sofia decided it was silly. He had every reason to stay here and be reassured their baby was safe and unharmed. "Niko, stay. You can see the baby for the first time with me."

His dark brows rose in surprise. "You're sure?"

"I am."

He moved to the opposite side of the bed. He stood a couple of feet away from her. It was as though there was a wall standing between them. How had they gone from laughing, flirting and making love to now being awkward parents?

Sofia's hands grew cold and clammy as she anxiously waited to see with her own eyes that her baby was all right. It seemed like an eternity until the doctor had the image up on the monitor. At first there was no sound. *How can that be? Please let there be a heartbeat.*

The doctor moved the probe around a bit more. And then a smile lit up the doctor's face. She turned the monitor toward Sofia and pointed. "See. Right there is your baby."

The doctor flicked on a switch, and the *swish-swish* of the baby's heart filled the room, bringing tears of joy to Sofia's eyes. *Thank goodness.*

She choked down the rush of emotion. "Is…is it all right?"

"Your baby appears quite strong and healthy. A lot like its mother."

Sofia blew out a pent-up breath. It wasn't until Niko took her hand in his that she remembered he was still by her side. She glanced up at him and saw undeniable happiness.

She squeezed his hand. No words were needed. They were both thinking the same thing. Their baby was safe. It was just a simple gesture—the joining of hands—but the warmth of his touch soothed something deep inside her. In the strength of his grasp, she received a boost to her flagging courage. And in his eyes, she found a depth she hadn't noticed before.

Her heart *tip-tap-tapped* in her chest, and she quickly glanced away. When she tried to pull her hand away, hoping to get her common sense back, he didn't let go. What did this mean? Was he just relieved about the baby's welfare? Or was there something more?

"Do you know if it's a boy or a girl?" Sofia couldn't help but be curious. She wanted every snippet of information she could get about the baby.

"I'm afraid it's too soon for that."

After printing out two photos for them, one for her and

one for him, the doctor turned to them. "We're going to keep you here for a bit longer."

"Is there something wrong?"

"No. I just want to make sure the cramping doesn't return. As soon as it's safe, I'm going to send you home, where I'm sure you'll rest better. The thing is I want you to stay off your feet and give this little one some rest. You both went through quite an ordeal today."

"You mean bed rest?" Niko spoke up.

"Yes, will that be a problem?"

"No."

"Yes."

Niko and Sofia spoke overtop each other. The doctor got a perplexed look on her face. Sofia glanced at Niko, wondering why he'd said no.

"We're traveling," Sofia explained. "The day after tomorrow we're taking off for the mainland."

Niko shook his head. "There's no reason we can't remain here, especially if it's best for Sofia and the baby."

"But you need to go on without me—"

Niko frowned at her. "Stop worrying. You heard the doctor. You can put your feet up, and I'll wait on you."

Was he serious? He was talking as if he were the one who'd fallen and hit his head. He was going to take care of her? She glanced down at their clasped hands, and her pulse raced. She was in his hands both literally and figuratively.

"Good. I'm glad to hear it's all taken care of." The doctor's gaze moved from Niko to Sofia. "I know it's tempting to rush back to your normal routine as soon as you're feeling better, but give it a little time. You had what could have been a serious fall today, and you got lucky. I want to see you in a week for a follow-up."

"A week?" She couldn't be that much of an imposition to Niko. She knew how much he needed to finish this trip and get back to work. "Could I fly back to New York and rest there?"

The doctor moved to the door. "I'd rather you didn't. Not yet. Besides, when you wake up tomorrow, you're going to be awfully sore. You'll be glad to stay put for a while."

"She'll be fine." Niko spoke up. "I promise to have her back for her follow-up."

"But I need to get back to New York—"

"And I'll take you as soon as you're ready."

"But what about your trip—your mission? It's important." Worry filled her eyes. "Promise me you'll see it through to the end."

He hesitated. "If you promise to follow the doctor's orders."

"I do."

"Good." The doctor smiled. "The nurse will be in with all of the follow-up information. But if you have any problems between now and then, don't hesitate to call my office or come back to the ER."

Once the doctor was gone and they were alone, Niko withdrew his hand from hers and walked to the other side of the exam room. Sofia clenched her fingers, still feeling the lingering heat from his touch. She struggled to keep from frowning.

"You don't have to do this." She wanted to give him an out. She was certain he wasn't the least bit thrilled with having to take care of her, not when he had more important things requiring his attention.

Niko continued to stare at the picture of their baby. "I said I would look after you, and I meant it."

"But I don't want you doing it out of obligation."

His head lifted and his gaze met hers, but she was unable to read his thoughts. "Why shouldn't I feel obligated? You're in Hawaii because of me. The baby you are carrying is mine. And the reason you fell is because of me. I'm taking care of you. End of story."

Really? That's what he thought? He was taking responsibility for her accident instead of blaming her. She struggled to keep her mouth from gaping. This man standing before her was much more complicated than she'd first assumed, and it made her all the more anxious to get to know him better—for the baby's sake, of course.

CHAPTER TEN

EVERYTHING WILL BE all right.

Niko assured himself as he once again checked on Sofia. She looked so peaceful napping in the master bedroom of the suite at the Honolulu Stravos Star Hotel. It'd been twenty-four hours since the accident, and so far there hadn't been any setbacks. It just had to stay that way.

He returned to the spacious living room and settled in a black leather chair behind a rustic mango wood desk. It wasn't nearly as big as his desk back in Athens, but it would do. A gentle breeze blowing in off the ocean sent the sheer white curtains in the living room rustling.

Niko stared at the monitor, watching the number of unread emails mounting with each passing minute. Something big was going down with one of the assets Niko was interested in purchasing. It was so frustrating to be halfway around the world from the action. He should be in the office leading the charge to fend off this takeover attempt. Instead his highly qualified, highly paid executives were handling the situation.

He wasn't used to being on the sidelines. His usual spot was in the thick of things. Under any other circumstances, he'd already be jetting back to Athens. But these were extraordinary circumstances to say the least.

He'd had no idea how much this baby meant to him until Sofia's accident. Once he'd known she would be okay, all he could do was will their baby to hang in there. And now not even an emergency at the office could drag him away from Sofia's side. He had to trust that the people working for him would do what needed to be done.

Niko pushed away from the desk. The chair wheels

rolled quietly over the wooden floor. He got to his feet and strode to the open doors leading to the veranda, needing a breath of fresh air. Being on the top floor of the Stravos Star Hotel gave him an unobstructed view of Diamond Head. He leaned back against the door frame and focused on the scenery, hoping it'd relax him.

He remembered as a kid wanting to climb Diamond Head, but his grandfather was always too busy. Niko had been left in the care of nannies—boring ones who preferred to watch their soap operas rather than entertain an energetic boy. Instead, he'd gotten into his own mischief in the hotel. His grandfather hadn't been amused, at all.

Niko recalled numerous times being chased through the hallways by the bellman. What was his name? It'd been so long since he'd recalled these memories that they were a bit hazy.

After a moment, it came to him. Mr. Kalama. How could he have forgotten that tall, lanky man, who wore the most serious expression? Niko didn't think he'd ever seen the man smile. It just made it all the more tempting to play harmless pranks on him, such as hanging out-of-order signs on all the elevators and forcing the man to take the steps. Or moving the wet-paint sign. But the thing Niko remembered most was when he ended up being caught in his pranks. Mr. Kalama would give chase. It was the most entertainment Niko had while traveling with his grandfather.

"And what has you smiling?" Sofia's gentle voice filled the room.

He was smiling? He glanced over at Sofia. Today her bruises had become quite evident on her olive skin. A purple bruise lined her jaw, while a brush burn left an angry red smudge down her right cheek and over to her dimpled chin. His gaze lowered to her right arm where her wrist was bandaged. Sofia had refused an X-ray, but the doctor was fairly certain her wrist was only sprained.

"Niko, did you hear me?"

He snapped out of his thoughts and stared into her eyes, trying to remember what she'd originally asked. Oh, yes, she wanted to know about the smile he'd been wearing. "Ah, it was nothing."

"It was definitely something if it actually had you smiling. Please tell me."

Had she just implied he didn't smile much? He'd never thought of that until now. Being around her had him considering things he'd never paused to think of before. What would it hurt to tell her the truth? "I was just remembering some childhood memories."

"Happy ones, I take it."

"Some were." *Happy* was a description he wouldn't readily attach to his past. Not wanting to go further down this path with her, he decided to change the subject. "You should be sitting down." He rushed to the couch and gathered the manila folders he'd been sorting. "Here you go."

Without an argument, she sat down. "I can't even imagine what it must have been like traveling the world as a kid. I spent most of my childhood in New York. We didn't vacation much. With so many kids, it got a bit costly." She stopped and pressed her lips together as though she'd said more than she'd intended.

"I guess traveling with my grandfather had its perks."

"You don't sound convinced."

He shrugged. "Sometimes I envied my roommate at school. He lived in a small village outside of London. He'd tell me about all of the things he did with his older brothers and his best friend." He shrugged. "You know kids— they always want something they don't have." It's what his grandfather always told him when he complained about not having any siblings or not being able to go to the mainland to play football.

"I'm so sorry."

"For what?" Niko wasn't accustomed to people feeling sorry for him.

"It sounds to me like you were a lonely little boy."

"I dealt with it."

"You mean you got used to it."

Was there a difference? Apparently Sofia thought so. He gave himself a mental shake. There was no point going down memory lane. He was no longer that bored kid. He was now a powerful businessman.

It was time to divert the conversation away from himself. "And how are you feeling now?"

"Better. That nap was exactly what I needed. But right now, if you aren't too busy, I'd really like to hear more about your childhood."

He sighed. "There's not much to tell."

"There's a lot to tell. I'd like to know more about the father of my child."

He shrugged. "You know everything that's important."

"Do I?" She arched a fine brow, challenging him.

Not about to be bullied into continuing to open up about his past, he pretended as though he hadn't heard Sofia's question. "Can I get you a pillow or a blanket? Should you even be out here?"

"The doctor said for me to rest. She didn't say I couldn't change rooms once in a while." She frowned. "Unless you're politely telling me to get lost."

"I'm not." And she did have a point. He knew she couldn't just lie around and do nothing. But it was for the sake of their child. "At least put your feet up and get comfortable." He followed her gaze to the coffee table littered with papers, files, books and a coffee mug. "I'll move them. Give me a second."

Just then the doorbell rang. When Sofia sent him a questioning glance, he said, "I'm expecting a delivery."

She nodded in understanding before he moved to the

door. As anticipated, there was a courier waiting with a box from Niko's office in Greece. He quickly signed for it, accepted the weighty package and closed the door.

When he once again met Sofia's inquisitive gaze, he knew she was expecting the box to contain something exciting. "Sorry. It's just some files from the office."

"Do they have something to do with these?" Sofia pointed to the papers surrounding her on the couch.

"My grandfather was from a different generation and relied heavily on paper copy. It's going to take me quite a long time until I have everything in the computer system, but I'll do whatever is necessary to digitize everything."

He carried the large box over to the desk. Then he returned to Sofia to help gather the mess of reference material. When he set the papers down next to the box, they slid to the side, spilling all over the top of the desk. With a sigh, he accepted that he would deal with them later. Right now, he needed to tend to Sofia. He could only wonder what that might entail.

When he turned around, she was staring at him with a strange look on her face. "What?"

"That's a lot of paperwork. You must be working on a really important project."

He raked his fingers through his hair. "It's the biggest one of my career. But it doesn't matter now." What was he saying? It was all he'd thought about for the past couple of years. "The only thing that matters now is making sure you have everything you need."

"I'm fine. You don't have to worry about me."

She didn't look comfortable. Niko moved next to her and pushed aside the books and candles adorning the coffee table. Then he gently lifted her legs.

"Niko, what are you doing?"

"Making you comfy. You're supposed to keep your feet

up." He carefully placed her legs on the glass tabletop. "Would you like to have a pillow under your feet?"

"You're being ridiculous. I'm fine. And I don't remember the doctor saying anything specifically about keeping my feet up." She started to move when Niko sent her a stern look. "Fine. You win. But I don't need a pillow."

"What else can I get you? Something to drink?" Without bothering to wait for her answer, he moved to the fresh pitcher of water that he'd gotten for himself. He dropped cubes of ice into a tall glass and filled it up. "Here you go." He held the glass out to her. "I read that pregnant women should have plenty of water."

"You were reading up on pregnancy?" There was a very definite note of surprise in her voice.

Niko took a seat on one of the plush white armchairs a comfortable distance from her. Because every time they touched, an electric charge raced up his arm and short-circuited his thoughts. "How about some food? Or the television remote?"

"Did you really read up on babies and pregnancy?" Her direct gaze met his.

"I did." Why did that admission make him feel so uncomfortable? It wasn't as if he'd done anything wrong. Wasn't that what expectant fathers were supposed to do?

"I'm impressed."

"Impressed? With what?"

"With you. Somehow you've managed to care for me and still keep up with your business. You work really hard, and I'm guessing you don't have to."

He'd never considered not working. It was never an option, and, even if it had been, he wouldn't have taken it. He loved his position running the Stravos Trust. "I like to stay busy. If I'm not working, I'm reading."

He caught sight of her smile. In that moment, a spot warmed in his chest and radiated outward. He couldn't tell if it was from her compliment or the smile that lit up her face and made her eyes sparkle. He did his best not to dwell on why either should affect him so much.

"Really?" She tilted her head slightly to the side. "I guess I can see that. What do you like to read?"

Was she really interested in his reading habits? He knew for a fact that no woman had ever asked him about his reading preferences. Other women had been more interested in what famous people he knew or if he had connections to Hollywood or the fashion houses in Paris or Milan. Sofia was so different from all of them that he didn't know exactly what to make of her.

"I like to read nonfiction."

She nodded as though computing his answer. "So you like biographies and that sort of thing?"

"I do. And recounts of historic events. I also read a lot of periodicals."

"But what about fiction?"

He shook his head. "I don't bother with it."

"But why? There are some really great fiction books out there."

"I'd rather stick with reality."

"There's something to be said for using your imagination. It lets you see beyond the here and now and imagine something bigger and better."

Was she talking about her life? Was she unhappy with it? The more he knew about her, the more he wanted to know. "And what sorts of fiction books do you read?"

"Cozy mysteries and…"

"And?"

"Romance."

He couldn't help but smile. He should have known. She always struck him as the puppies, posies and rainbow type. Always looking for the good, even when it came to him—

the man who'd gotten her pregnant. "So you believe in happily-ever-after?"

"You say that like it's some sort of crime."

"No. Not a crime. It's just that—"

He caught himself in time. He didn't want to ruin this friendly moment between them. It was a beginning, something he hoped they could build on. But not like the relationships in her books. He wouldn't sweep her off her feet and make a bunch of empty promises. But that didn't mean they couldn't be happy together—as friends—married friends.

"Just what?" Sofia sent him an expectant look.

He sighed. Why had he said anything at all? And then he realized it was easy to talk to Sofia. Too easy. "If you're looking to me for something romantic, you might as well know now that I'm not that kind of man."

"And why would that be an issue?" Her gaze narrowed. "I never once asked anything from you. I even told you to continue on your trip without me."

"And leave you here on your own?" He shook his head. "I don't think so. You need someone to make sure you listen to the doctor."

"And you've elected yourself to the task."

"I'm the only one around. And you're forgetting that I have a vested interest." A ding from his laptop alerted him of an upcoming Skype meeting. He got to his feet and moved toward the desk.

"You mean the baby?"

"Of course." What else did she think? He shut off the reminder. When he turned back to Sofia to tell her that he had a meeting in ten minutes, he was struck by her distinct frown. He inwardly groaned. He'd obviously said something wrong, but he wasn't quite sure what it might be.

"Oh." Her head lowered, shielding her expressive eyes from him.

And then it hit him. She wanted him to want to stay here for her. He wanted to tell her that he had, but the words wouldn't form.

He just couldn't get her hopes up that they'd walk off into the sunset hand in hand. Everyone he'd ever cared for had left him. He was better off remaining detached.

He'd been so young when his parents died that he couldn't remember much about them. And then his grandmother had died soon after. That left him with his grandfather, who Niko supposed loved him in his own way, but it wasn't the way a child needed to be loved. A string of nannies were not a suitable replacement. His child deserved better than that.

Niko wasn't going anywhere. And neither was Sofia.

For better or worse, they were in this together.

CHAPTER ELEVEN

WAS IT POSSIBLE to be bored in paradise?

Sofia sighed and thought of all the amazing places she could be exploring at this very moment, if only she'd been more careful. She gently patted her abdomen.

"A little boredom is worth it as long as you're safe, little one."

"Did you say something?" Niko appeared at the doorway of the bedroom.

She hadn't seen him since earlier that day when he'd made it abundantly clear that his only reason for being here was to ensure the health of their baby. She told herself that his response was exactly what she'd wanted him to say.

"I...I was just talking to the baby."

His eyes widened. "Do you really think it can hear you?"

"Maybe. Although at this stage, he's still pretty little."

"He? You think it's going to be a boy?"

She shrugged. "I don't know. But it's better than referring to the baby as an it."

Niko nodded in understanding. "I'm sorry to have been on that conference call for so long. You didn't have to stay in here the whole time. You must be hungry. What can I get you?"

"I need something, but it isn't food." When she noticed that she had his full attention, she said, "I need something to do." And she had an idea, but she wasn't so sure Niko would be agreeable.

He stepped farther into the room. "But you can't do anything. That's the point of bed rest."

"I'm bored." She groaned. "I at least need something to occupy my mind."

Niko rubbed his stubbled chin. "There are some more magazines in the other room. I'll get them for you."

"No, thanks. I've read most of them. And if I text Kyra one more time today, I'm pretty certain she'll block my number."

"I'm sure she understands."

She studied Niko. He hadn't shaved, and his hair was tousled. His usual "pressed suit" appearance had taken on a very casual look, which included a partially unbuttoned dress shirt with its fair share of wrinkles, dark slacks and bare feet. The man really needed some casual clothes, especially for times like this.

Not good at beating around the bush, she said, "Maybe I could help you."

"Me?" His eyes opened wide as though the suggestion came as a complete surprise. He shook his head. "I don't think so. You just rest. I have everything under control."

He turned for the door. He wasn't going to get away that easily. She slid her feet to the floor and stood. There had to be something she could do. She rushed after him.

"Niko." She called out his name from the edge of the living room.

He turned with a start. "What are you doing out of bed?"

"I'm serious about this. You obviously need help, and I need something to keep me busy."

He raked his fingers though his wavy dark hair. "What am I going to do with you? You're supposed to be relaxing." When she didn't say anything, he gestured to the couch. "Don't just stand there. Come sit down."

He moved his laptop to the side so she could have a seat. "Can I get you anything to eat or drink?"

"Some orange juice would be good. Thank you."

The suite had an open-floor concept, so it was easy for her to communicate with him while he got their refreshments. She couldn't take her eyes off him as he moved about the kitchen. He was so handsome even in his unshaven, shabby state. And there was something exceedingly sexy about a man waiting on her hand and foot.

But she felt guilty, too. She knew what a burden he'd inherited from his grandfather. The Stravos Trust appeared to be more like a life sentence than a blessing. Niko glanced over at her as he put together some finger foods with the juice. He smiled, but it didn't quite reach his eyes. She hated the thought that she was responsible for his exhaustion.

She turned to the papers on the couch. She started to gather them into an orderly pile to place on the coffee table, making room for Niko on the couch next to her. While she was straightening the papers, she noticed they were rows and rows of numbers. What in the world did he need with all of them?

"Here you go." Niko set a tray in front of her. "I thought you might be hungry."

She glanced down at the array of fruit, vegetables, crackers and dip. Now that she thought about it, she was a bit hungry. She reached for one of the plump strawberries. "Thank you."

"No problem. Here. Let me take those for you." He gestured toward the papers.

She relinquished the reports to him. "What are all of those papers?"

He waved off her question. "Nothing for you to worry about."

"But obviously you're worried about them." His handsome face was creased with worry lines, and his eyes were bloodshot from a lack of sleep. "I'd like to know, if you'll tell me."

He shrugged and then took a seat next to her. "If you really want to know, it's my support to justify changing the way the Stravos Trust does business. My grandfather was a big believer in spreading out our assets to keep them safe.

Not too much in one place so that if a sector went under, it didn't affect us much."

She nodded. "That makes sense. It's a very conservative way of doing business. But I take it you don't agree."

"I don't. I think the older my grandfather got, the more cautious he got. To the point where I believe he spread our assets too thinly. Without some risk, there can't be any real growth."

Sofia enjoyed their conversation. She loved listening as Niko explained his plan to sell off certain assets and focus more on the shipping sector by purchasing one of the world's largest containerships. She loved the passion that filled his voice when he spoke about the future he envisioned for his company.

"And these numbers, what are they for?" She gestured toward the papers and files that had been moved to the chair.

"They are the backup I need to consolidate and send to my advisers."

She found that interesting. "So you won't just forge ahead on your own?"

He shook his head. "There's too much at stake. That's why I have a panel of experts. They will analyze the data and advise me of their take on matters."

"But why are you personally compiling all of this data?" It was only after she'd uttered the words that she realized the answer. She was the reason he was here in a luxurious suite, slaving away instead of in his fully staffed office in Greece. Guilt weighed on her like a waterlogged coat— heavy and uncomfortable.

"It's best this way. I need to make sure everything is done correctly. If the numbers are skewed, even slightly, it could sway decisions one way or the other."

This was her chance to pay him back in a small way for caring for her since her accident. "Let me help."

His brows drew together. "Are you serious?"

"Of course I am. Why wouldn't I be?"

He shook his head. "You don't need to bother with this. Your job is to rest and take care of that baby. That's more important."

"And so is my sanity. I need something to do that will distract me."

"I'll go downstairs to the lobby and get you some more magazines. I'll also see if I can find you some books to read."

She realized he wasn't trying to be nice and watching out for the baby. He was rejecting her offer because he didn't think she was up to the task. He thought that a maid had no business helping him with something so important. And maybe he was right. Maybe it was beyond her current capabilities, but she was a fast learner. Instead of even considering her offer, he'd outright dismissed it. The rejection stung.

She averted her gaze, not about to let him read her thoughts as he'd done so many times in the past. Because there was no way she could hide the hurt at knowing he didn't think she was up to the task of assisting him.

Darn it. Now, the backs of her eyes stung. She would not cry. She flat out refused. Blast, these pregnancy hormones were making her so emotional. She blinked repeatedly, willing her emotions under control.

She pushed aside the rest of the fruit, vegetables and crackers. She'd lost her appetite. "You're right. I don't know what I was thinking. I think I'll go lay down for a bit."

She ignored the surprised look on his face and headed for the bedroom. When she got there, she sent the door flying shut with a resounding thud. It didn't make her feel any better like she'd been hoping it would.

All she wanted was to be alone with her wounded ego. If Niko thought so little of her skills, how was she ever going to get a college administrator to take her seriously? And without furthering her education, how would she do right by their child?

She'd just flopped down on the bed when there was a tap at the door. She wasn't ready to play nice—not yet. "Go away."

"Sofia, let me in. I didn't mean to upset you." A few minutes passed before he added, "Please, Sofia. Hear me out."

She had the distinct impression he wasn't going anywhere until she heard him out. She swiped at her damp cheeks and blew her nose. "Fine. Come in."

Was it possible he had a sheepish look on his face? The great and powerful Nikolas Stravos III looked as though he'd done something wrong. The ache in her chest eased a bit.

He cleared his throat. "Listen, about what I said. I only said it because…well, I don't want you doing my work because you feel sorry for me."

He thought she'd made the offer out of sympathy? *Really?* She searched his eyes, finding sincerity in them. He hadn't rejected her offer because he doubted her capability. It had nothing to do with her and everything to do with him. She struggled not to grin. Really, these pregnancy hormones lent themselves to big mood swings. It wasn't as though he'd said he loved her. Not that she wanted him to say anything like that.

"I don't feel sorry for you." She hoped that was the right response. "I truly wanted to help. I'm interested in learning more about what you do."

He didn't say a word for a moment as though considering his options. "There is one other problem. We only have one laptop, and we both can't work on it at once."

"Oh." That was a problem. And one she didn't have an easy solution for.

He glanced at her. "Were you serious when you said you wanted to lie down?"

She shrugged. Would it make her look pathetic if she were to admit she was sleepy? She hadn't slept well the night before as she kept having some bizarre nightmares.

"Tell you what. If you promise to stay in bed and take a nap or watch a movie, I'll run out and pick up another laptop."

"For me?" This time a smile pulled at her lips, and she didn't fight it. She loved the idea of working side by side with him. And she could use the access to the internet to move ahead with her college applications.

"Yes, for you. Do you promise not to move? I don't want to have to worry about you."

"I promise." When he started for the door, she called out, "Wait. Can you pick me up one more thing?"

His brow arched. "It depends on what you have in mind."

"Ice cream."

He smiled. "I think that's doable. What flavor?"

"Cookie dough. No. Um, rocky road. But cherry vanilla is good, too."

Niko laughed again. "I guess the cravings are kicking in. How about I get an assortment?"

She gave him a big smile. "Thank you. Not only for the ice cream, but also for trusting me with your work. I won't let you down."

"I never thought you would."

Her heart swelled. She would prove herself to him. She would do whatever he wanted, and she'd do a good job. After all, she'd excelled at math in school. She couldn't wait to get started.

CHAPTER TWELVE

THIS WAS GOING better than she'd imagined.

Sofia stared out the floor-to-ceiling windows at the Pacific Ocean. It'd been a week since her accident, and to her utter surprise Niko had stayed with her the entire time. He waited on her hand and foot.

The only movement she was allowed was bathroom breaks and to move her fingers over the keyboard. And even with that, he made her take breaks, which included naps. She hadn't realized how run-down she'd been feeling. Her aches and pains from the fall had eased, though some ugly green-and-yellow bruises still remained.

But Niko kept her distracted. All week he'd patiently explained her tasks in terms she could understand. He surprised her with his patience in showing her how to read the reports and how to input the data into the computer. He was teaching her to use a spreadsheet program, and that was a skill she could use to make herself more attractive to college administrators and future employers.

The only drawback to this new arrangement was that it got a bit lonely. Even with them cooped up in this luxurious suite, Niko made sure they didn't spend too much time together. When she was in the bedroom, he was in the living room. When she was in the living room, he was in the bedroom. If she ever needed a sign that he wasn't interested in her, this was it.

"Are you ready for lunch?" Niko strolled into the living room as though her thoughts had summoned him.

She glanced up, catching sight of his week-old beard. It was filling in nicely, but she preferred him clean shaven. "You know you don't have to fuss over me anymore. Didn't you hear the doctor this morning? I'm fine to return to my normal activities."

He nodded. "I heard her. But she also said not to overdo it."

"And I don't think preparing lunch is overdoing it. And then I plan to start cleaning the suite." When he didn't say anything, her curiosity got the better of her. "Aren't you going to say anything?"

"Why should I? You have that look on your face."

"What look?" She had a look? What did it say? She didn't like the thought that Niko was getting to know her well enough to read her expressions.

"The look that says you're about to do what you want no matter what I say."

"Is that what you really think? I've been the perfect patient."

"Hmph." Niko crossed his arms over his muscular chest. "Where shall I start? The laundry you insisted on doing when I stepped out to pick up a few items at the store? Or the beds that you had to make up—"

"It's my job."

"Right now, your job is taking care of that little one—"

"I am," she said defensively, still feeling guilty for the fall. That would never happen again."

"I know, and I just want to make things easier for you. I don't want anything to happen to you. Seeing you fall, well, I never felt so helpless. I've never been so scared."

Was it possible he cared about her maybe just a little? Before her imagination got carried away, she halted it. He meant he was scared about the baby's health. That had to be it.

"Don't worry. I won't overdo it. I promise. Now, I should make those salads." She moved toward the kitchen. "After lunch, I'll get started cleaning the suite. If you want to go through the rooms and mark everything that needs to be packaged and shipped back to Greece, that would be helpful."

Niko's phone buzzed. He checked the screen before returning the phone to his pocket. He frowned but didn't say anything. What was bothering him? The message on his phone? Or had she forgotten to do something?

She pressed her hands to her hips. "What's wrong?"

"Nothing." He glanced away. "I'm hungry is all."

She didn't believe him. "Is it something I said?"

"I swear it isn't you." When she continued to stare at him, prompting him with her eyes for a better answer, he added, "Fine. If you must know, I've been experiencing a lot of resistance to my proposal."

She breathed easier knowing he wasn't upset with her. "You mean the one I helped you complete?"

He nodded. "All but one of my advisers have outright rejected it."

"But why? The numbers are sound. We made sure of it."

"It's not that. They are opposed to my dramatic restructuring."

She was trying to follow him, but she was missing something. "I'm not understanding the problem."

"These are men my grandfather employed for many years. They are used to doing things in a certain way— my grandfather's way."

"And they are resisting what you are trying to do with the company?" When Niko nodded, she asked, "Can you hire your own people?"

"I've thought about it, but these people are experts at what they do. I don't want to let them go. They accepted the changes to the human resources policies, but they had issues with some internal restructuring I initiated. And now with the proposal to sell off some subsidiaries in order to invest heavily in the shipping sector, they don't even want to consider it—"

"Whoa. Slow down. That sounds like a lot."

"They are changes my grandfather should have implemented years ago."

"Did you ever consider you might be moving too fast? What if you slow down and give your employees time to catch on to your plan? Then they could be your strongest allies."

His brows scrunched together. "But I can't just stop."

"I'm not suggesting you stop everything, but maybe pick the most important change and focus on it for a while before moving on to the next item on your list."

"I don't know."

"It stands to reason that people naturally resist change. But time usually gives people a different perspective."

"And that would work for you? Giving you time to adjust to a new situation or a new way of doing things?"

"There's no promise, but it certainly wouldn't hurt." She smiled, liking that he was asking for her input.

Her ex had never asked her opinion about anything important. Bobby thought that business and money were a man's domain and cooking and laundry were a woman's. She'd talked herself into believing with time she'd be able to change Bobby's opinion. That had never happened. It was foolish of her to believe her love could change someone.

"Thanks for giving me something to consider." Niko's voice drew her out of her thoughts. "Now, how about I repay you by taking you out to eat?"

"I don't think it's a good idea."

Niko paused as though considering her words. "You mean because of the baby? Are you having pains again? You didn't say anything at the doctor's—"

"No, it's not that. The baby is fine."

"Honest?"

She nodded. She would never lie about something so important. "It's just that we've been in Hawaii much longer than anticipated. If I don't get started cleaning, we won't be able to take off tomorrow evening."

He waved away her worries. "The cleaning can wait. This is more important."

"You're serious?"

"I'm always serious when it comes to food." He ran a hand over his flat abs. "You've got to be hungry, too. Let's go try some local cuisine."

The eager look on his face said that fighting him would be fruitless. In all honesty, she'd been so nervous that morning before her doctor's appointment that she'd barely eaten a thing. She glanced down at her T-shirt and casual shorts. "Is the restaurant going to be fancy?"

"It doesn't have to be. There's a place along the beach that I've heard people raving about. So do we have a lunch date?"

Her lips pursed together as she tried to conceal her surprise at him using the word *date* where she was concerned. She was certain he hadn't intended any romantic connotation. So then why did she have this funny feeling in her chest?

He eyed her as though waiting for her response. She really did want to get out of the hotel. As beautiful and luxurious as it was, she'd been in the same suite for a week. She was going a little stir-crazy. "But what about your proposal?"

"I think I'll take your advice and let my advisers think about it for a bit before I speak with them again. And I'm sure my other staff will appreciate a break in the long string of emails I've been sending them."

She pulled her shoulders back. "Sounds like a good plan."

"Let me just get cleaned up. I won't be long." He started toward the guest room as he'd insisted she take the spacious master suite. Then he turned back. "Well, don't just stand there. Sit down and rest. I don't want you overdoing it today."

"Did anyone ever tell you that you're bossy?"

"Yes. But that isn't going to get me to change my mind. We don't want any return visits to the doctor, at least not any unexpected visits."

She shook her head. "The next thing you know you'll be wrapping me in cotton for the next six months."

"You know, now that you mentioned it—"

"Don't you dare!" She moved to the couch, grabbed one of the plush throw pillows and tossed it at him.

He caught it with ease and tossed it back to her. The deep rumble of his laughter filled the air as he moved back into the hallway. It was the first time she'd heard him laugh since that one magical night at the wedding. Why did it feel as if it were now a lifetime ago?

As close as she and Niko had become during this trip, she'd never felt so distant from someone. Except when it came to work, then Niko was 100 percent present and attentive. But when the work was done for the day, it was as though he put up a wall between them. No wonder he didn't want a family. He didn't have time for one—or he was purposely making excuses to avoid having one.

But during their banter, she'd noticed a subtle shift in their relationship. Was it possible that the protective wall around his heart had started to crumble? Maybe not completely. But even a crack or two was progress, wasn't it?

But to what end? Was he interested in developing some sort of relationship with her? Or was he just interested in her because she was the mother of his baby?

CHAPTER THIRTEEN

HE WAS A MESS.

Niko stared at his image in the mirror. *Wow!* His hair was unruly and his beard—well, he had one now. He'd never been anything but clean shaven in his life. And his eyes were bloodshot. No wonder Sofia had been giving him strange looks off and on this week.

He had been pushing himself hard—real hard. He'd been so eager to prove himself to everyone—most of all himself—that he could step into his grandfather's shoes at the helm of the Stravos Trust. In the process, he hadn't noticed the unhappiness he'd been inflicting on everyone—including himself.

He scratched at his beard. Between watching over Sofia and keeping up with the office via videoconferencing and emails, he hadn't had two minutes to call his own this past week. He reached for his razor. This mess was going to take a bit of time to tame, but he wanted to look good for Sofia.

He'd noticed how she'd perked up when he mentioned getting her out of the hotel. He couldn't blame her. They were visiting a tropical paradise, but instead of sightseeing and lounging about on the beach, they'd been huddled away in this suite working.

Sofia deserved to get out and enjoy some of Hawaii. And now that he'd finally completed his long-range business plan and had submitted it to his advisory board, he could afford to take a break.

Oh, who was he kidding? The thing bothering him was how Sofia pushed to get a move on their trip. Was she that anxious for their time together to be over? Once they reached New York, her home, he had a feeling he'd lose any chance to win her over. His hands moved faster, trying to eradicate himself of the bushy growth covering his jaw and upper lip.

He'd enjoyed this past week. Not the part where he'd been worried about Sofia and the baby, but the part of being there for her. No one had ever needed him before. His grandfather had been a solitary man who prided himself on his independence. Having someone rely on him in a personal way was new to Niko, and he liked it—he liked Sofia. She was very strong and determined, more so than he'd ever imagined. He respected that about her.

Time was ticking. And this time he wasn't contemplating a business deal. This time it was something so much more important. Sooner rather than later he needed to propose his idea of them getting married. But how would she react?

He rushed through the shower and soon appeared in the living room to find that Sofia had changed into a summer dress. It had a white bodice with some blue flowers on it and a dark blue skirt. It was loose fitting, obscuring her figure. He liked the way she looked. She was perfect, with curves in all the right places.

"Is there something wrong with what I'm wearing?" She smoothed a hand down over the skirt as though straightening a nonexistent wrinkle.

"Um, no. Not at all. It looks nice on you. Is it new?"

She shook her head, but her gaze didn't quite meet his. There was something amiss, but for the life of him, he couldn't figure out what was the matter. He wasn't good at circling problems. In business, he trudged forth and dealt pointedly with the issue. It was the most efficient way to resolve matters.

When she didn't answer him, he said, "Sofia, look at me."

When she lifted her head, her eyes glistened with unshed

tears. *What in the world?* His chest tightened. Tears made him feel so out of control, so unsure of himself. *Please don't let it be the baby.* "Are you feeling all right? If not, we can stay in?"

She blinked repeatedly and shook her head. "You're hungry. We should go."

"Not until you tell me what's the matter."

She shrugged. "You'll think it's foolish."

"Let me be the judge."

Her gaze moved to the white-tiled floor. "My clothes don't fit. I sat around this week doing nothing but eating, and now nothing fits. I had to wear this because it's one of the few things I could squeeze into. I'm fat."

That was it? That was what had her so upset? He let out a breath. "You are not getting fat." He stepped closer to her and placed a finger beneath her chin so their eyes met. "You are pregnant. Our baby is growing within you. Be happy. If it's clothes you need, we'll get you some."

"But I don't have the extra money—"

"Hush. Remember, you work for me. Between polishing up the suite in Tokyo and helping me complete the proposal, you've earned yourself a whole new wardrobe."

She sent him a hesitant look. "I don't want your charity."

"Trust me—it's not charity. You truly earned it."

"You really think so?"

"I do." She'd really impressed him. "Now let's go. We have a busy afternoon." He started for the door and opened it for her.

"I did do all of that, didn't I? I think I have earned a bonus." She sent him a playful smile.

"You do, huh?"

"Most definitely. After all, good help is so hard to find."

He chuckled, broadening her smile. "I'll give it due consideration."

"I knew you'd see things my way." As she went to pass

him, she paused. "You know, I could pick out some new clothes for you while we're at it." She ran a finger down the lapel of his suit jacket. "Something more casual."

There was a determined tone to her voice that set off an alarm in his mind. He had a feeling if he wasn't careful, she'd be updating more than just his wardrobe and at a faster pace than he was attempting to implement his plans at the Stravos Trust.

Now he understood what Sofia had meant when she said his employees would resist change. He liked his pressed dress shirts and suits. He felt in control in them. He didn't need casual clothes. He was fine just the way he was.

But when she gazed back at him, he found himself getting lost in her big brown eyes. Was it possible he'd already lost the battle and they hadn't even stepped in a store yet?

The next morning Sofia put on one of her new maternity outfits. She never thought stretchy material would ever have a place in her wardrobe. She'd always made a point of making sure her clothes fit perfectly, but that was no longer the case.

She ran a hand over her slightly rounded abdomen. "You're changing everything, aren't you?"

"I assume you're not talking to me."

She jumped at the sound of Niko's voice. She turned on her heels. "I didn't hear you come in."

"Sorry. I didn't mean to interrupt your conversation with the baby. You do that a lot. Is it important to the baby's development?"

"How much do you know about babies?"

He sighed. "Honestly, absolutely nothing."

"Then, Mr. Stravos, it's my turn to teach you a thing or two." She enjoyed the fact she knew more about this subject than he did. Somehow it made her feel as though they were at last on even ground.

"You're going to teach me? How do you know so much?"

"Did I mention the really big family I have in New York? None of my brothers have settled down yet, but I have a couple dozen cousins, most of whom have kids now. So there's always baby stuff going on. You don't have any extended family?"

He shook his head. "My only cousin is Kyra, and, as you know, we didn't meet until recently."

"I know. Let's stop by the bookstore. But we'll have to hurry. What time is our flight?"

"The flight?"

She frowned at him. "Is there a problem?"

Niko rubbed the back of his neck like she'd seen him do numerous times when his business plans hit a snag and he was devising a way to fix the problem. "About that. I didn't remember to contact the pilot—"

"What? But how?" She wanted to be angry with him, honestly she did, but she just couldn't muster the emotion.

"I guess I got distracted with all of the clothes shopping." He stepped back as though to admire her new outfit. "And we did a mighty fine job. You look beautiful."

She put her hands on her hips. "If we did so great, why are you wearing another suit? Why aren't you wearing any of the casual clothes we picked out?"

His gaze avoided hers. "I, ah, didn't think of it."

"You do know I don't believe you, right?"

"Tell you what. I'll change into some of those new clothes you picked out for me if I get to pick out what we do this afternoon."

"I'll be cleaning—"

"I don't think so. I have plans for you."

Well, that was certainly cryptic enough. And then she caught a gleam in his eyes. What exactly was he up to? And just how much should she trust him?

"Oh, come on," he cajoled her. "Surely I'm not that untrustworthy." And then he smiled, sending her heart tumbling.

Now why did he have to go and do that. His smile was like a warm sunbeam, and it dissolved her resistance to his charms like a hot knife through butter. Oh, she was so pathetic where he was concerned.

It was just a small delay. Not a big deal. "Okay. You have a deal. Go change."

She had no idea what she'd set herself up for, but something told her it'd be worth it. Just the thought of spending the day with Niko had her grinning and her heart beating faster. What adventure did he have in store for them?

CHAPTER FOURTEEN

Now, THIS WAS the way to spend a sunny afternoon.

The wind combed through Niko's hair, scattering it. And he didn't care as he sat next to Sofia on the sailboat he'd chartered for the afternoon. It'd come with its own crew, so instead of Niko manning the helm as he did back in Greece, he had time to spend with Sofia.

And his plan appeared to be a success. She was smiling as her eyes glittered with happiness. And the sun was putting some color in her pale cheeks. This was exactly what she needed. A distraction far from computers, cleaning supplies and baby books.

"Are you enjoying yourself?" He glanced over at her.

"I am. You know, this is my first time sailing."

"And it won't be your last." When her eyes widened, he realized he'd vocalized his thoughts. Still, it was a chance to find out if she was warming up to the possibility of them marrying—for their child's sake. "I have a boat back in Greece. You're welcome to use it anytime."

He didn't know until that point how much he wanted her to take him up on the offer. He'd thought he was fine continuing to live a solitary existence, but he'd come to find out how much he enjoyed spending time with Sofia, whether they were cleaning a suite, sharing a meal or boating. Some things were just better when they were shared with another.

Sofia pressed a hand to his shoulder, drawing him from his meandering thoughts. "It sounds like a lovely idea, but I don't think I'll be getting back to Greece anytime soon—not with the baby on the way, my job and going back to school."

"I understand. But know that the invitation is always open." He took it as a good sign that she hadn't outright turned him down.

Perhaps she'd be more receptive to his idea after their outing. He'd learned during his apprenticeship at the Stravos Trust not to hesitate when a prime opportunity presented itself. However, his gut was telling him this wasn't the time to propose. But it would be soon.

Sofia gazed out over the tranquil waters. "Growing up so close to the sea, you must have done this all of the time."

"Done what? You mean sailing?" When she nodded, he said, "I'm afraid not."

"Really? I assumed you and your grandfather would go boating almost every day."

"My grandfather had one love, and that was his work. He didn't have time for sailing or fishing or anything else that didn't pertain to an earnings or loss report."

"What about your parents? I know you mentioned your father passed away, but before that, did you two go boating or fishing together? Or maybe you did with your mother?"

He glanced at her. She really didn't know about his past? It wasn't any secret. Anyone with a computer could type in his name and pull up his family history. The look in Sofia's eyes said she was genuinely curious. What would it hurt to tell her a bit? After all, she was carrying the next Stravos.

"My parents died in a car accident when I was five. So I don't remember a whole lot about them."

"Oh, I didn't know. I'm so sorry."

All of this talk was too depressing and not what he'd intended for today. "I'm sure you don't want to hear about this."

Sofia reached out to him, placing her hand on his thigh. "I do, if you're willing to share. I figure if we're going to coparent, we should know more about each other."

"What about you?" he asked, turning the conversation away from himself.

"Okay, I'll go first. What would you like to know?"

He stifled a sigh, knowing already that she came from a normal family—something he'd never had. "Are your parents still alive?"

"Alive and still happily married after almost forty years. In fact, it's disgusting how much they are still in love. Talk about lots of PDA. Sometimes it's like they're still teenagers." Her face scrunched up into a grossed-out expression as she shook her head, making him laugh.

"They sound very happy." He couldn't imagine what it must be like to grow up in such a loving home. Her parents proved there were exceptions to every rule. He was glad for Sofia's sake that her parents were the exception. But love was still such a risk with very high stakes. "How about your brothers? Are you close with them?"

She shrugged. "I'm the little sister with four overprotective brothers."

"So you have a big family." He'd always wanted to be a part of a large family, but that was not to be. It was a possibility for their child. His heart *thump-thumped* at the idea of coming home from the office to Sofia and a houseful of kids. "Would you like to have more kids?"

"I...I don't know." She got a sad look on her face. "I thought so at one point, but everything has changed dramatically since then."

He knew she was thinking about the baby she'd lost. He had absolutely no idea what that must be like, and his heart went out to her. He reached out and squeezed her hand. "This time around will be different."

"I know." She expelled a sorrowful sigh. "But I've changed, too. I don't want the same things that I did at one time."

His gut tightened. "Are you talking about marriage?"

She nodded. "The baby and I will be fine on our own."

"I hope there'll be room for me."

"Oh, of course. I didn't mean to imply you wouldn't have a place in the baby's life."

"Good. I don't want him…or her growing up like I did, never getting to know my parents."

Sofia tightened her fingers around his, reminding him that they were still linked. "That won't happen with our son or daughter. They'll know us and how much we love them."

"Do you think by knowing your big family that our child will feel cheated by not having any siblings?"

"I don't know. I've never really given it much thought. A large family can be chaotic. This way our child won't feel lost in the shuffle."

"Like you did?"

She nodded. "I was the youngest and always felt left out of things because I was too small."

"Surely it couldn't have been all bad."

"It wasn't. We had a lot of good times, too. Especially when the holidays rolled around."

"Would your brothers approve of me?" Niko didn't know why, but it mattered to him.

"I don't know."

Not exactly the stellar endorsement he'd been hoping for, but Sofia was probably being realistic. "I bet they'd kick my butt for knocking up their little sister."

"They'd probably try."

"Do they know yet? About the baby?"

"I didn't think that was news to share over the phone. If I had, my brothers would have hunted you down already." Then she smiled, letting him know she teasing him.

He sighed. "You're lucky."

"Lucky? For having overprotective brothers?" She shook her head. "I don't think so. You have no idea how difficult it was to date with them lurking about. My mother at one point had to warn them off. If she hadn't, I'd have never had a date for the prom."

Niko didn't know what it was like to experience that sort of love, but he felt as though he'd missed out on something very special. The thought of his child growing up in such a loving family filled Niko with some comfort. He just had to make sure there was a permanent place in Sofia and their child's life for him.

Theirs wouldn't be a marriage of love. It would be better. From what he'd witnessed, most of the time love didn't last. Her parents were the exception. Even Sofia couldn't argue that point after her relationship with her ex had crumbled. Niko's body tensed as he thought of her coping with the loss of her first baby alone. He hoped for that man's sake that their paths never crossed.

No, his marriage to Sofia would be the best. It would be built on friendship and mutual respect. Those were things that could withstand the test of time, unlike love, which was here one day and gone the next—

"Excuse me, Mr. Stravos."

The sound of the crewman's voice stirred Niko from his thoughts. "Yes?"

"Sir, we're here."

"Thank you. Just give us a minute or two."

The man nodded and strolled off.

"Where are we?" Sofia's face lit up with interest.

"I thought we'd go ashore for lunch."

She glanced over at the small island and then back at him. "Here?" Her shoulders grew rigid. "But…but it looks deserted. Surely you don't expect us to catch our own lunch and cook it over an open flame."

He couldn't help but laugh at the appalled look on her pretty face. "Relax. I had a picnic lunch packed for us, including a big blanket."

"Oh." Her shoulders eased, and the smile came back to her face. "So it's an adventure?"

"Yes, it is."

She glanced out at the blue water surrounding the boat. "But how will we get to shore?"

He struggled to maintain a serious expression. "You don't swim?"

"Niko, be serious. I don't have a swimsuit."

"There's nothing wrong with skinny-dipping."

"Niko!" Her cheeks filled with color.

Her outrage was his undoing. He broke down in laughter. When she crossed her arms and frowned at him, he gathered himself. "I take it the skinny-dipping idea doesn't appeal to you?"

"No." Her voice held a tone of finality. She glanced at the blue water again as the sun's rays danced on it and then turned back to him. "Why don't we just eat here? The boat is huge. We could even eat out here on the deck."

"I thought you had an adventurous spirit."

She frowned. "I left it at home with my swimsuit."

"Oh. Okay. Well, don't worry. You'll dry fast in the sun."

Her very kissable lips puckered together as she glared at him.

He couldn't remember the last time he'd had such an enjoyable day. Growing up, he'd only had one friend in his life to joke around with, Adam, his roommate at boarding school. That seemed like a lifetime ago. Niko had forgotten what it was like to let loose and enjoy himself.

"Relax." He didn't want her getting seriously upset with him and ruining the day. "There's a dinghy on board. We'll take that ashore."

She lowered her arms. "Were you enjoying having fun at my expense?"

"Perhaps." A broad smile pulled at his lips. "It's just so

much fun. You get this little V between your brows, and your nose flares—"

"It does not." She fingered the tip of her nose.

"Don't worry. It's adorable."

"You are not funny, mister." She poked him in the chest. "I'm going to do with you what I do with my brothers and stop believing you."

"Is that so?"

She nodded.

"So if I told you I intended to extend our stay here in Hawaii, would you believe me?"

"No, I wouldn't. You're already so far behind on your schedule. In fact, we shouldn't even be here now. I should be cleaning the suite so we can leave."

"You'd rather be cleaning than enjoying this beautiful day?"

"I didn't say that."

"Good." He glanced around at the amazing view. He hadn't felt this free in years. "I couldn't think of anywhere I'd rather be."

"In the middle of the Pacific Ocean with no contact with civilization?"

"Don't forget about the amazing company." He loved making her smile.

"Are you always such a flirt?"

"Only on special occasions." He halted himself from saying more—from admitting that she was very special indeed. He didn't want to do anything to scare her off and ruin this moment. He got to his feet. "Now let me get our lunch. It's below deck."

He disappeared down the steps into the teakwood interior of the ninety-foot sailboat. Everything gleamed. His friend who owned it certainly took excellent care of it.

"Can I get something for you, sir?" A deckhand appeared before him. The young man in a pressed white shirt and shorts appeared eager to please.

"I just came to get our picnic basket."

"Certainly, sir. I have it right here."

Niko had to admit this truly was an adventure. He'd never once delayed work to entertain a woman. He'd never even considered it. And yet here he was in khaki shorts, short sleeves and deck shoes, getting ready to have lunch with the most amazing woman on a small deserted island. And he couldn't be happier. How did that happen?

This was some adventure all right.

Wait until I tell Kyra about this. She'll never believe it.

Lunch on a deserted island with the world's hottest billionaire. This must be a dream. And I sure hope I don't wake up any time soon.

Sofia turned to Niko as he leaned back on his elbows, staring out at the horizon. His long legs were stretched out in front of him on the blanket. This was one of those rare times when he looked at ease.

They'd picked a private spot on the beach that was shaded by palm trees. A gentle breeze came in off the ocean and scattered his hair. She loved how he wore it a bit longer than most in his prominent position. The dark strands were finger-combed back off his handsome face. His gaze met hers, sending her heart racing. He was quite a package.

"Did you say something?"

Was it possible she'd vocalized her thoughts? Surely not. "Um, no."

He cast her a sideways glance as though not sure he believed her. Then he turned away. "You know, I was doing some thinking about the trip."

And here it came, his announcement that it was time they got back to business. She knew this cozy relationship couldn't go on forever. The sooner she got back to reality, the easier it would be for all concerned. She braced herself for his next words.

He cleared his throat. "And I was thinking we should stay here a bit longer."

"What?" This was not what she was expecting him to say. Not at all. "But why?"

He shrugged. "Why not?" Then he sat upright. "You're enjoying yourself, aren't you?"

"Well, yes, but we both know that...that it can't last."

He arched a dark brow. "Are you referring to the trip? Or to us?"

"I...um..." There was an us? She searched his eyes, looking for answers. But there was a wall up, keeping her out. She must be imagining things, only hearing what she wanted to hear. "I meant that we need to get a move on with closing up the suites. You have to get back to your office, and I have to get situated back in New York."

"The work can wait," he said nonchalantly.

"Are you serious?" What had happened to the real Niko—the man who was connected to his cell phone, who had the courier service on speed dial and conducted Skype meetings daily?

"Perhaps the problem is I'm trying to micromanage every part of the company, to show myself that I'm worthy of stepping into my grandfather's shoes and living up to my father's memory. It's a lot of pressure—pressure I'm putting on myself."

"And now?"

"Now I'm starting to realize I could sacrifice my whole life and happiness and still not measure up to my grandfather's standards. He was a force to be reckoned with in the business world."

"But you are, too."

Niko shrugged. "Perhaps. But I think I'm making everyone at the office miserable in the process."

"And what's your solution?"

"To lighten up. To let people do their jobs and show them that I trust them to do what they've been trained to do without second-guessing them constantly."

She knew this was a huge step for him. She'd watched him ever since they'd left Greece. He constantly reviewed and questioned things. He knew every part of his business. Could he really take a step back? She had a hard time believing it. Once a control freak, always a control freak.

"You don't believe me." The corner of his mouth lifted, and his eyes twinkled.

"What? I didn't say that."

"You didn't have to. It's written all over your face. You don't think I can let go."

Darn it. Why did her thoughts always have to filter over her face? She'd never had this problem with anyone before. It just seemed Niko could read her so well. "You do have to admit that it's easier said than done."

"Then let me prove it to you." He sat up straight. "For starters, I'm extending our stay in Hawaii."

"But why?"

His shoulders rose and fell. "I have stuff to do here."

"Stuff, huh? Could you be any more vague?"

"Was that a complaint?" He arched a brow. "Are you saying you don't want to stay here in paradise with me?"

She glanced around at the blue skies and tranquil water, but quite soon her gaze was drawn back to him. Her heart pounded faster. It didn't matter where they were, his presence would make it special. "And if I said yes, would you work the whole time, leaving me to explore the island by myself?"

"I told you—I'm going to change my ways."

She wanted to believe him, but she just couldn't imagine

a man of his vast power and wealth kicking back and letting others make the big decisions. "I'm trying to believe you."

"What if I give you some proof?"

What would it hurt to have him put some action behind his words? "What do you have in mind?"

His hands moved over on the blanket. His fingers gently stroked hers, sending a tremor of excitement through her body. She searched his face for answers, but she didn't know the questions. Her mind was a frantic mess of fragmented thoughts.

His attention dipped to her lips. Her heart jumped into her throat, cutting off her breath. Was it wrong that she willed him to kiss her? It seemed like forever since their lips had touched.

Yet this was exactly what she'd promised herself she wouldn't do—fall for his charms. He would love her and leave her. She already had scars on her heart. She didn't need more.

The tip of her tongue moistened her dry lips. But he was here, and this place was like some sort of dream. A tug-of-war waged within her—logic versus a deep yearning.

Niko captured her lips with his, taking the decision out of her hands. And for that she was grateful. Because once their lips touched, her thoughts fled. All she had to do now was enjoy. She would deal with the ramifications later—much later.

She leaned back on the blanket, pulling him down on top of her. She would never forget this day—this trip—this man. Ever.

CHAPTER FIFTEEN

AT LAST HE had the answer.

Niko had researched his options. Thought it through. And had come up with a strategic plan. Now he just needed the perfect time to put it all into action.

He smiled. It'd been a week of sightseeing, a couple of luaus, moonlit strolls along the beach and that amazing picnic on the deserted island where they'd made love. Niko couldn't remember being happier. He liked making Sofia smile.

As they climbed to the top of Diamond Head, he felt as if he were climbing to the top of the world. He glanced at Sofia. "Sure you don't need to rest?"

She paused and turned to him. "No. Let's keep going. Unless you need to rest."

Her face was a bit flushed. Oh, no, had they overdone it today? He'd tried to talk her out of the climb, but she'd insisted she felt perfectly fine, and the doctor had given her the all clear to return to her everyday routine. Niko suggested that climbing to the top of Diamond Head wasn't part of her everyday routine, but she'd brushed off his concerns.

"Do you want some more water?" He glanced down at the bottle in his hand, finding it more than half full.

"That's okay. I'm good."

"Why don't we sit down?" Niko suggested.

"Here?" Her forehead scrunched up. "We'd be in everyone's way sitting on the steps. Besides, we're almost there."

"Are you sure you feel all right?"

"What's the matter with you?"

With him? She was the one who looked pale. "Maybe we should turn back."

"And miss the view? No way." She continued ascending the mountain, one step after the other. "I'll beat you to the top," she called over her shoulder.

Her voice sounded chipper. Perhaps he was worried about nothing. He had to admit that her fall the other week had scared him more than he'd been willing to let on to her or even to himself until now. And he'd do anything to keep her and the baby safe.

He paused on the steps as a sense of protectiveness settled in. This was new to him. He'd never felt this way toward another human. It left him feeling a little off-kilter and a bit out of control because no matter what he did, he could never fully protect Sofia or the baby. But his plan would go a long way toward ensuring their safety. Which made him all the more certain his plan was the right decision for all of them.

At last they were at the summit. They moved off to the side on one of the platforms where it was just the two of them. Niko stood next to Sofia. The view was stunning. There was so much to take in, from the lighthouse below them to Waikiki Beach off in the distance.

"Isn't this the most amazing thing you've ever seen?" Sofia smiled as she gazed around.

"Yes, it is." But he was no longer looking at the view. He was looking at her. The wind swept through the short strands of her hair as a smile lit up her whole face. She'd never looked more beautiful.

This was it.

This was his prime opportunity to keep Sofia in his life. His plan just had to work. By now she had to know just how good they could be together.

When Sofia glanced over at him, her cheeks grew rosy.

"You're supposed to be taking in the view. That's why we hiked all the way up here."

"I am taking in the view. And it's gorgeous."

"Niko. You're being impossible."

"No. I'm just being honest." Was that a bit of color in her cheeks? Had he made her blush?

She smiled and shook her head. "You best look around *at the scenery* because we can't stay up here forever. Other people will want this spot."

"They can wait for a bit." Long enough for him to make the biggest, most important proposal of his life.

Sofia arched a brow. "Niko, what's up with you?"

He drew on scenes in movies to figure out how exactly to go about this correctly. He was supposed to drop down on one knee. He could do that. Down he went on bended knee.

Sofia's mouth gaped, but no words came out. She pressed a hand to her mouth.

This was it. His big moment. "Sofia, I've been trying to figure out a solution to our problem, and at last I know the answer. Marry me?" When she still didn't say anything, but continued to stare at him, he added, "We make a great team. We can do this for our child."

The surprise faded from her face and was replaced by an expression he couldn't quite read. For a moment, nothing could be heard but the rustling of the wind. Why wasn't she saying anything? Did she understand this was the best solution for all of them? Somehow they'd make it work… for their child.

"No."

Surely he hadn't heard her correctly. Then, realizing that he'd forgotten the most important part of the proposal, he said, "If it's the ring, I promise to get you one when we get back to civilization."

She blinked repeatedly and shook her head. "I can't marry you."

And then she rushed past him toward the pathway, the one they'd just come up. She was leaving him there on bended knee.

This would be his first and last proposal. The memory of her so readily shooting him down was like a big kick in the gut. He refused to ever put himself in that position again.

And try as he might, he couldn't figure out why she'd turned him down. She had to see they made a great team. He got to his feet and turned to witness her hasty exit. It was then he realized a small crowd had formed. Their cell phone cameras were aimed at him.

Niko inwardly groaned. His most humiliating moment would be loaded onto the internet for all the world to see. It wouldn't be long before he went from the poor slob who'd been turned down to the rejected Greek billionaire. Where had he gone wrong?

Not about to stand there for any more photo ops, he set off after her. Did she realize who she'd turned down? The heir to the Stravos fortune. The father to her baby. How could she turn him down? Any other woman would have jumped at his offer.

Then again, Sofia wasn't any other woman. If she was, he probably wouldn't have made the offer. There was most definitely something special about Sofia. Or at least he'd thought so until just a minute ago. His steps slowed. Why should he chase after her when she'd made her feelings so clear?

She moved swiftly down the steps and through the little tunnel. He didn't push himself to catch up with her. In fact, he purposely lingered in the background. It was probably best he kept a little distance. The more time that passed, the more her rejection stung.

He'd never understand women. They continued to be an utter mystery to him. And he had no idea where he and Sofia went from here.

What's wrong with me?

Any other woman would have jumped at the offer to marry a billionaire. And it wouldn't matter the circumstances.

Why did she have to be the exception? Why couldn't she just make do with what Niko was offering her?

A life of luxury.

She could have anything her heart desired and visit far-flung places, things that would forever be out of her reach otherwise. It would be a dream come true for most people. Just not her. Was it wrong that she longed for more?

After they'd made love beneath the sun, she'd been sure it would make a profound difference in their relationship. But the words of love never came from Niko. It was as though he wanted to get close to her, but not too close. This realization made her heart sink.

Now back at the hotel suite, Sofia paused from wiping down the kitchen counter—the last room to be cleaned. The place was eerily silent without Niko around. The hour was growing quite late. She moved to the picture window that overlooked the ocean as the moonlight danced on the water. Where could he be?

She hadn't laid eyes on him since he'd dropped her off after their visit to Diamond Head. She tried to recall everything that had been said at the summit, but it was all a blur.

The truth of the matter was she'd never expected his proposal. There had been no telltale signs. No sense that he was about to pop the question. One minute they'd been having a good time together, and the next he was down on one knee.

For a moment, her heart had been in her throat. She

thought all her dreams were about to come true. And then he'd opened his mouth and spouted out what sounded like a business negotiation. Not a romantic proposal founded in love. The backs of her eyes stung with unshed tears. *Darn hormones.*

When they'd arrived back at the Stravos Star Hotel, he hadn't even gotten out of the car. The only words he'd spoken to her were to tell her to get her things packed.

It didn't come as any surprise. What remained to be seen was whether he'd have her booked onto a commercial airliner or whether he'd fly her back to New York on his jet. Why bother waiting when she could make the arrangements herself?

She moved to the couch where she'd left her laptop. Somehow the thought of being back in New York City didn't bring her the comfort she'd hoped it would. Her fingers moved over the keyboard. Oh, well, that really didn't matter at this point. She had to get on with her life.

The front door opened, and footsteps could be heard in the entryway. Sofia steeled herself, ready to deal with Niko's anger. After all, she had turned him down without any explanation. But what could she say? She refused to admit that she'd been waiting for a heartfelt proposal.

Niko's eyes widened when he found her sitting cross-legged at the end of the couch. "I didn't think you'd still be awake."

Countless responses came to her mind from sarcastic to sincere, but what passed her lips surprised even her. "Can I get you something to eat? There are some leftovers in the fridge."

He set his car keys down on the breakfast nook. "I'm not hungry. I'm going to bed."

When he started toward his room, Sofia called out to him. "Niko, wait." He paused but he didn't face her. *Fine.* At least he was listening. "We need to talk."

He turned around. His eyes were icy cold. "Do you want to explain why you turned me down? Because I don't get it. Was it because I didn't have a diamond ring?"

She shook her head. "It had nothing to do with the ring."

"You know I would have gotten you one. The biggest and best."

She didn't doubt that. After all, he was a Stravos. They were known for their fine taste. "It was nothing like that."

"Then I don't understand. I thought we were having a good time. Not to mention you're having my baby. The next logical step would be for us to get married. Isn't that what you wanted? What you've been waiting for?"

"No! That isn't what I've been waiting for. Not at all."

Niko sighed as his fingers forked their way through his hair. "Then I don't understand. What do you want?"

Sofia worried her bottom lip. How did she explain this to him? Didn't he know it took a strong, loving relationship to get through the good and the bad? Money wasn't a substitute. It wasn't even close.

At last she realized there was no way to say it nicely— to try to preserve his feelings. If he wanted the truth, she owed him that much. "I don't want you proposing to me out of obligation. That's not good enough—"

"I'm beginning to wonder if anything will be enough for you."

"Hey! That's not fair."

"And you think getting turned down in front of a crowd is fair."

"I...I didn't ask you to propose. I didn't even hint at it."

Lines formed between his dark brows. "You're right. You didn't. I thought I was doing the right thing." He swore under his breath. "I've given this a lot of thought, and it makes sense. You're just too stubborn to see it."

"I am not."

"You know what? This conversation is a waste of time.

You're going to marry me. And all three of us are going to be a family."

Sofia shook her head. "Baby or no baby, you're *not* going to dictate to me what I do. I am *not* marrying you."

His lips pressed into a firm line as his eyes darkened. Was that anger lurking in his gaze? Or was it pain? She couldn't tell. And at that particular moment, she didn't care.

"The suite is now clean. My bags are packed. I'll be ready to leave in the morning." Afraid this conversation was about to take a really bad turn, she set off for her room. With long, sure strides, she reached it in no time and slammed her door shut.

There was no way Niko or any man was going to tell her when or who she'd marry. *How dare he!* She was not an obligation that needed tending to. She was a woman who wanted to be loved and cherished. Was that asking too much?

She thought of her parents. Raising five children, they'd had their share of tough times, but somehow they'd stuck it out. And there were times when it would have been easier to just quit. But they never did. Through thick and thin, they held on. They couldn't have done that without a deep, abiding love for each other.

And that was what Sofia wanted. A man who would love her no matter what. She refused to settle for less. Even if that meant being a single parent and growing old alone.

CHAPTER SIXTEEN

TALK ABOUT AWKWARD. This is downright impossible.

Niko glanced over his laptop at Sofia. She sat across the aisle and continued to stare out the plane's window as though mesmerized by the blue skies and passing fluffy white clouds. He knew she was upset with him. He'd really botched everything.

The truth of the matter was he may have had his share of dates, but that's all they were—casual affairs. He knew nothing about relationships and making women happy. And with his grandfather gone, he had no one he was comfortable going to for such intimate advice.

Sofia had barely spoken more than two words to him since their argument last night. He had the feeling she was waiting for him to apologize, but his wounded ego wasn't so willing.

"Is there something you need?"

Her voice drew him from his thoughts. He cleared his throat. "What did you say?"

"You're staring at me, so I was wondering if you need something. Maybe you have some more spreadsheet work for me to do. If so, I'd like to get started." Her tone lacked emotion. It was as though their relationship had been reduced to nothing more than coworkers on a business trip.

"Um…no. I don't have anything for you to work on."

Her gaze moved from him to the mess of papers on the seat next to him. Okay, so maybe he could use a hand, but he wasn't ready to act as if nothing had happened between them. Not sure what to say to her at this point, he turned back to his laptop and started typing again.

"You're going to have to talk to me sooner or later."

He glanced at her over the monitor of his laptop again. "We don't have anything to discuss. You made that quite clear yesterday at Diamond Head."

"I tried to talk to you last night, but you weren't in any mood to hear me out."

"And you think I'm in a better mood today?" After a night of tossing and turning, he was exhausted. The truth of the matter was that while the rest of the world was in dreamland, he'd realized he'd been wrong. He'd just sprung the proposal on her, and that hadn't been fair. But did she have to shut him down so coldly and walk away without an explanation?

"I just think if we talk things out we don't have to part as enemies. After all, we're having a baby."

She was right. For the baby's sake, they needed to make peace with each other. But was that even possible? There was a spot in his chest that ached every time he recalled her turning down his marriage proposal.

He swallowed hard. "What's there to discuss? You turned me down. Plain and simple. There's even a video circulating on the internet of the event just in case I don't remember it clearly enough."

"What?" Sofia's jaw dropped. "But why? Who would post something like that?"

"Apparently a billionaire getting turned down is an internet sensation. At last count, it was over a million views."

"But surely we can have it taken down. That's not right. It was supposed to be a private moment between the two of us."

"In this day of technology, it would appear nothing is private." Niko closed his laptop and set it aside. "What I still don't understand is why you turned me down."

"I already told you. I don't want you proposing out of obligation."

"But what about providing a family for our baby? Isn't

that important, too?" He needed to make her see that she was wrong—that she'd made a mistake by turning down his well-thought-out offer. "And what about financial security? You'd never have to worry about money again."

She shook her head. "There's more to life than money."

"I know that." He'd learned a lot since spending time with Sofia—obviously not quite enough. He shrugged. "What do you want me to say? You want something from me that I'm obviously unable to give you."

"Are you sure about that?" Her gaze needled him as though searching for the truth.

"Listen, I gave it my best shot."

Sofia reached across the aisle, grasping his forearm and squeezing it. "I'm not trying to hurt you. It's just that maybe when you do find the right woman, you'll know not to make the same mistakes."

Mistakes? He pulled away from her touch. He was Nikolas Stravos III. He didn't make mistakes. His grandfather raised him to always do his best—to be flawless. Oh, who was he kidding? He'd blown this whole thing royally.

If he hadn't gotten excited and rushed things, he could have pulled it off. He could have had the flowers, a candlelit dinner, some mood music and whatever else went into a fancy evening. He mentally kicked himself for messing up this bad. Thank goodness his grandfather wasn't around to admonish him for rushing and not doing his due diligence.

He glanced across the aisle as Sofia fidgeted with her phone. He knew he was letting his pride get in the way. This was the time when he needed to be a bigger man—for his child's sake. Wasn't that what a good parent would do?

Niko choked down his pride. It was time to do the right thing. "I'm sorry."

Sofia's head lifted, and her startled gaze met his. Was it so strange to hear him apologize? If so, then perhaps he did have to make some changes.

"Apology accepted. Do you know how long it'll be until we're in New York?"

New York? Was that where she thought they were headed? Their trip wasn't over...not yet. He had a little more time to get this thing between them right.

"We won't be in New York for a few more days."

"Days? But I thought..." Her lips pressed together as though she were weighing her next words. "I just thought after everything that happened—"

"That I'd be anxious to get rid of you?"

She shrugged. "Something like that."

He couldn't help but shake his head. Here he was thinking that somehow, someway he could find a way to keep her in his life, and there she was thinking he wanted to get rid of her, the sooner, the better.

Maybe it was best they got back to their working relationship. "We still have an agreement, and not all of the suites have been closed. Unless you've changed your mind."

She hesitated. He willed her to stick out the trip until the end. He thought of sweetening the deal to entice her to stay on, but his pride held him back. If she continued on, he wanted it to be her choice—free and clear.

"I haven't changed my mind."

"Good." Niko shifted his attention back to transferring his grandfather's handwritten ledger sheets to the computer.

"Can I help?"

Niko glanced up, meeting Sofia's warm brown eyes. His heart slammed into his ribs, and he had the sudden urge to sweep her into his arms and kiss away her doubts about them. But he knew that would only exacerbate their issues.

Instead, he handed over some raw data and showed her where to find the databases that needed populating. He also told her what reports needed to be generated when she was done.

In an effort to keep from giving in to his desires to feel her lips against his, he began organizing the papers he'd discarded haphazardly during his foul mood. Things still weren't back to normal between them, but at least they were on speaking terms. He'd take that as a good sign.

He cast Sofia a sideways glance. As though she sensed him staring at her again, she glanced over. Was that a smile tugging at her lips? Or was he just looking for any sign of encouragement?

"Did you need something else?"

"No. Did I give you everything you need?"

"I think so." She fingered her way through the pages. "It looks like it."

"All right. I'll just put the rest of these away." He started closing files and inserting them in his briefcase, when he stumbled across a blue scrapbook from the Honolulu suite.

Niko had retrieved it from the safe as soon as they had arrived, but then he'd had a meeting, followed by Sofia's slip and fall. He'd been so distracted that he'd forgotten all about it. There were no words or pictures on the outside to indicate what he might find between the covers.

He undid the gold string holding the book closed and flipped open the cover. Inside he found a baby picture with his full name and statistics listed beneath it. The curvy print was familiar to him—it was his mother's handwriting.

Niko turned the page, finding a tiny bracelet with his name on it as well as the name of the hospital glued to the page. Next to it was a photo of his mother cradling him in her arms. There was a note next to the picture: *I never knew so much love could come in such a small package.*

Niko's eyes misted up, and he blinked repeatedly. He continued turning pages, learning about his first steps and his first word: *Dada.* And there were finger paintings from preschool.

When he stumbled across a handwritten letter, it drew him in for a close look. Again, it was his mother's handwriting.

Niko,
You caught us by surprise. I must admit that I was a nervous wreck when I found out I was pregnant with you. I had no idea how to be a mother, but your father was a rock. I leaned on him, and he leaned back. We helped each other through the tough parts, and together we celebrated the miracle that had come into our lives—you.

And now that you're here, our family is complete. Each day I watch you grow, and you amaze me with your fearless approach to life. I hope you never lose that sense of adventure, even when new things make you hesitate. Just keep putting one foot in front of the other. It will work out in the end.

I look forward to watching you grow into a strong man like your father. But never be afraid to listen to your heart. It will set you apart from the others. Use it as your compass in life, keeping you honest and happy.

I am so honored to be your mother and to call you my son. Remember that your father and I will always love you, no matter what.
I love you very much,
Mom

Niko's eyesight blurred. He ran the backs of his hands over his eyes as he swallowed the lump in his throat. This scrapbook meant the world to him. In fact, he planned to make a similar one for his child.

He glanced over at Sofia. She appeared absorbed in her work. Her brow was drawn, and her bottom lip was between her teeth. It was something she did when she was deep in thought. He couldn't help but smile. She was totally adorable. He didn't think he'd ever get tired of staring at her.

He went back to the scrapbook, but as he turned the page it was blank. He continued turning the pages until the very end, hoping to find some more snippets of his past, but there were no more. His mother hadn't had an opportunity to fill in the other highlights of his life. She'd been stolen away far too soon.

It was as though his family knew what was going on in his life as far as Sofia and the baby were concerned. It was as if they were sending him helpful hints. Niko had never believed in signs before, but his grandfather had definitely meant to teach him something about life on this trip. Did his grandfather have any idea just how timely his lesson would be?

Niko knew once he let go of this chance to be happy with Sofia that he'd never get it back. He didn't know exactly how to keep her in his life, but he had to try something different—something more enticing.

CHAPTER SEVENTEEN

D<small>ID</small> N<small>IKO</small> <small>HAVE</small> another adventure in mind?

Once their plane touched down in New Orleans, Sofia thought they'd be going directly to the Stravos Star Hotel. But instead the limo delivered them to the French Quarter.

As she followed him out of the car, the heat surprised her. For some reason, she thought with it being September the temperature would have dropped, but not in New Orleans. The warm breeze and humidity made it feel as though it was still summertime.

"Niko, what are we doing here?" He'd been acting suspicious ever since they'd arrived. He'd been on his phone and speaking in whispered tones.

"You'll find out soon."

With anyone else this bit of mystery would worry her, but during the time she'd spent with Niko, she'd come to trust him. Still, she couldn't imagine what had him so excited. The *clip-clop* of hooves drew her attention. She glanced down the street to find a fine white horse pulling a gleaming white carriage. It stopped in front of them. *What in the world?*

"Your carriage, madam." Niko waved his hand toward the carriage.

"Are you serious?"

"Of course I am. You said you've never been to New Orleans before, and I didn't want to rush in and out of town without giving you the grand tour."

"Really?" When he nodded, she continued, "Can we see Bourbon Street? The wax museum? Mardi Gras World? Oh, and maybe visit a steamboat—"

"Slow down. Where in the world did you come up with all of that?"

"Hey, you aren't the only one who knows how to surf the internet. While you were on the phone at the airport, I was researching the city. There's so much to do here."

He smiled as he helped her into the carriage. He took the seat opposite her, and they set off on their adventure. "You know, to squeeze everything in that you want to do, we might have to stay for a couple of days."

She shrugged, trying to act casual. Yet inside she was now the one who was excited. This city was full of energy, and she couldn't wait to go exploring. "It's okay. We don't have to stay. I know we have to keep moving—"

"I think we can make the time for some sightseeing."

"You do?" Her words were rushed as heat warmed her cheeks.

He nodded. "Just let me know if there are any other sights you'd like to visit."

She agreed as she sat back in her seat, taking in the colorful buildings lining the street. Even though she'd grown up in New York City, she'd never gone for a horse and carriage ride in Central Park. So this was a real treat for her.

As they turned a corner, the scent of Creole food wafted through the air. Sofia inhaled deeply just as her stomach growled. She sure hoped Niko would be up for trying some of the local cuisine.

A little ways into the ride, he moved to the seat next to her. The carriage wasn't all that big, so their arms and thighs brushed. Her heart picked up its pace. She willed it to remain calm, but that was impossible with Niko so close by. If she were to turn her head ever so slightly, they'd be face-to-face, lip to lip.

She remained facing forward, resisting the temptation. "Something wrong with your seat?"

"Yes. It's all the way over there."

The playful tone of his voice was yet another ding to her defenses. She tried to sound serious. "Did you need something?"

"For you to talk to me."

"I am talking to you."

"No. I mean I want us to be friends again."

How could she not be friends with him? He was the father of her baby and…and she truly cared about him. More than she wanted to let on even to herself.

She clasped her hands in her lap. "Who said we weren't friends?"

"Don't pretend like I didn't mess things up with that marriage proposal. We were getting along great, and then I thought I knew what was best. I'm sorry."

"Apology accepted. And I'm sorry I didn't respond better. You caught me off guard."

"It would appear I have much to learn about relationships."

"You and me both. I thought I had a clue with my ex, but I was so wrong." As she contemplated her next words, her heart pounded loudly in her chest, keeping time with the horse's hooves. "In a relationship, both people have to want the same things and…and feel the same way about each other."

There, she'd said it. She glanced away and stared out at the passing buildings and pedestrians. What he'd do with the information, she didn't know.

"Maybe we can learn together."

She turned to him, catching a gleam of desire in his eyes. "Niko, what do you have in mind?"

"Once we get to the hotel, you could teach me a thing or two. And I could show you what I know."

Leave it to Niko to turn an apology into an opportunity for flirting. She wondered if he knew how tempting she found his idea.

No matter how hard she fought it, this guy got to her on a totally different level than anyone else she'd ever known had. He was in her mind, her blood and her heart. *Whoa!* Did she just mention Niko and her heart in the same sentence?

When he leaned forward, she didn't back away. She knew he was going to kiss her, and in that moment, she couldn't think of any reason to pull away. She wanted him, too. Maybe it was just a fantasy that he could ever feel the same way about her, but what would it hurt to pretend just a little longer?

His lips pressed to hers, causing her heart to thump loudly in her ears. His fingers brushed along her cheek. As their kiss deepened, a moan swelled in her throat. It felt like forever since they'd kissed. So much had changed. And somehow even though they'd been driven apart, she'd never felt closer to him. She knew it didn't make any sense, and maybe just for this moment that was all right.

Much too soon the carriage rolled to a stop. Regretfully, Sofia pulled back. Trying to act as if Niko hadn't just totally rocked her world right off its axis, she glanced around. "Where are we?"

"Jackson Square. It's a mix of history and culture. I thought you might like it."

She was intrigued. A small street band filled the air with jazz tunes. Sofia resisted the urge to hum along with the saxophone. They certainly knew how to live down here.

A wrought iron fence surrounded the square with artists and their colorful work along the perimeter. "Do we have time to look around?"

"Certainly. That's why we're here."

Anxious to see absolutely everything, she set off at a brisk pace. Her hand was seized by Niko's much larger hand. His fingers laced through hers.

"Slow down." He leaned in close. "I don't want you getting away."

She didn't think that was possible—not that she had any desire to escape his presence. She glanced over to give him a reassuring smile, and then her gaze landed on his lips. Well, she did have some desires pulsating through her veins, but she suppressed them.

She didn't want to give Niko the wrong idea. Things couldn't return to the way they'd been on that deserted island in Hawaii.

She hadn't changed her mind about his marriage proposal. When she married it would be for love, not to make life more convenient.

They meandered around, taking in the numerous artists and their varying styles. Sofia loved the bright, cheery colors. The numerous canvases had images that ranged from a sax with drums to historic buildings in the French Quarter to a streetcar. They were all vibrant, just the like the city itself.

As Sofia passed in front of the gates leading to the park, she spotted a beautiful fountain and a statue of Andrew Jackson astride a horse. She'd explore it later. Right now, she was more interested in the beautiful and eclectic artwork. She was truly tempted to purchase a piece of art for her new home in New York—a reminder of this magical trip.

When they happened on an older man in a sunny-yellow T-shirt and faded denim overalls splattered in paint, he waved them over. On the railing behind him were sketches. "Have a seat? Let me sketch you."

Sofia ran a hand over her short hair, knowing with all the traveling that day she didn't look her best. "Thanks. But I don't think so."

"Go ahead," Niko encouraged. "Don't you want a souvenir from our trip?"

Yet again it was as if he'd been reading her thoughts. "I have some from Hawaii."

"Ah, but you don't have any from the French Quarter." And then she had an idea. "I'll pose if you do, too."

"I don't know if we have time for all of that."

"I'm fast." The artist smiled broadly.

Niko's gaze moved back from the man to Sofia. "That's not fair with both of you ganging up on me."

"Oh, please." Sofia pleaded with her eyes.

"Okay, but you go first."

"You don't understand. I want you to be sketched with me. It'll be for our baby." She just knew that Niko wouldn't be able to turn her down now.

And she was right. The artist set up another folding chair next to hers. With Niko's body pressed up beside hers and his arm draped over her shoulder, their image was sketched. She'd never admit it to Niko, but she wanted this drawing for herself—to remember this happy moment. Because all too soon he'd be halfway around the globe from her running his empire.

The next evening Niko sat next to Sofia on the jet bound for the Caribbean. It was to be their last stop before heading north to New York. Guilt weighed on him. He'd promised Sofia a memorable stay in New Orleans, but aside from that one kiss he'd stolen in the carriage, Sofia had kept him at arm's length.

He'd hoped with time she'd let down her guard, but that morning they'd been alerted to a storm coming in off the Gulf. He'd helped her, and they'd closed the suite in record time.

"I'm really sorry about this." He hoped she believed him.

Sofia's eyes widened in surprise. "You're apologizing for an approaching tropical storm with the potential to turn into a hurricane. What were you supposed to do? I know you're rich and powerful, but even you aren't any match for a storm that size. And don't forget that it had New Orleans in its crosshairs."

"Yes, but I promised we could do whatever your heart desired. I know—I'll take you back whenever you want."

"So if I said I want to go back next month, you'd just drop everything, jump on your jet and fly to the States to take me on vacation?"

"Yes." He said it without any hesitation, and the ease of his response combined with his utter honesty surprised even him.

She smiled. "Be careful or I might start believing you."

This was his moment to ask for a second chance. "Sofia, we're good together. What can I do to get you to reconsider my proposal?"

She shook her head. "Nothing. It's better this way."

Frustration pumped through his veins, but he forced his voice to remain neutral. "How do you get that?"

"Because all of this—" she waved her hand around at the luxurious cabin "—is nothing more than a fantasy. Once we return to our normal lives, reality will set in. We're from very diverse worlds with different expectations."

"But what we shared on this trip is a starting place—a foundation. We can build on it."

She shook her head again. "It won't work."

Niko's fingers tightened around the armrests. "Why do you have to be so stubborn?"

"Because I believed in forever once. And…"

"And?" Niko couldn't let her stop there. He had to know exactly what he was up against.

"And I found out that I was wrong. I thought I could change Bobby, and he thought he could change me. We both failed. I failed. I won't put myself through that again.

I like who I am. I don't want to change into a person I don't recognize just to try and be what someone wants me to be."

Niko sat forward in his seat so he could look her directly in the eyes. "I may mess up from time to time, but I'll never intentionally hurt you. And I think you're wonderful just the way you are." He smiled at her, trying to lighten the mood. "Maybe a bit too stubborn—"

"Ha! Listen to who's talking. You have stubbornness down to a fine art."

He couldn't argue. "But I'm serious. We could be a family for our child."

"What if…if later on you decide you're tired of playing family man and look elsewhere for fun?"

"Is that what happened with your ex?"

She nodded. "I caught him in our bed with someone else."

Niko swore under his breath. "I promise I'll never do that to you. First of all, I can't imagine ever getting bored of you and looking elsewhere. And secondly, if we didn't work out, I'd tell you straight up. There wouldn't be any guessing. I respect you too much to sneak behind your back."

She stared at him for a moment as though trying to decide if she believed him. "I don't know what to think right now."

"That's okay. Just relax. You don't have to decide anything right now. I want you to enjoy our visit in the Caribbean. Okay?"

She nodded. "I've never been there."

"Neither have I. At least not that I can remember. So we'll experience it together. Would you like that?"

"I would."

He reached out and took her hand in his. She hadn't said it outright, but this was his second chance. And he intended to take full advantage of it.

There had to be a way to convince her that he wasn't like her ex—but how? Especially since he'd already messed up the proposal. Niko was smart enough not to make the same mistake twice.

CHAPTER EIGHTEEN

THIS WAS AN ISLAND?

Sofia stared out the windshield at the passing green foliage. For some reason, she'd been thinking the Caribbean islands would be all beaches and sun. But this elevated area was lush with bushes, palms and flowers. It was definitely paradise—just different from what she'd pictured in her mind.

"Do you know where we're going?" She hadn't seen any buildings for a while now, and the vegetation was growing denser.

"Are you getting worried?" Niko glanced at her.

"You're following the GPS on your phone, aren't you?"

"It doesn't work out here."

"What? Are you serious?" *Say it isn't so.*

"Relax. I know exactly where we're going."

"How? Did you get directions back at the airport?" *Please, oh, please say you did.* But if he was the least bit like her father, then she knew the answer—he hadn't.

Niko just smiled at her. "You don't think I can get us there, do you?"

Did he really want her to answer that question? She knew he wouldn't like her answer. Instead she asked, "Shouldn't we be down by the beach?"

"You'd think so, but apparently my family wanted something different." He navigated the open-top, cherry-red Jeep down a narrow dirt lane. "Come on. Admit it. You think I'll get us lost."

The denial stuck in the back of her throat. She just couldn't get the words out. When it came to her experience with men and directions, well, the cards were stacked against Niko.

He stomped on the brakes and turned to her. "Come on. You can say it."

"I...I think you should turn around before we end up utterly lost." She pulled out her phone to see if there was any cell service. There wasn't so much as a flicker of a bar.

Her body tensed as she glanced around. Did that shrub just move? Sofia leaned forward, anxious to find out what else was out here in the wilderness with her. If it was some sort of reptile—she inwardly cringed—she would be jumping on Niko's lap. Goose bumps marched up her arms. *Let it be anything but a snake.* In this open-air vehicle, there was no safe place to go. Why did they have to rent a Jeep?

"How about we make a bet?"

He wanted to play games now? Sofia groaned. Set to grouch at him to step on the gas, she hesitated. It might just be easier to placate him. "What are we betting?"

His eyes lit up as though he loved a challenge. "How about we bet on tonight's dinner? If I get us to our destination without getting us lost, you make dinner? But if I get lost, then I'll make dinner?"

She wasn't so sure there would be any winning where this bet was concerned. If they got lost, they'd probably run out of gas and be left to walk out of here. And whatever was causing that bush to periodically shake would eventually come out. She wrung her hands together.

Not wanting to sit there any longer, she glanced over her shoulder at the crate of groceries in the backseat. "Fine. It's a bet."

Niko drove another hundred yards and then turned right into a clearing. In no time, a white villa with a red-tiled roof and green shutters appeared. The whole way around the perimeter was a wide veranda, just perfect for kicking back to sip an iced tea while reading a book. The villa was perched on a hillside, and it provided a sweeping view of the beach and blue waters of the Caribbean.

Relief flooded her body, and her muscles eased. Thank goodness they hadn't gotten lost. Instead, they'd ended up in this little slice of paradise. Maybe Niko wasn't so bad with directions, after all. Then suspicion set in.

Her narrowed gaze settled on Niko. "I smell a rat."

"A rat?" He chuckled." I don't think so. There are no rats here. Just a devastatingly handsome Greek businessman."

"Oh, you." She lightly swiped at his arm. He wasn't getting off that easily. "You knew exactly where we were when you made that bet. You just wanted to get out of cooking. That's cheating."

"No, my dear. That's called betting on a sure thing." He winked at her and then eased the Jeep along the drive to the front of the villa. "Well, now I understand why I never saw any listing in the Stravos Star Hotel papers for a property in the Caribbean."

"I take it this is your family's private residence?"

"So private that I didn't even know it existed." He continued staring at the modest structure as though searching his memory for some mention of it.

"I'm guessing this is different from your home in Greece."

He was no longer smiling as he nodded. "I didn't think it'd be so isolated."

"What's the matter? You afraid a croc might get you?" she teased, hoping to put the smile back on his handsome face.

"Not hardly. But I am worried about the proposal for the shipping line. After convincing my experts that my plan to expand the shipping segment had merit, I set a new deadline for them to formulate their thoughts. It's tomorrow. But I seriously doubt this place has internet access."

"Oh." She wasn't quite sure what to say. And there was

no way she could fix the situation. They were in fact in a remote area.

And then she realized that for the first time on this trip, she was totally isolated with Niko. There were no tourists, no staff, no nothing…except a snake or a crocodile.

She glanced around at the wide expanse of trimmed grass. She highly doubted any creature would willingly come out in the wide open. She hoped. The only thing she had to worry about now was the very sexy man sitting next to her. All it would take would be one kiss for her to forget her common sense.

The villa was definitely small by Stravos standards.

While Sofia enjoyed an afternoon nap, Niko decided to explore the house. His bare feet moved soundlessly over the wood floors. Each room had vaulted ceilings with a paddle fan. He made quick work of looking around two of the three bedrooms. Each had cream walls, potted palms, a colorful comforter giving it an island feel and glass doors that opened onto the veranda. All three bathrooms had skylights. An eat-in kitchen came furnished with modern appliances, and a spacious living room looked as though someone still lived here. It was really quite cozy.

Niko found this quaint house more appealing than his spacious island home. This place had a warmth to it. He wasn't quite able to put a name on it. Whatever it was, he immediately felt at home.

In the colorful kitchen, he found the cabinets fully stocked. And there wasn't a bit of dust anywhere. Either interlopers had moved in, or his grandfather had caretakers on retainer. Niko didn't understand why his grandfather had held on to this property—a place they'd never visited.

In the living room, Niko swung open the glass doors, letting in a warm breeze. He turned around to find the room filled with pictures. Some were hanging on the wall. Some were on the shelves. He approached them to have a closer look. He picked up a frame, and there smiling back at him was himself at a very young age. He couldn't have been more than two. Holding him was his father and standing next to them beaming warmly was his mother.

Niko didn't know how much time passed as he examined all the photos in the room. Each appeared to have been taken here on the island.

Then he took in the shelves. Most of the books appeared to be action/adventure titles, but a few were romances. He ran his fingers over the spines. Then he heard footsteps behind him.

He turned to her, unable to find the right words to describe what he was feeling at the moment—being in this house with his parents' mementos and having Sofia next to him. He'd never felt this way in his life. It was as though everything was at last right in the world.

Between the photos from Tokyo and the scrapbook including the letter from his mother, Niko felt as if the blank parts of his life were being colored in. In New Orleans, they'd recovered a photo album of his father's life, from his baby pictures through to Niko's parents' wedding. There was even a photo of his grandfather playing in the sand with Niko's father.

In the photos, there were so many smiling, laughing faces. Niko had only ever known his grandfather as a man who was reserved and set in his ways. Part of Niko was sad he'd never known that fun side of his grandfather, and another part wondered if Niko was about to miss out on the best time of his life. His chance to play in the sand, so to speak.

As Sofia had pointed out, the photos his grandfather had left him weren't so bad. They had actually answered many questions, some Niko didn't even know that he had. But somehow he felt his grandfather had bigger things in mind. He hadn't been a man to be subtle when a grand gesture would work. But what could it be?

"What have you been up to?" There was still a sleepy tone to her voice.

He turned around and smiled at her. "I was just exploring. I had no idea my parents brought me here when I wasn't much more than a baby."

Sofia glanced around at the pictures. "And a cute baby at that. Do you think our baby will be as cute?"

"Sure. If he's lucky."

"You've never been accused of being modest, have you?"

He sent her a playful smile. "No. But if our child is smart, they'll take their looks off their mom."

She smiled back at him. "Much better, Mr. Stravos."

"I thought you might like that." He loved making her smile. He loved it more than plotting and planning the growth of his shipping empire. "Anything special you'd like to do while we're here?"

She shrugged. "I can't think of anything."

"We could go sightseeing or shopping in the village." When she shook her head, he started to worry. "What about taking a boat tour of the islands?"

"I don't think so." She moved about the living room, examining all the photos. "I need to get back to New York. I've found some apartments that I want to see. I have an appointment for the day after tomorrow. Will that be a problem?"

The day after tomorrow. Less than forty-eight hours and she'd disappear from his life as quickly as she'd entered it. "Niko, if that's a problem, let me know. I'll try to reschedule the viewings. Or I could catch a commercial flight—"

"No." His voice came out much harsher than he'd intended. Her eyes flashed with surprise, and he immediately regretted it. "I mean, it's not necessary. I'll see that you get back in time."

"Thank you." She picked up a photo of him as a baby. "What will you do with this place? I take it that it's not part of your deal with Cristo."

He didn't want to talk about business. He wanted to know why Sofia wasn't interested in doing anything with him. After all, this was their last stop before New York, before Niko returned Sofia to her family—her big, loving family.

"Niko?"

Oh, yes. Her question. "I don't think I'll part with this place. It was obviously very special to my parents. And I feel at home here."

Sofia smiled. "That's good. See—something else has come of this trip. You've found a piece of your past—a piece you didn't even know was missing. Maybe someday you can bring your family here."

She talked as though she didn't plan to be part of that family. And he had absolutely no idea how to change her mind. He needed more time, but he realized he had no legitimate reason to linger on the island. And by the time they reached New York, any chance he had of making a lasting, tangible relationship with Sofia would be gone.

She glanced at the clock on the wall. "I'm going to start dinner. Since we had an early lunch, I'm hungry."

"Would you like some help?"

Her eyes widened. "What about the bet?"

"What bet? I don't recall one."

She laughed and shook her head. "You know, I think this is the beginning of a long friendship." She turned toward the kitchen. "Come on."

He followed her, all the while thinking what it'd be like if they maintained this friendship, but he knew the distance would take its toll. It'd soon deteriorate to emailing photos in between periodic visits. It'd be all about their child, not them. And the more time he spent with Sofia, the more he realized just how special she truly was, from making him laugh to getting him to loosen up and stop taking life so seriously.

And then a thought struck him. Maybe getting married didn't have to be an obligation—not when you were marrying your best friend.

CHAPTER NINETEEN

THE NEXT MORNING, he awoke before Sofia. The truth of the matter was he hadn't slept well at all, only catching snippets of sleep here and there. How could this place be kept so up-to-date and yet lack an internet hookup? He had so much riding on his proposal to expand the cargo shipping line and yet he was left with nothing but a landline to connect with his office.

As the coffee brewed, the sun crept up over the horizon. Niko's thoughts turned to Sofia. With each passing day, she grew more beautiful. Perhaps it was the glow of motherhood. And with each passing hour, he realized he was that much closer to losing her.

He latched on to a last desperate thought—his grandfather had left him a sort of life lesson at each stop. He wondered what his grandfather had left him here. And would it be anything to help him realize what he was doing wrong with Sofia?

Niko searched all over the villa for a safe. It wasn't exactly the sort of home to have a wall safe, but to his surprise, in the last bedroom he found a wall safe behind a mirror. The only problem was his grandfather hadn't left him the code.

Niko tried his grandfather's birthday. Nothing. And then, realizing that this was his parents' special place, he tried each of their birth dates. Nada. Their anniversary. No such luck. Niko groaned. This couldn't be happening.

He refused to give up. There had to be a way into that safe. But trying to locate a safecracker on an island this size would be an impossible task. And he just didn't have the patience to wait for someone to fly in.

In a last-ditch effort, he used his own birth date. The safe snicked open. What he found inside wasn't a stack of photos, but instead bundles of letters. Two to be exact. One was addressed to his mother. And the other stack was addressed to his father.

Intrigued, Niko carried them to the living room. He untied the first bundle. Inside the first envelope he found pictures of his parents' honeymoon right here on this island—in this very house. There were other photos of them dancing beneath the stars and staring at each other as though they were the only two people in the world.

And then Niko unfolded the first letter. It was from his mother to his father. It described the amazing ways his father had swept her off her feet from the bouquet of wildflowers to the walk in the starlight to the amazing meal his father had prepared his mother.

His father could cook? That was news to Niko. It made him wonder if he had some hidden culinary talent. He'd never tried. It was always easier to let the staff handle it or to call room service.

But there was no room service here. And he had picked up a few tips from Sofia the night before. He might be able to tackle something simple—at least to start with.

He continued reading the letters. They were like a detailed how-to dating guide. And though he felt uncomfortable invading his parents' privacy, there really wasn't anything inappropriate in them. They were more about how they had made each other feel and how his father hated leaving his mother for business trips and how he'd make it up to her when he returned. Apparently his mother preferred to spend much of her time right here in this villa versus the grand house on the island in Greece. *Interesting.*

The more Niko read, the more he knew about his parents. It was something he'd craved most of his life. And now at last he felt truly connected to them. And it was thanks to Sofia. Without her, he wouldn't have made it this far in the journey. He'd really thought it was a fool's errand. But now he saw things so differently.

Was it possible that his parents were somehow sending him a message? Was this what he needed to do to sweep Sofia off her feet?

Eager to read it all, he shuffled through the papers. When he came across his parents' marriage license, he paused. They'd been married here on the island. What struck Niko the most was learning that his mother had been pregnant with him when his parents had been married. It was as if his family was speaking to him through this memorabilia his grandfather had preserved for him. Now Niko just had to follow their advice.

Over a candlelit dinner, he'd make it known that he wanted Sofia in his life and it had nothing to do with feeling obligated because of the baby. He wouldn't pressure her about the future. They could just take it one day at a time.

Sofia couldn't believe how tired she was.

Globe-trotting must take more out of a pregnant person than she'd ever imagined. She'd slept in that morning, and then again this afternoon she'd taken a nap. Niko was going to think she was lazy.

She threw her legs over the edge of the bed and paused. She heard something. Was that music? She listened more closely. It was indeed, and it was a romantic tune. A smile tugged at her lips. Perhaps Niko had learned something about romance, after all. If nothing else, he had good taste in music.

She moved to the bathroom to wash her face and fix her hair when she heard a screeching beep repeatedly go off. Was that a smoke alarm?

Sofia ran to the kitchen, finding smoke rolling through it. Niko took a dish from the oven and rushed to the sink.

He placed the smoldering dish in the sink and turned on the water.

Sofia opened all the windows and turned on the overhead paddle fan. When she returned to Niko's side, his face was creased with a deep-set frown.

"What was that?" she asked.

"Your dinner."

"Oh, I see." She didn't, not really. Try as she might, she just couldn't make out what the charred remains had once been. "What were you trying to make?"

"Fish and vegetables." He raked his fingers through his hair. "I don't know what happened."

She moved to the stove. "Were you supposed to broil it?"

"What?"

She'd never seen him look so unnerved except for that one time in the hospital. "The oven is set on Broil, not Bake."

His frown deepened even more. Then his head lowered, and he shook it. "I ruined everything."

"Ruined what?"

He expelled a deep sigh. "I meant for tonight to be special, what with it being our last night on the island. I was going to cook you dinner and have this nice intimate evening."

"You know what they say, don't you?"

"That I'm an utter failure in the kitchen?"

She couldn't help but smile. "No. That it's the thought that counts."

His gaze met hers. "So you're not mad?"

She shook her head. "I'm impressed that you'd even try. Have you ever cooked before?"

"Never. I found this recipe in one of the drawers and thought I could surprise you."

"You did that all right." She glanced around the kitchen and realized he must have dirtied every dish trying to make her dinner. It was going to take a long time to straighten up the place.

"I know. It looks really bad. Why don't we drive into the village for dinner, and I'll clean this up when we get back?"

She scanned the room again. "I think we better work on it now." She moved to the sink to figure out where to start. "It'll be a million times harder if it dries."

"If you say so, but you're not doing it. Here." He moved to the table and retrieved a bunch of wildflowers. "I picked these for you."

"They're gorgeous. Thank you." There were shades of red, orange, yellow and white. As her nose and eyes grew itchy, she wanted to groan in frustration. But she didn't have the heart to tell him that she was allergic to most wildflowers, not after his dinner disaster. She pretended to inhale their sweet scent, all the while holding her breath and hoping she wouldn't start to sneeze.

"At least I got that part right."

"Yes, you did. Maybe you should put them in water." She held them out to him and prayed he wouldn't protest. The more distance between her and them, the better.

"Um, sure." He accepted them. "Any idea what I should put them in?"

"If you don't see any vases, I'd use a drinking glass."

He nodded. Something told her this was his first time picking flowers for a woman. She smiled broadly as she headed to the sink and discreetly rubbed her itchy nose. She would not sneeze.

Would. Not. Sneeze.

"Ha-choo!" *Darn it.*

She set to work clearing a side of the sink in order to rinse dishes off before cleaning them. One thing this villa lacked was a dishwasher. She set to work, and Niko was right by her side, doing everything he could to help.

An hour later with the kitchen put to rights, they sat

down at the table with a tossed salad and a side of fresh bread that Sofia had thought to pick up in the village earlier that day. Romantic music still played softly in the background.

Sofia couldn't resist adding some candles to the table. Once they were lit, she dimmed the overhead lights. "Is this more what you had in mind?"

At last a smile lifted his lips. "It is."

Niko made small talk about the documents he'd found in the safe. Sofia wasn't the least bit surprised to find that his parents enjoyed spending time here. It was cozy and comfortable. There were no formal airs or luxury furniture that would make anyone nervous they might somehow mar its beauty. This was much closer to what Sofia was used to—except for the view. It was awe inspiring.

"It's a shame you were too young to have memories of the time you spent here with your parents."

"Thanks to you, I have the photos."

"Me?" She set her fork down. "But I didn't have anything to do with it. Your grandfather is the one who orchestrated everything, including the upkeep of this villa."

"But it was you that made me promise to complete this journey. I was really tempted to cut the trip short and let someone else finish closing up the family suites, but you insisted I should see it through. And I thank you. I've learned so much—"

"Ha-choo! Ha-choo!"

Sofia's gaze moved to the beautiful arrangement of flowers. And then her eyes started to tear up. *Oh, great! Does this have to happen now?*

"Sofia, what is it?"

She shook her head and went in search of some tissues. Once she had her itchy nose under control, she returned to the table.

"You're allergic, aren't you?" Niko's voice held a don't-lie-to-me tone.

She nodded, not wanting to make him feel bad. And then she noticed the flowers had been removed from the table. "I'm sorry."

"You should have told me before."

"I...I didn't want to make you feel bad. I loved the flowers. Honest. It's just that I'm allergic to a lot of them."

"But at the wedding they didn't seem to bother you."

"There are certain flowers that don't bother me, like roses, lilies and orchids."

"Oh. I wish I'd known. I really made a mess of tonight."

The fact he cared this much touched her heart. She knew it would be best not to start up anything romantic on the eve of their departure to New York, but she wasn't ready to say goodbye yet. The burned food, messy kitchen and allergies wouldn't ruin this evening. It was touching to witness Niko going beyond his comfort zone and trying something new just to impress her. It was what a man did for someone he loved.

She got to her feet and held out her hand to him. His gaze moved from her outstretched arm to her eyes. His brows arched. "What do you have in mind?"

"Trust me."

"After what I put you through tonight, you might be ushering me to the veranda to sleep tonight."

She smiled broadly. "If you don't come with me, you might be right."

He jumped to his feet and clasped her hand in his. "Then by all means lead the way."

She grabbed one candle, and he grabbed the other. She led him to the living room, where she dimmed the lights. And then she moved into Niko's arms. Their bodies swayed together. Niko pulled her closer. The soft curves of her breasts pressed to the hard plains of his broad chest. Her head rested against his shoulder, and she inhaled the slightest hint of a spicy cologne. Its heady scent had an intoxicating effect on her.

"I don't want this night to end." Niko's voice was deep and soothing.

Sofia's heart pounded. "Me, either."

"You mean it?" His gaze searched hers.

"I do."

Tonight would be it. This evening would be the beginning of the rest of their lives—together. Because she knew what this whole evening was leading up to—Niko was going to tell her he loved her. At last, her dreams would come true. She would have one of those forever relationships that weathered the good and bad times. Like her parents and her grandparents.

Her hands slid up over his shoulders and stroked the back of his neck. Her heart *thump-thumped* in her chest. She pulled back just enough for her gaze to latch on to his tempting lips. As though he had exactly the same thought, his mouth claimed hers. There was certainty in the kiss. They both knew what they wanted—each other.

Her heart pounded even harder. Her head spun with the most delicious sensations. She planned to make this night last as long as possible. It'd taken them so long to reach this point that it needed to be savored.

Words of love rushed to the back of her throat. She wanted to tell him how she felt, but she couldn't. When he told her he loved her, she needed it to be because that was how he truly felt and not because he was following her lead. She needed the words to come from his heart.

She needed this to be real—to be genuine. For all of their sakes.

CHAPTER TWENTY

EVERY DREAM MUST END. There came a time when everyone had to wake up to the realities of life.

For Sofia, that startling moment came with dawn's early morning rays. After a delicious night of lovemaking, Niko never said a word about loving her. He cared. That was obvious. But Sofia knew it wouldn't be enough, not for the long haul.

She'd had a caring relationship with Bobby in the beginning, and it hadn't lasted. And Sofia loved Niko too much to end up in a relationship where they would one day end up hurting each other or, worse, hating each other. Niko deserved better than that. He was a great guy. Someday he'd find his forever girl. It…it just wasn't her.

As Sofia settled into the back of Niko's limo at JFK airport, her heart was heavy. Niko joined her, but he was absorbed in a phone conversation. The laughter. The teasing. The kisses. The whispered sweet nothings of the night before ceased to exist in the light of day. Everything they'd shared was like a dream now.

She couldn't even bring herself to meet Niko's gaze. She shouldn't have let things go so far last night. She'd let herself believe there was something lasting between them that never really existed, and it was now going to make their parting today so much harder.

In no time, their car eased into New York City traffic and headed toward her home. They only had mere minutes left together. She didn't know what to say, so she remained silent while Niko continued texting on his phone. She didn't have to ask; she knew he was working. Those couple of days without internet had really put him behind.

She should text Kyra and let her know she'd arrived in New York, but she didn't feel like it. Kyra would have questions, and Sofia didn't like the answers she would have to give her. She'd contact her later.

"Are you feeling all right?" Niko's voice interrupted her thoughts.

"Um…yes. Why?"

"You're just so quiet this morning. I was worried you might have morning sickness."

"No. I'm okay." *Liar. Liar.*

She did have an upset stomach, but it wasn't too bad. And right now it was difficult to tell if it was from the baby or from the thought of saying goodbye to Niko. Now that he'd revealed his gentle, caring side to her, he'd crept right past her defenses as though they weren't even there. If only—

"Just tell me if you need anything," he said.

Like getting away from you before you break my heart? But it was too late for that. Then she thought of the one thing they hadn't resolved on the trip—the raising of their child. "There is one thing."

"Name it." He sounded so formal, so distant this morning.

"It's the baby. We never set up any arrangements about raising him or her." She swallowed hard, clasped her hands together and tried to ignore the pounding of her heart in her ears. "I'd like it if you'd agree to let me raise the baby here in New York. My family is big and loud, but their hearts are bigger than the world. Once they know I'm pregnant, they'll be so excited about the baby, and I'll never have to worry about a babysitter." As Niko's frown deepened, she realized she'd failed to mention something important. "And you will always be welcome, as much as your schedule allows. I know how busy you are."

She just couldn't meet his gaze and risk him reading

the pain and disappointment in her eyes. She turned to the window. She recognized their surroundings. Their time together was almost up. And yet Niko wouldn't respond. She had no idea what he was thinking, and it was making her increasingly uncomfortable.

She forced herself to face him. "Niko, please say something."

"I don't have an answer for you."

"Oh." She knew he had enough money to hire a whole army of nurses to care for the baby and provide opportunities for their child that she could never afford, but he seemed reasonable. Surely he wouldn't want a long, drawn-out court battle like those she'd read about in the paper.

He cleared his throat. "Why don't you come back to the penthouse with me? You could see the hotel."

No. She couldn't. It'd be too easy for him to try to sway her with his mesmerizing blue-gray eyes or with his lopsided smile. Or worse, a kiss or two. She was already so confused. She didn't need to further complicate matters.

"I'm sorry but my parents are expecting me." It wasn't a lie. She'd called them from the airport. Her mother was probably already cooking pasta with meatballs as well as calling Sofia's aunts and cousins. Her mother's side of the family was enormous.

"You're sure?" When she nodded, not trusting herself to speak, he said, "Okay."

She wasn't sure. Not sure about anything.

Just stay busy.

That was what Niko had been telling himself all morning. If he stayed busy enough, it wouldn't bother him when Sofia left. And she certainly seemed anxious enough to get away from him today. He glanced down at the gaping space between them.

How could things have changed so drastically in the

light of day? It was as if they were back to being those two awkward people that had run into each other in his bungalow back at the Blue Tide Resort. And he hated that they were going backward in their relationship after how much progress they'd made.

He glanced at her as she gazed at the bustling city around them. For a moment, he considered proposing again, but she'd been so quiet and distant all day. She regretted their lovemaking. That must be it.

Yet, last night he'd been so sure that she'd been enjoying the closeness as much as him. Frustration churned in his gut. What was he missing?

Unable to figure out where things had gone astray with Sofia, he turned his thoughts to something he could control: the sale of the Stravos Star Hotel in Manhattan. It had always been his favorite. Maybe it was being in this particular city. It practically vibrated with energy. It'd be a shame to sell it.

He cleared his throat. "I'm thinking of keeping the hotel here in the city."

"But I thought you had an agreement with Cristo to sell all of them."

"We're still in negotiations. And Cristo already has a hotel here." And then he realized that Sofia already knew this. "The one where you work."

"Why would you keep it when you're selling all of the rest? I thought you planned to consolidate your assets into the shipping business."

He shrugged. "I can afford this indulgence. And since I'll be spending a lot of time in New York, it'll come in handy."

"You'll be here often?"

Why did she have to sound so surprised? Did she really think he'd end up like his grandfather, sequestered on that island with nothing but his work for company? He refused to let that be his future. "Yes. I'll be commuting between Greece and the States. I plan to expand the shipping business to the States."

"Oh. I didn't know."

Before Niko could tell her his main reason for coming back would be for her and the baby, the limo pulled to a stop in front of a townhome. It was well kept with potted plants lining the steps up to the black door with gold numbers. Suddenly the front door swung open, and smiling people rushed forth. Sofia's big, loud, loving family.

Unwilling to lose her, he uttered, "Sofia, come back to the hotel with me. We can make this work."

She shook her head and blinked repeatedly. "It won't work."

"Why not? We've learned so much about each other on this trip. If it's my business—"

"It's not. Not really."

"Then what is it?"

Sofia's gaze moved past him to the crowd forming on the sidewalk before returning to him. "Do you love me?"

His mouth opened, but no words came out. He wanted to tell her what she wanted to hear, but the truth was he didn't know. How was he supposed to know what love was when he'd never experienced it? Not really. Sure, he loved his grandfather, but that had been a very complicated dynamic. His grandfather had never been an easy man to get close to.

Niko had never been in love. He'd never allowed himself to go there. He did feel something for Sofia. He just didn't know how to put it into words.

When the silence dragged on, Sofia said, "That's what I thought. It'll be better for everyone, including the baby, if we end whatever it was here and now while we're still friends."

Her door swung open, and she stepped out, engulfed in hugs by a sea of smiling, laughing, talking-all-at-once people. So this was what it was like to be part of a large family. *Interesting.*

Niko wasn't about to leave. Not yet. He wanted to meet Sofia's family. She frowned at him as he exited the limo and moved to her side, but he pretended not to notice. He wanted to meet the people that would have such a big influence on his son or daughter.

An older woman with a bit of gray streaking through her dark hair eyed him. "Sofia, who's your friend?"

"Mama, this is Niko, erm, Mr. Stravos."

"Oh, he's the one you've been working for?"

Color tinged Sofia's cheeks as she nodded.

So that's what she'd told her family. He had wondered about that. And he was guessing they still didn't know about the baby. That would be one conversation he'd like to be a part of.

Realizing that his manners were lacking, he held out his hand to her mother. Sofia's mother took his hand and pulled him close. She hugged him. It was not a greeting he was accustomed to in his world.

When Sofia's mother pulled back, she sent him a knowing smile. So she didn't buy her daughter's story, after all. "It's nice to meet you, Mr. Stravos."

"Please call me Niko."

"And call me Maria."

An older man worked through the crowd on the sidewalk, calling out to Sofia's mother. It had to be Sofia's father. Niko steeled himself for a protective father. Niko would be the same way if he had a daughter as beautiful as Sofia. But someone stepped in front of her father, engaging him in conversation.

Sofia leaned over and whispered, "You don't belong here. Please go."

As he looked around at her loving family, he realized she had everything she needed right here. And he had nothing to offer her—not the epic love she deserved. Sofia should have a man who knew how to cook her an elaborate dinner and knew all the details of her life, big and small. Like the fact that she was allergic to flowers.

The weight of failure mingled with guilt pressed down on his shoulders. He didn't know how to turn his back on a future with Sofia, but he didn't see any other choice. He would contact her later about custody arrangements. At least they were still on friendly terms.

He leaned close to her, taking in one last whiff of her honeyed scent. "This isn't over. We will talk."

Her eyes widened, but she didn't say anything.

He'd meant they would talk about their child, but as he made his excuses to her mother, he wondered if Sofia had misunderstood. He should correct her, but he couldn't bring himself to do it. He couldn't admit that he wasn't the man for her. He climbed in the limo, never having felt more alone in his life.

CHAPTER TWENTY-ONE

WHAT HAD SHE DONE?

Sofia paced back and forth in her childhood bedroom. She hadn't been able to keep her dinner down. There was no lying to her mother, not that she'd planned to, but her mother was sometimes just too astute. She'd figured out Sofia was pregnant and that Niko was the father.

What her mother couldn't understand was why Sofia had turned him away. When Sofia attempted to explain her reasoning, the words didn't sound as convincing as they had in the limo. Had she made the biggest mistake of her life?

A knock at the bedroom door made her pause. She didn't want to talk to anyone. She felt physically exhausted and emotionally raw.

Without waiting for a response, her mother walked in. "Here." She held out a glass of what looked to be ginger ale on ice. "These saltines should help settle your stomach."

"Thanks, Mom."

"You know, I was sick my entire pregnancy with you. Might be one of the reasons you were the last. But no worries. This too shall pass."

"I don't think it's the baby." It was her own mess that was weighing on her.

"What's bothering you?" Her mother sat on the edge of the twin bed with the purple comforter that had been all the rage when Sofia was a teenager.

"Everything."

"That's a lot of stuff. No wonder you're not feeling well."

That was one thing she liked about her mother, she wasn't quick to solve her children's problems. She let each of them solve them for themselves and only stepped in when necessary. Her theory was that kids had to learn to stand on their own feet at some point. Only right now Sofia could definitely use some advice.

"I think I love him." Sofia's voice was soft, as she'd never admitted those words aloud.

"You think? You don't know?"

"Okay. Yes. I love Niko."

"So then what are you doing moping here in your old bedroom instead of being with him?"

"He...he doesn't love me." The pain of the admission pierced her heart. She moved to her window, which looked out over the quiet street, not ready to face her mother yet.

"Oh." There was a distinct pause as though her mother was digesting this information. "I take it he told you this?"

Sofia shook her head. "No. The problem is he wouldn't say the words."

"You, um, asked him?"

"Uh-huh." She sniffled, holding back a new wave of disappointment. "I thought he did. I really did."

"You always were quick to jump to conclusions as a kid—"

"But I didn't. Or at least I didn't think I had." She searched back over her memories of her time with Niko. All the signs were there that he loved her. Weren't they?

"So which is it?"

Sofia turned to face her mother. "I...I don't know. He took such good care of me after they released me from the hospital—"

"What hospital?" Her mother jumped to her feet. "What's wrong? Why didn't you call?"

Oops! She hadn't meant to let that part slip. She knew how her mother worried over her. So Sofia started at the beginning of the whole story, including Niko's journey to find the pictures and letters from his family.

"I'm so relieved you and the baby are okay." Her mother

moved to the door, about to leave. "You know, Sofia, you've been dealt a bad hand when it comes to love, but you can't judge all men based on Bobby. And for the part I played in that disaster, I apologize. I learned my lesson about sticking my nose in where it doesn't belong."

"It's okay. You didn't do anything but get excited about my engagement. I wouldn't have wanted anything different. I never blamed you for any of it."

"Thank you." Her mother hesitated as though trying to decide if she should stay or go. "You know, some men can say all of the right things and not mean any of them. Other men struggle with the words but do all of the right things."

Her mother slipped out the door, leaving Sofia alone with her thoughts. Why couldn't she have one of those mothers who told her kids what to do? It would be so much easier.

Sofia knew what she wanted to do, but was it the right thing? Her hands moved to her expanding midsection. There was more than just herself to consider now.

CHAPTER TWENTY-TWO

UNABLE TO SLEEP, Niko skulked through the penthouse.

He'd never felt so profoundly alone. Being with Sofia had shown him what it was like to be part of a team—to have someone to lean on and to talk to. Now the silence was deafening.

How could he have let her get away? Why couldn't he just tell her what she wanted to hear? That he loved her.

Because he honestly didn't know how to describe these feelings he had for her. They were so strong at times that they scared him. He'd never felt this way before. Was it real? Or was it infatuation? How was he supposed to know the difference? He just couldn't mess this up. He had to be certain.

He turned on the desk lamp in the study and sat down at the desk. If he wasn't going to sleep, at least he could get some work done. He turned his laptop on. That would help. He'd be able to center his thoughts on his shipping business—a project that would mark his name on the world.

His fingers moved over the keyboard, but he soon found it wasn't business that kept him typing. Instead he was researching business schools, wondering which ones Sofia would apply to. And then he started searching for information about babies. It was amazing how much information was online. There were even pictures of how the baby might look at this stage. The breath caught in his throat. He was going to miss out on so much.

He clenched his hands and groaned in frustration. How was it that he could lead one of the world's biggest companies and make million-dollar decisions that would affect many lives and yet he didn't know how to deal with the emotional land mines of being a family man?

In that moment he realized he wanted to learn to be the man Sofia and their baby could count on. He wanted that more than running the Stravos Trust and more than heading up his shipping business. He wanted to be a part of Sofia's life now and forever.

And then he realized why he wanted to marry Sofia, and it had nothing to do with obligations or that it was the right thing to do. And it wasn't even the little baby she was carrying. She was his family. It was her—Sofia was his home. Plain and simple.

He loved her.

At first the admission scared him. The more he thought about it, the less scary the concept became. He, Niko Stravos, loved Sofia Moore. He smiled. Why did he have to make something so simple into something so complicated?

Now he had to prove his love to her. Would words be enough? Or was it too late? No, he couldn't believe that.

Wishing there was someone he could go to for advice, he wondered if his grandfather had left him anything in the penthouse like he had at the other stops on the trip. Niko headed straight for the floor safe in the bedroom closet. Inside he found an envelope with his name on it. The bold letters were in his grandfather's handwriting.

The last letter his grandfather had written him had sent him on the journey of his life. Something told him this letter was going to affect him just as profoundly, but he had no idea in what way.

Niko moved to sit on the bed. His finger slipped through the opening at the edge of the envelope. He ripped it open, anxious to find out what his grandfather had to impart to him this time.

Niko,
By now you have completed the journey I have set
out for you. I hope you were able to appreciate your
heritage in a way that I never shared with you. I am
sorry I wasn't able to open up about the past. I made
too many mistakes and had too many regrets.

Learn from my errors. Don't get so obsessed with
the company that you forsake those you care most for
in life. The lesson I learned too late was that in the
end, love is what counts. It's the important total on
life's balance sheet. Don't let it pass you by.

It won't be easy. Nothing in life worth having will
come to you easily. Don't give up. If it's important
enough, stick with it.

Don't end up old and alone. The company is no
substitute for an amazing woman by your side.

I love you.

Immediately Sofia's face came to mind. And then an
image of her holding their baby. Niko vowed then and there
not to give up. Because as much as he loved his work, he
loved her more.

And then Niko noticed a note scrawled at the bottom
of the letter:

In the back of the safe is a small box. It is yours now.
Make sure you put it to good use.

Intrigued, Niko rushed back to the safe. In the dark, he
felt around until his fingers came in contact with the box.
He pulled it out and surmised it was a ring box. There was
a message attached.

This first belonged to your great-grandmother, then
your grandmother and lastly your mother. It is now

yours, for your bride. Take it and create your own happiness.

Niko opened the box, finding a beautiful diamond solitaire. It wasn't fancy, but there was something appealing in its simplicity. And it would look perfect on Sofia's hand. He snapped the box shut.

Tomorrow he'd beg her to forgive him for being so slow with figuring out the truth—he loved her with all his heart. He sat back on the bed, opening the ring box again.

There was no way he was going to fall asleep. Not now. He was too anxious. Too worried. What if Sofia rejected him again? But what if she didn't?

He glanced at the clock. It was after midnight. Much too late to go pounding on Sofia's parents' door. But this couldn't wait. Surely they'd understand. He had to seize the moment—

A knock sounded at his door. An insistent knock. A knock that went on and on.

What in the world?

CHAPTER TWENTY-THREE

Sofia wasn't leaving until she had her say.

She realized Niko had every right to turn her away, especially after how she'd shut him down not only on top of Diamond Head, but also in the limo. In truth, she realized she didn't deserve another chance, but she had to try.

Her clenched hand continued to pound on the door. *Please let him be here.*

At last the door swung open.

"What the h—"

The words stopped as Niko's narrowed gaze settled on her. Immediately his tense stance eased. That had to be a good sign, right? She couldn't resist taking a second to appreciate that the only thing he was wearing was a pair of wine-colored boxers. She did seem to have perfect timing where he was concerned.

When her gaze returned to his face, she noticed that his hair was mussed up. "Did I wake you?"

"No. Come in. We need to talk."

So he couldn't sleep, either. *Interesting.* She stepped past him, careful not to touch him. She was already nervous enough.

"Sofia, listen I—"

She turned to him and placed a finger on his lips—his very tempting lips. So much for keeping a safe distance. A tingling sensation rushed up her arm and settled in her chest. Her heart pounded so loudly that it was hard to hear her own thoughts.

"I need to say this." She pulled her hand back. "Just listen." When he nodded, she continued, "I'm sorry." Her gaze met his. "I didn't realize it, but I was so afraid of you hurting me that I didn't see what was right in front of my eyes. I love you—"

Niko swept her up in his arms and pressed his lips to hers in a needy, hungry kiss. She didn't fight him, forgetting her speech. This said so much. It soothed her worries that he would turn her away. There was passion and undeniable need in his kiss. They'd figure out the rest as they went along.

Tangled limbs. Endless kisses. Pounding hearts. This was where she belonged. She knew it in her heart. And at last, Niko knew it, too. He was showing her in every loving touch.

Niko was the first to pull away. His forehead rested against hers as he drew in one unsteady breath after the other.

"I need to tell you something, too." Niko continued to hold on to her as though afraid if he let go, she'd disappear like a dream.

"I'm listening."

"I was just about to head out the door and go to your parents' house."

"Well, that would have been quite a scene."

"Because it's so late?"

"No, because of your lack of clothes." She tugged on the waistband of his boxers.

"You're so funny."

"I try."

"And that's one of the reasons I love you."

"What?" This time Sofia did pull away. She had to be sure of what she'd heard. "Say that again."

"I love you, Sofia Moore. I love the way you smile. I love the way you care for others. I love everything about you. And I'm sorry it took me so long to figure it out."

"You...you mean it?" When he nodded, she added, "And

you're not just saying this because you know it's what I want to hear?"

"I would never do that. This is too important. If we're going to make it through the years like your parents, it has to be genuine."

Tears of happiness sprang to her eyes and she blinked repeatedly. "I love you, too." Then she took Niko's hand and placed it on her tiny baby bump. "Did you hear that, baby? We're home for always and forever."

EPILOGUE

Four months later, Athens, Greece...

"DID YOU EVER see such handsomeness?"

A smile tugged at Niko's lips as he listened to the nurses whisper back and forth. He was used to the attention, but he didn't want their admiration to bother his wife after she'd worked so hard to bring their son into this world.

Their son.

The words still sounded so unreal to his ears. He was now a father. He sat on the edge of his wife's hospital bed, holding her hand. Her eyes were closed as she rested while they cleaned up the baby.

"He really is handsome," came another female voice.

He'd have to put a stop to this before Sofia heard it. After all, he was a happily married man now. He didn't have time for flirting, no matter how cute the nurse. He only had eyes for one lady, and she was lying next to him. She'd opened up a whole new world to him.

Niko slipped off the bed, trying not to disturb his wife. He turned to the women as they continued to whisper more compliments. In truth, he was extremely flattered, but he just couldn't let it go on.

"Excuse me." He stepped closer to the cluster of nurses.

The women moved apart and turned to him with smiles on their faces. His gaze landed on his son in one of the nurse's arms. Realization dawned on him. They were oohing and aahing over Ari.

"Would you like to hold your son?" The nurse approached him. "He's so darling."

"Um...yes. Thank you." Embarrassment hit him like a

brick wall. He was starting to realize he was no longer in the forefront of people's attention—from this point forward his son would be the shining Stravos star.

And that was totally fine with Niko. He never knew having a wife and a baby could feel this good. Being a family man meant more to him than buying his first megacargo carrier, which he'd just christened that week the *STC Ari*, named after his son, Nikolas Ari Stravos IV.

"Niko, bring him closer." Sofia's voice was anxious.

He moved swiftly to her side, and, knowing exactly what was needed, he eased Ari into his mother's arms. Nothing had ever looked so good.

"He looks just like his father." Sofia smiled up at him.

"You think so?" Niko glanced down at his handsome son. He didn't know how much he resembled him, but if his wife said so, that was good enough for him. "He looks happy."

"Of course he is—he's with his mom and dad." Sofia ran her finger over their son's chubby cheek.

Niko was awed by the immediate bond between mother and son. "Are you sure you'll be able to part with him now that you've been accepted into the university?"

"I don't have classes for a few more months." She continued to smile and make cooing noises.

He knew Sofia followed through on things, but he also knew separating mother from son, even for a few hours a day, would not be easy. Even he didn't know how he'd go back to the office and leave both of them. He was already planning to work from home as much as possible. Their trip around the world had taught him many things, including how to work remotely.

Niko cleared his throat. "Not to ruin this moment, but are you ready to see the godparents? I think you made them a little nervous when you went into labor a month early."

"They were nervous? How about you?" Her accusing stare landed on him.

"What? I wasn't worried at all. I knew you had everything under control." *Yeah, right.* He'd never been so scared in his life. He'd had no idea what to say or what to do, but somehow Sofia seemed to keep it all together as if it was all natural to her.

"Well, then that makes one of us because I was really worried. I've never had a baby before, let alone delivered a month early and in a different country from the one we were planning. You know my family is going to be really upset about this. We were supposed to deliver Ari in New York."

Niko hadn't thought about that. When Sofia said she had a big family, she hadn't been kidding. He could barely keep her brothers' names straight, and when it came to her cousins he was at an utter loss. There had to be at least twenty—no, make that thirty—of them.

"Let me get Kyra and Cristo."

In no time, he was ushering his cousin and her husband into the private hospital room. Niko took his rightful position next to his wife and son. Nothing had ever felt so right. "Say hello to your godchild."

"Really? You want us to be his godparents?" As Niko and Sofia nodded, Kyra's eyes glistened with unshed tears. "Aww…thank you."

Cristo held out his hand. Niko shook his hand before pulling him into a hug. He was just so darn happy and proud of his family. The men quickly pulled apart just as Kyra scooped Ari up in her arms. She immediately placed a kiss atop his head. That boy was going to have all the women wrapped around his finger in no time.

Kyra's gaze moved from the baby to her husband. "Maybe you're right."

"Right about what?" Sofia sat up in bed, her face aglow with curiosity.

Color bloomed in Kyra's cheeks. "Cristo thinks we should start a family, but I wasn't so sure. But now after holding little Ari, I'm starting to think he might be right."

"That would be great." Sofia smiled. "Our kids can grow up together."

"They'll be the best of friends. Just like us."

"Yes, just like us."

Niko couldn't think of anything he'd like better. His family was expanding in ways he'd never thought of, and yet it was growing closer. And he couldn't be happier.

As Kyra and Cristo fussed over the baby, Niko leaned over to his wife and whispered, "I love you."

She glanced up at him. "I love you, too."

* * * * *

LET'S TALK
Romance

For exclusive extracts, competitions
and special offers, find us online:

f facebook.com/millsandboon

🐦 @MillsandBoon

📷 @MillsandBoonUK

Get in touch on 01413 063232

For all the latest titles coming soon, visit
millsandboon.co.uk/nextmonth